Infinite Risk

ANN AGUIRRE

FEIWEL AND FRIENDS
NEW YORK

A Feiwel and Friends Book
An Imprint of Macmillan

INFINITE RISK. Copyright © 2016 by Ann Aguirre. All rights reserved.
Printed in the United States of America by R. R. Donnelley & Sons
Company, Harrisonburg, Virginia. For information, address Feiwel
and Friends, 175 Fifth Avenue, New York, N.Y. 10010.

Library of Congress Control Number: 2016937595

ISBN 978-1-250-02465-7 (hardcover) / ISBN 978-1-250-08683-9
(ebook)

Feiwel and Friends logo designed by Filomena Tuosto

First Edition—2016

10 9 8 7 6 5 4 3 2 1

fiercereads.com

For the believers:
Never let the magic die.

THE DEFINITION
OF INSANITY

For me, the definition of insanity was not "doing the same thing over and over and expecting different results." Instead, it was getting within a few months of graduation and then enrolling as a sophomore at a different school. I barely made it out of Blackbriar Academy alive. I hadn't been to public school since fifth grade, and nerves clawed at my stomach lining until I tasted extra bile.

I can't believe I'm doing this.

Bitter wind blew, cutting through my jacket. As I studied the building, the parking lot was louder and more chaotic than I'd expected, guys horsing around despite the January chill. Sock hats, rubber bracelets, plastic chokers, people with words on their butts, bright T-shirts, heavy eyeliner, skater boys, people with un-smartphones—I'd forgotten that the world had once looked this way. But when I was twelve, I didn't exactly pay attention to the details.

The school swam in cement and pavement. There seemed to be two or three parking lots, one dedicated entirely to students.

A couple of fast-food places had sprung up across the street, probably catering to people who left for lunch. As for the building, it
was made of faded stone, casting the red trim along the windows
and roof into sharper relief. Somehow it seemed like the whole
place was dripping with blood. *Damn, you're not Carrie. Settle down.*
There was also a bizarre sense of déjà vu, since I'd skipped back in
time; only in this timeline, I was eighteen pretending to be sixteen, and everything was impossibly screwed up. *But I can fix it.* That
belief had propelled me to jump, and I couldn't let doubt chew
through my resolve. Considering the shit I'd seen in the last six
months, I shouldn't be fazed by a new school. But it was difficult in
a different way, making myself cross the lot and climb the steps to
the front office.

Inside, the place smelled of sweat and industrial cleaners. The
gray-speckled tile floors were dingy and scuffed beneath fluorescent
lighting, and three-fourths of the space in this entry was devoted
to trophy cases. On closer scrutiny, I found the majority of them
came from sports teams. Two shelves offered other victories from
other clubs, but I could already see the focus.

Students hurried by, joking with and bumping one another.
One group that went past definitely smelled like pot. Steeling myself, I shoved through the door marked MAIN OFFICE. There were a
couple of girls in there already—one crying—and two people I
took to be teachers hurried out with their arms full of papers. This
place could not be more different from Blackbriar, but I liked the
bustle and anonymity. It took me a minute to catch the attention of
the harried secretary. I'd cobbled some transfer documents together, which I hoped would pass inspection long enough for me to
do what I had to. Fortunately for me, if not the other students,

Cross Point High seemed both underfunded and understaffed, so the secretary barely looked at my forms. For a minute and a half, she clicked rapidly on her keyboard.

"We can't fit you into all your first choices since you're starting in the middle of the year. Better luck next time." She slid my schedule across the counter, picking up a ringing phone with her other hand.

I took it and pretended some concern over my classes. Really this was just an excuse to be here. My only interest in this school came from needing to meet Kian. If I'd planned better, I could've learned his schedule beforehand. Now I had to rely on luck and intuition.

Clearly, the secretary was surprised to find me still standing there when she hung up. "Something else you need? We don't have a welcoming committee, so if you were expecting a student guide—"

"Ha, no. An old family friend goes here too. I was wondering if you could tell me what lunch period he has?"

She sighed, likely weighing whether it was faster to refuse or just tell me. "Name?"

"Kian Riley."

After clicking a few keys on the boxy computer, she said, "Freshman? He's on A lunch, same as you."

"Great, thanks." I waved and headed out before she could ask why I didn't just text him. There was no reason to spin a story when leaving served just as well.

Thanks to the map in my class packet, I found first period while mentally shaking my head. *Sophomore English. God.* On the plus side, I could do the work in my sleep, so at least I wouldn't be distracted by teachers complaining about my performance and wanting to talk to nonexistent parents. Every move in this timeline had to be cautious and well conceived; I couldn't afford to make things worse and need to leap again, as time wasn't on my side.

I thought I was prepared for everything high school had to offer—Blackbriar Academy had put me through the grinder—but when I stepped into my first class and everyone stopped talking, it was a fresh sort of awful. A quarter of the girls did a lip curl and then deliberately turned away while a portion of the guys sat up straighter and tried to make eye contact. And I'd come in intentional down style, no branded clothes, standard hoodie and T-shirt, cheap sneakers, no makeup, nothing that should make me stand out.

"New student?" the teacher asked, cutting into the whispers. She was a middle-aged woman with salt-and-pepper hair worn in plaits, given to hippie style, if her fringed blouse and swishy skirt offered any insight.

"Chelsea Brooks," I said, offering my schedule.

"Ah, a transfer from Pomona, California. You'll miss the nice weather, but we do have tornadoes." She grinned as if that was funny somehow, and indicated a seat in the third row from the door, near the back. "That one is empty."

"Thanks."

"But before you sit down, introduce yourself to the class."

Ah, Christ, this really is hell. Changing how I looked hadn't given me any additional skill at public speaking, and I certainly couldn't tell the truth. Best to pretend apathy, slacker magic at work. With a shrug, I mumbled, "I'm Chelsea Brooks. I used to live in Pomona; now I'm here."

"Sucks to be you," someone called.

I took that as my cue and went to my desk without adding anything. The teacher read the room and started the lesson, likely figuring that if she let them, the class would seize this excuse to delay cracking the books. Around me, everyone opened their copies of *A Tale of Two Cities*, which I read when I was nine and found incredibly boring. With the exception of *Jane Eyre* and *The Count of Monte Cristo*, the classics never interested me.

"I'll share with you," the guy at the next desk said.

Before I could argue, he moved across the aisle and spread out his dog-eared copy of the alleged Dickens classic. Students took turns reading while I stared out the window. There were enough eager beavers that the teacher didn't have to beg for answers, but she apparently enjoyed picking on people. I dodged until nearly the end of the period, but she called me out eventually.

"What are your thoughts on the book, Miss Brooks?"

"It's really obvious that Dickens got paid by the word," I said.

Half the class laughed. I didn't mean to be a smart-ass; that was my actual opinion, but the teacher sighed. "Would you care to elaborate?"

"He wasn't exactly subtle with the allegory. If you want symbolism, the transformation and resurrection motifs are pretty obvious. Carton is meant to be a Christ figure."

"Interesting." But she didn't look pleased with my analysis.

The bell rang, however, freeing me to escape. I rushed out in the first wave, joining the throng of students surging to their next class. The guy who'd shared his book fell into step with me. He was short and thin, had light brown skin, and wore a cream beanie, black skinny jeans, and a cable-knit sweater. I had zero interest in fitting in or making friends, so I didn't speak.

Finally, he said, "You have a serious dislike for Dickens, huh? Mrs. Willis probably won't forget that."

"I'll survive."

"I'm Devon Quick, by the way."

"You already know who I am."

"Right, Chelsea from Pomona." He smiled, and I couldn't bring myself to be a complete icicle in light of such niceness.

So I waved as I cut into my next class. For the next three periods, the teachers seemed content to let me pretend to be a houseplant. And then lunch arrived. All my nerves prickled to life at once. Finally, I had a chance to look for Kian. I raced through the halls, skirting clusters of students, and didn't stop until I hit the cafeteria. My stomach felt too knotted to eat, but it would be weird to sit down with nothing, presuming I could even find him. So I went through the line and got pizza sticks, salad, and a fruit cup, along with everyone else.

From what I knew of being a social outcast—and it seemed like Kian had occupied that stratum as well—I picked a path through the crowded tables. *He'll be near the garbage cans or the doors in case he needs to make a quick getaway.* I spotted him at table in the back corner and headed that way, conscious of my heart pounding in my ears.

I tried to tell myself to calm down, but younger Kian was still Kian. In theory, the fact that I was older and out of my time stream should be enough to keep me focused, but I couldn't stop looking at him as the distance between us lessened. Ten feet. Five feet. His hair was longer than when I knew him and badly cut. From the way he was hunched over his tray, I couldn't see his expression. Thick glasses obscured his beautiful green eyes and half his face. He had problem skin, and he was so skinny it didn't look like they fed him at home. Oblivious to me, he stared to his left, watching some girl with shiny hair.

Tanya, I remembered.

"Is it okay if I sit here?" I asked, setting my tray down.

Kian's head jerked in my direction, and I couldn't help smiling. At this distance, I could see him. His eyes were the same beautiful green, thick lashed and stunning, but most people wouldn't notice. For a long moment, he stared, mouth half open, and it was like looking into an awkward mirror. Instead of waiting for a response, I joined him.

"You must be new," he said.

"How'd you guess?"

His mouth twisted. "Because you're sitting here. I won't take it personally when you assimilate into a better group."

"I'm not much of a joiner." I poked at my pizza sticks dubiously; they looked like normal pizza cut into thin strips. "Rectangles are better than triangles for some reason?"

He looked puzzled for a few seconds and then a half smile slipped, only for an instant; he swiftly locked it down in favor of the blank expression that I knew from experience hid a lot of pain. He scanned the cafeteria as if my presence heralded some badness he couldn't yet envisage.

My heart pinged. *Been there, lived that.* But I couldn't show any of those emotions as I studied him. *We're strangers; he doesn't know you.*

Finally, he mumbled, "Maybe the cafeteria supervisor had her heart broken by somebody who played one."

"Could be." Though I hated lying, I couldn't meet him as Edie. Not in this timeline. So I said, "I'm Chelsea . . ." and was about to let that stand when a better idea occurred to me. "But you can call me Nine."

"Why?" He made eye contact again, his interest piqued by the nickname I'd chosen.

I held up my hand. "It's better not to make a big thing of it. If I act like it bothers me, it'll be worse. You know how people are."

He took in my missing ring finger and seemed to relax a little, as if imperfection was easier for him to process than a pretty face. "Yeah, that's true."

It was too soon for him to ask, but I could tell he was interested. And since he was already firmly set as the skittish, wary one, I'd have to be friendly and open. "It was a dumb accident."

"What happened?" Curiosity evidently got the best of him.

"To be blunt, I stuck my hand somewhere I shouldn't. And I would've died if I hadn't chosen to lose the finger."

"So you did this to yourself?" His face reflected equal measures of awe and horror.

"Not for fun," I pointed out. "But, yeah, to survive."

"Wow. That's hard-core."

"Not really. What's your name anyway?"

The casual question sent his eyes skittering from mine. He ate a few bites of his salad before muttering, "Kian Riley."

"Are you a sophomore too?" I asked.

Like you don't know.

"Freshman." By his terse response, he expected me to know something about his family background. And *I* did, but Nine would remain ignorant of his past until the day she transferred, offering him a clean slate.

"So give me the rundown on the school. Who should I avoid?"

"Me, if you listen to everyone else."

I laughed like he was joking. Since he wasn't, it took a moment for Kian to return the smile, uncertain as sunshine on a cloudy day. "No, seriously. I can already tell you're awesome."

"Excuse me?"

An exquisite ache went through me as I remembered how I'd felt when he praised my smile, back when I didn't see any good in myself. "It's your eyes. They're fantastic, and they prove you're a kind, honest person." I added some New Agey stuff about how the eyes were the windows to the soul and then closed with, "I'm from California," as if that explained everything.

From his bemused expression, it was pretty much exactly the opposite. Yet I was committed to this Manic Pixie Dream Girl impersonation. If I came across a bit flaky, that was fine because I didn't want him to fall in love with me so that it would break his heart when I left. Just by *being* here, I'd already changed things.

"Are you on any psychotropic medication?" he asked eventually.

"Nope."

"*Should* you be?"

I snickered, drawing the attention of the surrounding tables. From Kian's reaction, their stares ranked right below Armageddon, but I made eye contact and offered indiscriminately bright smiles that said I was having a blast. Eventually, they went back to their lunches, and I caught Kian trying to pack up his stuff while I wasn't looking.

"Did I do something wrong?" I asked. "And please don't say, 'It's not you, it's me,' because whenever someone says that—"

"I wasn't kidding about the meds."

"If you're trying to drive me off for some reason, it won't work. I've already decided we're going to be friends."

"How can you just decide that?" He seemed torn between pleasure and irritation. "It's your first day at a new school, so you pick somebody at random?"

"It wasn't random."

Until now, it didn't occur to me how resistant Kian might prove to this idea. I'd thought I could just sweep into his life like the winds of change, and he'd be happy to see me. But he appeared to be getting pissed at my invasion of his silent world.

"Huh?"

"You were sitting alone. Either all your friends are sick today or you could use one." Maybe it was a mistake to be so blunt, so I went from there to straight up lying. "Me, I've been in fourteen schools in the last two years, and I'd rather hang out with someone who's happy to have me. If that's not you . . ." I acted like I was about to leave.

Stop me, you have to stop me.

At the last possible second, he whispered, "Wait."

"Okay."

"This is a little weird and really sudden, you know? This . . . Things like that just don't happen to me." He didn't even sound depressed, just . . . resigned, and that was worse. With every fiber in me, I wanted to hold him, but that couldn't happen.

I can't let it.

"People transferring to your school?" I kept my tone light and teasing.

10

"Never mind." But he clearly wasn't thinking about those watching and judging anymore—a step in the right direction.

"Do you want my number?" That was *way* pushier than I'd ever be, but the MPDG part of me didn't blink at the offer.

I could see Kian struggling to frame a reply. Like, *for what,* or *seriously, is this a prank?* Because I had been there. So I took his phone and entered my contact info. The thing seemed ancient compared to the smartphone I'd been using, and it actually flipped open. Since I'd acquired mine at a pawnshop two days ago, it looked no better than his.

"Now mine?" he asked, taking my phone like this was some kind of bizarre dark ritual that could only end in blood and tears.

"Yep. It'll make it easier for us to hang out." That was pretty much my whole plan: saving Kian, which would in turn save me, my parents, and all the assholes at Blackbriar.

"I really don't get it. But okay." Kian tapped out his digits with the precision of someone who hadn't done this much.

I tested the number to make sure he didn't give me a fake one, and his phone rang. He stared at it, as if he couldn't believe I cared enough to do that.

I smiled. "Awesome. Everything is working as intended."

A UNIQUE SORT
OF HEARTBREAK

At the moment, "home" was a shit-hole three-story historical building that never got gentrified. In fact, Cross Point had the air of a steel boomtown that lost all hope when the mills closed. The small downtown was more than half boarded up, and the businesses hanging on were mostly liquor and convenience stores, along with a thrift and wig shop. I shivered as I passed the head models draped in other people's hair.

I went to the Baltimore after school because I didn't have a choice. Using cash from Buzzkill's go-bag, I'd rented a room in a no-tell motel that advertised hourly, daily, weekly, and, as it turned out, monthly, as long as you paid up front. I had haggled a deal that offered me shelter, but when I let myself in, it was hard not to let the soul-deep loneliness seep in, just like the brown stains on the ceiling. Looking at the faded red carpet made me think they had chosen it because it could soak up bloodstains.

Peeling floral wallpaper, plastic furniture, and a minuscule kitch-enette were only a few of the charms my temporary home had to offer. I also got bonus screaming from the thin walls and the constant threat of invasion via the rusty fire escape right outside my window. I didn't like cooling my heels here, but I'd already been plenty forceful in the initial meeting. If I called Kian tonight, he'd think I was both crazy and desperate.

When I'm only the last thing.

But it was definitely a unique sort of heartbreak, being the only person in the universe who knew my story. I touched the watch on my left wrist; if I could remove it without dying, I'd already have it off, but it was firmly affixed to my skin like a parasite. If the medallion I'd taken from Raoul's body didn't conceal me, my only extracurricular activity would be killing immortals. So far, things had been quiet, but I knew not to get complacent.

I dumped my backpack and headed out with only a few necessities in the front pocket of my jeans, covered by my hoodie. A CTA bus delivered me to the small public library, a cream stone building underwhelming in both size and scope. The librarian at the front desk smiled at me, so I risked a question.

"Do you have computers for public use?"

"To use the print lab, you need a library card, but we do have a couple of old machines in back that are free for anyone."

"Thanks." I followed her directions and found them already occupied.

Slouching into a nearby chair, I waited my turn since the sign said PLEASE LIMIT YOUR USE TO TWENTY MINUTES. I didn't think I'd need that long. Finally, an old man stood up from his hunt-and-peck typing of a Hotmail something or other, and I slid in. Forums were the place to find info like I was looking for, so I dove into local-scene sites and keep going through sublevels until I found a

13

quasi-underground site that recommended a vintage vinyl shop for "additional services." Memorizing the address, I checked the bus routes and decided I still had time to get there before closing at five.

Seven minutes, not bad.

A twentysomething with pink hair was waiting for my machine when I checked over my shoulder. Before I got up, I cleaned the history and cache. She rolled her eyes as I slid by.

"You think anyone cares about your business?" she muttered.

More than you'd expect.

Not that the immortals would follow my trail that way but still. Right now I was out of my time stream and off the grid. If possible, I'd stay that way. Since the bus stop was a couple of blocks away and the computer said I had five minutes until the next one, I ran as soon as I left the library. As it turned out, the bus was six minutes late, so I could've taken my time, but missing this one meant putting off my business for another day.

Psychedelic Records had a LEGALIZE MARIJUANA shirt in the front window on one side and a giant poster of Bob Marley on the other. The smell of patchouli nearly knocked me out as I pushed through the front door. Row upon row of old records filled up plastic crates, along with rock-and-roll memorabilia that might've been "classic" when my parents were in high school. A signed guitar hung in a place of honor behind the counter, but I couldn't make out who had scrawled on it from the doorway.

There was no point in pretending I was a retro-music hipster, so I went straight to the guy behind the counter. "I'm interested in your additional services."

He scrutinized me head to toe. "Show me your chest."

"Excuse me?" This reminded me a little too much of the whole *show me your belly button* test I had going before I jumped.

"Just a quick flash. If you're not wired, I guarantee it's nothing I haven't seen before."

"Fine." I lifted my hoodie and shirt, giving him a peek at my plain white bra. "Satisfied?"

"Yeah." To his credit, he did seem pretty disinterested in anything but verifying that I was a customer, not a narc. "What can I do for you?"

"I want two IDs, one that says I'm sixteen and, the other, twenty-one."

"That's weird," he noted. "Never had anyone ask me to prove they're underage before."

"What do you care? It's your job to make IDs and collect the money."

Basically, I needed the first ID in case my current identity came into question at school, and if the authorities grilled me elsewhere, I'd whip out the adult ID and make a quick getaway. There was also no telling if I might need to meet someone in a bar. Being a time traveler had ridiculous constraints, as it turned out, since my real self was twelve and completely obsessed with anime and rock tumblers.

"True. Questions are bad for business. How high-end do you want these?"

"Basic is fine, just something to pass first inspection."

"That's easy enough." He named a price that was less than I expected. Buzzkill's cash would pay for this too. "Half now, half on pickup."

"Sounds good." I handed over the money.

"Excellent. Come in back for a minute. I'll take your picture."

He had a compact setup, though nothing so overt that anyone would notice his side business. It was all fairly typical office equipment. The various backgrounds for the photos were hidden behind an enormous framed Led Zeppelin poster. I posed but didn't smile, and he nodded approval.

"Good call. People always look surly in government ID photos. It's because they've all been waiting for over an hour at the DMV or whatever." He smirked at his own joke.

I gave a pity chuckle, no point in pissing him off. "When should I come back?"

"Wednesday, after three."

"Okay, thanks."

"Let me check the front, give me a sec. We'd have heard the bell, but I like to be careful."

I waited in back until he called the all clear; then I emerged. Just in case, it seemed like a good move not to leave empty-handed, so I bought a peace-sign keychain from the counter display. He acknowledged that with a knowing grin as he bagged it up. Since the Baltimore had actual metal keys, I even had a use for this. On the bus back, I snapped the two together. An old man fell asleep on my shoulder, and I stared out the dirty window at the crumbling cityscape, hoping I could achieve all my goals.

Jostling the shoulder sleeper, I got off at the stop that in no way felt like home. My stomach growled, reminding me that I hadn't eaten much of my pizza sticks at lunch and that breakfast had been a granola bar. *There's a bodega on the way.* I was thinking about what I could afford to buy—because Buzzkill's cash wouldn't last forever and the credit card couldn't possibly work—when I bumped into someone coming out of the thrift/wig shop.

"Sorry," I said in reflex.

I moved to step past, then realized that this was the guy who had shared his Dickens with me earlier. He seemed frozen in horror, like seeing me here was the worst-case scenario. Other people passed us on the sidewalk, collars up, heads down against the wind. *One of us needs to say something. What's his name again?*

Devon.

"Don't tell anyone," he finally mumbled.

"That you buy your clothes here or you have a wig fetish?" Since he wasn't carrying any packages, I figured that was a safe joke.

But he scowled. "You think that's funny?"

"Apparently not."

"If people at school find out my mom runs Madame Q's House of Style, I'll know who to blame," he snapped.

Oh.

"So this is your family business?"

"Shut the hell up."

Now that was surprisingly rude compared to how nice he was before, but he must think I was making fun of how his mother made her living. Which wasn't my intention at all. But I had no reason to correct his misconception. It wasn't like I'd be here long enough for it to matter.

"Okay, I'll pencil you in as my nemesis. I was kind of hoping I'd find one without looking on Craigslist."

From his blank look, that joke didn't land, either. *Shit, when did Craigslist become a thing?* I couldn't remember, but it must not be mainstream knowledge yet. With a mental shrug, I moved to pass him.

"It won't help you either if people find out you hang around downtown."

That sounded like a warning . . . or maybe a threat. So I turned. "Are you going to tell everyone I'm poor? And here I'm maintaining my image so carefully with haute couture." I struck a pose, tugging on my hoodie strings so the front conformed to my skull.

He relaxed a little then. "Okay, fine. But you know what dicks people can be."

"Seems like the haves would be pretty fiercely outnumbered in a town like this. Maybe we could organize and burn all their Gucci in effigy or whatever."

"You have *no* idea what's popular, do you? But . . . that sounds magical."

I shivered as the wind gusted stronger, with a frosty edge that hinted at snow. *Please, let this be normal winter, and not the winter king, searching for me.* "Okay, good talk, but I have to go buy dinner at the bodega. So . . ."

His brows went up at that, but he didn't try to stop me. I felt the prickle of Devon watching me until I went into the shop on the corner. This was the closest thing to a grocery store in this neighborhood; there was a small prepared-foods section, packaged so that I was pretty sure the owner's wife must cook it in her home kitchen. A tiny shelf of fruits and vegetables stood in the corner near the back, one section of canned goods, and the rest was liquor and snacks. After crunching some numbers in my head, I bought bread, cereal, apples, milk, peanut butter, jelly, and some instant noodles. Not the best diet, but until I figured out how to get a little more money, it would keep me alive and on the right path.

It was dark by the time I got back to my room. Putting the chain on helped for psychological reasons, though I could deal with any threat better than the flimsy door. I touched Aegis on my wrist for reassurance and then made a sandwich. Darkness didn't make my room more appealing, so I turned on the old-school, boxy TV for company. No free cable here, so there were four channels, all blurred with static.

I listened to the couple next door fighting until I fell asleep.

• • •

In the morning, I did my homework on the city bus, so it was messy but legible. Five minutes per subject did the trick. Another three blocks, and I was crossing the parking lot. Today, it was easier. My hoodie and jeans uniform granted me anonymity, or so I thought, until a group of letter jackets blocked my path.

"Hey, new girl. Hold up. You haven't met me yet." The guy who delivered that deathless classic was clearly the alpha, Cross Point's answer to Cameron Dean.

Though this guy had dark hair and hazel eyes, he radiated the same seamless confidence, as if life had never failed to deliver exactly what he wanted. Yes, he was built. Yes, he was hot. And I kind of wanted to kick him in the shins for assuming that my life couldn't be complete unless he acknowledged me.

I decided to be an asshole. "But we totally met last summer at that party. Remember? And you *never* called me. What's up with that?"

His smile froze. "Uh . . ."

One of his friends nudged him. "She's cute, Wade. Why didn't you call her?"

"Don't worry, I won't hold it against you." I gave a cheerful smile and extricated myself from the biceps fencing me in.

As I reached the relative sanctuary of the front hallway, I noticed Kian watching. No question he'd seen the exchange. I hurried to catch up with him.

"Can you smell the testosterone burning, or is it just me?"

"Did you just screw with Wade Tennant's head?" he asked, looking incredulous.

"Maybe a little. Which is probably cruel and unusual because I suspect he mostly uses it as a counterweight."

"Don't say shit like that. Maybe you can get away with it, but I'll get my ass kicked."

"I'll protect you," I promised.

"Well, that's emasculating." But he was smiling, not as tentative as the day before, either.

"Bullshit. It's way more egalitarian for people to take turns being heroic." I launched into some heartfelt commentary about Hermione and Harry, which Kian heard with growing interest.

"Wait, what did you say? I don't remember that scene."

Crap. I always get the books mixed up. Has the last one been published yet?

I hurried to distract him. "Never mind. My point is, it's totally cool for girls to be heroes. See you at lunch," I called as he went toward his first class.

By third period, everyone was calling me Nine. Which was weird, but I figured it was because of my hand, until I heard some guy say, "She's *totally* a nine, all good except for that missing finger. How do you think—"

His friend covered the dude's mouth when he realized I could hear. I raised my brow. "The answer is, obviously, that I crammed it up somebody's ass so far that it broke off. Probably because he was objectifying me, but I forget."

"Bitch," he mumbled from behind his buddy's palm.

As I walked off, the friend proved himself to be an ass too by whispering, "Dipshit, you can't say that in *front* of girls."

God, I hate high school.

Only Kian could make me stay here. The classes were no challenge, compared to Blackbriar's curriculum, though, so I coasted to lunch. My pulse ticked like a clock, reminding me that I had a deadline. If I didn't improve Kian's life and his state of mind by his fifteenth birthday, everything would happen all over again. The prospect of getting stuck in a loop as awful as this chilled my blood.

Not happening, not again.

After I went through the line, I skirted the room, but before I could reach Kian, Devon stood up at a table near the window. He gave me a tentative smile; his friends looked nice, a mix of smart, friendly people, and if things were different, it would be cool to get to know him. So I was already braced to shut him down.

"Want to sit with us?"

Six pairs of eyes in a variety of hues met mine. Four of six offered smiles that said they were totally okay with making room. So I waved as I said, "Thanks for the invite, but my friend is expecting me."

"Where?" Devon scanned the room, seeming surprised that I'd gotten a better offer.

Nosy much?

But there was no point in hiding it because I intended to make it super obvious that I thought Kian Riley was fantastic. Beaming, I raised my hand. "Over there."

Kian reluctantly waved back, then ducked his head, clearly hating the attention. Style-wise, he looked worse than the day before. I started toward him, but Devon grabbed my arm.

"Okay, fair warning. That kid is so freaking weird; he never talks to anyone. I'm not kidding." He invited the table to weigh in with a speaking look. "Nobody's ever heard him say a word, right?"

"He's a future school shooter," another guy agreed.

My heart twisted. If they knew him, they'd never say that. Deep down, he wanted to be a hero, so he'd never hurt people, even if they made him feel like a worthless shit. No, given time, Kian would implode, taking all that pain and turning it on himself. I swallowed hard, fighting sudden tears. God, I wanted instant intimacy so he'd share those feelings with me instead, but we had to build a relationship first, and these jackoffs were standing *in my way.*

"Maybe you should get to know him." With a pointed stare, I added, "Funny how people who worry about being judged can do it to someone else."

This time I won't fail; this time I'll save the boy I love.

MANIC PIXIE NIGHTMARE

At 3 a.m., I woke to find the Harbinger perched at the foot of my bed, head cocked in apparent fascination. At first, I thought I was dreaming, but when he leaned forward, I scrambled back, nearly knocking over the lamp on the bedside table in my hurry to turn it on. But he didn't vanish with the feeble glimmer of light. So close and unexpected, his aura scraped across my nerves like unchained lightning, so I couldn't get my breath.

Terror, dread, and awe fought a cage match until I managed, "Stop."

He dialed it down so I could focus. Dark cloak, red vest. My heartbeat steadied as his boots vanished from his feet and reappeared on the floor. He came up in a crouch, looming in a way that was probably supposed to be terrifying. Without the aura, however, I could cope.

"What are you . . . *how* are you here?" Since I'd jumped, the Harbinger in this time stream shouldn't even know who I was, right?

"Time doesn't have the same hold on us, dearling."

"Are you saying you followed me?"

"Not exactly. You know how a rock of sufficient size can be both in a stream and out of it at the same time?"

"Time being the river in this analogy."

"Precisely." He seemed pleased as he went on. "Like that rock, I exist here, just as I do there, and I retain awareness of those connected to me."

"You're asking me to believe in cross-dimensional memory? Or that you can remember things that haven't yet happened, will . . . did happen, or will not have happened . . . ?" I trailed off, giving up on figuring out the correct tenses for this convo.

It's three in the morning; I can't handle this.

"Is that so much stranger than nightmares given life by human credence?"

Sighing, I allowed, "Okay then. That doesn't explain how you found me. Isn't the medallion working?"

"Remember, it has limitations and I have eyes everywhere."

"Flipping birds," I muttered.

"Even without them, I'd have located you in time. Our prior exchange did more than just nourish me, and . . . some bonds cannot be broken."

"Awesome, so there's some kind of ethereal tether between us?"

"You could say that." He shifted from the predatory crouch and folded his legs lotus-style, as if settling in for a cozy chat. "Admit it, you're pleased to see me."

I didn't want to give an inch, so I said, "Do you remember how things turned out there?"

"The longer I focus here, the blurrier it becomes. Despite immortality, we are not omnipotent or omniscient. So it's a bit like multitasking. You know how an old woman knits in front of the television, most of her mind on the scarf? Little bits from elsewhere slip in, snips of dialogue, noise from outside, but mostly she only notices what's in her lap."

That actually made sense. Otherwise Wedderburn wouldn't have locked up the Oracle; he would've turned his attention on the future and learned things without needing technology to travel. But fixating on the future would be like disconnecting plugs in the present, leaving the winter king vulnerable to attack, and he had too many enemies to make that feasible.

"Interesting. But that doesn't explain *why* you're here." His arrival felt like a boulder suspended on a fragile chain. After all, the word *harbinger* meant "bearer of bad tidings." At least, I'd never heard anyone called a harbinger of *good* omens.

He leveled an assessing stare on me. "Would you believe it if I said I'm curious? You've done so many foolish and fascinating things. I'd like to know how your story ends."

"I guess that depends on whether you intend to place bets against me, help other immortals track me down, that kind of thing." With Aegis on my wrist, I could probably end him before he realized I'd made the decision.

But I don't want to.

"Technically, there's still a contract open between us, you know. Fell made it impossible for me to complete it as originally intended, and that is . . . bothersome. But I *know* you don't believe I'm here as your protection."

"Not really," I admitted.

"Honesty has never been a friend to me," the Harbinger said.

"But perhaps I'll try it this once. The bond I mentioned before . . . you're the closest thing I have to kin now."

"Because you fed from me?" I didn't get it. He took energy from Nicole too, but he wasn't camped outside the mental health facility waiting to see if she recovered.

When I pointed that out, a lopsided smile carved into his lean cheek. "You gave of yourself willingly, dearling. That is the difference. What I have from you is born of free will . . . and that is a sweetness I cannot otherwise experience."

Oh.

"I'm glad," I said, though I wasn't sure that was the right response. "But I won't assume you're on my side since caprice is kind of your deal. As long as you don't get in my way, I won't complain if you want to watch the show."

"An excellent summation of my intentions."

"Just to be clear, I don't have to worry about the others finding me like you did?"

"They lack our connection, but they have other resources."

"So don't get comfortable?" I'd already come to that conclusion myself, so that wasn't exactly invaluable advice.

He nodded, letting himself topple sideways on my bed. The light didn't touch him, as if he was a shadow too deep for the photons to penetrate. Really I should get him out of here, but at this hour, the Baltimore was creepy enough that the Harbinger qualified as comforting in comparison. The woman next door had been crying for two hours when I finally fell asleep, and her silence was somehow more ominous than the despairing sobs.

"Why are you staying in such a hovel?" he demanded then.

"It's a protest against our consumer culture."

The Harbinger's look said he wasn't even slightly amused. "Karl Marx would be charmed, I'm sure. Power to the proletariat."

"Okay, this is what I can afford on Buzzkill's stash. And to avoid starvation, I'll need to get a job while I'm here."

"I could help you," he said.

Shaking my head, I backed off that offer so fast I got vertigo. "No thanks. I'm pretty sure I know how it goes, once I start accepting favors from you."

"You wound me with your cynicism." But he didn't deny that there would be terrifying costs associated with his assistance, even given to someone he dubbed "kin."

"Bullshit. I've just gotten better at anticipating the fine print."

The Harbinger snapped his fingers, and the tired bulb on my bedside lamp guttered out.

His voice came soft and low, but also terrible like the groan of a beam before it gave way. "The woman in the room next door . . ."

"Yeah?"

"She's dying." Two words, cool as a sealed tomb.

That launched me from bed, and I went out the door at a run. Though he was the trickster, it didn't occur to me to question. In the hallway, the carpet was gross and sticky beneath my bare feet; nobody answered when I pounded with both hands, so I ran back and dialed 911. When the operator answered, I gasped, "I think my neighbor OD'd," because that would surely get the right people out here. But after the man took all the info, time ticked away. I called the night desk clerk, but he had no interest in the situation and wouldn't agree to unlock room ten so I could check on the tenant.

The Harbinger watched my anxiety with inscrutable interest. Eventually, he said, "Would you like *me* to open the door?"

27

And then I knew. "She's gone, right? If I say yes, I'll owe you a favor, all for nothing."

"It's like Schrödinger's cat, dearling. You'll never know unless you open the box."

Before I could decide, however, sirens finally sounded and paramedics pounded up the stairs at the end of the hall. My door wasn't the only one that cracked open as they ran into room ten. Five minutes later, they came out with a body, not a patient. Sheer fury sparked inside me. I balled my hands into fists, turning on the Harbinger in the darkness.

"Was that *fun* for you?"

"A little."

"Thanks for reminding me how awful you are. I'd almost forgotten." Even if that woman's life was miserable, it was worth saving. Death was the final answer to second chances . . . because as long as you were alive, you could always turn it around.

"Does that mean you won't pet my hair and assure me I'm not a monster?" He danced out of reach when I swung. "My heart is breaking. *Broken*, even. I want your approval almost as much as I want to sow misery and discord."

On the verge of activating Aegis, I stilled . . . because his final statement carried the unmistakable ring of truth, a sort of hopeless longing. In my life, I'd often felt exactly that, watching people laughing with their friends, warm and effortless. It was like there was an invisible wall dividing me from the things I wanted most. Now I had cast everything off except for this one absurd, impossible mission. The worst part was, even if I succeeded, no one would ever know. At that moment, I understood the Harbinger well enough *not* to kill him.

28

Again.

"You're such a child," I said.

His tone sparkled with puzzlement and wonder. "Am I? Then . . . will you raise me?"

"Get out."

I didn't wait to see if he'd listen, slamming into the bathroom. The tub was awful and gross with dark stains on the grout, but I climbed into it anyway, fully clothed, and wrapped my arms around my knees. For some reason, it was hard to breathe, as if an iron band had wrapped around my chest, tightening with each desperate pull of my lungs. I didn't even know that woman, but the fact that I didn't save her felt like the promise of failure.

You can't do this. Everything will play out exactly as it did before.

My sense of self receded until I might've been a speck of dust beneath the bed, a small and impotent mote. The tears didn't come, but each gasp shivered through me in dry sobs. Closing my eyes didn't help, either, because I only saw the slim outline of a body, being wheeled away by people who didn't know her or care.

But I should've known a simple door wouldn't stop the Harbinger, though I didn't register him until his hand rested on my hair. "You let me give you so much grief."

I slapped him away. "Leave me alone."

"What a wonder. Why do you care about such a miserable husk?"

"She was a *person*, and everyone matters. Don't you get that? Even if she made bad choices, she mattered, and you made her a damn game or a test or—"

"Edie."

I stopped talking because I couldn't remember the Harbinger ever saying my name precisely like that. "What?"

"I lied. She wasn't dying before. When I arrived, she was already gone."

My breath went in a wheeze. Hadn't I thought that the silence was worse than her incessant crying? I might have even noticed the moment of her death and counted it a relief—*Thank God I don't have to listen to that anymore.* While the Harbinger did screw with me, *I* was the one who should've done better. There was no way I could sustain the rage at him, considering the weight of my own faults.

I lifted my gaze to meet his star-shot eyes. "Is this what you wanted to teach me? That I'm awful too?"

Something like regret flashed over his face; then he swept me up in a swirl of dark fabric and carried me back to the other room. "Come away; you'll catch something." Once we reached the bed, he set me down and drew back as if I was a pillar of flames. "You're the only one who would seek meaning in my myriad cruelties."

"I can't know your intentions," I said. "But it felt like a warning. There are lots of ways to become a monster, and the *easiest* is to look the other way when you see people in pain."

"You give me too much credit."

"I'll do better. And . . . I think I understand now. Life is about connections. To save Kian, I have to help him meet other people. Me, alone, it's a start, but not enough."

"Your ramblings have become nonsensical. For you to imagine I'm *helping* you without recompense, that is madness." He sounded annoyed.

I stifled a smile. "Of course not. You're the Harbinger."

"It would behoove you to remember that."

As I glanced at the clock, I sighed. Almost four, school would

30

suck more than usual tomorrow. "Right. Well, I'm going back to sleep. Either get out or keep quiet."

He stared. "You'd let me stay?"

"What do I care?" It occurred to me that the Harbinger was the closest I had to a friend in this timeline. *Is that awesome or terrible?* Full of bravado, I went on. "Stand guard in the corner, watch TV, or eat my instant noodles. But replace those if you do."

"I'll stay for a while," he said softly.

The TV flickered to life. When he sat down in the grubby vinyl armchair, I didn't expect to sleep. But it was better than being alone, and I was tired. In the morning, he was gone, along with two packs of ramen. In their place, he had left two cherry Danishes and yogurt, along with a note. *Cup Noodles are delicious. Why did no one inform me? See you soon. —H.*

I had the Harbinger's offering for breakfast and then ran for the bus. More homework on the ride to school, and then I pondered the adaptation of my original plan. It wouldn't be easy to integrate Kian with Devon's group, considering what they thought of him, but—

To my surprise, Kian was waiting near the bus stop when I hopped off. I could tell he had tried extra hard since he'd tucked his paisley polyester shirt into his jeans and was wearing a belt. Overall it didn't help much. But it was so good to see him, alive and healthy, instead of dying in my arms that my smile must've been about a thousand watts—to the point that it startled him. He blinked, pausing before he took a step toward me. Awkwardly, he fiddled with his backpack straps.

"I thought we could walk to school together."

"You ride the CTA too?"

31

He nodded. "Different route, though, I guess, or I'd have seen you."

"Which means you were looking," I teased.

Kian's eyes widened, and he stumbled back a step like I was about to declare him a stalker. "What? No. I mean—"

"Relax." Only by interrupting could I put him at ease. "So what do you do on weekends? I don't know anything about this town." And then I used personal intel to sweeten the deal. "You know what would be cool? A theater that showed the classics." I ached a little, remembering all our dates in Harvard Square, precious memories that only I shared.

But as I hoped, that distracted him. "Are you into golden-age cinema?"

His eyes were so, so bright and hopeful, that I wished I *could* be Nine, not Edie the Echo, out of time. If I really was a transfer student, things would be so different. Getting to know him like this— and not as part of the game—would be incredible. As we walked, I tried not to let the wistful feeling overwhelm me.

"Totally. *Casablanca, North by Northwest.*" I named movies that I already knew Kian loved. "*Notorious. To Catch a Thief. Indiscreet.*"

"I'm sensing a Cary Grant theme here," he noted.

Of all the old movies I'd watched with Kian before, Cary Grant *was* my favorite. I could understand why people loved Humphrey Bogart, but Grant had a dashing, urbane quality I appreciated more. So I nodded, hugging the truth to my chest—that Kian was the only reason I knew about any of this. Suppressing a smile, I wondered what he'd say if I straight up confessed to being his girlfriend from the future, a la *The Terminator*, and then the dialogue wrote itself:

Make out with me if you want to live.

Okay, maybe not.

Oblivious to my weird, born-of-desperation humor, Kian was saying, "I've never been, but there's a cool place in Lofton. It's an old theater that's been converted to a bar. They kept the screen and show classics on Saturday nights. It's over twenty-one only, though."

"Not a problem," I said, feeling cool for the first time ever.

He lowered his voice like the students nearby might report us. "You have ID?"

"I'm picking it up tonight, actually."

"You move to a new town and, first thing, you find someone to make you a fake ID?" His eyes widened, and he looked like he couldn't decide if that was awesome or if I was the irresponsible maniac who would ruin his life.

But most important, he didn't look sad at all. He seemed . . . intrigued. *Like me, Kian, like me a little. Enough to forget the girl who breaks your heart.*

I grinned. "So? You never know when you'll need to get into a bar."

"If you say so."

"I'm heading there after school to pick up my ID. Come with me. If you do, you'll get yours on Friday, and then we can check out the classic movie joint on Saturday."

We reached the school parking lot, and the warning bell was about to ring. I could predict all the reasons why he couldn't trembling on the tip of his tongue. But what finally came out was, "How much is it?"

I did the math, then said, "Don't worry about it, you can pay me back later."

"Okay. But I don't understand why you're being so nice to me. BT-dubs I'm out of here if you say weird shit about my eyes again."

That sounded *so* like what I said to him in the diner that I had to strangle the urge to kiss him. "Don't worry about that, either. Just be sure of one thing, Kian Riley." As if he sensed I was dead serious, we locked eyes, so sweet it hurt. "I'm going to change your life."

ALL OUR YESTERDAYS

After school, we took the bus to Psychedelic Records. The lack of business made think the owner paid his rent with fake IDs. But Kian seemed really into the vinyl, which shouldn't have surprised me, considering how much he loved old movies. So I browsed the store for a few minutes, trying to see the magic through his eyes.

"Oh my God, look . . ." He showed me a beat-up album with three guys on the front, clad in strange costumes sporting facial hair and shaggy beatnik style.

I'd never heard of the band, but apparently they were British, and this was hard to find. "You should totally get it."

"It's twenty bucks."

From what he'd said, his uncle wasn't well off and his aunt disliked him, so they probably didn't give him much allowance, if any. It looked like his aunt had spent five dollars at Goodwill for Kian's current wardrobe. But one problem at a time.

"Maybe he'll make us a deal."

The beardo behind the counter flicked a look at Kian, as if to ask me what was up. "It's cool. I'm here to pick up, and he's interested in additional services."

"Chest," the guy said.

"Flash him," I told Kian.

"What?"

"Come on, hurry up. I'll turn around."

A few seconds later, the owner said, "Okay, what do you need?"

Kian shot me a helpless look, so I answered, "Basic ID, over twenty-one."

I handed over half the cash for Kian's ID and my two, which cut significantly into my stash. At the rate I was spending money, I wouldn't last long on my own. But budgeting wasn't a skill my mom and dad taught me before everything went pear shaped.

The owner handed me an envelope; then Kian headed back for his quick photo session. Afterward, I confirmed, "Pickup on Friday afternoon?"

The guy nodded. "Thanks for the referral, but don't post a flyer at school."

"After this, you won't see me again," I promised. "But I was wondering, is there any way you could give us a discount?" I held up the album.

"Sorry. If this town wasn't such a shithole, I could probably get more than twenty."

"All right. Thanks."

Disappointed, I put the record back. Unfortunately I couldn't grant all of Kian's wishes like a fairy godmother; my resources were decidedly limited. I had to save bus fare to get to school, which was a huge priority. Skipping would not only get me in trouble but it would also limit my access to Kian. How else could I see him every day without it being weird?

"I'm so excited. I wonder what's playing," I said.

"I can check tonight if you want."

"That would be awesome."

The wind was cold, and we really needed to get on our respective buses. But as we walked toward the stop, I could only think of keeping him with me a little longer. Inviting him to my place would probably make him call family services or at least open the door to some serious concern on his part. Yet I wished we could hang out like we did before, none of the barriers between us. Now I understood how Kian must've felt, falling for someone he'd watched on Wedderburn's orders.

"I can't believe we're doing this." His words came out in a rush. "It's like something I'd read about, happening to *me*."

"Life should be an adventure," I told him.

Not a constant struggle for survival.

"It must have been awesome in California," he started, and then he appeared to remember the lie I'd told. "Oh, wait, fourteen schools, two years. So you probably didn't leave a ton of friends behind."

"Not many. Do you still have time tonight? There's somewhere else I want to go."

He raised a brow at me. "How exactly do you envision my social calendar looking?"

"Well, you might get in trouble for being late."

"It's fine. I already texted my uncle that I was hanging out after school, and my aunt probably wouldn't care if I didn't come back at all." Those words should've been laced with bitterness, but instead, there was only this matter-of-factness that bothered me more.

I ignored the implications, however, because he didn't want sympathy. "On the plus side, it means you can do what you want, right?"

But I'd been on that side of parental freedom, and it sucked because it meant nobody gave a shit.

"I guess. But mostly all I do is go to school, read, and watch movies in my room."

That's a lie. You write poetry too. But that wasn't something he'd tell me so fast because it wasn't cool and he was probably still focused on how I might judge him, like friendship was a chipped porcelain cup—one wrong move, and it would all be shards on the floor.

"Come on." I dragged him on the bus and dinged my pass twice.

Since he had no idea where we were going, there was no reason for him to pay. Hopefully, this idea wouldn't hurt his feelings. It wasn't like I planned some big makeover or that I didn't like him exactly as he was. But to fit in a little better at school, he needed to dial down the vintage.

"You know, I'm not big on surprises." But he settled beside me without further complaint, and I totally noticed when his knee brushed mine. He jerked back, though. "S-sorry. I didn't do that on purpose."

"Relax. A little human contact won't hurt us." Teasing, I tilted my head to the side to let it rest on his shoulder for a few seconds.

Kian froze. Then he slowly turned his face toward mine, so I could see the ridge of his nose, his inky lashes, all the imperfections in his skin. Mostly, though, I saw the stunning disbelief in his jade eyes behind those lenses. I didn't pull back, though I shouldn't be close enough to kiss him. It was kind of weird, and he was too young, which made me feel like a creeper. I mean, obviously *he* thought I was only a year older, not four. *Okay, three and a half.* At Blackbriar, there were seniors who dated freshmen, but everyone kind of side-eyed over it because it seemed like they only did it because it was easier to get into their pants.

But he didn't lean in, exactly. He rested his head on mine briefly and then dug into his backpack. "Not sure if you're interested but I have some music we can listen to . . ."

I took the earbud and put it in my left ear, leaving him the right. It didn't surprise me to learn that his favorite listening could've been featured on the soundtrack of Fallout: New Vegas. As the bus carried us closer to our destination, I listened to a mad soulful version of "I Had the Craziest Dream." The song would've been the perfect choice for him to make a move, but Kian didn't have the confidence for that. His gaze lingered on my lips for a few seconds, but I made the decision to shift away.

You can't.

"You like it?" he whispered.

"It's fantastic. Who is this?"

"Nat King Cole. He's best known for 'Unforgettable.'"

"Oh yeah. I've heard that one."

We listened to another song before I nudged him that we had to get up. Kian glanced out the window in surprise. Apparently, he would've been happy to ride around the city with me all night on this crappy bus. My heart turned over. *Don't let him fall for you all the way.* But I didn't listen to that cautionary voice; I grabbed his hand and towed him toward the doors. The solitary point of contact made me feel like singing. His fingers were cold when he wrapped them around mine. *He's holding my hand. Not dead. Not gone. Not in extremis.* The tears I couldn't cry in the tub last night threatened at the worst possible time. I couldn't let him think I was unstable; it might scare him away.

"This way," I said, swinging our hands like little kids.

There, that's the opposite of romantic.

When he saw the neon MADAME Q'S HOUSE OF STYLE sign, he paused. "Are we actually going in here?"

The wigs in the window were a little creepy, but . . . "My wardrobe could use some augmentation, and my budget doesn't stretch to the mall. I didn't want to go shopping alone, though. Do you mind?"

"I guess not," he said.

The bell tinkled when we stepped inside. A willowy woman wearing one of her wigs—or so I suspected—came out to greet us in a drift of colorful scarves and lilac perfume. *This must be Devon's mom.* She beamed as she realized she had two customers.

"Anything I can help you find?"

"T-shirts, if you have any."

"Sure, over here." She forged a path through the racks to a table near the back.

The store was crammed full to the point it was hard to maneuver with racks of old dresses rubbing up against vintage suits. If I ran the place, I'd organize the clothes by style instead of putting all the pants together. But maybe space didn't permit a better system. I glanced at Kian, still standing awkwardly by the door, and beckoned.

"Help me pick something out."

"You don't want *my* help," he mumbled.

But he still came over as I picked through the offerings. Eventually, I dug up a couple of cool ones near the bottom, one black Grand Funk Railroad, one white Who shirt. They were priced at five bucks each, though, so I hesitated.

"I need to move some merchandise to make room for stock in back," Mrs. Quick said. "So if you want them, I can cut you a deal. Two for six?"

That seemed like a good deal. "You have three bucks?" I asked Kian.

He nodded. "But I don't listen to either of those bands."

"It's a shirt, not a testimonial." I paid for my part in crumpled singles; then Kian added his bills.

"Need a receipt?" Mrs. Quick asked.

"No, it's fine. Do you take stuff as trade-in or on consignment or . . ." I was already plotting to get Kian into some better-fitting jeans.

"As long as the clothes are clean, I can sell them for you on consignment or I can give you store credit."

"That would be cool, thanks."

"Do you want a bag?"

I shook my head, taking the Who shirt and stuffing it into my bag. Kian did the same with his black one. With a pair of Chucks instead of those grubby white Walmart sneakers, skinny jeans, and that band shirt, he'd fit in better at school. A wardrobe change didn't require a ton of money, but I could tell his aunt didn't care by what she bought for him and Kian probably felt too guilty to object.

As I headed for the door, I had to step out of Devon's way. He looked straight up horrified to see me here; then he noticed Kian. "Can I talk to you?"

He dragged me out the door into the bitter wind before I could protest. "What?"

The neon threw an orange glow over us, making our skin look ruddy and weird. It was starting to get dark, and a few flurries swirled down, shining as streetlights caught them. I rubbed my hands together and stuffed them in my jacket pockets. Gloves would've been a smart investment; I didn't even think to look. *Next time.*

"How come you're here?"

"I got a shirt. Is that okay?"

"You promised you wouldn't tell anyone."

"And I didn't. We're shopping. But you acting like this is more likely to tip Kian off than anything I say. Plus, it's kind of weird that your friends don't know—"

Devon sighed. "Of course *they* do. But assholes like Wade Tennant give people shit all the time for less."

Since I had been the Teflon crew's favorite target, I understood his concern. Once bullies locked you in their sights and saw wounds appear, it was like some kind of collective madness infected them. Individually, they might not even be that bad, but combine mob mentality with peer pressure and shit got scary.

"I understand, but we're just shopping. I swear."

Since it was true, I had no other defense. Devon studied me for a long moment, then appeared to believe me. "Okay. You like my mom's store?"

"She's got some cool stuff."

"Vonna and Carmen shop here too, to be honest."

"So you're protecting them. Well, no worries on my account."

We exchanged a tentative smile then. Kian stepped out and pulled up the hood on his puffy maroon jacket. He started to ask me a question, but it was like his voice shriveled up and died when he realized I wasn't alone. *Wow, he really* can't *talk to people. So why didn't he clam up at lunch that first day?*

To smooth the awkward moment, I said, "Devon's in my English class; he had a question. Do you know him?"

Kian shook his head, not making eye contact. The pavement might've been inscribed with hieroglyphics based on his intent fascination. I stepped closer so he had no choice but to look at me, and I tipped my head in encouragement.

"Hey," he finally mumbled.

Devon's eyes widened. "Hey."

"Happy shopping," I said. "We're out of here."

Devon waved, seeming surprised. "See you."

Kian let out a long breath as we moved away. "I hate seeing people from school. It's like, I don't know, a sudden punch in the face when you least expect it."

"I'm from school," I pointed out.

His eyes lit on my face, skimming my features like he still couldn't believe I was real. "You're different."

"How?"

"I'm not sure. Just . . ." He stopped talking and shrugged, unable to put it into words.

It seemed better not to press, as he was just getting comfortable with me. "Okay. I live near here, so I'll walk you to the stop."

"Wouldn't it make more sense for me to see you home?" he asked.

"It's okay." *Because then you'd see where I live.*

43

We walked in silence for those two blocks, his expression pensive. Finally, he said, "So we're going back to Psychedelic on Friday . . . and to the movies on Saturday. Right?"

"That's the plan."

"Sweet." It was like he just wanted verbal confirmation or something.

Though he said I didn't have to, I waited with him. The bus shelter was open to the wind on one side, so after he sneezed the first time, I huddled against him, remembering when he held me like it was the most natural thing in the world. But he was so nervous with each puff of breath that I feared he'd hyperventilate.

"This was the best day of my life," he whispered.

I said that once too. Because of him. Lights appeared in the snowy night, bus brakes screeching as it slowed. It was hard to let go of him. Kian stepped away and climbed aboard, and each step felt like a thousand miles. He pressed his face against the window and waved for much longer than made sense. But then, I could've turned and walked off. The sidewalk was slick with new snow by the time I raced back to the Baltimore. Passing through the grimy gray lobby always made me feel dirty by association. So far, I hadn't seen the clerk wear more than a stained undershirt and tan trousers; the only way the place could be more disreputable was if they had Plexiglas on top of the counter.

I meant to pass through quickly, but the guy stopped me with a phlegmy throat clearing. "You're the one who called about the woman in ten." It wasn't a question.

"So?"

"Better mind your business." That sounded like a threat, and I wouldn't get a refund if he kicked me out.

"Okay."

If he planned to say more, I didn't wait for it. I ran up the stairs to the second floor and locked myself behind the chain, like *that* was secure. The pleasure I'd gotten from hanging out with Kian chilled like the lonely swirls of snow frosting my window. My reality was bleak; the best I could hope for was to return to my time, but I didn't even know if this device worked that way. By leaving my world, I might've erased it and replaced it with this reality.

I sighed. The weather made me want to buy a mask and cape, then go loom broodingly—or brood loomingly—atop a tall building. The note the Harbinger had left was still on my pressboard table. Reading it again cheered me a little. Since he was right, and Cup Noodles were delicious, I had some for dinner, along with an apple and a slug of milk. *I should buy a multivitamin. Can time travelers get scurvy?*

After waiting an hour, I texted, *Did you get home okay?*

No problems. Kian responded fast enough that I wondered if he was holding his phone, thinking about me.

Probably I should let it go for now, but my room was so quiet, hard not to think about the woman next door who died alone. So I sent, *today was fun,* just to keep the conversation open. My phone was silent long enough that I felt like a dipshit staring at it.

Kian: *You wearing your shirt tomorrow?*

Me: *Definitely. We should clean our closets and go back there. I bet she has some cool stuff buried.*

Kian: *I'm up for it.*

Me: *We could go Saturday, before the movie.*

I stared at the screen, wondering if that was too much. Maybe he'd think it was weird that I wanted to glom on to him constantly.

45

Normal people should have other stuff to do, family activities, but Kian must be lonely too. And I'd go crazy if I hung around the Baltimore all weekend. Damn, just the prospect of Sunday made me want to crawl back in the tub.

K. Meet you at the Broad Street stop? Not that we couldn't plan this at school.

Laughing, I sent, *See you tomorrow.*

Tomorrow, and tomorrow, and tomorrow. The full speech from *Macbeth* popped into my head, so I murmured it aloud.

Shakespeare was wrong. Life was far more than a shadow, and it signified everything.

WINTER'S WRATH

Friday I went with Kian to Psychedelic Records. He'd scraped together the other half of the cash somehow, which was good, as I couldn't have paid for the rest. *I need to quit being so impulsive.* He also had an extra twenty for the record he'd wanted. The guy behind the counter smirked at us.

"Pleasure doing business. Remember, if someone realizes your IDs aren't kosher, you never heard of me."

"Got it," I said.

He bagged Kian's album and offered the colorful plastic sack. "Thanks for your patronage. Stop by again."

The owner followed us to the door and flipped the sign to CLOSED as we stepped out. There were only a couple of other businesses still open on this street. The weather was colder than it had been, more snow piling up in the streets. It would probably affect the buses until the plows went around. From what I'd noticed, Cross Point didn't have enough equipment, nowhere near as efficient as Boston. Shivering, I grabbed Kian's arm.

"We have twenty minutes until the next bus, assuming it's not late. Let's not wait here."

I slipped and slid across the street, weirdly deserted for six on a Friday night. But the better parts of Cross Point lay farther from the town center, subdivisions and malls built away from evidence of industrial failure. The flickering lights from the convenience store offered a welcome oasis, and I sighed as the warm air rushed over me.

The girl behind the counter spared us a glance but not a smile; she was watching a small black-and-white TV. I paid for a packet of sweet rolls and two cups of bitter coffee. I added nondairy creamer and packets of sugar to mine until it turned caramel instead of sludge brown. There were three plastic stools near the far window and a narrow counter where you could set Cup Noodles or a beverage, so we went over there to wait.

"It's kind of amazing," Kian said, stirring his coffee.

"What?" I split the cinnamon rolls down the middle and slid his half toward him.

"This should be awful." He glanced around at the dingy store with a half shrug. "With someone else, it probably would be. But anything *we* do seems like an adventure."

"It's all about the company," I agreed.

Sipping the coffee, I decided it was just below adequate with all my additions. More important, it was hot and it warmed me up from the inside out. I nursed it, suspecting the clerk might ask us to leave if we weren't eating or drinking items purchased in the store. For the same reason, I pecked at the sweet bun in tiny bird nibbles. It didn't taste as delicious as I remembered from childhood, gummy more than yummy.

Maybe it's stale.

"Do you think the buses will be on schedule tomorrow?" he asked.

"I hope so. Otherwise my weekend will suck."

He paused, studying me intently. "Mine too."

Since I didn't want him to fall for me all the way, I nudged him. "Are those headlights?"

Peering through the slanting snow, the shine resolved into a bus shape, still about a block away. He nodded, and I raced out of the store, determined not to miss it. The snow in the street was above my ankles, and my fabric sneakers were sodden. I made it to the bus stop with Kian right behind me a few seconds before the bus groaned to a stop, sliding as it did.

Probably because of the awful weather, there was nobody else on board. The driver said, "You're lucky, kids. The CTA ordered us back to base, so this is the last run of the night."

Kian's eyes widened. "But I need a transfer to get home."

"Sorry. Your family will have to pick you up."

The bus started with a jerk, and the floor was slippery. I'd have fallen if Kian hadn't grabbed me. We tumbled together into the nearest seats. He didn't immediately let go and since the bus wasn't that warm, I couldn't object. I shoved my hands in my pockets, trying to ignore the fact that my feet were freezing.

"This sucks," he murmured.

"You can't get a ride?" I already had an idea of the answer, but Nine didn't.

"Probably not. My uncle is away this weekend for work and my aunt . . . well, she won't go out in this weather." He didn't say *for me*, but I sensed the unspoken addendum.

Before I could think better of the offer, I said, "You can stay at my place if you want."

He glanced at me, eyes wide. "Are you sure? Won't your parents mind?"

"My mom is . . . gone," I said. "And my dad doesn't pay much attention. He's not around tonight anyway."

That was surely pathetic enough to discourage questions. A flash of sympathy glimmered in Kian's green eyes. Then he said, "That's my situation in reverse. My dad's dead and my mom has . . . issues." A polite way to describe her drug habit. "But I'm with my aunt and uncle. How come . . ." He trailed off, likely unable to figure out how to frame the question.

"We don't stay in one place long enough for anyone to notice," I said softly, expanding on my *fourteen schools in two years* story.

This might be a bad idea, if feeling sorry for me made him want to save me. I wasn't sure if his white-knight complex had emerged yet. But it was my fault we'd come out tonight to get his ID, and I couldn't let him sleep in the bus station. My room might be shitty, but it was better than that. Probably.

"If you're sure it's cool, I'd appreciate it. I'll text my aunt." From his expression, that was more of a courtesy than necessary for permission.

And sure enough, five minutes after he sent the message, he got back *OK*, and that was it. No questions about his friend or the family he'd be staying with. I had the feeling he could text *Moving to Siberia*, and the response would be the same. Though I'd never met this woman, I already didn't like her. Even if she hated Kian's dad, that wasn't *his* fault.

With the bus creeping through the snow, it took half an hour longer than usual to get to my stop. The snow was coming down even harder, nearly blinding me as the wind whipped it sideways, catching the light from the streetlamps so it looked like a white stream. Kian grabbed my hand, probably so he didn't lose me. A few cars parked on the street had six inches on them, and if it wasn't for the fact that the whole city was caught in this, I'd think Wedderburn had something to do with it.

Maybe he does.

Kian was a catalyst he hoped to acquire. So Raoul must be watching and reporting. By hanging out with Kian, I'd certainly expose myself if Wedderburn focused on the future at all. The snowstorm seemed like a reflection of ire more than a planned attack, though. So that meant he was pissed that Kian had stopped inching toward extremis.

It's working. I'm changing things.

So despite the shitty weather, I was smiling when I led Kian into the Baltimore. For once, luck was on my side, and the front desk clerk was in the toilet or something, so I didn't have to face his leers or gross remarks when I went up to my room. Kian was trying not to look horrified, I could tell, but he kept glancing over his shoulder like something terrible was chasing us.

I unlocked the door and gestured. "Home, sweet home."

Through his eyes, this must be one of the lower levels of hell, though I'd gotten used to the awfulness of it. I showered on a towel, not wanting to put my bare feet in the tub, and the only good thing that could be said about the sheets was there were no bedbugs, though they certainly didn't believe in discarding stained linens here. I went inside first, seeing his hesitation.

"If you're uncomfortable, you can call for a ride," I said.

"No, sorry. I was just wondering if this would be okay. I mean, there's no privacy."

I smirked. "If you were expecting your own room, I have to disappoint you. But the radiator works pretty well. Usually."

"It's fine," he said.

Shrugging out of my damp jacket, I tinkered with said radiator until a blast of hot air caught me in the face. Then I hung up my coat by the door and stripped out of my shoes and socks, arraying them by the heater to dry. My hoodie was damp too, so I hung that up as well. Kian just watched me, mouth half open.

"You should dry your stuff too. Otherwise it'll be awful in the morning."

"Right." He followed my lead until he was barefoot.

The plain gray T-shirt he had on was better than the polyester stuff he usually wore, and it made me think I was influencing him subconsciously. When you liked someone, you wanted to fit in with them better. *A good sign*, I thought.

"Are you hungry? I have ramen."

By the way his eyes lit up, you'd think I had offered filet mignon. "That would be great."

So I boiled the water in my kettle and filled the cups to the line. We waited three minutes, then added the season packets. I'd done this a lot alone since my kitchenette didn't lend itself to fancy cooking, nor did my budget, but it was a little better with Kian perched on the other side of the bed mixing his noodles with complete concentration.

We slurped them down in unison, and he looked into his cup, wistful, when they were gone. Thanks to the Harbinger, I couldn't offer seconds, but . . . "Want something to drink? I have apples and yogurt too."

"I can't eat all your food."

"It's okay. I can buy more."

"If you're sure."

By recent standards, we had a feast. I made cups of hot tea, lightly laced with milk, and we had those, along with the apples and yogurt. If we ate the granola too, that would be pretty much it, except for the makings of a few PB&Js. *That'll be breakfast.*

"Better?" I asked.

"Much."

The black tea perked me up considerably in conjunction with the bad coffee, so I wasn't remotely tired. Plus, it wasn't even nine. Without asking his opinion, I switched on the TV. "Don't expect much, I only get four channels."

On one of them, an old movie was about to start, one I'd never heard of called *The African Queen.* The picture was shitty, but Kian seemed excited. "You'll love this."

I almost said, *Will I?* like a smart-ass and then recalled that I was supposed to be a classic-film buff. "I've wanted to catch it; this must be my lucky night."

For some reason, that pulled his attention from the screen and he flushed. "I think that's my line."

"Really? You wanted to be snowed in at the Baltimore with ramen for dinner?"

"Remember what I said before—you, me, adventure? Still applies." With the sweetest, easiest smile I'd seen from him, he bumped his shoulder lightly against mine.

"Then let's get comfortable."

I climbed into bed and pulled up the covers because the radiator wasn't winning against the storm outside. Pillow tucked behind me, I settled in to watch the movie. Kian followed suit, though I could tell he was nervous, pretending to be nonchalant. But I acted oblivious, and he soon relaxed, swept into the adventure unfolding on screen. Truthfully, it wasn't the most riveting thing I ever watched, mostly because World War I wasn't my jam, so I got sleepy as I warmed up. My mind wandered to the nights I'd spent in Kian's apartment with his arms around me, dozing through something he loved.

"How do you like it so far?" he whispered.

"It's good."

"You've been asleep for the last five minutes."

"I was watching with my eyes closed. To better engage my imagination."

Kian laughed. "Ah, so that's where they lost you—all the visuals. Maybe we should check into some old radio shows."

"Maybe."

"Seriously, though, you can sleep if you're tired. Just tell me where I'm supposed to—"

"Here is fine. I trust you not to do anything, but if you try, I'll kill you." Because I smiled when I said it, he couldn't tell if it was serious.

"I w-wouldn't," he stammered.

"Kidding. I do trust you."

Somehow I stayed awake for the epic conclusion where Charlie and Rose escaped execution via torpedoes or something. By then it was after eleven, so it didn't seem as lame to call it a day. I went to the bathroom first, brushed my teeth, then waved Kian in. "You can use some of my toothpaste if you want."

"Thanks."

By the time he came out, I was already snuggled in bed under the blankets. They were thin and raspy, and I'd piled all of them on the bed. At least the much-washed top sheet was soft, if pilled with age. Kian slid in on the other side as if we did this all the time.

And in another world, another life, we might.

"The mattress is kind of lumpy, and there's one spring—"

"Found it," he groaned.

"I'd offer to flip the mattress, but the other side is worse. Just take my word for it."

"Nine . . ." He sounded like he wanted to ask something.

"What?"

"I noticed there's only one set of everything in the bathroom. When you said your dad doesn't pay much attention . . . I mean, how long has it been since you saw him?"

"Three weeks? Maybe a month." I kept my voice matter-of-fact.

"So who pays the rent on this place, buys food . . ." Kian seemed to realize the answer was obvious, so he let that go. "Are you even *safe* here?"

"Maybe not, but I prefer this kind of danger to living under somebody else's roof, where they have all the power, and they can do anything they want to me. I'm emancipated, okay?"

He paused, probably calculating the likelihood that I had actual documents putting me in charge of my own life. "You mean you ran away."

"It's basically the same thing."

He made a sound that said he disagreed with me, but he finally whispered, "I can see your point. Sometimes I'd rather be alone than burden my uncle any more. It's really hard when you feel so unwelcome."

"You don't get along with your relatives?"

"My younger cousins are okay, but I get stuck watching them whenever my aunt feels like going out. And that's the only time she ever talks to me—to tell me to do something. It's like she thinks I work for her."

"People are assholes," I muttered.

"No, that's seriously it." He sounded like he'd come to some realization. "I'm in her house, eating her food. So she figures I should pay it back. No wonder she gets mad that I spend so much time in my room. She wants me doing housework when I'm not at school."

"Your uncle is nicer?"

"Yeah. He was my dad's younger brother, and I always liked him. But he's gone two or three days a week. He's in sales and the market is tough, so . . ."

"That might be part of why your aunt is so awful. If they're strapped for cash already."

In the dark, I sensed more than saw him nod. "Could be. Doesn't make living there any less awkward. Sometimes I pretend my dad didn't die and I have my old life back. Other days I imagine my mom getting her shit together and coming for me."

"Does it help?" I whispered.

"Not really. Because I know nobody's coming to save me. I just have to stick it out until I graduate. College will be better, right?"

"Definitely."

"Tell me something?"

"Depends on what it is." I rolled over because it felt weird not to face him when we were having this intimate conversation.

"Why don't you just drop out? Isn't it hard moving all the time?"

"It's a milestone. And it's come to mean something to me. If I quit, then that's like accepting I don't have a future."

That was the one true part of these lies; back when the headmaster had agreed to let me finish my senior year on independent study at Blackbriar, I'd known I could pass the equivalency exam right then and save myself the bother. But I couldn't, not after everything that happened. It was too much like giving up.

"You could get your GED and still go to college. It would be better if you had roommates and a nice place to stay."

"Places like this don't care, as long as you can pay. I can't get into college or an actual apartment with a fake ID." Luckily, there were logical reasons to back up my presence in his life.

"Right, you need to be eighteen. So you might as well graduate while you're waiting?"

"Basically."

"I really respect you. Nobody's looking out for you and yet you're still doing everything you need to. So many people would do crazy shit in your situation."

"You mean like invite guys to sleep over?" I said, smiling.

Kian laughed softly. "Okay, you got me. But I appreciate you taking the risk. I might've frozen to death waiting for my aunt . . . and I'm actually having an awesome time."

"Here?" My skepticism was obvious.

"Hey, I live in an attic. It's not a cupboard beneath the stairs, but it's freaking close. My aunt wants *me* to nail up the paneling to cover the insulation."

"So she wants you to build yourself a room to live in?"

Damn, it's worse than he ever told me. Oh, Kian.

"Basically. I keep telling her I don't know to hang paneling or dry wall, and she's all, *You're supposed to be a genius or something, right? Figure it out.* Like I have nothing better to do than teach myself DIY construction."

"Isn't that kind of hard to learn from a book?"

"Probably. And if I don't keep my grades up, I'm not going to college; that simple." His voice contained all the yearning in the world, picturing his escape from Cross Point.

Time to plant a seed.

"There are a lot of great schools in Boston," I said.

Kian sighed. "Harvard obviously. But there's no way I'm getting in there."

"It's not the only one, though, and Boston is a cool city. I lived there for a while. It was probably my favorite out of everywhere I've been. I'd like to go back someday."

"I'll bear that in mind. So . . . how long will you be here?" Somehow he seemed to realize there was a certain transience about me, maybe from the room I was staying in.

"Until the end of the term." It was better if he knew up front not to get too attached; I had to change his life just enough, not imprint on him.

"But you'll keep in touch, right?"

The vulnerability in his voice made me reckless. "Definitely."

With deepest winter setting in, I wasn't sure if I could keep that promise.

ANYTHING IS
POSSIBLE

In the morning, I woke to find us curled together like puppies.

I lay there for thirty seconds, trying desperately to remember that this Kian was *not* mine. In time, he'd grow into a version of the person I'd loved, but they would never be one and the same. Like my very existence here, I had to look on my feelings as an echo, a might-have-been. Yet it didn't stop me from staring at the thick curl of his lashes, the dark hair falling in a tangle against his cheek. The slope of his nose was the same; so were his eyes. Really, Raoul hadn't done a lot more than refine his features into the supernatural beauty that was so startling.

He's not yours, I reminded myself, and rolled out of bed before I could be tempted to linger. If he woke and caught me staring, it would break one of two ways. *Option A: He concludes I like him and makes a move. Option B: He thinks I'm creepy and starts pulling back.* Both were bad for different reasons, so I went into the bathroom to wash up. When I came out ten minutes later, Kian was awake. He managed a bashful smile as he sidled by for his turn.

"Hungry?" I asked ten minutes later, as the door swung open.

"Yeah, but I'm feeling guilty."

"Don't worry about it." I shoved a napkin with a PB&J on it toward him. "Breakfast of champions, so eat up."

After a makeshift meal, I peered out the window, relieved to find the streets plowed. As a result, three-foot dirty gray drifts partially blocked the sidewalk, but at least vehicles were moving on the wet streets. Honking horns and the red glare of taillights made things seem more normal than they had the night before, eerie in the winter desolation. It was hard not to see Wedderburn's fingerprints all over that storm, but maybe I was paranoid.

"I should get back," Kian said, sounding reluctant.

"I need to stop by the store. So I'll walk you to the bus stop."

"Do you still want to do the thrift shop and the movie tonight?" he asked.

"Definitely. Let's meet at the stop nearest the House of Style."

Kian laughed. "That name kills me. But, okay, around four?"

"Yep."

My hoodie was still damp when I shrugged into it, but I didn't say a word. At least my sneakers were dry, thanks to their night by the radiator. This room had no closet, but since I had like four T-shirts, two pairs of jeans, three pairs of panties, two bras, a hoodie, and a jean jacket, I didn't need much space. I wished I had thicker socks and a proper coat, though.

Frowning, Kian watched me layer up. "You dress like you're still in California."

More like, this was what I could pick up quick and cheap, but my *I'm a time traveler, so I pack light* rationale probably wouldn't play well. So I shrugged.

"It'll do until May, I'm sure. I'm thinking of heading south next."

"Sounds awesome. Or terrifying." He seemed like he couldn't make up his mind.

"It's scary."

I'd never encourage him to run away; the streets would definitely be worse. While it might suck at his aunt and uncle's house, he seemed to be safe physically, at least. I wished staying didn't mean emotional neglect, but I couldn't fix everything. Much as I hated it, some hurts he just had to suffer through and keep fighting.

"Can't you stay?" he asked then. "I mean, isn't it hard starting over every four months?"

"It is. But if I stick around, I risk being found. And I can't have that. It would be bad for me and a disaster for anyone I care about."

Kian's eyes widened, as if it had never occurred to him that I might run because I was being chased. It was even true in a manner of speaking. Every moment I spent with him, I worried about the other timeline catching up to me. With Raoul watching, Wedderburn might wonder about my interference. If he looked to the future, he'd know. And then shit would start all over again. I might have to kill gods I'd already slain once, and how messed up was that?

"Sometimes I don't know if you're being honest or if you're completely full of shit," Kian said finally.

I offered an inscrutable smile. "Probably better that way. Let's go."

The bus stop was past the corner store I usually shopped in, but Kian didn't know that. So I went with him and waited until his bus came. By the brightness of his smile, he thought I just wanted to hang out a little longer. And that was true enough, but I also watched for Raoul, scanning the sparse crowd with a wary eye. Across the street on a diagonal, I glimpsed him curled up on a grate huddled against a building beneath a mound of old newspaper. His derelict guise offered the perfect surveillance cover, as nobody ever paid attention to homeless people. I watched six pedestrians stride right past without ever glancing in his direction. But since spotting him, I sensed the sharpness of his attention.

"My ride's here. See you this afternoon." Kian summoned my attention with a wave as he got on the bus.

I raised a hand, standing guard until the vehicle moved away from the curb and down the street. Keeping an eye on Raoul in my peripheral vision, I headed back toward the Baltimore; I expected him to follow Kian, but instead, he silently stepped out of the newspaper and circled the building in the opposite direction. My puzzlement lasted exactly half a block, as a grimy hand locked onto my arm and dragged me into an alley littered with needles and broken glass.

Though he was filthy on the surface, Raoul didn't smell like he belonged on the streets. He was leaner than he had been when I first met him, with an aura of palpable menace. Dark, glittering eyes raked me from head to toe; then he narrowed his gaze on my face. I stared back, determined not to give an inch. *The medallion will shield me, and I have Aegis.* As a double agent for the Black Watch, he'd have no compunction about making me disappear from Kian's life, if it looked like I might keep him from extremis.

"Who do you work for?" he demanded, twisting my wrist. "Dwyer? Fell?"

"Let me go, or I start screaming."

In answer, he lunged to slap a palm across my mouth, probably intending to drag me to a more secluded location for interrogation. I responded with a move he'd taught me, twisting his arm behind his back so hard that it would break if he struggled. But before he could question that, I slammed him face-first into a building, conscious of how hot Aegis felt on my wrist.

Govannon didn't give me some cursed sword, I'd said to Rochelle.

Did he not? Have you tried to put it down?

An odd, alien sensation prickled over my arm, as if the weapon was urging me to end Raoul here and now, and it struck me as eerily similar to the mirror where Cameron's spirit dwelled. I hadn't been present when Govannon forged this blade, so how could I be sure what went into its crafting? He'd used the sun god's heart to create it after all.

"I don't know what you want, asshole, but don't assume girls make easier targets." For good measure, I knocked his head once more against the wall.

It should've been enough to daze him, but he was steady enough to chase me back onto the street. A couple of passersby gave us uneasy looks, and a woman muffled in an ugly homemade scarf crossed the street to avoid whatever conflict might be brewing. I balanced on the balls of my feet, ready for Raoul to come at me, but he was frowning.

"You're human," he said, puzzled.

"And you're high as hell, apparently." That was the only reasonable response; I had to make him believe my arrival was a coincidence.

Go tell Wedderburn I'm a normal girl. They might still try to kill me because there were no rules protecting random mortals, but they

63

wouldn't be prepared for the strength of my resistance. If Wedder-burn learned I'd wreaked havoc on his headquarters and killed four gods in the game, he would never stop until I was a smoking stain on the concrete.

"Whatever," Raoul muttered.

He whirled and retreated into the alley. I didn't chase him, hardly daring to breathe until a full minute had passed. Then I turned and went to the corner store in case he was still watching. *Nothing unusual to see here.* My food budget was down to a few crumpled singles and change.

"You're here a lot," José said, ringing me up.

I knew that was the owner's name because he had it embroidered on the bowling shirts he wore. At first I only nodded, waiting for the total, because that seemed like a rhetorical question. I paid the requested $3.52, and was about to leave when he added:

"I can't pay, but if you want to clean and stock shelves for a couple hours, I could give you some groceries." By his expression, he wasn't too sure about the offer.

So I said quickly, "That sounds good. I don't know if I can come every day, though."

"It's not like I'm making a work schedule."

A woman called from upstairs, "Did you talk to her?"

He yelled back, "I'm doing it right now."

Something about the exchange reminded me of my mom and dad. It was always my mother nudging him in the right direction. So I was smiling when José made an apologetic face. "Sorry, Luisa gets impatient. She noticed you're new in the neighborhood and thought maybe . . ." He trailed off, only to start again. "It's hard to be sure if you should offer help, you know?"

I nodded. "People might get mad or take advantage or you could be inviting their troubles into your home. I get it."

"Anyway, I said what I was supposed to. Have a good day."

Though I had been cagey, I intended to work on Monday. Before that, I had a number of other things to do. Back in my room, I dug up a clean sponge under the kitchen sink and a can of cleanser. It wasn't meant for bathrooms, but I couldn't stand the grunge a second longer. It took me two hours of nonstop scrubbing, but by the time I finished, the room even smelled clean. For the first time, I took a shower without worrying about contact infections.

Wish I'd known Kian was coming over; I'd have done this sooner.

As I dried my hair with a stiff, scratchy towel, I wondered what Raoul was telling Wedderburn. *As long as I act normal, they can't prove anything.* But if they saw the Harbinger sniffing around, it would definitely raise the alarm. Probably I should tell him to get lost, but I'd promised he could watch the show, so I hesitated.

Why is it so hard to cut him off?

No ready answer sprang to mind, and my phone pinged, distracting me. Unsurprisingly, it was from Kian, the one person who had my number. *I have way more fugly clothes than I can fit in my backpack. This may take two trips.*

Sweet, plenty of store credit for you, I sent back.

That night, I wore my hair down, not because I was trying to look pretty, but because it was significantly warmer. The usual suspects sat on the bus: women in uniforms coming off cleaning shifts, a couple of homeless men, three teenagers who took turns staring at me and shoving one another. I wished I had some headphones but staring out the window did almost as well in sending the UN-AVAILABLE message.

At 3:56, I got off at the stop nearest to Madame Q's House of Style to find Kian already waiting. His cheeks were red flagged with cold, and he was pacing with a backpack stuffed so full that it seemed like one good shove would topple him. When he spotted me, his face brightened with a smile that was relief and delight commingled.

"Ready for some shopping?" I asked.

"To unload these clothes anyway."

The thrift shop was open until six, so we had a good two hours to browse. But first Mrs. Quick inspected Kian's clothes, muttering in delight. "My God, this is vintage, all vintage."

Holy shit, did that mean they never bought him anything, just dug into the attic and gave him stuff his uncle wore in high school? Well, no wonder he looked like a perpetual fashion victim in outfits from the seventies nowhere near his size.

"Is that good?" he wanted to know.

"Not for you," I mumbled.

"It means a better trade-in value," she replied.

Kian blinked. "It does? Why?"

Mrs. Quick went into a long explanation involving hard-to-find styles and cosplay and hipsters who didn't want vintage *look*, but I tuned out long before she came to the end of it. The upshot was that Kian ended up with forty-five dollars in store credit as opposed to my pitiful $2.50, as I'd only brought one T-shirt to trade. I suspected the owner was being kind too.

I went nuts picking out stuff for him to try on: black jeans, faded jeans, gray cargo pants, striped button-up, oversize hoodie, T-shirts so quirky they were cool. In the end, he took everything I suggested and still had five dollars left over. To my surprise, he led me to the outerwear section instead of telling Mrs. Quick he was ready to check out.

"I'm getting you a present," he said firmly. "Don't argue."

I didn't. After browsing a little, I chose a matching hat, gloves, and scarf in dove gray. They were so gently used I couldn't tell anyone else had ever owned them, and when I lifted the set to my cheek, it was whisper soft. *Perfect.* It was priced at $7.39, which meant we could afford it if I kicked in my measly $2.50.

"All set?" Mrs. Quick asked as we came over.

Kian nodded. "If you could, ring everything together and combine our credits, please."

"Not a problem."

She added everything up, confirming that we had eleven cents left. "I don't give out cash on credit purchases, though."

"It's fine. Leave it on our account." Kian grinned like we'd opened a store charge card together or something. "I have more vintage to swap, so we'll be back."

"I'm looking forward to it," she said. "In fact, I'm about to call a buyer I'm fairly sure will be interested in some of your shirts. You'd make good money if you sold on consignment."

He shrugged. "I'm not worried about that. You're helping me a lot already. Is it okay if I use the changing room?"

"Of course," Mrs. Quick said.

When he came out, he had on the gray cargo pants and blue hoodie. "Better?"

"It only matters how *you* feel." But he did look handsome. The casual fit of clothing purchased in his size lent his thin frame a gangly grace.

His answering smile made his eyes shine like the green waters of a deep forest glade, glimmering with flashes of sunlight. "When you're around, I feel like anything is possible."

My heart turned over, and I fell a little in love with *this* Kian, who was not—and never would be—mine.

OF
CONTRADICTIONS
AND DARK WISHES

Outside, I put on the hat, wriggled my fingers into the gloves—the tiny kind that seemed like they'd never fit human hands—and wrapped up in the scarf. Despite still not having a proper coat, I instantly felt warmer. Kian watched, not quite smiling, but I could tell he was glad. At first, I only noticed the flaws that made him so different from the boy I fell in love with. But now he was familiar enough for me to see that he didn't need perfecting: from the sharpening of his chin when he smiled, to the lean line of his jaw, to the nervous way his Adam's apple bobbed when he caught me looking.

"What?" he asked.

"Nothing."

Fortunately, our bus arrived just then.

Somehow I held it together long enough for us to reach Lofton, a neighborhood near downtown, but not close enough to walk. Kian practically thrummed with excitement. It was harder for me to summon the same level of enthusiasm while looking over my shoulder.

Yet I couldn't appear *too* nervous because, as far as Nine knew, the weird guy I met downtown was a meth head or whatever. I shouldn't be on the alert for a stalker, but I could let my guard down.

So my nerves felt raw when we hopped off the bus. I scanned the area, trying to look like any girl who might be uneasy as dark closed in. Cans and bottles littered the sidewalk, along with crinkling plastic wrappers, half buried in the slushy remnants of the snowstorm. There were a few pedestrians, likely headed toward the Marquee Bar. They'd kept the old signage that used to list NOW SHOWING but instead had been replaced with drink specials and theme nights. Apparently, they always showed movies, but only focused on classics on Saturday.

Getting in turned out to be way easier than expected. There was nobody posted at the door, and the lobby had been turned into a standing bar with an industrial vibe. Ten people stood around with beers, but since I didn't want to drink, I led the way through the open double doors. The big room that had been a theater still had a sloping floor, but it had been terraced so that a handful of tables sat on each level, and most seemed to have been rescued from an old diner, mostly four- and two-seater booths. At the back/top, they had free-range tables with regular chairs, probably to accommodate bigger groups.

Nobody offered to escort us, so I grabbed a small booth near the middle. Eventually, a waiter came over. "What'll you have?"

The lighting was dim, so he probably couldn't tell how young Kian was. It helped that he was tall too.

I glanced at Kian, who shrugged. So I peered at the menu, seeking the cheapest options, answered for both of us, "Two Cokes and a basket of fries."

"Coming right up."

Since we didn't order booze, he never checked our ID. Technically, we needed to be twenty-one to get in here, but I was a little let down over how easy this was. I mean, I didn't want to get questioned or kicked out, but still. After dropping the money at Psychedelic Records, it would be nice to put the licenses to use.

Other people filed in and kept coming, even after the lights went down. Leaning forward, I whispered, "How come they don't have a cover or sell tickets?"

"Pretty sure they make their money off drink markups."

That made sense, but since we'd gotten here early enough to snag a table, they couldn't exactly refuse to serve just because we weren't drinking expensive cocktails. Soon our Cokes and fries arrived. Kian still loved his with a ton of ketchup. I nibbled, aware of my own heartbeat like it was the tick of a clock. When the previews started, they included all the vintage stuff on the show reel, like going back in time. Which I'd done recently, just not this far. I settled in to watch *Casablanca*. The first time I'd watched it with Kian, I was riveted and it even made me cry, but this time I was more interested by the expressions that swept his mobile features. My heart felt like it was being squeezed in a vise as I memorized each smile, each intake of breath.

But around the halfway point, he glanced over, seeming to notice that my attention wasn't on the movie. "Are you bored?"

"Not at all. I love this movie. I've seen it like ten times."

And always with you.

That seemed too much to bear; I was alone in my love story, whispering the secret to myself in the dark. Somehow I mustered a smile that must've convinced him, and I tore my gaze away and locked it on the screen. *You can't ruin this by being sad and weird. His life is already different because of you.*

As the credits rolled, I wiped the tears from my cheeks. Fortunately, the ending made it credible, so Kian patted my shoulder. "I know, right? No matter how many times I watch it, it always gets me. Part of me wishes they could have a happy ending but—"

"If Ilsa stayed with Rick, she wouldn't be the woman he fell in love with. She was always fighting for a cause that mattered more than her own happiness." In that moment, I identified with her *so* hard.

"Exactly." His green eyes sparkled with the pleasure of talking to someone who got it.

In the lobby, moviegoers seemed in no hurry to leave. The magic of the Marquee was that afterward, you could drink in the lobby and chat people up. They were showing another movie in twenty minutes, but it was a seventies college comedy, so it drew a different audience, mostly middle-aged men, some of whom stared at me creepily as I bundled up.

Outside, it had gotten colder. My lips felt like they were freezing as I fought for a breath that didn't hurt my lungs. Someone swung away from the wall, a stranger in a long dark coat with an inky waterfall of hair adorned with a red knit hat. His face was lean and lovely, sharply sculpted, eyes gray as a thundercloud. When he smiled, my stomach dropped.

"I'm here for Nine." That was unmistakably the Harbinger's voice, and by the sweetly malicious smile curving his pretty mouth, I was in so much trouble. Since he was pretending to be human, his aura didn't stagger me.

Shit. Why didn't I cut him off?

72

Kian took a step back, his expression equal measures hurt and puzzled. "You're—"

"Her boyfriend. Colin." He offered a black-gloved hand in a semblance of manners while I ground my teeth.

There was no way to argue without this encounter getting weird. The guys shook, and I could already tell Kian was hastily evaluating everything we'd done together, wondering if any lines had been crossed. *Am I getting my ass kicked?* was practically written on his wrinkled forehead. I needed to take control before the Harbinger screwed things up further.

"She hasn't mentioned you," Kian said, studying my face.

"I wasn't sure where we stood," I bit out. "Colin has this habit of vanishing when it's convenient and showing up later to cause trouble."

"I always come back, don't I?" The Harbinger tapped my nose in what might approximate an affectionate gesture, but I felt more like a dog being swatted with a newspaper.

My gaze slammed into his as I choked down all the shit I really wanted to say. Like, *What the hell are you doing?* "So far, yes."

"I should let you two—"

"It's fine," the Harbinger said, smiling. "Why don't I buy coffee? It's the least I can do since you've looked after my lovely girl so well."

Despite my halfhearted protests, we ended up in a diner four blocks away. The garish fluorescent lights stung my eyes, throwing the faults in the décor into sharp relief, a sort of chiaroscuro in neglect. The place reminded me a little of the place where Kian made me an offer I couldn't refuse, only these people weren't pieces set in place by Wedderburn. Most of them were layered in worn winter gear, counting coins to pay for their coffee.

I rubbed my fingers across a tear in the beige vinyl booth seat as the Harbinger shoved in beside me. *Should've seen that coming.* He waited until the tired waitress took our order, and then he shrugged out of his coat in a swirl of silky hair. This was such a bizarre echo of a scene, only last time it was Kian pretending to be my gorgeous boyfriend. The Harbinger could look however he wished, so this was just salt in the wound. There was no reason for him to come across so ethereal and rock-star perfect, unless he intended to make Kian feel shitty.

Probably.

"You . . . you're not in high school?" Kian ventured.

The Harbinger laughed. "Hardly."

"He just graduated," I cut in, hoping to discourage more questions.

A look of dancing gray amusement swung my way. "Don't be so nervous. You know I don't mind if you make friends."

That seemed to put Kian a little more at ease, though he didn't say much. Instead, the Harbinger monopolized the conversation before and after our drinks arrived. Kian appeared to regret his hot chocolate; he stirred it more than drank.

"Not good?" I asked.

He shrugged. "Powder mix, a little too much hot water."

It did look gray instead of rich brown. My coffee was fine, if bitter and strong, definitely better than what I'd bought at the convenience store. The struggle to be sociable lasted for half an hour before the Harbinger polished off his second cup and curled an arm around my shoulders in a graceful slouch.

"We should go before the buses stop for the night. I'll take you home." Then he added, "You can put yourself back where you belong, Ian?"

"Kian," he corrected.

"Right. Sorry." It was the sort of passive-aggressive bullshit a jealous boyfriend might pull, so I couldn't bitch in present company. *Just wait until I get you alone, "Colin."*

We headed to the bus stop together, but Kian's came first. From his apathetic wave and the way he didn't turn to look at me from the bus, he wasn't pleased. As soon as the vehicle trundled out of sight, I shoved the Harbinger away from me.

"What is *wrong* with you?"

"Should've killed me when you had the chance?" He didn't shift to his customary appearance, however, and I wasn't used to him looking so young.

"Don't tempt me. Why are you messing around like this? What's the point?"

"It'll be easier to finish the mission if people think you have a boyfriend, no? Weren't you worried about crossing a line with the young nerdling?"

I stared up at him, his face wreathed by the mist of my own breath. "How do you *know*?"

"Didn't I already tell you that we're bound?"

"What the . . . *seriously*? Can you read my mind because I fed you in a different timeline? How does that even—"

"You'll drive yourself mad, trying to impose logic on monsters. Our world was crafted in layers, over time, born of contradictions and dark wishes."

"If you can read my mind, I might actually end you." I touched the gold weight of Aegis beneath the layers of fleece, yarn, and denim.

To my annoyance, he laughed. "Then I'm safe. Sometimes I just *know* things about you, dearling. Not thoughts but a flicker of desire or fear."

The bus headlights shone in the dark, and it slowed as the driver spotted us. Smiling, the Harbinger took my gloved hand in his, and then we were gone in a swirl of darkness, just as he'd transported me after Kian's death. This time, we appeared in my room at the Baltimore, definitely more convenient than the CTA. I switched on the light, fiddled with the radiator, uncomfortable with the intimacy he'd forced me to acknowledge between us. Sometimes I found myself thinking of him at odd times, almost *missing* him when he wasn't around, and none of it made it any sense. *But maybe it's not my fault, a side effect or something.*

"Can we stop it?" I asked finally, turning to face him.

He lifted his shoulders in a careless shrug. "Why would I want to? Your life is infinitely amusing, and now *I* get to participate in the drama."

"It's not . . . You can't do this. This may be hilarious to you, but if the others notice you sniffing around, it'll get me killed. And if that happens before I fix everything . . ." My hands curled into fists as I trailed off.

"You're not fixing anything," he said.

"Huh?"

"You've created a new possibility; that's all. The world you left still exists. All the awful things have still happened. The details are fuzzy, but do you think you're wiping the slate clean somehow? That's not how it works."

His words hit me like a tire iron, and I collapsed on the edge of the bed. I'd suspected, of course, but I knew shit about time travel before I used my dad's device, other than what I read his notes and had seen in science fiction. Of course, since the Harbinger was a trickster, maybe I shouldn't believe him. He'd lied to me before, like when the woman next door died. But . . .

"In stories, people believe you're wicked when you lie," I said softly. "Fomenting misery, chaos, and discord with deceit. But *I* think you're cruelest with the truth."

He sank down beside me, slipping into the shape most familiar, like someone else might change their shoes. In contrast with the pretty boy he'd chosen before, tonight he seemed haggard, eyes sunk deep, and there seemed to be more silver in his hair. Since he didn't age, his form must reflect his present mood.

The Harbinger stared at his folded hands. "And this is why I always come back. Such acuity is like an incision. It always hurts, but I've come to savor it."

"Excuse me?"

"You see the coal where my heart should be, and you don't turn away. You speak it."

It took me a minute to parse, but I thought I understood. He was drawn to me because I saw him as he was, not as legends described him. Knowing that, it got harder to cling to my wrath over his interference. Truthfully, the existence of "Colin" would make my life easier, helping me toe the line so I didn't break Kian's heart.

"Want to hear something funny?" I asked.

"Always."

"When you talked about making the mission easier, that's kind of what Kian said in the other timeline, when Wedderburn told him to get close to me, so he pretended to be my boyfriend. It was supposed to get guys off my case at school and let me focus on revenge." I had no idea why I was sharing this, maybe because solitary memories felt like sacks of cement strapped to my back. Loneliness could be distilled to this—*I'm the only one who remembers.*

If I was expecting sympathy, clearly I'd mistaken my audience. "That makes it even more delicious. I do so love theater of the absurd."

"I deserve that. For thinking you care about anything but your own entertainment."

His voice dropped, signaling a somber air. "You shouldn't worry. My presence won't raise any red flags; this is hardly the first time I've played with a human for sport."

"*That's* supposed to make me feel better? Wedderburn already has one asset snooping around. Won't Raoul wonder about your interest in me? If this escalates—"

"I will protect you. There is one thing you should never doubt, and it is that I guard my treasures well."

That was so infuriating, I could only laugh. "I'm not your treasure."

"Of course you are," he said, as if a priceless vase had objected to being set on a shelf. "Until I weary of you anyway."

"And so we circle back to the broken-toys allegory." He looked blank, so I guessed he didn't remember. I went on. "We've been over this. You don't have the power to protect me from all the immortals who will want me dead if they find out about Aegis."

"What's Aegis?" he asked with birdlike tilt of his head.

"Are you screwing with me right now?"

The Harbinger lowered his chin, so the silver-shot hair veiled his face. "I've forgotten the details. They were clearer when you first came, but I've been here and now with you and not there and then for long enough that it's going. Tell me again." He flopped backward on my bed and stretched like a cat.

"You really want me to turn what happened in the other time-line into a bedtime story?" Sighing, I decided aloud, "I guess it won't be any worse than old-school fairy tales."

He cracked one eye open, offering a lopsided smile. "Truly. The stories your people make up for children are frightful."

"So if I tell you here and now, you won't forget?" It seemed prudent to ensure he wouldn't ask for this once a week; I couldn't handle the Harbinger in my bed on a regular basis.

His starry gaze met mine fully, laced with weights and implications I couldn't interpret. Then, like the cat I'd compared him to earlier, he rolled onto his side and rested his head in my lap. I remembered how he had said *Just . . . do this a bit longer*, when I was petting his hair, and predicted he would break my heart. Later he changed it to me breaking his.

In that case, one piece of coal becomes two, right? But . . . coal under sufficient pressure turns into a diamond.

He sighed softly. "Other than space-time tomfoolery, I *never* forget."

"Sounds like a blessing and a curse."

His eyes closed then, an ancient creature weary beyond bearing. "No, dearling. Just a curse. Now it's important . . . so tell me everything."

A TSUNAMI
OF NOPE

Monday during lunch, Kian was so silent that I could tell he was still pissed. He looked only at his food, not at me, to the point that I might as well not have been there. I tolerated it for five minutes, and then I jerked his tray toward me. His milk sloshed, and I ate two tater tots as a form of protest. The gambit worked, forcing him to make reluctant eye contact.

"Something on your mind?" I asked.

"Don't worry about it."

There was nothing for it but to pretend to be obtuse. "This is bullshit, Kian. We haven't known each other that long, but I thought we were friends."

His jaw clenched, and he spoke through gritted teeth. "So did I. Funny how you didn't mention having a boyfriend. You think he'd be okay with our sleepover? It's fine for you; I'm the one getting my ass kicked for no reason."

I pretended sudden comprehension. "He *is* cool with it, actually. Colin isn't the type to beat someone up."

More likely to kidnap you and keep you in a cage or have birds peck out your eyes.

Kian seemed to deflate, a sheepish expression dawning as he lowered his eyes. "I guess that was kind of unfair, huh?"

"When we met, there was no reason to mention Colin. I hadn't seen him in a while. He and I . . . well, our history is complex and inexplicable." There, that should do it.

"But you just take him back the minute he shows up?" Kian sighed and shook his head, stabbing his fork into the chicken patty with enough force that the plastic tines broke. He plucked the white shards from his food with evident annoyance.

"Actually it's more like I leave and he follows."

His eyes widened. "Seriously? You take off and he drops everything to chase you?"

Put that way, it sounded bad on both our parts; it painted me as heartless and him as a stalker. "I'm not running from *him*," I said finally.

"Your life is so complicated."

I smiled faintly. "Tell me about it. So you're not mad anymore?"

"I was mostly worried about the fallout. It's not like I don't have my own secrets." He tore off a piece of his roll, compressing it into dough with nervous fingertips.

If I read the situation right, that was my cue to dig. "Such as?"

His gaze flickered to the girl in the middle of the cafeteria, currently tossing her shiny brown hair. "There's someone I like a lot . . . since I first moved here."

Wow, that's been years. Talk about a long crush.

I followed his gaze. "Have you ever talked to her?"

"God, no. That's part of the problem. Until you showed up, I never talked to anyone."

"How come?" Despite the question, I didn't expect him to show me all the skeletons in his closet over bad school food.

So it surprised me when he eventually answered.

"I was pretty messed up when I first moved in with my aunt and uncle, definitely in no mood to make friends. It's hard to explain now, but it's like I thought, if I don't engage, if I don't make any move to adapt, then it's like none of this is real?" His tone went up at the end as if he was asking for confirmation of his past emotional state.

So I said, "That makes sense. You were in denial."

His smile surprised me with its brilliance, brightening his eyes. "Exactly. By the time I rebounded, it was too late. I already had an unshakable rep as a weirdo. So all I could do was mark time and do my work."

"It's never too late," I said.

He laughed, until my expression made it clear I was serious. The rest of the noise might as well be gibbon monkeys as he stared. Then Kian shook his head. "I know you're trying to make me feel better, but I'll be bottom of the barrel socially until college."

Maybe it was too soon to argue. "With that attitude, you definitely will be. So tell me about the girl." Tanya . . . I'd forgotten her last name. "Or should I guess? She's a cheerleader, dating the sports superstar, probably excels in academics but more because she's good at working the teachers than for actual achievement."

He scowled. "Wrong. She's in science and math with me."

Shit, I should've realized. Just being pretty wouldn't be enough to make him like her.

"Sorry, that was unfair."

"The other stuff is true, though. See the guy sitting next to her?" Kian didn't need to turn around apparently to know exactly where she was. His devotion gave me a pang, even as I told myself, *Good thing he's not falling for me.*

I shifted, peering past his shoulder. "Blond hair, generic handsome?"

"Yeah. That's Jake Overman."

"Quarterback?"

"Nope. Wait until he stands up before trying again."

That could've taken a while, but Tanya sent him to get some napkins. As he uncurled from his chair, I realized he was considerably taller than six feet. "Basketball, then?"

"You got it. JV squad."

"Don't expect me to figure out his position. I barely know anything about sports."

Kian grinned. "That's one of my favorite things about you. I won't ask you to guess anything else."

We finished lunch while I pondered what I'd learned. Though he didn't watch her as obviously now that we were hanging out, Kian still had a thing for Tanya. I shouldn't have expected *everything* to change just because I was here. From what he'd told me, he spiraled into an impenetrable depression after this girl rejected and humiliated him, until he hit extremis. After that, his decision to accept Raoul's offer ended badly for poor Tanya. While the immortal game was screwing up people's lives all over the place, this was where I'd chosen to stand and fight. , I couldn't permit events to unfold as they had before.

But how can I be sure I've done enough?

The obvious answer was to stay until his birthday in June, but I had no idea what the ramifications were for living five months in the wrong time stream. From what little Kian had said, Wedderburn had agents experienced in time travel, but I doubted they stuck around for long; what Kian said sounded more like quick in-and-out jobs: artifact retrieval or timely executions. And that was out of the question here.

"What's got you so perplexed?" Kian asked as we cleared our trays.

"Just some time-travel paradox stuff." I expected him to leave that alone, but he leaned closer in apparent interest.

"Is it about wiping yourself out of existence or becoming your own grandma?"

I laughed. "Not that complicated, thankfully."

"I didn't know you were into science fiction. Smart, classic-film buff, a bit of a geek . . ." Kian nodded as if he'd come to a difficult conclusion. "You're perfect."

"For what?" I wondered aloud.

"The role of my best friend." He stressed the last word, maybe because of Colin.

"I'm glad to hear that," I said, quietly aching.

He bumped his shoulder against mine as we headed out of the cafeteria but the move caught me off guard, so I stumbled. Somebody steadied me, and I turned reflexively to say thanks, only to find the uber-tall Jake Overman behind me. The rest of his group stood nearby, polished and shiny in designer labels. A few sported smirks as if they expected me to be embarrassed, but these people were amateurs compared to the Blackbriar elite. Pretending I didn't understand that they were school royalty, I offered a friendly wave.

"Thanks."

One of the girls, not Tanya, edged to the front. "Can you settle a bet? Everyone's so curious, are you going out . . . ?" She gestured at the two of us, lip curled.

Smiling brightly, I said, "I wish. But he just made it really clear that I'm friend-zoned."

"No way," a guy muttered.

"He likes someone else," I added, and Kian nudged me so hard that it hurt, since I caught the elbow square the ribs. I ignored him because it was better for them to think *he'd* rejected me.

"You have a boyfriend anyway," he finally mumbled. "So it's just as well."

"Wade was asking me about you," Jake put in.

The name sounded familiar, but I couldn't place it. My blank look must've annoyed the not-Tanya girl because she said, "He's the captain of the football team, senior, best thing ever to happen to this school."

"I disagree. I'm going with electricity and flush toilets. Didn't I see a plaque that says the original building was constructed in 1912 or something?"

"Everything was torn down," Jake told me. "And they rebuilt in 1967."

I beamed at him. "I'm impressed you know that. Nothing like local history."

He made eye contact long enough for me to realize he was smiling a little warmer than the exchange warranted. Tanya noticed too and grabbed his hand, giving an impatient tug. "Weren't you about to walk me to class?"

"I . . . guess?" Overman seemed startled by the question, but he went along.

When the power couple rolled out, the others followed, and Kian let out an audible sigh. "That is the closest I've ever been to her. Did you see how pretty her eyes are?"

"I admit, it escaped me. She's got great hair, though."

That opened the floodgates to a lot of Kian's private paean on Tanya, and I listened until the first bell rang. "Gotta go. See you later."

Truthfully, it sucked more than a little hearing him wax rhapsodic over someone else. I reminded myself that romance had no part in this mission. I'd nearly persuaded myself when school let out, so I was smiling when I stepped into the hall. The contrast to Blackbriar, which was more like a private college campus, seemed especially sharp today. This school was struggling with outdated equipment, broken fixtures, and floors that needed a good scrubbing.

"You're new, right?" For the second time today, Jake Overman loomed over me. I could see how some girls enjoyed feeling tiny and fragile beside him, but it wasn't my thing. "I'm sorry I didn't introduce myself earlier. Tanya was in a hurry."

I wasn't great at reading people or judging intentions, but since he'd mentioned his girlfriend, this interaction didn't seem skeevy. *Maybe he's a nice guy?*

"Chelsea Brooks," I said. "But you can call me Nine."

"Yeah, I got the scoop from some assholes in my Bio 2 class. If it bothers you, I'll call you Chelsea."

"No worries. Kian told me your name already."

"Did he?" He seemed honestly startled to be known, unusual in a school athlete. "I didn't realize he followed basketball."

"Everyone is capable of surprising you," I said.

I didn't mean for it come out flirtatious, but judging by his slow, appreciative smile, that was how he took it. "I'll bear that in mind. Anyway, I just wanted to tell you that I'm having a party this weekend. Stop by if you can. Can I text you my address?"

"Sure." I gave him my number. "But to be honest, I probably won't come."

"Something I said?"

"No, I'm just not much of a party person. I'll probably go to the Marquee with Kian." That was an intentional name drop to raise awareness.

"Isn't that a bar?" Jake seemed *really* impressed, enough that I felt like rolling my eyes. Apparently the key to popularity as a new kid was true indifference along with projecting a convincing aura that your life was more interesting than everyone else's.

"Sort of. But they're not picky about ID. We were there last weekend."

"You and that kid? Went to a bar."

"Yep. We watched an old movie, drank a little." I didn't have to say it was Coke, right? The point was to raise Kian's social footprint. "Nothing huge, it was chill. And we didn't have to worry about being raided by the cops for a noise complaint."

Jake frowned. "My parties never get busted. We live out in the country, and my parents are gone this weekend."

"Cool. I'll keep that in mind." Waving, I headed for the front doors.

The halls had thinned a little, and I didn't find Kian anywhere. *He probably already got on a bus.* But in the weirdest echo—and maybe because of the story I'd told Saturday night—the Harbinger was waiting for me, leaning up against an electrical pole just past the edge of the parking lot. In his Colin guise, he attracted a lot of attention from students who lived close enough to walk to school. Today he'd come as a musician with a violin case on his back, and even *I* had to admit he was irresistible layers of gorgeous: black shirt, claret leather vest, black trousers tucked into maroon combat boots, black trench coat over everything. The final touch, a dark red knit beanie contrasted beautifully to the raven spill of his hair, and as I processed the soft sighs and longing looks, it was like replaying how everyone reacted to Kian at Blackbriar.

Seems I'm destined to be envied for loves that aren't mine.

"Nine!" he called.

Six heads swiveled in my direction. *I have to get him out of here before he makes somebody go full Nicole.* I hurried toward him, face locked in a grimace of a smile.

"What're you doing here?"

"Picking you up, of course. I understand it's the thing to do."

"More like marking territory," I muttered.

"Don't be absurd, dearling. I don't need to mark for you to be mine."

That was both annoying and wrong, but I didn't have the energy to argue. "Are you planning to ride the bus with me?"

The Harbinger laughed. "Hardly."

But before I could speak, the talkative girl from Tanya and Jake's group stopped beside us. "I heard you might come to the party on

Saturday." While she was allegedly talking to me, her gaze never left the Harbinger.

Shit.

"You are?" I prompted.

"Lara. Sorry." As far as she knew, I could be a doll made of pepperoni sausage. So much for thinking Wade was the best thing ever to happen to this school. "Is this your boyfriend?"

A little of the Harbinger's aura shivered through me, but either I'd built up an immunity or he was shielding me somehow. Yet Lara must be getting the full impact. If he asked, she'd probably run out into traffic. I grabbed his arm, annoyed that I probably looked jealous and possessive, when my main goal was delivering a vicious pinch. The Harbinger smirked, setting his hand briefly over mine, and Lara didn't notice how he squeezed the fingers together, a little painful while seeming intimate. That pretty much described all our interactions.

"Yes," he said. "You said something about a party?"

I stepped on his foot, but it didn't faze him. Lara enthusiastically explained how awesome Jake's parties were, kind of legendary despite him only being a sophomore, and we should *both* totally come. By his gentle smile, I could tell the Harbinger thought this was all delightful and tremendously entertaining. He could probably find at least twenty people to feed from.

Lara finished, "Normally I think the violin is boring and weird, but I bet your music is awesome. So you can even play if you want to."

Finally, I understood why he was carrying one, the whole fiddle of gold against your soul thing had to be massive in-joke. I sighed. "We have to go. See you around."

It took all my strength to haul him away from the conversation, and I didn't notice I had a hold of his wrist until he resisted, staring at where my fingers held him. I let go at once.

"Sorry, but you can't complicate my situation. You're supposed to be a spectator."

"How am I interfering?" he asked softly.

"Forget butterfly wings causing a hurricane; you're a tsunami of nope. You just being here will screw things up."

"How can you be sure? Maybe you need chaos on my level."

"We're not going to the party," I said. "And that violin—"

"Is not a prop."

"What?" Caught off guard, I stared while he opened the case, withdrew a burnished instrument, and played a few gorgeous bars. His music tore through me like an anguished, exquisite cry. My breath went. "Wow."

Satisfied with this response, the Harbinger put it away. "You underestimate me. I learned to play in Dublin, a long time ago. I was pretending to be human then too, and there was a red-haired girl, various misfortunes, and a dingy pub. It ended badly, of course," he added with a flinty kind of tenderness. "Sometimes I still like to go out and play. It amuses me to seduce a few coins from people I could drink like a cup of tea."

"That's a terrifying metaphor."

The Harbinger snapped the case shut without looking at me. He obviously didn't want to talk about taverns or red-haired girls; I remembered the shawl and gown he'd let me borrow before and wondered about all the sad stories he'd wandered through alone, set on his course by our tales, and then abandoned. It was hard to feel nothing for him. Hesitantly, I put out my hand but he stepped away as if acid coated my fingers. An unexpected chill seeped into my bones despite my hat and scarf.

"Where shall I deliver you?"

"To the corner store near my house."

He asked no questions, only beckoned for me to follow. I had the incredible impression that I'd wounded him somehow by being agitated by his arrival. *No, that's crazy.* Hard-pressed to keep up, the Harbinger rounded a corner ahead of me. I stepped over a slick patch on the cracked sidewalk, and he grabbed my wrist. The world whooshed away, and we reappeared in an alley near the Baltimore.

"Close enough?"

I nodded. "Thanks. And look, I'm—"

"You have your business to tend and I've mine." With that, he was gone.

Sighing, I made my way to the store, pausing to wipe my feet so the bell jingled nonstop. José glanced up with a crisp snap of his newspaper. "Ah, you're back?"

I nodded. "If the offer's still open, I'm here to work."

A PENCHANT FOR INNOCENT EYES

I worked at the bodega twice more, enough to keep me in noodles, bread, and yogurt for the week. José and Luisa were nice people, and by Wednesday, she was sending me home with a plastic container of tamales. I devoured them for dinner that night, and they were pretty much the most delicious thing I'd tasted since I made the leap. For some reason, sweets didn't have the same savor these days.

On Thursday, I talked Kian into sitting with Devon and his group, overriding his protests that it would be awkward. For the first ten minutes, it was, and Devon glared at me over trays of macaroni and processed cheese. Kian stared hard at his food and didn't talk to anyone, so I considered conversational first aid and hoped someone at the table liked classic movies.

"So who's seen *Casablanca*?" I asked, during the next lull.

Five out of six shrugged and shook their heads, but Vonna said, "It's pretty fantastic."

Score.

Devon mentioned her the other day. She was short and a little chubby with brown skin and hair in braids. I could've hugged her, but that would have been weird. I made sure to mention we'd watched it last weekend at the Marquee, then added my two cents in evaluation, hoping to lure Kian into the discussion. That spurred some interest from the rest of the group, and soon Kian was fielding questions about the place. At first, he spoke so softly that people had lean in to hear, but I could tell the minute he realized they were honestly curious.

"Have you always liked classics?" Vonna asked eventually.

"Pretty much as long as I can remember. And, yeah, I know it's gross nostalgia and that history isn't the way those movies make it seem—"

"Some things you have to appreciate apart from the ugliness," she said, eyes glinting. "I mean, Hollywood is still a hot mess for people of color, and back then . . ."

"Exactly." Kian was nodding, and they went into a deeper discussion of progress that still needed to be made in the movie industry.

The rest of the table seemed pretty shocked, but I couldn't stop grinning. *Yeah, he's smart. He's articulate. He's got ideas worth hearing.*

Fifteen minutes later, Vonna was saying, "I'd like to direct someday, but damn, I might as well decide to be an astronaut with the glass ceiling so firmly in place."

When the bell rang, everyone seemed startled, including Kian. His gaze met mine, and I could just about hear him saying, *Holy shit, that went a lot better than I expected.* As I passed him, heading for the hallway, I bumped my shoulder against his.

"Hold up," Vonna called. "What's your number? I can't geek out with just anyone about old movies."

Eyes wide, Kian stopped, and I whispered, "Give it to her."

Devon caught up with me as the others filed out of the cafeteria. "Hey, Nine, wait. I owe you an apology."

"Why?"

"Because I was wrong about you. My mom works really hard to keep us fed, and I want to face punch anyone who judges how she does it."

"I like HOS," I said, tugging at my Who shirt. "I'm wearing something I bought there."

He sighed. "I know. My mom saves the best stuff she gets in my size, but I worry if it comes from somebody here and if some asshole like Wade is gonna yell, 'Hey, Devon, nice sweater, gave it away last week,' and then I'll be the secondhand kid for life."

"Understood. People care so much about image at this stage. It'll be nice to leave that, though I guess some folks never get past it."

"There's something odd about you," he said, thoughtful.

"You're just noticing? I'll take it as a compliment."

He smiled then. "I also need to say sorry for what we said about Kian before. Seems like he's just shy, huh?"

"Basically. I'm glad you didn't make a big thing when I brought him with me. I mean, you *did* invite me to have lunch with you guys and all."

"Heh, he was all but kicking and screaming when you two sat down. But once he loosens up, he's okay."

"And now we're on the same page. I'll be happy to one-plus-one into your group now, assuming that's still on offer."

"You make it sound like we have limited memberships."

"Well, the tables only seat eight," I pointed out.

"True. Makes you wonder how the A-listers decide who are the shiniest that week."

I snickered because I *had* noticed that there were upper- and lower-class royalty, two neighboring tables, in the center of the cafeteria, but while four seats were set, the others seemed to rotate depending on who was in favor with the core group. It was like getting voted off the island on *Survivor* or something, the way people vied for seats at those tables.

"Maybe it's sports-related. High scorer?"

"They also ostracize breakups. Like if a couple splits, one stays and the other goes. No idea how they decide who to keep, though."

"To be honest, I don't care," I said, smiling.

"Me either. I'm this way. Talk to you later." With a wave, Devon went down a different hallway, leaving me to collect stuff from my locker and dash to class.

Jake Overman fell into step with me halfway there. "Given any more thought to my party? I hear Lara met your boyfriend on Monday."

Raising a brow, I asked, "Why is that worth mentioning?"

"Apparently he was hot like whoa and damn."

"Are you repeating her, or is that *your* opinion?" I smirked.

Jake laughed, which made me like him a little more. While looks might fade, a sense of humor lasted a lifetime. "Sadly no, *I* haven't seen him. But I could quote more from her if hearing your man praised is good for your self-esteem."

"Nah, it's not a big deal."

"That's a weird attitude for a girlfriend," he noted.

"Why? If he's hot, it's nothing to do with me. Same with talent."

"But per Lara, someone that awesome chose you, right?"

"Maybe *I'm* that amazing and he's lucky I chose him."

"Maybe so," he murmured.

Ignoring that, I marched into class, only to be deflated when Jake followed me and sat down near the front of the room.

Huh, I never noticed he's in here too. Not surprising, since when I first arrived I only had Kian on my radar. But now that the mission had evolved, I had to take other people into consideration. Maybe I should test how far Jake's goodwill extended.

Since he was waiting for me after class, it didn't take long. "About your party . . ."

"Change your mind?"

"Not sure yet. Can I bring some people?"

"That Kian kid?" he guessed.

"Yeah, and a few others."

"You haven't even been here that long, how many people do you know?"

"Well, you and Tanya, Lara, Kian, Devon Quick's group . . ."

His brows shot up. "You want to invite all of them? It's not even your party."

"Good thing too. I'd make everyone drink Kool-Aid because it's cheap, and force them to do geometry to figure out the trajectory of various astronomical objects."

That startled another laugh out of him. "I have no idea if you're screwing with me right now, but I'm kind of into it. Tell me why you want to invite so many people, and I'll consider it."

"Because I'm opposed to systemic elitism," I said simply. "Logistically speaking, I know you can't invite the whole school to rock out at your place. The cost alone . . ." I shrugged. "But I've made some friends here and I don't want to go where they're not welcome."

"Not even if it means other invitations, more parties . . . ?"

"I don't care about that. I won't be here long enough for it to matter."

That snagged his attention hard, enough that he stopped walking and a short kid plowed into his back. With a mumbled "sorry," the boy scuttled past, but Jake wasn't looking at him. "Are you . . . dying or something?"

"Heh, no. Do you have a secret addiction to Lifetime movies?" That existed, right?

"Guilty as charged. I love to watch them and cry."

"Now it's my turn not to be sure if you're messing with me. But it's a good flip."

Jake licked one fingertip and etched a hash mark into the air. "One point for me. Anyway, it's fine if you want to invite people. I can't guarantee everyone will get a warm welcome, though they won't get shit from *me*."

That was about as generous as I could expect him to be, considering he was talking about his own friends. Sometimes you liked people even knowing they could be assholes to everyone else or maybe there were childhood bonds or secret pacts, whatever. I understood where he was coming from anyway. Turning, I spied Tanya watching us, but she didn't have the possessive vibe from the other day. Which likely meant Lara had regaled her with tales of Colin's excruciating hotness.

"Hey," she said brightly.

The greeting clearly included both of us, and I saw why Kian had spent his junior high years silently pining for her. Her eyes were this amazing hazel, gold when the light hit just right, and her hair, as I'd admired before, fell in tawny, sun-streaked waves. Her skin was gorgeous, flawless, lightly tinged with gold. When she stepped into the sunlight, I was kind of attracted to her; she had a radiance that made you want to step closer. In some ways, she reminded me of Allison Vega, but I detected no malice in Tanya, at least no more than usual in a human.

It's so weird that I have to make that distinction.

"'Sup." After I said it, I regretted it, but maybe I could blame California if anyone gave me a weird look.

"I didn't know you two had class together," she went on.

"Me either. I'm usually asleep." That wasn't too far from the truth.

"Yet the teacher never catches you. You have to teach me that trick," Jake said.

"Me too." Tanya took Jake's hand, and he bent down to kiss her forehead. They were actually kind of sweet together, which made me feel sorry for Kian.

It also reassured me that while our conversation had been kind of flirty, Jake didn't necessarily mean for it to go anywhere. Since I had so little romantic mojo, sometimes I thought nothing was something and something was nothing. In this scenario, I was willing to ruin Tanya's relationship if it would help, but I didn't want Jake to be easily distracted. He seemed like such a decent guy that I'd be disappointed to learn otherwise.

"Well, Colin is probably waiting," I said, mostly as an excuse to get going.

But it backfired spectacularly.

"Would it be super weird if I went with you?" Tanya asked.

"Excuse me?" I stared at her, wondering how that request sounded okay in her head.

"I'm right here," Jake pointed out.

Tanya waved him off. "Go to practice. I'll text you later."

"Fine." He sighed, but lifted a hand and jogged toward the gym, evidently well-versed in her eccentricities.

Once Jake was gone, she continued. "Lara made such a huge deal about your man candy that I want to verify. She made it sound like Justin Timberlake was here or something."

"I have no idea how to feel about this. It *is* super weird. If you decide that her hyperbole was justified, do I get a prize?" But I didn't try to stop her from accompanying me.

"You already got him," she said, as if that was obvious. "And I know this must seem bizarre, but this is Podunk, PA. I have to make my own excitement."

"With *my* boyfriend," I noted in a wry tone.

Mostly because it would be peculiar if I was totally cool with other women coming to check Colin out. Only he and I knew the truth, so I swallowed a sigh when I found him leaning up against the same electrical pole. *This is such an odd echo.* Today he was a wistful dream in shades of blue, though he still wore the black trench. Beside me, Tanya stopped, and while her mouth didn't quite drop open as the Harbinger sauntered toward us, it was a close call.

Then she swore.

I cut her a surprised look. "Something wrong?"

"I owe Lara ten bucks."

Now I understood why she needed to see "Colin" with her own eyes, and it finally made sense. "You bet he wasn't all that?"

99

"Sorry." She had the grace to look chagrined. "It's not very classy, huh?"

"It's fine," I said as he reached us.

"What is?"

"Never mind," I mumbled.

The Harbinger startled me by leaning in for a fleeting kiss. He was so natural about it that I almost tipped over, and he steadied me with a hand on my waist. "You can't get used to this, hm? Our chemistry is so—"

"Oh my God, shut up."

Tanya laughed. "Well, I'm done third-wheeling. Talk to you guys later."

She seemed to mean it, all friendly smiles as she jogged back toward the school. Kian wouldn't have liked her for this long if she wasn't smart, pretty, and nice, the intersection of feminine accomplishments. But the last item on her list of good qualities made me wonder why she'd been so *mean* about rejecting him, cruel enough to destroy him. From what I'd seen so far of her, she wasn't like that, and it made me think—

Wedderburn.

While he couldn't force Kian directly to extremis, he could shape the factors in play. My hands curled into fists, and it was all I could do not to head to Boston right now. Mounting an assault on the winter king's stronghold didn't seem like the smartest move, however. I jumped when cool, gloved fingertips tipped up my chin.

"You seem more than usually distracted." The Harbinger slung an arm around my shoulders, ostensibly in affection but his touch felt like a target on my back.

"You think? I wonder why." Unable to help myself, I glanced around, pondering if Raoul would recognize an immortal playing human. There didn't seem to be anyone in the vicinity who fit his profile, even in disguise, but as I'd learned in the game, just because you didn't see them did not mean they weren't watching. A chill crawled down my spine.

The Harbinger dug his fingers into my shoulders and leaned over to whisper, "Stop fretting, it bothers me. I may take your lack of trust personally."

"Everything you *do* bothers me, so we're even."

"You're an execrable lover," he observed with a worrisome glint in his eyes. "No concern about my day, no delight that I came to fetch you from educational imprisonment."

"It's awesome that I don't have to pay for the bus."

"That's the best you can do?" He sighed and pulled away, quickening his step, so I had to trot to keep up. Normally, he'd pull me into a quiet corner and transport us, but we hiked two blocks with no indication that he planned to stop anytime soon, not a single word spoken between us. The wind sliced through my hoodie and jean jacket like icy knives. No question about it, the Harbinger was sulking.

I shouldn't find this endearing.

"You're right. I'm sorry. I'm a terrible girlfriend. I appreciate you coming to get me when you have more important things to do."

He stopped, casting a diamond glance over one shoulder. The bright blade of a look nearly stopped me in my tracks because it was equal measures sweetness, longing, and malice. Each third carried equal impact, stealing my breath and withering my voice. It wasn't his aura exactly, more the weight of the eons he carried, as though he was a marble plinth carved from mountains and left to wear away beneath the wind.

"The last woman who apologized to me was called Saiorse."

"Redhead, dingy pub, and you were a humble fiddle player," I remembered aloud.

"I love that you collect my crumbs and try to make a loaf of them."

"Even the fragments are fascinating."

He took both my hands in his, crunch of leather against the soft knit covering my fingers. "That time . . . I said it ended badly."

"I remember."

"It wasn't my fault. For some reason, I feel impelled to share that much. I never . . . I didn't play with her. We just kept company for a time. She reminded me of Sigyn. I've always had a penchant for innocent eyes."

Knowing the Harbinger, he might even have a collection of them; I chose not to pursue that disturbing avenue of inquiry. Nor did I yield to the impulse to ask if my gaze fit his criteria. "What happened?"

"Human frailty," he said gravely. "In those days, they called it consumption."

"Tuberculosis? I'm sorry. It must have been hard."

He let go of me then. "No, it's the easiest thing in the world to watch someone die, dearling. What's hard is continuing on. After."

Contemplating my losses, I decided those might be the truest words he had ever spoken.

SILKEN ROPES AND UNSEEN SNARES

"I am *not* going to Jake Overman's party," Kian said, as if I'd suggested he head for Mars in a one-man craft.

Actually, he'd probably be more willing to take that risk. I nudged him, trotting out my best imploring look. "C'mon. Everyone else said they'd check it out. Carmen even said she'd drive . . . her mom has a minivan so everyone can pile in. We're meeting up at the bus stop nearest House of Style."

"No way. This won't end well," he predicted.

"How can you know that for sure?"

"When I'm not watching golden-age movies, I'm all over eighties teen comedies. I know what happens when the nerd goes to the jock party."

Despite my sense of urgency, I laughed. "Those movies are brain candy, but they don't write the script for reality. Jake seems like an okay guy, and Tanya is nice too."

"What about the twenty other people?"

"Well, we're bringing eight. The odds are in our favor." Normally,

Kian would've made a Hunger Games joke here, but the first book hadn't come out yet.

"I don't understand why this is so important to you. What difference does it make if I go to a party or not?"

"Life is all about new experiences. You should try things, even if they scare you. If it turns out to be fun, then it's a win."

"And if not?"

"Then you know for sure it's not your deal and can tick it off the list."

"I can do that right now," he muttered.

Sighing, I said, "Then I guess you don't like Tanya that much."

He grabbed my arm and tugged me out of the stream of people passing from the cafeteria to their next class. "Are you crazy? Don't say that."

"It's true, though. If you cared that much about her, you'd be willing to take risks."

"She has a boyfriend, genius." It was the first time I'd heard such a scathing tone from Kian, and in all honesty, it cut deep.

Ignoring my personal discomfort, I shook free of his grasp because a new friend like I was pretending to be wouldn't be affected so much by his anger. "Whatever, dude. If you'd rather watch from the sidelines, it's your call. But *I'm* going to the party. Maybe it'll suck and I'll have no desire for an encore, but life is for living."

"Carpe diem," he said quietly.

"Exactly, seize the day."

He seemed to be talking to himself more than me as he went on. "It's pretty gutless to complain about my situation while I refuse strategic changes."

"I don't know if it has to be *that* much of a thing," I said, because Nine probably wouldn't understand.

Remembering how scared I was before Cameron Dean's party, how Davina practically had to shove me bodily through the gates, I got his angst. Kian squared his shoulders and tipped his head as if the ceiling tiles offered resolve and inspiration. Then he let out a deep breath and nodded, some inner turmoil resolved.

"Fine, I'll go. But I'm not expecting to hook up with anyone; it would just be nice to prove that I'm not a total loner."

Anyone had to mean Tanya. But it would be cool if he talked to her. In three years of this endless crush, he'd never managed that. The first step to getting over this girl was realizing she wasn't the pinnacle of perfection. I considered telling him that she'd bet Lara ten bucks that my "boyfriend" wasn't as hot as she claimed, but he wasn't ready for Tanya to climb down from her pedestal yet.

"Sounds good. We're meeting at seven on Saturday night." Since I'd already given the location, that should be enough.

"I'll be there. But . . . do you think I should get a haircut before then?" Kian peered at me through shaggy bangs, undeniably anxious.

"Yeah. There's a beauty school downtown with a sign for five-dollar cuts."

"Is that a good idea?"

"The students are probably more worried about doing a good job than stylists that charge fifty bucks while texting as they work on you."

That seemed to soothe his misgivings. "Want to go with me?"

"Sure. I could use a change too. Did you want to get it done tonight?"

"Unless you have something planned with Colin?"

The Harbinger was strange yesterday . . . and that was saying something. After his surprising confession that Saiorse had died of consumption, he dropped me off at my room and vanished with no mention of when I'd see him again. That left me with surprisingly conflicted emotions. On one hand, it was a relief not to stress about him signaling Wedderburn's agents that I was more than I seemed, but a kernel of concern wedged itself into my heart. It was weird to care how he felt, but now that I'd started, the roller coaster didn't look to be letting me off anytime soon.

"No, he's got a gig."

"Violin, right?" I nodded, and Kian made a face. "I always heard musicians are irresistible. Guess that's true."

"You're a clever guy. Learn to play the guitar."

"Maybe I will." He grinned.

The vibe was so different than it had been. Before Colin appeared, there were signs Kian might transfer his devotion from Tanya to me. Now I'd been firmly friend-zoned. I had . . . mixed feelings, but I reminded myself that was for the best while choking down memories he didn't share. No matter what, he would always be my first love.

"That would be awesome. Then you can jam with Colin."

By Kian's expression, that wasn't what he wanted to hear, but it etched the boundary between us anew. I was just the spontaneous girl who crashed into his life and would dart away like a hummingbird when the time came. Before then, however, I had to leave him in a good place with enough support to survive whatever Wedderburn threw at him. I couldn't accept the idea that Kian might be made to be broken, and that the loop would repeat, no matter what.

"Anyway, I'll meet you after school?"

The warning bell rang, drowning out any verbal reply, so I gave him two thumbs up and dashed toward my class. I dozed through the rest of the day, and when I headed to the front, Kian was waiting. Notably, the Harbinger was not. A little pang went through me. Not because I missed him, but he was even more isolated than me. I imagined him curled up in his rocky pile on the coast, licking ancient wounds. There was nothing I could do, however, so I slung my bag over one shoulder and hurried toward Kian.

"Let's catch a bus," I said.

This time, he didn't lean his shoulder against mine or offer to share his music with me. We joked around until our stop and got off to walk the four blocks to the student salon. There were five people already in the chairs, so we waited half an hour before they called Kian. He cast a nervous look over one shoulder, but I didn't go with him. Telling the stylist what he wanted would be good practice, and it wasn't like I could intercede for him forever.

Ten minutes later, a girl with spiky green hair came to get me. "Your turn. Don't let my look worry you. I funk people up by request only."

I laughed as I sat down. "Actually that would be cool. I've always wanted to try a bob, something a little edgy?"

She picked up a magazine and flipped through it. "Something like this?"

"What's that even called?"

"Asymmetrical bob with heavy side bangs."

"I'm glad it's something so easy to remember," I said.

"You'll be losing a lot of hair—you sure you're okay with that?"

"Totally. It's time for a change."

That settled, she went to work, but she was slower than the stylists I'd had before, probably because she had a teacher inspecting her efforts every ten minutes. But an hour later, my hair looked fantastic. She gave me a mirror so I could check out the front, and went over how I could achieve this careless look on my own.

While listening to the instructions, I glanced around for Kian, but he must've finished and gone back to the waiting room. I slipped her some crumpled singles. "You did a great job."

"Thanks." She pocketed the money and started cleaning up her station. "You'd look cute with some streaks. Come back if you decide to go for it."

"I'll think about it."

Out in the lobby, I spotted Kian right away. He'd gone for a style similar to the one he'd worn when I met him in the other timeline: short on the sides, shorn in the back, with a little flip of a quiff up front. It was such a huge improvement that I beamed. Maybe Tanya wouldn't fall for him at first sight, but other people would definitely be checking him out at the party.

"How is it?" he asked, anxious.

"Good. I like being able to see your face."

His mouth twisted. "Funny. I see you weren't kidding about changing things up."

I resisted the urge to ask his opinion. "I'm hoping it'll be easier to manage."

"Since you lopped off eight inches, it'd be pretty messed up if it was harder."

"Smart-ass. Ready to go?"

"Yeah, I need to get home. My uncle will be around this weekend, and he said something about hanging out." Kian seemed stoked for that, practically running to the bus stop so we could catch the next one.

We got off at my stop, but he had to wait for a transfer. I waved as I headed for the Baltimore, but instead of going straight there, I stopped at the bodega. José had a line of customers and somebody had broken a bottle of beer, so I got the mop while he focused on the register. After I removed the glass, it seemed like a waste to do only one spot, so I mopped the whole store. Soon the crowd thinned out and I finished cleaning, then left the yellow WET FLOOR sign out just in case.

"You showed up just in time," he said.

"What else do you need me to do?"

Glancing around the small shop, he locked onto the aisles of canned goods. "The shelves haven't been cleaned in a while . . ."

"Okay, I'm on it."

It took me a couple of hours to move everything, wipe the grime off the metal units, and replace the stock. The bodega would be open for hours still, but I was tired. The awkward thing about working under the table was, I couldn't just put what I wanted in a basket. First José had to tell me what he thought my efforts were worth. He came out from behind the counter and walked down the narrow aisles, checking out the situation.

"This is fantastic. And you did the floor earlier. If you restock the drink cooler before you go, I can give you thirty in groceries."

Wow. That was the most I'd gotten so far. "Thanks. That'll help a lot."

"You ever gonna tell me your story?" he asked as I headed for the cooler.

"Probably not."

"How come?"

"It's implausible," I said. "So you wouldn't believe me anyway."

"Try me. I got a cousin who was abducted by aliens, my hand to God." José went on a five-minute digression only interrupted by Luisa coming in the front door, tired from a long day of doing whatever she did for the city of Cross Point.

"Are you telling her about your cousin? Paco has problems; everybody knows this."

That started a small squabble about whether his history of mental illness made him an unreliable witness, which I used to escape into the cooler. This was mindless work—fill from the back, ensure the old stuff ends up in front. Half an hour later, I stepped out, shivering but done. Luisa had gone upstairs, but José had a care package for me in addition to the staples I took my time in selecting.

"I probably won't be in this weekend," I said as he bagged my stuff.

"Somehow I will soldier on."

His sarcasm made me smile; it took the edge off accepting help that I wasn't sure he truly needed, and that put this job half a step above charity. Still, today I'd finished some gross chores that were off his plate. I doubted he and Luisa were getting rich from the bodega, but since it was the only shop in the neighborhood, they seemed to sell a steady stream of drinks, liquor, snacks, cigarettes, and lottery tickets.

I waved, stepping out into the bitter wind past the tinkle of the bell. There were a few others out in the gloaming, two waiting for the bus, and one probably just got off it. Everyone had knit hats on with their collars pulled up. Returning to the Baltimore didn't even bother me; I'd gotten used to my temporary life. The cleaning cart was sitting in the middle of the hallway when I reached my floor, but the housekeeper was nowhere in sight. With a mental shrug, I borrowed the vacuum and hauled it to my room, where I ran it over the carpet and then used the hose to suck up the dust everywhere I could reach.

She was waiting with a ferocious frown when I returned it. "Are you trying to get me fired? You're not supposed to do that."

"Sorry. I thought I'd save you the trouble." Also, she didn't really *clean* the rooms, though she was supposed to do so once a week. From the way she walked, I suspected she had back problems, likely from a lifetime of scrubbing.

"Ask first next time." But she didn't seem quite so pissed.

Deciding that was as far as the conversation went, I retraced my steps to lock my door, then jogged down the stairs. I'd memorized the bus schedule, so I knew the one I wanted would be there in seven minutes. As I stepped out into a drizzle of freezing rain, I tugged up my hood and increased my pace, hoping to reach the stop before the sky opened up. *Any colder and this would be snow,* I thought. *Am I making your life worse, Wedderburn?* Probably not, but I smirked anyway, picturing his frustration as one of his anticipated pawns started making unanticipated moves, thus messing up his game.

An elderly woman was already waiting when I skidded up, sneakers losing traction on the newly slick sidewalk. "Careful, there," she chided with a faint accent.

"Sorry."

"It's been such a winter. I haven't seen this much ice and snow since we left Siberia."

I couldn't tell if that was a joke, but she looked like she *could* be

Russian, though it was hard to tell with the handmade muffler wrapping most of her face. "It's bad all right."

"And you're running around without a proper coat. Do you want to catch pneumonia?"

This conversation was weird, but sometimes old people came across like life-choice missionaries, obligated to point out everybody's failings. I was in no mood to listen to it, however, so I said, "Of course not. But some people can't afford coats."

"Oh dear." It horrified me when she dug into her purse with trembling fingers.

"Look, my bus is here." I fled before she could offer me a dollar. Nice people made it impossible to be a practicing curmudgeon.

Exhaling in relief when she didn't get on, I picked a seat near the back and leaned against the window. Six stops later, I got off the bus, silently mocking myself. *Only I would test a fake ID to see if it can get me a library card.* Friday night, an hour before closing, the place was pretty much deserted apart from the staff.

"I'd like a—"

Before I could finish, the librarian gave me a form. She glanced at my ID, keyed some information, and then gave me a plastic card with a barcode on it. I took it, along with two stapled pages. "Here's all the pertinent info, including branch locations and hours."

To me, this was way more exciting than getting into a bar. Even if shit got rough, as long as I had unlimited access to fiction, I could power through to the end, whatever that might be for me. I spent half an hour browsing and chose two books with a happy flutter in my chest. Books had always, always saved me, time and again. This timeline would be no exception.

Darkness wreathed the city when I came out of the library. The bus was full of excited people heading to a club or maybe a sporting event. From what I could tell, most of them knew one another, and I stood near the front, hanging from a strap. Funny how lonely it was here. Now. The more people Kian knew, the less time he'd have for me. That was a good thing, right?

Right.

My parents were alive, but I couldn't talk to them. Yet that didn't stop me from pausing at a payphone and feeding coins into it. *I shouldn't dial this number.* My fingers did it anyway.

On the third ring, Mom picked up and her crisp "hello" cramped my chest so I could hardly breathe, let alone speak. *She's alive. She's really alive.* Tears froze in my eyes and didn't fall. I heard my dad murmuring about dinner getting cold in the background. Twelve-year-old Edie would probably be annoyed when she had to stop fiddling with her geode collection to eat brown rice and poached fish.

Mom repeated the "hello" with rising annoyance.

"I'm calling to ask if you're happy with your long-distance carrier." That was a safe gambit, no matter the year.

"Not interested," she practically sang.

Dial tone hummed in my ear. Slowly, I hung up the receiver and turned. The Harbinger was waiting in the shadow of the closest building. He pushed away from the crumbling brick to close the distance between us, something sweet and sinister in his aspect. Tonight he was Colin, an ageless musician holding a battered violin case in one arm like a bouquet of roses.

"Your heartache is excruciating," he said.

"Sorry." And I was, for so many things.

"Don't apologize. The fact that it abates a bit when I appear? There are no words for such a gift." His tone was silken ropes and unseen snares, and—

I didn't care. When he set down his case and opened his arms, I went.

THROWING A
KILLER PARTY

When I arrived at the meeting point, a full fifteen minutes early, someone was already waiting. It took me a few seconds to realize it was Kian, mostly because he had on a different coat and new glasses. They were blue and rectangular with a definite hipster air, and more to the point, they completely changed his look. He turned and caught me staring; freezing, he ran a sheepish hand through his hair.

He's adorable.

Between the glasses, the belted jacket, and the cargo pants, I saw echoes of the person he would become. *If he survives.*

He has to survive.

"You're making me feel weird," he mumbled.

"Sorry. I like the upgrade. Your uncle took you shopping?"

"Yeah. I . . . talked to him about some stuff."

"Like what?"

"Things I need . . . and the fact that I want to spend more time with him." He offered a half smile and went on. "I took a page from your book. I mean, you're so fearless. I figured I didn't have any-thing to lose by opening my mouth."

"How did it go?"

"We went to a basketball game last night . . . and then he took me to a one-hour optical place this morning. He also said he'll talk to my aunt." He didn't sound hopeful, but any progress on the family front relieved the hell out of me.

"That's great," I said.

"Yeah, it was a good talk."

"How come you didn't say anything before?"

"I don't know." He hunched his shoulders against the bitter wind, and I could tell there was something he didn't want to confide.

I haven't known him that long after all.

"Well, I'm glad it helped a little."

"I think that's Carmen," he said, obviously wanting to change the subject.

But I turned to look and spotted a blue minivan pulling up near the bus stop. Carmen waved to us from the driver's seat; she had a couple of passengers already, but we were waiting for three more yet. Kian and I piled in and crawled all the way to the back. Evidently, Carmen had a bunch of siblings because the floor was lit-tered with toys that suited kids of all ages, plus fast-food wrappers and empty soda cans.

"You'd think these lazy asses could show up in time for a free ride," Carmen said five minutes later.

"They're probably on the next bus," Devon guessed.

Vonna nodded, then said to Kian, "Cool glasses."

I suspected he was blushing when he said, "Thanks."

It turned out that Devon was right, as Nathan, Amanda, and

Elton arrived together, getting off the number twenty-seven, which came from the north side of town. Once everyone settled in, Carmen took off. This was the most I'd seen of Cross Point, as we left the downtown area, passed the school, and kept going west into suburbs and then finally countryside. Leaning forward, I measured the distance between houses and had the eerie feeling that anything could happen out here. Of course, I *had* been raised in Boston, so I was used to lots of people and buildings, not wide-open spaces.

"Jake wasn't kidding when he said his parties never get raided, huh?"

Vonna nodded. "Their nearest neighbors are like a mile away."

"Have you been to one out here before?" Kian asked her.

She shook her head. "Nah. We don't rate high enough . . . or at least we *didn't*."

"I'm not sure why you got us added to the A-list," Devon said, "but this should be a night to remember."

Famous last words, right?

The house came into sight around the next bend, an impressive Federal-style home set behind an even more impressive fence. Perimeter lights blazed like beacons along the paved road that led up to the redbrick structure. A pool house sat adjacent, newer construction. I'd thought Cameron Dean's place was fancy, but this was a whole different level. I'd pictured an upscale four-bedroom in the middle of suburbia or maybe a farmhouse. This was more like an estate.

"Holy shit," Devon said.

The gate opened after a brief conversation with Jake. Inside, twenty cars were lined up single file down the drive, and music thumped with insistent bass, cracking the stillness of the winter

117

night. Snow piled up on either side of the walk created a sense that we were entering a winter fortress, an impression that freaked me out for oh-so-many reasons. Beyond the house, the grounds were wreathed in white, so the lights reflected in tiny crystals of brightness. We went in the front, stepping into an impressive foyer that led into an enormous space, complete with fireplace, multiple couches, marble floors, chandelier, and wet bar. The locale was more upscale than I'd anticipated, though the dress code didn't seem to be.

"Check this place out." Devon nudged me.

"It's crazy," I agreed.

"What time are we heading out?" Vonna asked.

Carmen looked at her phone. "If you're riding back with me, meet up here at eleven fifteen. I have a curfew, and some of you need to catch the midnight bus home."

"Sounds good." Devon squared his shoulders and locked on a target I couldn't pick out of the crowd.

Kian put a hand on my arm. "You won't ditch me, right?"

"Of course not. I'm the one who talked you into coming tonight. Relax, it'll be fine."

The others drifted off, in twos and threes, probably not wanting to seem so nervous that we had to rove in a pack like wolves. With black lights and multiple strobes, the room possessed a surreal air, making it hard to recognize anyone. Though I'd likely seen most of these people at school, I couldn't ID Jake or Tanya. In fact, the whole place gave me a weird vibe. From the corner of my eye, I caught odd movements and sourceless shadows. Sometimes a guest seemed to have mouths too big for their faces, or too many teeth, but when I shivered and peered closer, they seemed human.

I'm freaking out over nothing.

Just because the one party I'd attended in Boston ended with the host being devoured by demon dogs, it didn't mean this one was cursed by association. A tall figure skirted the crowd, some of whom were dancing, but their movements were weird. I attributed that to drinking as Jake's features clarified. The strobe made it seem like his smile was cut into his face with a serrated knife. One blink, and that impression faded. He seemed genuinely pleased to see me.

"You made it. That's awesome."

"What the hell are you playing, though?"

"It's a mix of Skinny Puppy, Frontline Assembly, and NIN."

"I haven't heard of any of that," I said.

"Not a fan of industrial?"

"Not so much. But in all honesty, music isn't really my jam anyway." I had to practically yell to be heard over the growl and grind of the song.

"It's too loud," Tanya whisper-yelled.

She slipped her hand into Jake's in an affectionate gesture. I noticed Kian tense at my shoulder, but he didn't react otherwise. *Come on, say something. I won't be around to pass you perfect segues forever.* Jake rolled his eyes. Across the room, I watched a dark shape approach Carmen in staccato movements. *It's a guy, it's just some guy.* She disappeared from one flash to another, and I stared hard at the space where she had been, chills crawling up and down my spine. The foreboding from earlier rebounded and intensified.

Probably because Tanya agreed with me, Jake went over to the iPod dock and shifted to a different playlist. The first song that came on didn't drown out all attempts at verbal communication at least. She smiled at him, but the strobes made her expression seem strange and predatory. I had the urge to ask to see their belly buttons. Not just Jake and Tanya, either, I pretty much wanted to inspect every-one in the room. But that would ruin what social cred I'd managed to accrue and I couldn't be branded an outcast for Kian's sake.

"Your boyfriend isn't coming?" Tanya asked.

"It's hard to tell with him. I told him, but . . ." I shrugged, not wanting to talk about the weird conversation I'd carried on while the Harbinger hugged me, which was like surviving a close encoun-ter with a lion.

"Does he have a gig?" Kian wanted to know.

"Maybe. Full disclosure isn't his style."

"I'd put up with a lot for a guy that hot," Tanya said.

Jake strolled up just in time to hear that. "I could get a complex. Every time I turn around, you're looking for an upgrade."

"Like that's possible." She grinned, stretching up to kiss his cheek.

Kian shifted beside me, and I read his discomfort, but I didn't know what to do about it. If anyone did, I understood the pain of hiding your feelings; my emotions were a hot pot bubbling with conflicting impulses. But before I could make an excuse to break away, Carmen reappeared across the room. She seemed a little mussed, and if I found her smile slightly alarming, maybe I'd just never seen someone who just got laid before.

That was fast.

A frisson of unease prickled the skin on the nape of my neck. Glancing around the room, I caught someone—or something—staring our way, but the focus wasn't on me. Whoever—or whatever—had locked onto Kian like a laser targeting scope. *Some-thing terrible is going to happen tonight. Wedderburn can't let him get too far from extremis.* The insight didn't feel like a hunch, more of a certainty.

I stopped trying to convince myself that the bad feeling came from my imagination and frantically tried to factor damage control.

"I think we have bio together," Tanya was saying to Kian with a friendly smile. "You took best on that last test. Thanks to your ninety-nine, I got a B."

He didn't freeze up. "I guess you have to try harder."

Her eyes widened. "Oh, I will. You'll be eating my bell curve next time."

Smiling, he said, "I doubt it. You have extracurriculars to worry about while I'm focused on grades."

"How come?" Jake asked.

"Not everyone lives in a house like this," I reminded him. "Some of us need scholarships, or we'll be asking if you want fries with that for life."

"Come on. I'm pretty sure I could land a job at Staples even without college." Kian seemed to be relaxing, even as terrible anticipation wound me up like a clockwork ballerina.

"Best Buy," Tanya suggested.

"Sorry." Jake had the grace to look embarrassed.

"No worries. You're tolerable for a rich brat."

"Whatever. I have to mingle. Hope you have fun tonight."

I thought Tanya would go with him, but she showed no signs of being tired of our company. For Kian, this had be heaven and hell combined. He could finally talk to the girl he'd liked for so long, but she was firmly off-limits. I'd keep an eye on him to make sure he didn't drink some spiked punch and then make a drunken declaration.

"I always wondered what your deal was," she said.

"Mine?" Kian's eyes widened.

"Yeah. When you transferred, there was a lot of talk, but some of the stories . . ." She shook her head. "Anyway, I'm glad you're not as weird as they say."

"Uh. Thanks?"

"Oops." She flashed a charming smile. "Guess I should lay off the schnapps."

"Maybe so." I hadn't touched any of the liquor on offer, and I devoutly hoped Carmen hadn't either since she was our ride.

Maybe I should check on her.

But I couldn't leave Kian, and he wouldn't thank me for dragging him away from his first contact with Tanya. *Makes it sound like she's an alien species.* For him, that might not be too far from the truth, as long as he'd idolized her. In his defense, she *was* smart, pretty, and nice, way more approachable than any member of the Teflon crew at Blackbriar, so maybe it was the difference between public and private school attitudes.

"Crap, Lara's about to make a poor life choice. Catch you guys later." Tanya hurried to the stairs, stopping a burly guy from hauling Lara off.

"Let's circulate," I said to Kian.

He nodded, sticking to me like I was his bodyguard . . . No doubt, Aegis's weight on my wrist in the form of a gold bangle gave me the confidence to push deeper into the crowd. Whirling colors joined the strobe effect, tinting people blue, red, and then green. The flashes tinted their eyes, imbuing a demonic glow, and I reached for Kian, remembering the Harbinger's bash. *Whatever happens, don't let go.* But my hand found only empty space. I spun, but he was gone. *What the hell?* My heart went into overdrive.

Carmen stood a few feet away, so I hurried over to her. "Have you seen Kian?"

Her eyes were wide and glassy when she smiled at me, and the bruise on her neck looked exactly like the one that I'd acquired at the Feast of Fools when the time slip happened and something awful fed from me. *Damn it, the monsters are here.* I set my hands on her shoulders and jostled her a bit, hoping she'd come out of it on her own, but the vacant smile lingered.

Devon came over, disengaging from the guy he was chatting up. "Is she okay?"

"I don't think so."

"Shit, did someone lace her drink?" He spun in a slow circle as if the culprit might be watching the show.

Which would've been likely at Blackbriar.

But immortals didn't operate on the same level as bored kids. While they used humans for entertainment, we were also food. I fought a frustrated scream, swallowing it like necessary medicine. I located the other members of our ride share, but still didn't see Kian. Devon seemed to sense my anxiety.

"This party is a lot to take in, even if you're used to . . ." He trailed off, likely not knowing how to put it. "You think he found a quiet corner?"

"I don't know, but I have to find him. Can you stay with Carmen? I don't think she's in any shape to drive."

"Me either." He put an arm around her and led her over to one of the leather sofas.

I searched the whole room but didn't find Kian. The rest of our group hadn't noticed a problem, and they were playing beer pong with some of the more popular folks. Trouble was, this house was so damn huge that I had no idea where to start. Plus, if an immortal had taken Kian, there was no guarantee he was on the property. The Harbinger couldn't be the only one with the ability to whoosh through time and space.

Fifteen minutes, I'd checked out the kitchen, formal dining room, pantry, laundry room, and every other space the downstairs had to offer. I found a few people making out in dark corners and one couple on their way to third base, but no Kian. Bracing myself, I jogged up the stairs. If the displays of affection were so intense in public areas, the bedrooms would be like Cirque du Soleil. Two locked doors later, I stepped into what had to be the master suite. Apparently, people felt weird about doing it in the parental bed.

It was a gorgeous space, decorated in dove gray and lavender, a low yellow light emanating from the walk-in closet. It was quiet enough that I heard my own heartbeat, the rasp of my own breathing. The prickle of unseen eyes made me turn around, but there was nobody in the hallway. As I stared, the door swung shut of its own volition and the temperature dropped, cold enough that I could see my next exhalation.

"Is someone there?"

In answer, the closet door creaked open and the lights went out. Below, the music stopped, bathing the house in eerie silence. Then the screaming started. Stumbling forward, I set a hand on Aegis. The switch didn't respond when I flipped it.

This was my idea. Kian didn't even want to come.

I waited, because someone—something—was clearly setting a mood. At this point, a normal teenage girl would be pissing in terror, too frozen to defend herself. And I couldn't break character unless my life depended on it. *And it might.* The slow thunk of boots on a hardwood floor came from the closet, and in the murky light shining through the window, I made out a shadowy form. A flashlight clicked on, highlighting a white face with a smeared red mouth and sharp yellow teeth.

Buzzkill. Someone's dying tonight.

"It's not your lucky day," he said.

"Nobody told me this was a theme party." The tremor in my voice came naturally; I'd barely won our last fight, and I hadn't been training lately. Plus, even if I managed to take him out, it would alert Wedderburn, assuming he didn't already know.

"Hold still, I'll make it quick."

As I was about to activate Aegis, the pane in the nearest window exploded and the Harbinger arrived in a shower of glass and the frantic beating of black wings. He was full on, radiating power like a nuclear reactor. With him on total wattage, it hurt to breathe, and I staggered, catching myself on the bed. Buzzkill didn't react.

"This is a bad move," the clown said. "Unless you're here to watch the carnage."

"I think you already know she's mine." Shivers raised goose bumps on my exposed skin at the iciness of his tone.

"She may be your latest pet, but she's also interfering in Wedderburn's business. That makes her a snafu that I *will* eliminate."

"Over my dead body," the Harbinger said.

"I'm ninety percent positive Boss won't have a problem with those terms. You sure you want to do this? Making an enemy like him over a meatsack is a dumb shit move."

The Harbinger wrapped his arm about my shoulders, his eyes all lightning anticipation. "Do your worst, scary clown. Let's go to war."

UNNATURAL DISASTERS

Buzzkill took a step toward me, and I could tell he was thinking about forcing the fight here and now—without waiting for Wedderburn's approval. Aegis burned on my wrist, whispering that I should unleash. And I might have if not for the Harbinger digging his fingers into my shoulder. How odd for him to serve as the voice of reason.

"You should know better than to interfere with what's mine," he added.

"Flesh puppets are easily replaced." I'd never heard a conciliatory tone from Buzzkill before. Interesting that he seemed to respect or at least remained wary of the Harbinger.

A chill wind blew over us, gusting the gauzy panel as if this was a haunted house, not a sophomore's party with nervous laughter echoing through the halls. *They probably think the blackout is a joke. They have no idea what's coming.* For the moment, the greatest threat was contained as the Harbinger studied Buzzkill with eyes like two downed electrical lines sparking at passersby.

"Did I fail to communicate in some fashion?" He bit the next words as if they were ice cubes, cold and grinding. "Mine is mine."

The killer clown didn't budge. "Yeah, and orders are orders."

"Have you no ambition? How long do you intend to hunt as Winter's hound?"

"Eh, I'm not much for long-term planning, and I like the perks. Lots of carnage, good hours, benefits package." He grinned, showing stained, scary teeth. "Plus dental, obviously."

"Then I am through wasting my precious time since you've chosen to be a minion instead of a power."

"You should talk. All *you* ever do is flit around the fringes of the game. There's a word for assholes who consistently go after low-hanging fruit."

The Harbinger dug his fingers into my shoulder, likely not realizing that his protection was starting to hurt. A normal girl wouldn't utter a sound, terrified out of her mind, hopelessly bewildered, and maybe wondering if somebody had slipped something into her drink. So I did my best to cower and look bleary. Forty crows cawed and shifted behind me, a palpable air of malice settling over the room like a death shroud. The tension clung to my lips and frosted my eyelashes. If the Harbinger had been half playful in his defense before, he was amused no longer.

"Take care," he said softly.

"You think I'm scared of some angry birds? I beat that app like five years ago. But see how far this pissing contest gets us? You're starting to piss me off, Trick." Buzzkill cracked open his go bag, revealing an array of knives.

"Starting? *I'm* finished. Scuttle back to your master before the choke chain throttles you."

The clown let out an exaggerated sigh, kind of like an evil balloon deflating slowly. "Be reasonable. The Oracle fingered this one as screwing up the timeline, blocking the boss from acquiring a necessary asset."

That explained how Buzzkill knew I was here, and the trouble I had breathing because of the Harbinger's aura intensified, resulting in near hyperventilation. My heart raced so hard, it hurt, and it wasn't hard to act like I was passing out. Head rush sparkles popped as the Harbinger caught me in one arm. His strength was absurd and effortless, belying his lean frame.

"She dead?" His heavy boots clonked a few steps closer. "That would solve everything. We'll find a replacement, no problem. This is the style you like?"

The sound of beating wings engulfed me, and to my astonishment, through my lashes I saw the birds had formed a feathery wall, fluttering together in a formation so unnatural that it filled with me a sort of grateful revulsion. Playing the damsel in distress sucked, but if I deviated, then all the Harbinger's bullshit would be for nothing, and I had to hang on here somehow, long enough to get Kian past his personal nadir. But it was tough letting them talk while all hell broke loose downstairs. Every muscle in my body quivered with tension as I resisted the urge to break free and run—not away from Buzzkill—but to help the terrified people below.

"You reek of blood and bratwurst, cretin. Another step, and you shall see why the others find it wise to leave me be." His tone rang like sharped blades over smooth ice.

"Don't be dramatic. I'm just trying to do my job."

"Does it seem as though I'm interested in your employer?"

"Not really." Buzzkill seemed to make a decision and snapped

128

his kit shut, hiding the silvery glimmer of multiple blades. "See you soon."

"You'd better gear up and come heavy," the Harbinger said gently. "Your little knives will barely scratch the surface."

"Don't worry about *my* firepower. See you later, asshole."

I kept quiet until the clown faded into the shadows and then for a minute more, just in case. "Is he gone?"

"It seems so." The Harbinger let go of me and phased into Colin.

"Was it smart to talk about that stuff in front of me?"

"He thinks I'm draining you. By the time I finished, you'd be incoherent and broken, if not deceased."

"But a slow death isn't good enough. They want me facedown immediately." A shiver went through as the screaming intensified downstairs. "We have to help them. Buzzkill probably brought monsters."

"I'd be surprised if he didn't, though some things just slither in greater shadows, hoping to feast off the carnage that others provoke."

Fear made my words run together in a desperate rush. "They'll try to frame Kian, force him back into the role of school pariah."

"Probably," he said.

"Will you help me stop it?"

The Harbinger thought for a second, the pensive look illuminated faintly by the moonlight shining through the window. "I've already rescued one person tonight, dearling. I'm over my limit already."

I sighed. "Never mind."

"Then . . ." He swept out of the room, probably thirsty to drink in the chaos and fear.

I followed, conscious of the chill that pervaded the upper story. The bedroom doors weren't locked anymore, but the couples were half dressed and trembling as they clung to one another, likely not even positive why they were so terrified. On some level, they must grasp that this wasn't a normal power outage and that things were prowling the dark, even as they tried to convince themselves it was all in their imaginations.

In the kitchen, I found Vonna and Devon standing guard over Carmen, who gazed around with a blank stare. "Something truly screwed up is going on here," Devon said softly.

"Get to the car. Give me fifteen minutes to find everyone else. But if I'm not there, get out of here, don't wait. You can drive, right?"

"I don't exactly have a license, but yeah. I know how."

Vonna held out her hand. "I have mine. Give me Carmen's keys."

I went over and fished them out of her purse, dangling limply off her shoulder. "I think you know this but don't leave her alone. It'll take her a while to feel like herself again."

"You seem pretty sure what's wrong with her," Devon said.

"It happened to me once."

Vonna studied Carmen with an increasingly worried look. "She hasn't been—"

"No," I cut in. "It's kind of like a roofie, but nobody raped her."

Not physically anyway. I didn't have time to get into the particulars of how she'd feel after being psychically drained. That was definitely a violation, but not the sort they were worried about. After checking that we had our meeting time straight, they led Carmen out the back door onto a snowy patio, and I turned back toward the enshadowed house.

How many people am I looking for? Nathan, Amanda, Elton, and Kian.

The Harbinger didn't need *me* to rescue him. So four. In the hallway leading to the laundry area, two human forms cowered. Someone sobbed, low and breathless, as darkness crept closer, amorphous with red eyes in a blob of a face. I almost made out claws atop thin, elongated arms. *I can't just watch. I brought these monsters here.* Silently cursing, I touched Aegis, and it sprang to life in a shimmer of a gold. I swept the thing from behind, piercing it with a hiss of dark steam. It wheeled on me, and I slashed again. This time, I passed through the thing's core, and it dispersed like a malevolent cloud. More unsettling, the darkness whirled around me like a tornado of evil, until Aegis drew it all in.

Oh, shit. It's . . . Am I feeding *it?*

Suddenly, I wished I had asked more questions of Govannon or paid more attention when Rochelle tried to warn me. But before worry could lock me down, a rush of a pure energy shot up my arm. I'd never mainlined any illegal drugs, but this must be what it felt like. Euphoria crackled through my veins like fireworks, and I bounded away from the cowering humans on the floor. *They're safe, good enough. I have more killing to do.*

Stepping into the laundry room, I nearly tripped on Jake Overman, on his knees and scared shitless of the shadow fiend that had him by the throat. Kian lay unconscious in front of the washer and dryer, and that checked my reckless fervor. *Dammit, I'm not here to fight. I'm supposed to be saving people.* But sometimes there was overlap between mission and inclination; Jake's gaze locked on mine, but I could see the smoke tightening on him like an ethereal noose. I didn't hesitate; the creature noticed too late, dropping its prey to face me, but I executed it in two sweeps of the blade. These creatures posed no challenge, just scavengers.

"What . . . how . . ." Jake was breathing, but not getting much oxygen.

If he kept huffing like that, he'd pass out. Which might not be bad for me. Bruises ringed his throat, and his eyes were glassy but he didn't have that vacant look yet. The thing hadn't finished feeding on him when I interrupted it. I had a feeling the shadow might've killed Jake since Kian was unconscious nearby and he wouldn't be able to explain *anything* later.

"You throw a weird-ass party. Pull yourself together and look for Tanya."

"Oh, shit." He hauled himself to his feet, nearly pulling down a metal shelving unit in the process. It wobbled and so did he, but fear for his girlfriend distracted him from the sword in my hand and the fact that something deeply disturbing had just happened in his utility room.

Once he ran out, I sheathed Aegis and knelt beside Kian. He didn't respond when I shook his shoulder, so I rolled him over and found the same bruise Carmen had, in multiples, like three shadows went at him at once. *No wonder he passed out.* When I checked his pulse, it was weak, like a dying bird fluttering against the glass. *But . . . he can't die, right? Wedderburn would flash-freeze all these things and make coasters out of them.* Trembling, I used the rage-strength Aegis granted me to get him over my shoulder, but I couldn't stand. Seven minutes had already elapsed, and I still didn't know where the others were.

As I staggered on one knee, trying again, Jake burst back in. "I can't find Tanya, and people are passed out everywhere, and they're talking about calling the cops. Lara's saying I roofied everyone or put some hallucinogenic shit in the beer or—"

"Slow down. What's the plan?"

"Damn, I don't know. You're not panicking?"

"First, we need to get the power on. Where's the breaker box?"

"In here. That's part of why I came back." He went over to it, flipped some switches, but nothing happened. "Damn. What the hell is going on anyway? The generator should be running after five minutes or so. My dad has it on a timer, so it doesn't start right away in case of a brief fluctuation in the grid." Talking seemed to calm him down; he was breathing better now.

So I asked, "Is he a survivalist or something?"

"Nah, he just doesn't want his steaks to spoil."

"Rich-people problems," I mumbled.

When we had blackouts in Boston, we always ate the ice cream first. The memory came at me hard like a tackle, but I held steady as Jake took Kian from me. He had no trouble with the fireman's carry I had been attempting; I led him out the back as the others had gone. Nathan and Amanda were ten feet ahead of us, slip-running down the drive toward the van. When Jake put Kian down outside the minivan, he was stirring vaguely, and I nearly fainted with relief. Devon and Elton hauled him in; then Amanda and Nathan jumped in after.

"What're you waiting for?" Devon asked.

Vonna revved the engine in emphasis; she was more than ready to take off. "Hurry up."

"One favor, Devon. Kian's got the same issue as Carmen, but . . . maybe worse. If you send them home like this, we're all in deep shit."

"How long before they recover?" Vonna asked.

"For me, it was about four hours. I think Kian got more, though, so it might take longer. Would you mind taking them home with you? If they're not better in the morning, take them to the hospital."

"We should go now," Amanda muttered.

I could tell Vonna and Devon were weighing the risks of trusting me. Then she nodded. "If Carmen's not talking sense in a few hours, I'll call her mom and drive her to the ER."

"I'll give Kian until morning," Devon added. "He can stay at my place tonight. My mom should be asleep when I get home anyway."

"Get in already," either Elton or Nathan called from the back.

I stepped away from the minivan. "Take off without me. I promised Jake I'd help get things in order here. I can find my own way back."

Vonna didn't wait. The door slid shut, and she backed down the drive, eager to get away. Damn if I wasn't lucky all the people who had come with me were leaving in one piece. *I won't be so reckless again. I can't afford to wreak havoc in this timeline.* Jake was already pulling me toward the house. As we raced up the slick path, the generator kicked on, illuminating the windows to golden rectangles. That would help in driving off the shadows. Anything that lingered might take on human form, though, like the Harbinger as Colin.

Lara had everyone gathered in the living room, and like half the guests had bruises on their necks. "Why don't you just admit you did this to scare us, Jake?"

At that accusation, he stopped in the doorway. "Excuse me?"

"You're always looking for ways to make your parties memorable. I'm guessing you dosed everyone, turned out the lights, and waited to see what would happen. Have you heard what people are saying? Monsters, demon shadows; I mean, seriously. It's obvious you gave us something. Maybe you rimmed the red cups you passed out at the start?" She peered at the Solo cup in her hand suspiciously.

I had to admit, it was plausible. "If that's what you think, take the cup to be tested. Get a full checkup while you're at it. Then bring back the proof."

"Why are you encouraging her?" Jake demanded.

"It's not like *you* can prove you didn't do anything wrong, but science will."

He relaxed a little. "True. Has anyone seen Tanya?"

"I think she was passed out in your sister's room," someone volunteered.

"Then I need to check. Can you clear these assholes out?"

I wondered how he expected me to accomplish that, but the words started an exodus with people muttering, "Like we want to stick around" and "Worst party ever." The ones who seemed too dazed to drive, I found someone willing to take their keys and make sure they got home okay. Fifteen minutes later, the property was mostly clear. Jake came down carrying Tanya, who had two bruises, one on each side of her neck. It was odd, though, because Jake's neck was marked all the way around, different than what I knew of their feeding habits.

It wasn't eating . . . it was just killing him. Since Wedderburn couldn't ruin Kian's life the other way, he tried a new method. How long can I possibly keep it from happening?

Maybe . . . it's inevitable?

Not in the sense of fate, which I firmly thought was bullshit. But in the sense that the winter king just had too much power for me to block all the avenues. Frustration, fear, and despair united to weigh me down. It was all I could do to meet Jake halfway and check on Tanya.

"How's she doing?"

"I wish I knew. Nothing that happened here makes any sense, especially you killing that balloon smoke thing with a sword."

"That didn't happen," I said.

He stared at me, one brow arched. "Excuse me?"

"Somebody was choking you when I came in. I shoved him, and he ran off. I'm not sure how it happened, I'm not saying you did it, but somebody passed out some bad shit tonight."

Don't argue. Don't question. This is for your protection. Trust me, the less you know about this, the less you wonder, the better off you'll be.

"Then what if Lara gets her cup tested and it comes back with something? You know I'll take the blame."

"They can't find drugs you don't have," I pointed out.

"But . . . my reputation . . ."

I shrugged. "Nothing I can do about that. The people who believe in you won't care what everyone is saying."

"You're a bucket full of charm."

"Isn't she?" The Harbinger stepped into the great room wearing a smile that was all fondness and anticipation. "I'll thank you for an interesting night and take my lovely girl off your hands now that it's done."

Tanya stirred then, distracting Jake. "You're here. I had the strangest dream . . ."

"Is it safe?" I whispered.

He nodded, which I took to mean he'd made sure the house didn't harbor any supernatural surprises. I waved to the other two and followed the Harbinger out into winter's chill. He tucked me beneath one arm, and we vanished in a swirl of snow.

THIRD-EYE
BLINDSIDED

The morning after, my cell woke me up with multiple text messages. Last night, it was *so* hard to turn Kian over to relative strangers, but I couldn't let myself be his everything. Each time I walked away, it felt like the conflict between *must* and *want* would break me. When the Harbinger took me home, I hadn't expected to fall asleep, and there was an abrupt break in my memory, a conversation with him that I couldn't retrieve no matter how hard I tried. Rubbing the grit from my eyes, I picked up the flip phone to see what was so urgent.

Unknown, 1:00 a.m.: *This is Devon. K woke up for like 5 min, drank some water & passed out. If he's not OK in the AM, I'm kicking ur ass.*

Unknown, 2:23 a.m.: *Carmen is fine, thought you'd wanna know. V.*

I saved Devon's and Vonna's numbers and kept reading. There were more updates from Devon, the latest time-stamped five minutes ago. This one read: *K just got on a bus. He's a little shaky & doesn't remember shit but an ER visit would've been OTT.*

I sent back, *Glad to hear it. That was crazy, huh?*

Devon: *Note to self, avoid rich-people parties.*

A few more texts, one to Vonna and another to Kian, checking in, then I hopped in the shower. I'd told José I likely wouldn't be in this weekend, but the store needed some work. Just then, I didn't need groceries, but they had been so good to me that I *wanted* to clear out the back room as a way of saying a silent thank-you. This dump was paid for several months, long enough to get me by, but food would be a serious issue without the bodega and the kindness of strangers.

Though my heart ached with bittersweet, it was good that Kian had spent the night with somebody besides me. Devon probably considered him a friend now, which would help after I was gone. I swung out of the Baltimore, trying to convince myself of all the reasons why I shouldn't call Kian to make sure he was fine. *He's probably sleeping that off.* From my own encounter, he'd feel loopy and exhausted until his natural energy built back up. So preoccupied, I didn't notice anything wrong until I took the blow to the back of the head. My vision cut out, feet sliding on the icy sidewalk, and someone grabbed me. I tried to fight, but it hurt so much. Another hit, and I knew nothing else.

It was dark when I woke, full-on countryside darkness, or maybe we were underground. Panic stirred inside me like a thousand butterflies set free at the same time. A light flashed on, shining directly into my eyes so I couldn't get my bearings, discern any details, or recognize my captors later. That gave me a *little* hope, just a smidge. Jerking back and forth, I discovered no play in the bonds that secured my hands behind me. My shoulders burned with a low-grade but deep discomfort, suggesting I had been out for a while.

"That will only wear you out, Miss Brooks." This voice . . . I'd heard it when the old zealot tried to recruit me.

I've been taken by the Black Watch.

Of all the complications I'd foreseen, this one never factored into my plans. But it should have. In hindsight, I realized the omission right away. I mean, Raoul had his orders as a double agent and the Black Watch had been planning his movements long before I jumped. They wanted Kian in extremis as much as Wedderburn, just for different reasons. While I might not be able to scheme like an immortal, I should've known humans could be just as awful. Historical precedent alone offered countless examples.

Well, shit. At least they don't know who I really am . . . or where I came from.

The old man went on. "It's odd, though. You don't look much like the Chelsea Brooks who ran away from Pomona when she was fourteen."

Fortunately, the makeshift gag spared me the need to respond. People probably didn't think that very often, huh? *Thank God my mouth is duct-taped shut.* Defiance would be wrong in this situation since I was still pretending to be a normal girl. So I remembered everything that had happened in the other timeline: my mother's murder and Kian's loss, the untimely death of so many Blackbriar students, all because of me, because I didn't think before I made a wish on a monkey's paw even though I thought I was so smart, too smart to be taken in by an obvious sucker bet. And the tears came, streaming down my cheeks in a way I'd rarely let them, pretty much only that night with the Harbinger.

"There's no point in pretending. We've been watching you, and we already know you're involved in the game somehow. You'll tell the truth. Eventually."

The lights went out, and his footsteps rang out over stone, impossible for me to tell if it was cement or natural. In the darkness, I heard other sounds, but none of them belonged to people. No rats, either. No, these were distant gears, machine noises, and the rumble of . . . something. We might be underground, but I didn't think it was a cave, maybe a bunker. Noting these details occupied me for a couple of minutes, no more. I struggled until I was tired, but the chair was fastened to the floor somehow, and I only succeeded in making my wrists bleed. After that, I counted the seconds and got confused somewhere in the upper eight thousands, and then I had no sense at all of how long I sat alone in the cold, in the dark. At some point, I slept again, and I'd been bound long enough to piss myself. The smell drenched me in shame.

My captor returned a little later, and he wasn't alone. The interrogation lights switched on again. "Are you ready to communicate with us, Miss Brooks?"

They hadn't given me anything to drink, so when rough hands tore the tape off my mouth, my lips tore. Blood trickled from the cracks down my chin, but I couldn't swipe it away. It dripped down onto my chest like a coppery portent of pain to come. His companion didn't speak, merely looming to increase tension and dread.

I wanted to spit the remaining blood and unleash every insult that occurred to me while counting the seconds, but it didn't fit the profile. Instead, I wept some more. "What do you *want*? Is it sex? We can do it. I won't tell anyone, just let me go after."

"That's delightful," the old man said, likely to his partner. "Funny, you seemed much stronger when you encountered our agent on the street."

"Huh? You mean the creepy meth head?"

"See, you're a clever little thing. Why act otherwise?"

"Look, I didn't realize you were stalking me. *Anyone* would act different on a public street than tied up in your sex dungeon."

"It's not a sex dungeon." The snappish tone told me I was getting to him, which was satisfying, until he growled, "Persuade her."

A fist slammed into my jaw so hard that it snapped whatever tethered me to the floor, tipping the chair over. Then a boot hauled back and caved in my pelvis. At least, that was how it felt. Red-hot pain radiated through me from top to bottom as the silent asshole worked me over. He was thorough and methodical until I couldn't speak, drooling and sobbing through each blow. Tied to the chair, I couldn't curl in on myself, but I tried, chafing my scabrous wrists and nearly dislocating my shoulder in the process.

Finally, the old man said, "Stop."

From a distance, I heard myself crying. The light blazed everywhere, even under my eyelids when I tried to cower behind them. Visceral shudders wracked me until it felt like they might turn into seizures. *People are doing this to me. People.* That desperate thought echoed in my head like a rubber ball. *This is another way to become a monster, pursuing a goal with such focus that you don't care how you achieve it.*

"Should I get the knives, master?" The dispassionate tone frightened me almost as much as his name for the old man.

"Give her some time to reflect. She's human, so she won't be able to hold out much longer. This one will break in another day, maybe two. She'll tell us who she works for."

In parting, one of them dumped a bucket of icy water on me and left me lying in the puddle, still shivering, still on my side. Broken ribs, dislocated shoulder, fractured ankle . . . maybe. I couldn't move my arms enough to tell how badly they were hurt. My face had to be a swamp of bruises, and my jaw . . . best not to think about it.

"Aegis," I whispered.

Nothing happened. With my hands tied at this angle, I couldn't touch the spot on my bracelet to activate it. Wishing I'd thought to request voice activation didn't help now. *What's the chair made out of?* I bounced and was rewarded with a streak of pure anguish and the clack of wood. *Thank you, it's not metal. Maybe I can work with this.* Again and again, I threw myself against the floor, slamming sideways with all the power I could muster. The pain made me black out twice, and when I woke, I was still in that congealing puddle of piss, blood, and stagnant water. *I can't quit now. I can't let them bring the knives.*

I went back at the chair, and with the fifth strike, I heard a telltale snap. Since it was so dark, I couldn't see what I'd broken, but it was clearly not one of my bones. Twisting and rubbing around, I found a crack in the left arm, so I focused on it, rocking and knocking until it fell all the way off. That gave me enough wiggle to bring my arms around in front of me, though I had to swallow a thousand screams in the process. They had been smart enough to use multiple bonds, but this was a better angle and, with some gritting of teeth, I angled my thumb enough to tap my bracelet. This time when I said, "Aegis," the sword came in a glimmer of gold, hungry enough to light up a circle five feet in diameter.

With some judicious slashing, I got my hands and feet free and then struggled to my knees. There was no way I could fight my way out in this condition, and I had no damn idea where I was or how many assholes were committed to my imprisonment. Still, even if escape was impossible, I had to try. Aegis lit my path as I stumbled in the direction I thought the other two had gone. Blood dripped into my eye from a cut on my forehead, and I smeared it away.

I had gone twenty steps or so when the light barely prevented me from tripping over a pile of supplies covered by a tarp. Bracing myself, I leaned on what felt like a stack of trunks for a good thirty seconds before I had the fortitude to go on. *This is a huge room.* The floor was definitely cement, and as I crept toward the far wall, it seemed to be concrete block. Tremors ran through me on loop— pain, fear, exhaustion, hunger, thirst—but I couldn't let my knees buckle.

It took forever to circle looking for a way out, but at least I could lean and rest when I had to.

Finally, I came to a military-grade metal door. Bad news, the lock was engaged, and it had all kinds of bells and whistles, including a control panel and analog dead bolt and chain, just in case of power failure. *Damn. They're taking no chances.* Since I had only a sword that was good for killing cocky immortals and no security skills, I fought a wave of despair and leaned my head against the wall. Planning my next move seemed fruitless; it took nearly all my remaining strength to get out of the chair in the first place.

As I pounded my fist on the wall, an alarm went off, muffled by the steel and concrete, but I still heard it. Impossible that I'd set it off, which meant some bad shit was going down at the Black Watch compound. Footsteps pounded down the corridor toward the warehouse/prison, and I positioned Aegis in a terrible attempt at readiness. The locks disengaged, and I sliced straight through the person stepping through the door.

The master of the Black Watch stared at me in stupefaction as he slid to the floor. Hurting people bothered me, but *they* took me captive; it wasn't like I'd invaded. He opened his mouth, and blood poured out as I stepped over his prone form. Quickly, I rifled through his pockets and took his wallet and his keys. If—no, when—I got out, I could commandeer his vehicle. That seemed like poetic justice, considering what they planned on doing to me.

Low-wattage fluorescents lit up the corridor beyond. Dingy gray walls and ancient tile made me think this had been built as a bomb shelter. Impossible to say what level I was on. The alarm cut out. Was it was shut off because the threat had been neutralized, or the invaders won and were tired of the noise? Either way, I'd cut a path out or die trying. But . . . I *hated* fighting people. Diving into a storage closet, I hid from six followers, four men and two women, who ran past in gray clothes that looked more monkish than military. *This feels like a cult.* Given what Raoul had told me about the Black Watch, that seemed like the right word.

Cautious, I tracked them to an elevator and then waited around the corner. One of them used a pass to activate the lift. I rummaged through the old man's wallet and came up with a card that had to open security doors—and hopefully—unlock the elevator. They probably had cameras, so unless the guards were too busy fighting to keep watch, I had to be ready for an ambush as soon as I got off. *If there's a lot of them, I won't make it.* Hands trembling, I swiped the bar code, and the doors opened.

There were six corpses on the floor, four men and two women.

The Harbinger stepped out like an ancient avenging god, covered in lightning and the blood of his enemies. The red spatters didn't even faze me when he reached out, pulling me close with gentle hands capable of such violence. My tongue felt too thick to speak, and the shakes got worse, until I could only think, *He came, he came again, oh my God, he came for me. Again.*

He studied me, wordless, for an infinite moment, tilting my face to assess the damage. "They will pay for this. I shall strip flesh from bone and grind even that down to dust. For you, I will burn this place until its shadow can never form again."

"Why?" I got out.

"Stop asking." He helped me into the elevator, still littered with the dead, and I stood in a circle of shock and terror.

I knew he could kill; I'd never *seen* it. But for the first time, I imagined him as a glittering scythe, the reaper on a human battlefield surrounded by death birds. That human life meant so little to him didn't surprise me, but the scene unmoored me. *I'm not special; he'll tire of shielding me. Soon I'll be a broken toy.* And the rush of pain did surprise me because it was emotional, not an echo of the prior beating.

The Harbinger shook my shoulder as the elevator dinged. "Stay with me. If I could whisk us away, I would, but this devil's den is warded against my ilk."

That revelation stopped the whirling of my thoughts, sending the brain cyclone in another direction. For the first time, I noticed his exhaustion, the glitter of his stormy eyes, his countenance wan yet frenetic with expended power. The lines on his face were real, and it seemed as if they'd *wounded* him. He favored his side when we stepped onto solid ground and the lift doors swished shut behind.

"Don't," I said softly. "Stop saving me. Stop now. You can't fight all my enemies alone. If you don't stop, at some point they'll overwhelm you."

"Who wants to live forever?" he wondered aloud.

"If you don't leave, you'll *die*." Desperation made me shrill. While I'd made peace with the idea that saving Kian would probably be the last thing I ever did, it seemed unforgivable to doom the Harbinger too. He might be a monster, but he was *my* monster.

"And I'll die if I do." Such a sweet, rueful tone. His look simmered with an awful, possessive sweetness that stunned me with its implications, an intensity I couldn't trust or accept. "Haven't you worked it out yet, dearling? I mistrust the estimates of your intellect, truly I do."

He'll die if he leaves me? I couldn't speak the question aloud because more cultists charged at us with the complete confidence of true fanatics. Dread pooled in my stomach as I watched the Harbinger summon what seemed like the last of his strength. A shudder worked through him, and then lightning appeared in his palm.

Beside him, I raised my sword and prepared to fight.

A WORLD OF INFINITE RISK

When the Harbinger launched the volts, they settled as an electrical barrier instead of frying the cultists. Confused, I stared as he grabbed my hand and pulled me in the opposite direction. At first, I took the choice for mercy, but that didn't fit what I knew of him or his promise to grind their bones to dust. He seemed impatient when I stumbled, but it was hard to match his pace, given my current state.

"I don't understand; I thought we were fighting."

"That will slow them down, any that might be left on this level. I've already dealt with the ones outside." He cut me a sharp look. "And you don't have the energy for a battle."

"True. But I have car keys and a clearance pass."

"That may come in handy," he said with a half smile.

I tried to ignore the bodies as he led me out through the bloody path he'd carved. The Black Watch might think the end justified the means, but they were fighting against Wedderburn and other immortals. Guilt swirled in my stomach, but I kept moving. It wouldn't bring any of these people back if I got captured again. Maybe I just had one of those bloody fates, and no matter how hard I tried to change it, there would always be carnage in my wake.

"They don't care that they hurt you," the Harbinger said. "So please don't mind that *I* hurt them."

"I'd be an ungrateful asshole if I bitched about your rescue methods."

"Precisely. Keep moving. Two more flights of stairs, and we'll be at the main exit."

The bunker seemed huge, though that might have been my cracked ribs talking. My side burned where the boot had first made impact, and I pressed a palm to it as I took the steps laboriously, one by one. He kept one hand on me, like I was a corn-husk woman that might blow away at the first strong wind. In all honesty, I didn't feel a lot stronger than that.

I'd expected to need the passcard to get out, but the heavy doors were blown wide open and half melted to slag. *Damn. He did this for me?* It looked like a bomb site with dust and smoke still simmering, obscuring visibility. I stumbled over the wreckage and pitched forward; the Harbinger hauled me upright. Lights shone all around me, reminiscent of a prison yard, but as my eyes adjusted, I saw it was night. Beyond the debris lay a parking lot, and from this perspective, it looked like we had left a simple warehouse. Nobody would ever guess that it extended several levels belowground.

Digging into my pocket, I clicked the unlock button but no lights flashed, so I went farther and a black Buick responded, the kind of car an old man would drive. I glanced over at the Harbinger, and he looked so fragile, as if the surrounding lights shone through him. *If he could whoosh us out of here, he would. No point in asking.*

So I staggered to the driver's seat, my head spinning with fading adrenaline, pain, and probably low blood sugar.

"Get in," I said.

"You don't even know where we are. How do you plan to extricate us?"

"Away is a start. Don't argue with me, okay?"

The Harbinger's mouth thinned, but he climbed into the car like an actual person. That had to rankle, but with his powers at low ebb from a fight whose aftermath left me queasy, there were no better alternatives for either of us. When I put the key in the ignition, a screen powered up when the engine kicked on. *Nav-star . . . oh, this will help a lot.* But the problem was, if I recalled correctly, if the master recovered enough to order his minions check the lot, the service could shut this down remotely, so there was no telling how far we could drive before it turned into a giant paperweight.

"Holy shit, we're in Minnesota? How long have I been gone?"

"Three days. Three very long days." The Harbinger closed his eyes, turning his face away to lean his cheek against the frosted window.

I shook myself out of the daze that news threatened to create and adjusted the defroster settings. *Kian must be freaking out.* It took all my self-discipline not to check my pockets; I already knew they hadn't left my phone with me when they tied me up. Taking a deep breath, I backed out of the space and headed for the gates. Luckily, the car had a sticker on it, so the metal arm went up and we didn't draw unwanted attention by ramming it.

While checking the rearview mirror obsessively, I put ten miles behind us before the trembling stopped. I still hurt all over, but driving was bearable. As I settled down, I pulled into a gas station lot to input Cross Point, PA, into the Nav-star, and it spat out a route that would take us seventeen hours. I didn't intend to stay with this vehicle that long. Even if I'd killed the boss man, he doubtless had a second-in-command who would continue this bullshit seamlessly. The attack might have hurt them, but they wouldn't implode because of it. Over a long career as a secret society, they'd probably pissed off other immortals through the years.

"What's your plan?" the Harbinger asked eventually.

"We're a hundred miles from Minneapolis. I think it's safe to head there. We should ditch the car and take the slow route to Cross Point."

"You're going *right* back where they found you?" Anger didn't begin to express the force of his tone.

"I got careless. It won't happen again. But either way, I have to finish what I started."

It was only February. Somehow I had to stick around for four months more, though the way odds were stacking up against me, I didn't see how I'd survive. But since Kian died for me in the other world, it seemed like a fair deal for me to go out trying to save him here. Maybe Wedderburn would kill me, or possibly the Black Watch. At this point, I gave no shits who finished me off.

Rummaging through the car turned up almost ten dollars in small bills and change, and there was a half a tank of gas. Good enough. I put my hand on the door handle. "Do you want anything in here?"

"From the Kwik Stop? I'll pass." He angled a disturbingly playful look on me. "Unless you'll let me have the cashier."

"Um. No."

"I didn't think so."

"Sugar and caffeine for me, it is. Be right back." I pulled my hood up, hoping to hide the worst of the damage.

My luck held. The clerk was more interested in the miniature TV behind the counter than what a bad day I must be having. He rang up my food and drinks, and I handed over the amount in coins that he sighed over. His annoyance meant I didn't get a bag, so I cradled the jerky and chocolate and energy drinks like my beloved pets on the way back to the car. The pavement was wet, so I almost fell twice before I collapsed in the driver's seat.

"This is the strangest thing I've ever done," the Harbinger said.

"Rescuing somebody?"

He shook his head with a faint smile illuminated by the neon beer sign in the front window of the store. "Never mind. By all means, let's continue this ill-advised adventure."

"Okay, well . . . you rest up, if you can. You probably need to feed, but I don't have the energy to spare right now, and I'm not okay with you draining someone else."

I started the car, conscious of him staring at me like I'd grown horns. "Are you jealous?"

I laughed. "No, genius. It hurts people who don't know what's going on. I'm trying to limit your collateral damage because, whether you admit it or not, that destruction bothers you. You carry those scars everywhere."

"You're worse than Saiorse," he said quietly. "Worse than Sigyn, even. You know all my truths and then act as if they can be rewritten."

"Excuse me?"

He sighed. "You cannot save me from myself."

"Maybe not, but if you hadn't noticed, I've got this Quixote thing going on anyway. It's kind of my deal."

"So . . . you're implying that you'll feed me again? Of your own free will. It's extremely *odd* that you'd strengthen the bond between us when you're always telling me to go."

I squirmed, turning as the Nav-star instructed, toward Minneapolis. "You're helping me, no, saving my ass constantly. It's quid pro quo or something. Don't make it weird."

"The weirdness is none of my doing," he muttered.

To cover the fact that I did register these mixed messages, I switched on the radio. Men talking about politics came on an AM channel, so I fumbled with the buttons until mellow music filled the car. This sounded like a station Kian would listen to, big band era or something like that, all smooth and jazzy, so I left it. I realized then that I had no idea what kind of music the Harbinger liked, and clearly he did love it, if the violin he carried offered any sign.

"Is this okay?" I asked as a torch song came on.

In answer, he changed the station, pausing, skipping onward, until he found a livelier offering. It sounded like folk music but had a toe-tapping quality. "Existing is hard enough without wallowing in sorrows that cannot be changed."

"I agree with you, actually."

We exchanged a look, oddly in harmony, as I tore open a packet with my teeth. "Sorry to be gross. It's hard to eat and drive."

"Let me help," he said.

And before I could ask, he placed a cookie in my mouth like a priest offering communion, only it was slow and careful, and just a little explicit. I ate the cookie pretending he hadn't just touched my lips and tongue, and that it hadn't felt sweet and strange, and almost like the precursor to a kiss. *No. No, no, no. I am losing my mind. No.* But I didn't say anything when he did it again. He fed me the whole pack, and it wasn't just the sugar that left me quivering with the subsequent rush. My hand trembled when I opened the energy drink. I downed it in one long swallow, eyes locked on the road.

Only seventy-odd miles to Minneapolis. We can do this.

He broke the silence in a peculiar, musing tone. "Do you know how revolting it is, how you process food into energy? And yet I'm *feeding* you."

"That's because you're going to eat me later," I said.

As soon as the words popped out, I wished I could swallow them back. His low laughter filled the car, a pleasant vibration beneath the bouncy folk song on the radio. "Is that why? How clever of me to cultivate my own crops."

At least he didn't take that the dirty way. Could be worse.

I kept quiet after that, preferring to listen as the Harbinger sang. His voice could have charmed birds from trees, and he wasn't even using his aura. No, he was too drained for that, hardly more than an echo of his usual strength. We drove for half an hour before the car delivered a warning from Nav-star and then it slowed down on its own. Nothing I did to the gas pedal helped, so I pulled over to the shoulder and parked.

"The police will be on the way," I said, scowling. "We have to walk from here."

"Truly harrowing, the indignities I suffer for you."

"If you can whoosh away now, go for it. You've done enough."

"Your determination to banish me like an evil spirit is becoming hurtful."

Sighing, I filled my pockets with the goodies I'd purchased and climbed out of the car. The remote area gave me hope that it would take law enforcement a while to reach the vehicle. Yet it was also freezing, well below thirty degrees, and as people had noted in Cross Point, I didn't have a proper coat. No reason to let reality bum me out, however. I'd been doing reckless, impossible things for the last month; why stop now?

The Harbinger set off ahead of me, his strides long and graceful. "Hurry. This is hardly my idea of a picturesque haven."

I had to admit he was right. "Sorry about this. Really, you can . . ."

He wheeled, some twenty feet ahead of me. "No. I cannot. To draw sufficient strength to travel, I would need to drain you dry. So for now, we walk."

Rarely had I heard him sounding so pissed. Chastened, I shut up and limped after him as fast as I could. Soon my shivering took on a life of its own. The sky was a swathe of black velvet above, dusted heavily with diamonds, but the natural beauty like the trees framing the road didn't make up for the raw blade of the wind cutting through my thin, damp layers. The Harbinger must have regretted signing that deal since it looked like protecting me might be the last thing he did. I lost track of how long we'd been walking, but my feet felt like blocks of ice.

"There's a building up ahead," he called.

It turned out to be an abandoned motor lodge, exactly the kind of place where a mass murderer would use his mother's corpse as a marionette while lying in wait for hapless travelers. Yet I couldn't last much longer in the cold. Most of the rooms were damp or wrecked, but after peering through six or seven windows, we found one where the roof hadn't collapsed and the furnishings seemed relatively intact. Shuddering, I stepped through the doorway, wishing I didn't want to crawl all over the Harbinger for reassurance. Oblivious, he checked the room, looking for anything useful. I stared at him so hard it was a wonder his hair didn't catch fire.

What . . . how? When did I start feeling safe with you?

Putting the chain on was ridiculous in these circumstances, but I did it anyway. The room was rustic bordering on creepy; a dead deer stared at me from across the room with glassy, baleful eyes, and a stuffed squirrel occupied a place of honor on the bedside table. Shadows only made the room worse, nearly bad enough that I wanted to go back out into the cold. While I let the décor freak me out, the Harbinger started a fire in the hearth. The wood smoked a bit, but not so much that I needed to worry about asphyxiation.

"You should sleep near the hearth. There are things nesting in the mattress, but this rug looks relatively clean."

"Things," I repeated.

"Would you care to know more . . . ?"

Hastily, I shook my head as he opened the closet. An owl swooped out, and I saw moonlight through the hole above the storage area. Any spare blankets must be covered in bird poop, so he shut the door before turning to me with a faint frown. Still shivering, I dragged the top quilts off both beds, as it was a double room. In the bathroom, the taps didn't work, and I wanted to cry when I realized I couldn't do anything about my piss-stiff jeans. I'd had them on so long that they'd stuck to my skin, and the urea in the dry fabric had irritated my skin until I had a humiliating case of diaper rash.

It's okay. You thought being the Beantown dog girl was the worst thing ever. You were wrong. You can get through this.

"I'm sorry," he bit out.

"For what?"

I edged out of the bathroom, avoiding a dead thing on the floor. Okay, not dead—it scuttled behind the sink, all long tail and scrabbly claws. Somehow I swallowed the scream and slammed the door, but I couldn't stop shaking.

"You're in pain. Frightened. So weak you can barely stand. And I can't do anything. I might as well be human." He spat the last word like a curse.

"If you were, I would've died in that bunker. Nobody could've come in and got me alone like you did."

"If I was human, I needn't worry that you'll freeze. I'd have heat, at least, to offer."

Bracing against the paneled wall, I tried to smile. "Hey, you love when mortals suffer."

"Not you," he whispered. "When you hurt, I bleed."

"Sorry."

Before, I'd thought he was wounded. I'd noticed . . . *Oh my God, no.* Horrified, I stared at his side, and before I could think better of it, I lifted his shirt and coat away from where I hurt the worst and found a black spot in the shape of the boot that broke my ribs. *I had no idea the bond ran so deep. It's like I'm his Horcrux or something.*

I touched the wound lightly, but he still flinched. His skin felt like iced marble, form without feeling. "If you knew this would happen, if you *knew* I'd make you vulnerable, why did you agree when I offered to feed you?"

The Harbinger pushed my hands away and wrapped me up in the musty-smelling quilts and led me over to the guttering fire. "This is a world of infinite risk," he said. "In my stony barbican, I abide with birds and bones and memories. Suffering is always better than nothing. I've gorged on nothing until I'm sick with it. So when you offer beauty, I'll choose that, even if it comes at a cost. Pain proves that I exist, that I *am*."

I could think of nothing to say.

He pressed cool lips to my forehead. "Don't fret over me, darling. I've been making bad choices since a thousand years before you were born and yet I'm still here. I'll probably be prowling the wreckage long after you clay mannequins have blown one another to bits."

THE KINDNESS
OF STRANGERS

In the morning, I was a little surprised to wake up. My whole body hurt, and other discomforts had gotten worse. Real food, a hot shower, and clean clothes . . . there was very little I wouldn't do for that trifecta. I stirred, astonished to find that I had been resting against the Harbinger all night. At my movement, he let go and folded to his feet with the preternatural grace of one who suffered no stiff joints or cold muscles. Despite tucking my hands against my chest, they still ached with the frost that made my breath visible as puffs of steam. I couldn't stop shivering, and I couldn't seem to wake up fully.

Not a good sign.

"We must get moving." The gentle tone told me I must look horrible.

"Okay." But I couldn't stand up without him physically towing me upright, like I was a capsized boat at the mercy of stormy seas. "I'll eat on the move."

It was unlikely the Black Watch would be combing this stretch of road, so it should be safe to flag down a car, provided one would stop. I stumbled through the broken parking lot, but this wasn't exactly a busy thoroughfare. Only three vehicles passed us by the time we went a mile, and none of them showed any inclination to be Good Samaritans. One energy drink stuffed my pocket, but it was so cold, I couldn't bring myself to drink it. My chapped lips already burned in the chilly wind; that would only make it worse.

"You're dehydrated," he said.

"Stop reading my mind."

The Harbinger ignored that. "I think I'm causing trouble in my current incarnation."

With a faint shimmer, he shrunk in size, retaining many of his Colin features, but now he looked to be around five years old. *Clever.* While people might hesitate over picking up a stranded couple, it would take a special sort of heartless to leave a little kid out in the cold. I took his hand because that felt natural, and for the first time, the Harbinger felt *warm* to me. Combined with my other symptoms, I probably had a mild case of hypothermia, and if I didn't warm up soon, it wouldn't be Wedderburn or Buzzkill that did me in.

"If you have the energy to shift, can you take us back now?" I managed to ask through chattering teeth.

He shook his head. "Some feats are nearly cost-free. Folding space is not one of them."

I guessed that meant changing his aspect didn't drain much energy since it was a matter of tweaking human perceptions, not altering the world itself. While it made sense, it didn't alleviate our suffering. We walked another half a mile before the next vehicle approached, a semi with a red-and-orange custom paint job thundering down the two-lane highway. I waved one arm frantically while the Harbinger did the same, and I thought for a minute the driver meant to zoom by without hesitation. But no, it just took longer to stop a rig this size. It shuddered to a halt fifty feet past us and I ran, nearly falling twice because my legs felt numb, but I couldn't let the person change his or her mind.

To my relief, it was a woman in her late fifties with bottle red hair and gray roots coming in. She was portly and concerned as I lifted the Harbinger in. It was so weird for him to let me manhandle him, but he had to know that if he complained, it would seem odd. We couldn't afford to set off her danger alarms. I scrambled in next and shut the door. A shudder went through me at how warm the cab was.

"Thank you so much," I whispered.

"You kids might've been in deep doodie if I hadn't been forced to detour. This road doesn't get used much anymore."

"We really appreciate it."

The Harbinger climbed up on my lap and put his little arms around my neck. *God, this is weird.* I patted him with clumsy hands, wincing as the needles invaded my extremities. He rested his head on my shoulder, just like a tired kid would, and I stroked his hair, wondering if he was enjoying this. Before, he'd liked it when I petted him while assuring him he wasn't a monster.

"No worries. Where you headed?"

"Minneapolis," I said, after deciding it couldn't hurt to tell the truth. It wasn't like that was our final destination anyway.

"I'm going right through there. Name's Nadine. I've been doing long hauls for almost twenty years, and I recognize when people are in real trouble. Was it so bad at home?" Her tone was gentle as she diverted attention from the road for a few seconds to offer a kind look.

In answer, I pulled back my hood so she could see the severe bruising on my jaw. "Yeah, we had to get away."

She sucked in a swift breath. "I should probably drop you off at—"

"No, I'm twenty-one. I have ID." It didn't take a genius to guess she was about to send us to child protective services. Though they'd taken my phone, they hadn't found the fake ID hidden in my shoe. "He's mine, and you can see I didn't let anybody hurt him."

A tremor of laughter went through the Harbinger at that claim, but he obligingly turned his face toward the truck driver for inspection. This story we were crafting on the fly should make her sympathetic, right? Her demeanor softened, probably because wee Colin was cute as hell with his tousled hair and big eyes.

"Lord, you must've been a child when you had him. But kudos for getting out. People often don't understand just how hard it can be."

"It sounds like you know." That should be safe enough.

She nodded, both hands on the wheel. "It's been twenty-five years, but the scars don't go away. People say, 'She's so dumb, why didn't she just leave? I'd never let anyone treat me that way.' They don't understand how alone you are, how you start thinking you did something to deserve it, and most of the time, there isn't any money to travel on. It takes so much bravery to do what you did, just grab the baby and go, not knowing what's out there or how you'll survive once you're away."

Now I felt bad for exploiting her personal pain, but I couldn't tell her that my abuse didn't come from a domestic partner. If I told her I was involved in a supernatural chess game and I had been kidnapped by their mortal enemies, she'd drop me off at a mental health facility so fast it would make my head spin. So I just kept quiet and hoped it would help her to talk; then I realized she must be waiting for a response from me.

"You give me something to aspire to," I said softly.

And it was true. I imagined Nadine fleeing her home in the night with the clothes on her back. If she could rise from those ashes and reinvent herself as a long-distance truck driver, then maybe I could still save Kian. It couldn't have been easy to find a place to stay or get the training she needed, but from the look of this truck, she was doing well. I'd take heart in her success.

"I didn't do it alone. People gave me a hand along the way, so that's why I stopped for you and your boy. Paying it forward, you know?"

"We wouldn't have lasted long out there."

Her tone became brisk. "You need hot food and a shower. Lucky for you, I was planning a break at a truck stop in five miles."

The travel plaza was big and rustic with a restaurant, a driver's lounge, general store, and a fleet of trucks in the lot. There were also some tour buses as Nadine expertly parked her vehicle and then flipped down the sun visor to get something.

Offering me twenty dollars, she said, "That's far less than relative strangers did for me. I'll be here for an hour. If you want to ride on with me, meet back here on time."

I let out a slow breath. "Okay. Thank you."

With that, she climbed out of the truck, and we followed so she could lock up. The Harbinger didn't let go of my hand even after we got to the entrance. It was a sprawling place done up in country-style décor with lots of wood and Americana memorabilia, photos of athletes in black and white, men in suits shaking hands. I didn't pause to admire any of the homey touches since I had a lot to do and only fifty-seven minutes left.

First I went into the general store and bought the cheapest clothes they had: a pair of sweats and a novelty T-shirt. Next stop, personal hygiene. But when I asked how much, the woman said, "Nadine already reserved you a shower room. Here's your key, honey."

I'd expected a dormitory sort of thing, but it was a full bathroom with a lock on the door, clean tan tiles, a sink and mirror, hooks for my clothes, a bench where the Harbinger could wait, plus toilet and shower stall. I got in, pulled the curtain, and undressed. Inside, the place offered the same basic amenities as a cheap motel: tiny soap and shampoo, plus a scratchy towel. There was a plenty of hot water, and I moaned as it sluiced over me.

"Are you all right?" It was the first time he'd spoken since turning into a little kid, and his voice was more than a little disconcerting with me naked and only a thin vinyl curtain between us.

"Yeah. It just stings a little. This is way better, though, don't worry."

I spent a good ten minutes scrubbing and rinsing until it felt like my skin was raw in certain places. There was no money to spare for soothing creams, however, so I reached out of the shower feeling around for the towel, only to have the Harbinger place it in my hand. That startled me so much, I laughed.

"Something amuses you?"

"This whole situation just feels fairly absurd."

"Imagine my dismay," he said dryly. "I never pictured myself playing lady's maid to someone like you."

"What's that supposed to mean?"

"Just get dressed. We only have forty minutes left before the kindly driver abandons us."

"She wouldn't mean it that way. I think she just didn't want us to feel obligated to stick with her out of gratitude. But I doubt we'll get a better offer."

"Unlikely," he admitted.

He passed my clothing through. Going commando was the only option, but the fleece felt so good on my raw skin that I almost cried. In this timeline, I didn't have clothing to spare; otherwise I would've stuffed these jeans in the garbage can. Instead, I folded them and hoped a good washing could save them. My dirty things I stowed in the bag they'd given me for the items I bought at the general store, and then I was ready to eat.

"See, it's good you're not human, or I'd have to figure out how to feed us both on eight dollars and sixty-four cents."

"Small mercies indeed."

After I towel-dried my hair, we headed down the hall, past the store, and into the restaurant. I didn't see Nadine anywhere, but we still had time. She might be upstairs in the lounge watching TV or something.

A busy waitress waved from the counter, where she was topping off a man's coffee. "Take a seat anywhere," she called. "I'll be right with you."

The room was pretty packed, a good indicator that the food must be tasty, so I chose a couple of stools at the counter. It wasn't like we had time to linger over lunch. Based on the specials written on the chalkboard, I guessed it must be around that time. I ordered some coffee and a bowl of vegetable beef soup, surprisingly cheap on both counts. Certain franchises would be astonished that $1.09 could buy unlimited refills. My meal came with a basket of bread and crackers, and it was hard not to empty it in the first thirty seconds.

"Doesn't he want anything?" the waitress asked.

I glanced at the Harbinger sitting quietly beside me. "We'll share."

"Okay, hon. But kids get a free dessert. I'll get him a play mat."

It took all my self-control not to break out into giggles when she set a battered plastic bucket full of chewed and broken crayons in front of the trickster god. He immediately plucked out a purple one and solved the maze puzzle, getting the goat out of the corn-field.

"Good job," I said.

"If I can save annoying schoolgirls, why not goats? The sky is the limit." He kept his voice soft to avoid attention.

Smiling, I devoured the soup, half of what was in the bread bas-ket, and downed two cups of coffee. And when the nice waitress wasn't looking, I ate the small slice of cake she brought for my "son." Anyone paying close attention would be horrified at what a terri-ble mother I was, but luckily, the patrons were far more interested in their phones or the game playing on the big TV. Once I finished, I felt almost strong enough to face another round of sudden death against my varied opponents. We made it back to the truck with two minutes to spare, and I wished I could hug Nadine in pure grat-itude. She waved away my thanks as we climbed back in.

"Nothing somebody else didn't do for me at one point or

another. If you tell me where you're going in the city, I can drop you off."

"Any bus stop should be fine," I said.

"Greyhound or local?"

"We're going a long way, so Greyhound."

"Whereabouts?"

I trusted her as much as any relative stranger, but I was wary of dragging her into my problems. The longer we stayed with her, the greater the chances my troubles could explode all over her generosity. So I resisted the temptation to find out exactly how close she could take us to Pennsylvania. *Of course, on a public cross-country bus, it might be even worse, and those people would just be bystanders who are in the wrong place at the wrong time.* Chewing my lip, I wished I could ask the Harbinger, but he'd clammed up again.

But maybe . . .

"Should I . . . ?" I whispered.

He nodded ever so slightly.

Yeah, things are already messed up enough. No point in making life more complicated. I already couldn't stop worrying about what might be happening to Kian in the aftermath of the party. If everyone blamed him for it—*oh, shit. It might already be too late.* My stomach knotted. *No, I can't think that way. Everything will be okay. Right?* But he must be wondering what happened, why I just disappeared, even if people at school weren't blaming him for the crazy shit at Jake's party.

"Pennsylvania," I said finally, hoping her patience and goodwill didn't run out.

"I'm heading through there on my way to New York."

Relief surged through me. Now I didn't need to worry about scrounging bus fare somehow. I had been holding on by a thread, trying not to obsess over problems before we got to that point, but it felt like a huge weight slid off my shoulders. The Harbinger squeezed my hand as if he sensed my shifting mood. Wait, not if. From what he'd said before, he did, no doubt.

"Then if you don't mind the company, we'll stick with you as far as you'll take us."

"It's a nice change and your little one is so well-behaved, quiet as a mouse. Probably skittish around strangers, huh?"

"A little," I mumbled.

"He'll get used to me. We'll be together for a while yet."

"Thanks again. You probably don't know Cross Point? It's in northern Penn."

"I'll find it. I can't promise door to door service, I hate city driving. But I'll get you to a safe bus stop there."

"You have time?" I thought there were usually delivery deadlines.

"Sure thing. The weather was okay coming through, so I'm ahead of schedule."

"I wish I could offer to drive to help out, but . . ."

She laughed at that. "Forget it. I'll be fine. But I do nap from time to time, so you and your boy will have to make do in front. I only have one bunk."

"No worries. You've already done too much for us."

"Stop, you'll give me a big head." She flicked on the radio, making me think she was done hearing what a heroine she was.

Okay, message received.

For like two hundred miles, we sang along with the radio instead of chatting. Her taste in music ran toward oldies, but thanks to Kian, I actually knew some of the songs. Funny how meeting him colored so many of my interactions. By the time we stopped at a rest area,

I felt pretty good, all things considered. I went to the bathroom and pretended to take the Harbinger, who seemed less than enamored with all the subterfuge that came with acting like a human child.

Maybe I'll get back to Pennsylvania before everything explodes.

As I emerged from the brick restroom, the killer clown stepped into view.

DEVIL AND THE DEEP BLUE SEA

"Funny how much trouble your pet gets into," Buzzkill observed. "Though from where I'm standing, you two sure play some twisted games. Jesus. And I thought *I* was messed up."

His arrival meant all manner of terrible things, but I still choked the urge to laugh. The killer clown had always struck me that way, all carnage and inappropriate humor. Honestly speaking, he'd made an awesome ally when I could trust him not to murder me in the most gruesome manner possible. I froze, sensing that this encounter wouldn't stop at clever repartee.

The Harbinger morphed into the appearance I'd grown accustomed to, when he wasn't pretending to be someone else. At this point, I had been exposed to his aura so much that I only shuddered in discomfort. Or maybe it was more that his strength had been so depleted fighting into that warded warehouse that he didn't have the juice for a powerful display.

"You have an unprecedented fascination in my business," the Harbinger said.

"Sucks for you. From here, I can tell you're running on empty. You won't win this fight, and I can't end you. So let's save the posturing; just give me the girl."

Weird. In my experience, Buzzkill was always eager for a battle, but this was the second time he'd tried to reach a resolution through verbal means. *Either he likes the Harbinger or he's wary of him.* But that question didn't change the fact that we were in a bad situation.

"I take it your master gave his blessing."

"Obviously. How would it look if the boss backed down from some indie asshole who doesn't even play the game?"

Just then, I couldn't factor what it would mean for my mission, but the time had come to stop pretending to be a helpless, normal girl. The Harbinger could burn himself into a shadow trying to fight Buzzkill, and in the end, the clown would still drag me out off by the hair to see his boss, presuming he didn't execute me on the spot. I tapped Aegis and called it to me in a whisper; the bracelet shifted into the glowing golden blade that slain so many immortals in the other timeline.

"What the hell," Buzzkill said.

"Enough bullshit. Let's go." I stepped forward.

"Edie." Actual fear vibrated in the Harbinger's voice.

Ignoring that, I positioned the sword before me as Raoul had taught me, sparing a moment to mentally shake my head over the irony that the Black Watch's training might save me from a murderous immortal as I tried to flee from a kidnapping attempt by the former. *My life has become a Gordian knot.* Yet I didn't feel confident about this fight. Luck let me win last time, and I couldn't count on that again. Since it was daytime, however, the clown wouldn't be able to strike from the shadows. He excelled at stalk-and-kill tactics, so maybe I had a shot.

Maybe.

"Don't stop, little girl. Let's play a game. You show me yours, and I'll show you mine." Blades appeared in the clown's hands, twin serrated knives that would hack through bone in a messy aggressive slash.

He came at me so fast I barely had time to block, and both knives slammed against my sword hard enough to knock me backward. I didn't make the mistake of rushing him; instead, I readied myself for his next run, and this time, I sidestepped and twirled my blade in a move that would've disemboweled anyone else. But I left my flank open, so his lunging blade opened a long jagged cut on my arm. One minute he was there, and then he was just . . . gone. Blood poured from my slashed biceps, a white-hot throbbing that affected my ability to guide Aegis. The injury seemed to inflame my weapon, though, because it trembled in my hand . . . like it was hungry, even for *my* blood.

What the hell did Govannon give me?

Laughter echoed all around us. "This is fun. I can see why you're so desperate to keep her, Trick."

"You cannot win," the Harbinger snarled, low. "Not alone. Let me in."

"Huh?"

"If you trust me even a little, say yes."

Then a clown-shaped monster nearly beheaded me from behind; the speed and force of the attack left me reeling. I ducked and swiveled, going for Buzzkill's knees, but I only sliced the air. *Next time, that's the end.* There was only one decision I could make.

"Yes," I said.

A swathe of darkness filled me, and it was *excruciating*, like swallowing a car. Every fiber of me throbbed with the Harbinger, his eyes, my eyes, his hands, my hands, and then he wrenched control of my body from me. I watched as he ignored my various injuries and readied Aegis with far more grace and precision than I could have mustered, even when I was training with Raoul. He crouched, ready to strike, and the killer clown paused.

"Foul," he muttered.

"Come on, then. You wanted a war."

The Harbinger leapt. This battle might kill me anyway. Surely my body wasn't meant to twist like this, bounce off walls, or flip in midair. Sparks rang out repeatedly as the weapons struck home, a flurry of feints, parries, and strikes too fast for me to track, let alone match. Buzzkill tried his there-and-gone tactics, but against the Harbinger, it proved fruitless, as he seemed to know exactly where the other immortal would appear. The clown landed a few more strikes, glancing slices that would wear us down.

It couldn't have been more than two minutes, but it felt like an eternity trapped in my own head. As the Harbinger anticipated another move, he swung, and in that same motion, he relinquished control so it was me severing Buzzkill's head from his neck. For the second time, he dissolved in a burst of black smoke. And I fell over. Every inch of me hurt, as if I'd pulled all my muscles simultaneously.

"Aegis can't leave your hands," he said, as if I'd asked for an explanation.

I didn't have the breath to discuss the implications of him using me as a marionette. In all likelihood, he'd saved us both, but it hurt to breathe and I was bleeding in three places, plus all the injuries I'd received from the Black Watch now felt worse than ever. Somehow I clawed to my feet and stumbled a step toward the parking lot.

"Thanks."

He stilled. "I didn't expect that."

"Should I complain about making it through another day?" This should buy some time, as Wedderburn didn't have the same sense of time as mortals. The winter king trusted Buzzkill, so he'd assume his chief enforcer had a good reason for going incommunicado. If I was lucky, it would take a few months for him to wonder what went down.

The Harbinger didn't respond to that. Instead, he inspected my wounds wearing an inscrutable expression. "You're in poor condition."

"Thanks. I hadn't noticed."

If he registered my sarcasm, he gave no sign. "We should return to the vehicle, or she might leave us behind."

"I think she'd look for us first."

Sure enough, Nadine was headed this way. "Do you have enough power to camouflage my wounds?"

"That I can manage. Tweaking human perception is a small matter. She already expects you to look a certain way. I'm only fulfilling those expectations."

"So completely changing my appearance would be tougher?"

"Yes, but not impossible."

Since he'd created a simulacrum to keep my father company in the other timeline, I didn't doubt it. By the time Nadine noticed us, he was a child and I wasn't limping. Okay, I totally was, but she didn't notice. She offered a cheerful wave.

"I was afraid you fell in," she said to the Harbinger.

His expression was priceless, but somehow he didn't respond. He pulled on my hand, likely wanting to get back in the truck and put some distance between us and this supernatural crime scene. *Would the Oracle be able to tell Wedderburn exactly what happened?* Her purview was the future, not the past, though. He could send someone to find out using the same tech I traveled here with, but that was where shit got confusing. Because if they intervened, they couldn't change this, it would only create an alternate possibility. However, if he sent someone to watch, then theoretically, the agent could report back on Aegis, me, and the Harbinger.

These convoluted thoughts in conjunction with awful physical pain occupied my focus for several hundred miles. For obvious reasons, we couldn't talk about what went down, and the words clustered thick and heated in my throat. I had so many mixed feelings about being used that way; even now, the sense of him lingered, like I was alone in my head, but . . . not. I'd had him crammed in every possible space, from the tips of my fingers to my toes.

"I'm stopping for a nap here," Nadine said eventually.

"No problem."

We paused for two hours at the next rest area, and then she drove straight through. When she got off the interstate at Cross Point, I was mostly numb. I recognized the south side somewhat, so I said, "You can let us off here. We're not far now."

A single bus ride would get me back to the Baltimore. Probably I should be more effusive in my thanks, as we'd been together for like twenty hours all told, but my energy level dipped to subzero, like I might pass out at any moment. That would extend our relationship in ways that would be desperately unsafe for such a kind woman.

"Here's my card. If you need anything, let me know. I probably won't be nearby, but I know lots of people, a perk of traveling. Also, once you're settled, maybe drop me a line?"

"Okay. Thank you for everything." Gathering my pathetic plastic bundle of stinky clothes, I opened the truck door, and the Harbinger scampered out. He was getting better at pretending to be a little kid.

As Nadine pulled away, we crossed the street at the corner and walked half a block to the nearest bus stop. Once she was gone, he slipped seamlessly into his Colin persona. Good thing it was too cold for a ton of pedestrians to be out, as one guy did a double take, and then shook his head. The Harbinger wrapped an arm around me, not in affection, but to keep me upright. Sitting in the truck for so long made my bruises stiff, and I'd hit the wall, endurance-wise.

"Hang on." Surely I was imagining how worried he sounded.

But my head swam as we climbed on the bus. The Harbinger did something to the driver, so he didn't say anything when we didn't pay the fare. I collapsed near the front and floated most of the way through downtown. In fact, the Harbinger nudged me when my stop came because I didn't even notice. Stumbling, I fell off the bus more than stepped down; he took my arm and guided me to the Baltimore. I didn't have my key, so we climbed the fire escape, and it turned out that breaking into my room was every bit as easy as I'd once imagined.

"Take a hot shower," he ordered.

I mumbled a protest.

Really I just wanted to flop on my bed, which was actually made. That meant the cleaning lady had come in while I was gone. They promised weekly maid service, but her efforts had been hit or miss. Checking around, it seemed like nothing was missing, not that I had much.

"You're covered in blood. Would you rather I scrub you down?"

That galvanized me into action. Somehow I mustered the energy to get in the tub and turn on the water, but I didn't do much more than rinse off. He brought me clean clothes and checked my cuts. Like a wax figure, I let him and then stumbled to bed.

I passed out.

When I woke, I had no idea what day it was, and there were two people in my room. For a moment, I wondered if it had all been a dream. *Am I in Boston?* No, same shitty room at the Baltimore. Checking my wounds showed old scabs instead of raw flesh. To my astonishment, I felt a thousand times better. Sitting up, I recognized Rochelle, the healing goddess I'd met before. *No wonder I don't feel like microwaved death anymore.* She smiled at me and beckoned, indicating the food on the table, the only real meal this dingy room had ever seen.

"You must be special. He cashed in his single remaining favor for me to make a house call. Come and eat. I can only do so much; your body must do the rest."

Rubbing the sleep from my eyes, I picked up a bowl of oatmeal. "What day is it?"

Rochelle shrugged. "They're all the same to me. Maybe check your cell?"

"Wish I could," I mumbled.

The Harbinger rose from the ripped vinyl armchair and offered a battered flip phone similar to the one the Black Watch had confiscated. "Will this work?"

"How . . . ?"

He seemed uncomfortable, unable to meet my gaze. "The birds are always finding things. This should serve while you're here, as long as you need it. I also liberated a spare key for you from the cretin behind the desk."

"Damn. You've been busy. How long was I out?"

"Almost a day," he said softly.

He was worried, I realized. *That's why he called Rochelle.*

"Thank you."

"Please let her eat. The girl can't regain her strength without proper nutrition. And you should refrain from riding her for at least a month." She didn't sound judgmental, but hearing it put that way made me blush furiously.

Fighting the urge to react like a manga heroine, I lowered my head and devoured oatmeal, bacon, fruit, toast, and yogurt. The Harbinger went over to Rochelle and made conversation in a tone too low for me to catch. Since I didn't know how I felt at this moment, I enjoyed the respite from supernatural intervention.

"She'll live," Rochelle said, loud enough for me to hear, after a few minutes. "But don't call me again. We're even now, and I don't want your feuds spilling onto me."

"Understood."

He went to the window and opened it. At first, I only stared in bewilderment because it was like fifteen degrees outside; then Rochelle shifted into a blue bird and darted out. I guessed all the supernaturals didn't travel the same way. *That's pretty cool. Wonder if it takes less energy than folding space.* But that wouldn't have permitted the Harbinger to get us both to safety, unless he could transform me too? *Unlikely.*

But . . . he could have left you behind. And he chose not to.

It would be a shitty rescue to break someone out and then be like, *Good luck getting home,* but still. The Harbinger turned with his usual air of faint disdain. "Your adventures aren't as enthralling as I'd hoped."

"When was the last time you colored with crayons?"

"That would be never."

"You shouldn't have burned your last favor with Rochelle for me. I know you stockpile those like currency."

"If you feel guilty, then acknowledge that you owe me."

That was a dangerous admission to make, given his nature, and our interactions to date, but honesty wouldn't let me lie. "I definitely do."

His eyes widened ever so slightly, infinitesimal surprise. It wasn't that his features gave no sign of his reactions; rather, they were micro-expressions, minute shifts, and apparently I'd gotten better at reading them. A surge of affection surprised me, strong enough that I fought the urge to hug him. The Harbinger's favor might kill me, but I was starting to think maybe ending up as one of his broken toys might not be the worst fate.

Or maybe I have Stockholm syndrome.

"This means that if I call the marker due, you must honor the debt, dearling. You *do* understand that?"

"Yeah, I got it. Write me down in your debt ledger."

"Even if repaying me means you cannot save your beloved boy?" His voice went sweet and silky, sending a fearful shiver through me.

That was exactly the sort of devil and deep-blue-sea choice that would amuse the shit out of him. "Please don't put me in that position."

"If you deny me in my hour of need, there will be a forfeit. Perhaps you've forgotten, but I *am* a petty, jealous god."

"Here's the thing," I said quietly. "You claim to enjoy being around me because I see you as you are, because I'm not scared of you. But here you are, trying to freak me out."

"You know the story of the frog and scorpion, I trust?"

I nodded.

"The scorpion never claims his actions make sense, does he? Sometimes one's nature conflicts directly with other desires."

"True. Well, whatever you need, I'll be there. You've been my only friend for what feels like forever." *Who knew time travel was so lonely?* It definitely lent me a new understanding of Doctor Who, and *I* had only been doing this for a few weeks, not a thousand years.

"I don't take such promises lightly," he said.

A shiver of prescience tingled down my spine, like this moment hung us both over a precipice, and if he didn't catch me I'd fall. Catching the Harbinger's gaze, I held it, and a static charge gathered between us, like a gathering storm. *Fate couldn't be so cruel, right? I won't be asked to choose between Kian and the Harbinger.* Yet even uncertain of the outcome, if I could truly shape a different future for my first love, there was only one answer I could give.

"Neither do I."

THE TRUTH ABOUT CONSEQUENCES

After the Harbinger left, I slept more, though I didn't mean to. On awakening, my body felt weird and slightly numb. My fingers tingled, so I flexed them. A glimmer of gold showed through my fingernails, but when I blinked, it was gone. *Did I imagine that? Wonder if that's a side effect of the healing? Or maybe it has to do with Aegis?* When I rolled out of bed, I ached with bizarre pain flashes in my joints, places that weren't even wounded before.

Well, that's new.

Filing the issue under "things I can't understand or change," I added Kian to my bird-acquired phone. I didn't remember anyone else's number, but this was the only one I needed. According to the time, it was just after four on a Thursday, so I had been gone almost a week. Biting my lip, I tapped out a text.

Sorry, this is Nine. New phone number. Ran into some trouble. Everything OK?

His reply came back immediately. *OMG, cant believe ur asking ME that. What happened? R U OK?*

I'm basically OK. Told U my life is complicated.

Guess so, he replied. *U home now? Can I come over?*

Yeah, if U want.

Be there in an hour. So much to tell U.

I stared at the phone, wondering why I felt let down. Kian hadn't known me that long, and I *didn't* want him falling for me, but he seemed fairly casual about my vanishing act. I compared it to when my dad was kidnapped by Cthulhu monsters and Kian mobilized everyone we knew searching for me. Since I understood that circumstances were different, it shouldn't hurt, but . . . I cut the thought before it could blossom fully.

He's not your boyfriend. Forget it.

Around five thirty, a knock sounded at my door. The Black Watch would probably break down the door and the Harbinger always appeared wherever he wanted, like my space belonged to him, so I opened the door. Sure enough, Kian stood there with take-out bags. He put them on the table and hugged me, a startling move. For a few seconds, I let him, breathing in his scent, crisp wintry woods; then I pushed him away.

"You couldn't call?" he complained, shutting the door.

Kian shrugged out of his jacket, and he had on the new clothes we'd picked out together, cargo pants and sweater. Adding in the new haircut and glasses, he definitely registered as attractive. People who went after the intellectual type would be after him for sure, but the most appealing thing about him had to be his confidence. He didn't shrink in on himself anymore, his shoulders were straight, and he met my gaze head-on without flinching. That was such a big change in a relatively short time.

I pictured myself tied to the chair and shook my head. "I really couldn't."

His look grew serious. "It sounds like you need help. One of these days, you might go missing and not come back."

That's truer than you know.

But I didn't want to discuss *my* issues, so I changed the subject. "Thanks for dinner."

"No problem. I brought a list of assignments from your teachers, by the way." He handed it over, and I set it aside to check out later.

"That was nice of you." Honestly, it was more than I expected. "So what's going on at school now? Man, that was a weird party, huh?"

"Oh my God." Kian's expression shifted, becoming avid as he set out the deli takeout, sandwiches and various small salads. Not surprisingly, I was ready to eat, but it didn't taste as good as I expected. As I dutifully munched pastrami on rye, he elaborated. "You wouldn't believe how that shook the social order. Jake is officially out; they're basically shunning him."

I put down my plastic spoon. "What?"

"Gossip isn't normally my thing, but then again, nobody talked to me before, so maybe I didn't know how intriguing it could be."

"Just tell me what's going on."

"Geez, you won't even let me build the suspense, huh?" At my look, he continued. "Lara told everyone that he had some weird new drug at the party and slipped it to everyone. At first, people didn't believe it, but there was just so much bizarre shit that night, eventually it seemed like the only explanation."

This was exactly what Jake had been worried about on Friday

night. "Why did they assume it had to be him? There were tons of people."

Kian shrugged. "Probably because he's got money. They assumed he wouldn't hesitate to spend it to make his shindig memorable, only the theory is that it backfired in a huge way and sent everyone on a bad trip."

I had to admit, as far as unsubstantiated bullshit went, this was more credible than most. "Poor Jake. How's Tanya holding up?"

"Dude, that's the craziest part. She broke up with him." Kian probably should have checked that level of excitement around anyone else.

"Wow. I thought they were solid."

"Me too. But I guess the pressure was too much for her. I have to admit, seeing her buckle made me . . ." He trailed off, seeming unsure how to finish that sentence.

"Think less of her?" I offered.

"Not exactly. She seems real now, I guess. Before, she felt like a goddess or something, somebody I could never even talk to."

"I'm confused, do you like her less or more now?"

"Both," he said. "I don't get nervous or tongue-tied around her anymore. Yesterday we discussed our homework."

"Riveting."

He looked sheepish. "Hey, this might not be a big deal to you, but for me, it's major progress. I sat with Devon's group at lunch this week too, and it was okay. I really like talking to Vonna about old movies."

"You're a changed man," I said.

Which was exactly what I wanted for him, but I felt a little left out. Yet this was the reality check I needed. Kian could make other choices, now that I'd given his fate a shove. Possibly things would be fine from this point, even if I disappeared for good, but I couldn't take that chance. Calling the mission a success four months before his birthday qualified as premature. Somehow I had to hang on until then. With Buzzkill MIA, so far as Wedderburn knew, and the Black Watch gunning for me, I didn't like my chances. Plus, I officially owed a debt to the Harbinger, further complicating my situation.

"Sure, make fun of me." Kian sounded a little hurt.

"I'm not. I'm happy for you, seriously."

"Sorry. I realize this probably seems incredibly trivial, considering the shit you're dealing with. But I don't know what to do, and you don't seem to want to talk about it. So it's not that I'm trying to be self-absorbed or whatever."

I smiled. "You read me right. There's nothing you can do, so it's better for you to act normal. I've been dealing on my own for a long time."

"But you shouldn't have to. We're friends, right? I wish you'd confide in me."

"We are. But only time can solve my problems."

"When you turn eighteen." He made the natural assumption, and I silently pretended to agree while finishing my food.

I live in a world that I never want you to encounter. Stay this way.

"Are things better at home?"

"Yeah." Sighing, Kian shook his head. "It honestly never occurred to me that my uncle didn't *know* how my aunt treats me when he's not around. Oh, and we're going to the lumber yard together. He's got some vacation time coming, and I'm helping him finish the attic."

"That should be . . . fun?"

"It will make me feel more at home . . . finally. I have to accept my situation and make the best of it. Things will never be the same. My dad isn't coming back. I don't know if my mom will get better. But I can still live, right?" His green eyes glinted with a quiet anxiety, and I knew what he needed to hear.

"Totally. Organisms adapt or they die. It doesn't make you a bad person if you don't grieve forever." At the way he tensed, I added, "I'm not saying you should forget the people you lost. But maybe think about using your life to honor them? I bet your dad and sister would be really proud to see you make something of yourself."

Kian's hand jerked, knocking over an empty soda can. Then he sucked in a sharp breath, looking like I had stabbed him. He jolted to his feet. "What did you say?"

I tried to figure out what was wrong.

"How did you know? I never told you about my sister. I've never told *anyone*." He shoved at his hair, eyes livid. "You disgusting asshole. You read about me and set out to make friends? I should've known girls like you don't just appear out of nowhere. Are you writing an article or something? Are you even a high school student?"

Ice formed in jagged shards around my heart, but I tried to play it off. "You think nobody warned me about you? Tragic loner, troubled history. I heard all of that on the first day. I didn't let it stop me from getting to know you, but thanks for the faith."

He collapsed in his chair, burying his head in his hands. "Oh God. So . . . they know? They all know."

Dammit. I got careless, and I hurt him.

Tentatively, I rounded the rickety table and rested my hand on the nape of his neck. "Thing is, that's old news. Nobody cares. When you go to school tomorrow, nothing will have changed. It's only your perception."

"Easy for you to say. Your dad didn't shoot your sister."

Dropping to my knees, I made him meet my gaze and told a small snippet of the truth. "No, but I made some really poor life choices and got my mom killed."

Shock drove away all thoughts of his predicament out of his head. Kian stared. "Are you for real right now?"

I nodded. "If it wasn't for me, she'd still be alive."

And I'm working to change that in this timeline. Please don't let me fail. Not just for Kian's sake, but for my mother, and all the people at Blackbriar. They might've tormented and humiliated me, but those weren't capital crimes.

"Holy shit, Nine. I'm starting to understand the scope of what you're running from. Are you sure you shouldn't call the police?"

"They wouldn't believe me." That was the literal truth.

"I'm sorry for flipping out before. I just . . . I've never talked about my sister with anyone. I guess you could call it a trigger."

"It's okay."

"Friends?" When he offered a hug, I leaned against his shoulder. He was bonier than he had been when we were together, all angles and gangly arms. It still felt good.

"That didn't change just because you got mad. Maybe you're unclear how this works?"

"Possibly. Not only are you my best friend, you're also the first I've had in years."

"But not the last. It sounds like you're leveling up socially just fine."

"Yeah. It's weird. I'm not sitting at the popular table or anything, but people say 'hey' when they see me and Devon is really cool."

"I'm glad. Don't be lonely when I'm gone, okay?"

He hugged me a little tighter. "Can we not talk about that right now? You'll be here until June or something, won't you?"

"If everything goes well."

"And if it doesn't?"

"I'll probably vanish without a trace."

He pulled back to level a stern look on me. "That's not funny."

I stared back.

"Oh, you're not kidding. Well, I choose not to think about life going catastrophically wrong. Want to go out?"

"Where did you have in mind?" I needed to be careful on the street, but I could hardly spend the rest of my limited life in this room.

"Psychedelic Records. That album I got before was sweet, so I was wondering if he had any more rare vintage stuff."

"I'm game. Let me get ready."

In the bathroom, I leaned my head against the door to settle my nerves. *That was too close. I almost ruined everything.* I couldn't be so careless again. Once my heart thawed somewhat, I got dressed, brushed my teeth and hair, then called it good. Kian was watching a cop show rerun on my shitty TV, but he clicked it off when I came out.

"All set?"

"Yep. Let's catch the bus."

Despite my fears, the trip went off without a hitch. He didn't buy anything this time but he admired several albums, and I suspected he must be saving up. Amusingly enough, the beardo behind the counter pretended he didn't know us. Afterward, we got convenience-store coffee like we had the night of the freak snowstorm. The clear but unnaturally frigid weather today said Wedderburn was pissed but holding out to hear from Buzzkill that his problem had been solved. The best thing about the winter king had to be the fact that he had so many irons in the fire, and with his chief enforcer tending to the problem of me, he must be dealing with other matters, other game gambits, as Kian couldn't be the only asset he was trying to acquire. That multitasking might buy me the time I desperately needed. *Maybe.* Hope was basically all I had. Well, that and the Harbinger, but it wasn't like he belonged to me, more like a wild animal who chose to circle me for its own reasons.

"I'll see you at school tomorrow?" Kian asked as we got off at my stop.

"Definitely."

Since I'd slept so much, I had a hard time drifting off that night. The weird noises at the Baltimore seemed more ominous than usual, and I wished the Harbinger would show up for a three a.m. chat, but that didn't happen. At four, I gave up and showered, then tackled all the assignments I had backed up. It seemed ridiculous and surreal to do homework, considering my situation, but I had to play normal until Kian's birthday. Getting kicked out of school would severely limit my ability to see him and, of greater significance, protect him. The immortals on either side might move against him. Wedderburn seemed like a sore loser; he might decide that if he couldn't have Kian, nobody could.

The mere thought sent a shiver through me. *Not happening. Not on my watch.*

Once I wrapped up my work, I forged an excuse note from my father. Hopefully, the attendance officer wouldn't try to follow up on the phone or in person. It wasn't like I set out to miss four days of school. Slightly worried, I headed out to catch the bus and rode through without encountering any danger signs. Weird that the world could be so normal for other people when mine was completely topsy-turvy.

The school looked just like it had the first day, not sure what I expected, but I marched through the parking lot ignoring a few cat calls. Normally, Kian would be waiting for me, either out front or near the lockers, but today I didn't see him. Instead, I spotted Jake Overman looking depressed as hell as he spun the combination. He hadn't shaved, and his hair was sticking up. Ruining his life had *not* been part of my master plan.

"You okay?"

He jumped, evidently not hearing my approach. When he realized it was me, his expression darkened into a scowl. "That's all you have to say? You realize everyone thought I did something to you that night."

"Huh?"

"Think about it. You stayed behind and then, suddenly, you vanish in thin air. I told everyone you left with your boyfriend, but nobody believed me. Maybe now I can be absolved of that crime at least."

"Sorry, I had no idea. It's really unfair they're blaming you for everything."

"Tell me something I don't know." Jake slammed his locker and stomped away, done with the conversation.

Across the hall, I noticed Kian chatting with Tanya. She flipped her shiny hair and laughed at something he said. His responding smile was shy but adorable. *Damn. He's not even looking for me.*

That's fine. Totally fine. I'm not jealous. I have no right to be.

Before I could decide what to do, if anything, Devon waylaid me. "You're alive. People have been taking bets, dude. You wouldn't believe the stories circulating about you and Jake. On Tuesday, Tanya broke up with him over it."

"Kian mentioned that, but he didn't say it was because of me."

"This school sure got exciting. I blame you."

"That's fair," I said, heading for the attendance office.

"Where you going? Isn't your first class the other way?"

In answer, I left my fake note with the assistant and comprehension dawned. "Oh. Were you really sick?"

"I had some family problems." It was probably best to keep it simple. Otherwise, I might lose track of my lies.

"Sorry to hear that. Anything I can do?"

"Not really. Come on, we don't have much time before the last bell."

Sure enough, we barely slid into our seats before it rang. The teacher gave me a dark look. Apparently, I didn't qualify as a good student anymore. Somehow that didn't rank high on my list of things to worry about. There had to be something I could do for Jake. If I saved Kian's future at the expense of someone else's happiness, I couldn't leave with a clear conscience.

Why is time travel so complicated?

Unfortunately, instead of an answer, I got a pop quiz.

LIKE COMING
HOME

The next week was blessedly uneventful, though I remained on high alert.

On Thursday afternoon, Kian messaged me during class, an absolute first. The teacher was droning on, so I surreptitiously checked my texts. *You have to do me a favor.*

Nine didn't care if she got in trouble, so I sent back, *What?*

Tanya asked if I wanna hang out tomorrow but there's no way. I'll choke. Will U bring Colin and double as my wingman?

Wow. That was something I never thought I'd hear from the first boy I ever loved. But the pain only twinged, no searing anguish; I must be getting used to my role in his life. Yet I couldn't assume the Harbinger would go along with this. I didn't even have a way to get in touch with him, and how could I request such an absurd favor when I already owed him?

I'll ask, I sent back. *He might already have plans. It's short notice.*

Kian replied with a sad face and added, *Yeah, she just mentioned it today. Sorry.*

No worries.

Once the initial shock disbursed, I realized what this meant. *Things have already changed. They can't happen as they did before.* Last time, Kian asked Tanya out, and she rejected him with such cruelty that it resulted in extremis. In this timeline, I boosted Kian's confidence, then broke up Jake and Tanya unintentionally, so events were already off script. *I just have to keep nudging.* Belatedly, I remembered what Kian told me:

In my optimum future, I end up with Tanya. She pushes me through law school, and I eventually go into politics.

A sick feeling swirled low in my stomach. *Is that what I have to do to make things right?* When I jumped, I never imagined that I'd have to play matchmaker. I'd thought stopping his suicide would be enough. *Okay, slow down. This probably isn't a date. Tanya just broke up with Jake, so when she said "hang out" she meant exactly that.* Just then, the teacher moved away from the front, roving the aisles to check our work, so I hastily slid my phone into my hoodie pocket and whizzed through the math problems on the assigned page. By the time she got to me, I had nine out of ten finished.

She paused, scrutinizing my work, and then she gave me a startled once-over. "You have a real knack, Chelsea. Why aren't you in one of the accelerated classes?"

"They were full," I mumbled.

"Do you want me to get you on the waiting list? I can already tell that the work in here isn't challenging enough for you."

"It's fine. I'm what you'd call an underachiever."

The guy next to me snickered while her brows came together in a disapproving frown. "Only hard work can secure you a bright future."

"It'll take more than that," I mumbled.

"Let me make you an appointment with the school counselor. Between your attitude and the number of absences already accrued . . ." She lowered her voice to advise me she'd noticed my emotional struggles and wanted to be there for me.

If I was a normal student, I'd just be mortified, but this could be deeply inconvenient. Arguing over a counseling session would just present me with more attention than I could handle, so I ended up in a stuffed armchair while a bearded guy in wire-frame glasses studied me over a can of chewed pencils. His oral fixation probably needed some analysis, but it was my turn on the couch.

"Are you having some trouble at home, Chelsea?"

Oh lord.

"My mom passed away recently. It's why we left Pomona." I felt shitty saying that, but since it was the truth, after a fashion, it was the best I could do.

"I'm sorry for your loss. It's just you and your father now?"

"I guess. But he works a lot, probably as a distraction from the loss, you know?" I offered that snippet of vulnerability, hoping he'd take the bait.

"Everyone has their own way to process grief," he acknowledged. "But I imagine that leaves you feeling pretty lonely."

I nodded. All of this was true, and it applied to my old life. The discomfort of talking about it with a complete stranger didn't matter, as long as it won me some wiggle room at this school. Teachers shared information, so Dr. Miller would spread the word about my bereavement. The slack should last until end of the semester.

"Sometimes grief can turn into depression. When we feel like that, it's hard to get out of bed. Everything feels like too much effort."

"I know what you mean." Clearly, he thought that was why I'd missed school.

"I'll talk to Mrs. Palmer. She had good intentions, but it might be too soon to increase your workload. She doesn't like seeing wasted potential, but you still have two years to build your academic record. It's important to do what you can, even when it's tough."

"I get it," I said, lowering my eyes. "But I need some time."

"Of course." He casually nudged the tissue box closer like I might break down.

"Thanks for listening." Maybe that was too much?

He smiled, probably thinking he'd made a difference today. Fine; I wouldn't disillusion him. Miller could go home and drink some Shiraz while basking in a job well done. "I'm here when you need an ear. Have you considered a creative outlet, poetry or a thought journal? It doesn't have to be formal or structured. Sadness is okay; you shouldn't try to stifle it. The important thing is not to let your feelings strangle you."

"That's a good idea," I said.

"Anytime. I'll write you a pass for your last class."

I arrived ten minutes late and slipped into my seat mid-lecture. *God, school is such a pain in the ass.* Once the final bell rang, I bolted from my chair like an Olympic runner. It would've been convenient if the Harbinger was waiting for me, but today I found Jake lingering in front of the school. When he spied me, he pushed away from the building.

"I'm wondering if you can answer some questions for me."

This couldn't be good. "About what?"

194

"The night of the party, obviously. I keep playing it back, and you're the only one who wasn't completely freaked out, like you knew exactly what was going on."

"You're accusing me of what exactly, not panicking?"

"If you dosed everyone and let me take the blame for it, I'll find out." His expression had been friendly and kind before, even occasionally flirtatious. It wasn't anymore.

"Leave her alone," Kian said.

I hadn't heard him come up behind me, but the timid, skittish boy I'd met initially had vanished. In his place stood a confident young man, not preternaturally beautiful as he had been, but better, because he was wholly himself. Since I didn't want this to escalate, I waved him off.

"It's fine; we're just talking. I'll see you later."

Kian didn't like it, but he left. Tanya beckoned him from across the parking lot, and they headed out together. Jake followed them with his eyes, and then the anger drained out of him. His hands curled into fists, not to lash out, but as if he needed something to hold on to.

"I wish there was something I could do," I said.

He sighed and shook his head. "After I blamed you for everything? I knew you were cool the first day we met. I just . . . I can't figure out how everything fell apart so fast."

Wedderburn, I thought, but didn't say it out loud.

Jake didn't seem to need my input to continue the conversation, though. "I used to think I was *too* lucky, you know? Life's been easy for me so far."

"Maybe you're supposed to learn from this."

"I guess. But I could've lived without knowing how fast supposed friends can turn on you. Even Tanya . . . She said she loved me, but when people started talking shit, she listened."

"In my experience, athletes get forgiven a lot. So even if it doesn't blow over on its own, when you start playing varsity basketball next year, everyone will come around."

"I don't want to be forgiven; I didn't *do* anything," he snapped.

"Then I don't know what to tell you. Life isn't fair."

"Not a news flash, not helping."

Despite residual guilt, I had no more patience for his personal problems. Jake didn't seem to get it; sometimes shit went horribly wrong through no fault of your own, and you had to cope with the fallout. He was still tall, white, cis male, handsome, and athletically gifted. This shouldn't be more than a small bump in his road. A little adversity built character, right? I jogged to the bus stop, wondering how the hell to ask the Harbinger on a double date, and it wasn't even solely a question of how to frame the request. I pondered it on the way home but didn't come to any solutions. He always showed up at his pleasure, not according to my convenience, though I had to admit; lately, I came perilously close to counting on him. Which made no sense, considering how well I understood his nature.

I sighed as I hopped off the bus.

"The Japanese say that sound is happiness escaping," the Harbinger said.

In Colin guise, he drew looks from people passing by. More than a few smiled or made eye contact, and he encouraged them with bedroom eyes. From the spark of his aura even in human form, he seemed much stronger than he had when he left my room. Remembering how he drove Nicole mad with unrequited longing, I didn't want to think about what he'd done to siphon that energy. But a small part of me eased at realizing he hadn't disappeared, even if it meant strangers might be hurting. My inclination to look away didn't make me unique; entire empires had been built on that premise.

"You've been tugging at me for a while now. I collect you require my attention?" But he was smiling, so it seemed he didn't mind.

"So here's the thing . . ." I explained the situation in a rush.

"This is too delicious. But . . . it will be excruciating for you to watch, will it not?" His delicate tone didn't change the meaning of the question.

"Uncomfortable is the word I'd pick. No, it won't be awesome seeing Kian bask in Tanya's glow, but . . ." I shrugged.

"I suppose I should cooperate, having volunteered my services as your love interest."

"True, I didn't ask you to tell everyone that."

"And why I'll do it without you incurring another debt. I suspect it will be diverting. Now if you'll excuse me, I have an engagement." He stepped into the shadows and disappeared.

With who? I knew so little about his habits and his existence, if he had friends in the immortal realm or if everything was checks and balances. It actually agitated me to discover this. *Okay, I'm losing my mind. The Harbinger is not my business.* Getting attached to him would be like falling for a tropical storm. All at once, I remembered . . . and then I couldn't believe I had forgotten, even for a moment.

Aaron.

The Harbinger who came for me, who rescued me, was also the same one who kept someone as a pet. Disappointment crashed down on me, a baffling mixture of pain and chagrin, both at myself and him. Rubbing my chest, I set out unsteadily for the Baltimore. As I passed the bodega, José caught my gaze through the shop window. To my surprise, he darted from behind the counter and out into the cold without a coat.

"You okay?" he asked.

I shrugged. "What answer would satisfy you?"

"Luisa was worried when you went missing," he muttered.

But in his dark eyes, I saw an echo of his wife's concern. The awareness that normal people could find something to like in me acted as a balm on my aching heart. So I softened and managed a smile. He returned it and gestured toward the store.

"Come in. I just made coffee."

"That's it? No questions."

"Sometimes that's the last thing you need," he said.

"You got that right."

What I needed, he offered—and that was a warm respite from a cold world. After I drank some coffee and ate a plate of Luisa's tamales, I fetched my cleaning supplies without being asked. It almost looked like he'd saved up chores just to make me feel needed; the floor didn't look like it had seen a thorough mopping since I'd been gone.

"You don't have to," he said. "That's not why I invited you in."

"I know. But I could use the company."

So he stopped protesting and made casual conversation as I worked, nothing too personal or intrusive. It was, frankly, perfect. José tried to give me a sack of groceries once I finished, but I shook my head. "No thanks. I have plenty of food at home."

"Then why . . . ?"

"You're not the only one who likes doing good deeds."

"I'm glad you're okay."

Okay was a relative word. The discomfort from other day rebounded, filtering a phantom pain throughout my body. Maybe I'd overdone the physical exertion while my body was still healing. Rochelle had said she had done as much as she could and that the rest of my recovery would take time. Whatever the reason, I hurt as I trudged back to the Baltimore. For so many reasons, it bothered me that the only reason I could even get into my shitty room was because of the Harbinger. It was like he was trying to infiltrate my life on an atomic level. When I should be focused on Kian or worrying about my myriad adversaries, my head was full of the Harbinger, to the point that my skull felt like it might explode.

By the time our double date rolled around, crankiness settled its teeth into my neck. I set out for the meeting point without much caring if the Harbinger even showed. I hadn't told him where we were meeting or what time, but if he was coming, he'd find me. He'd tracked me down almost two thousand away after all, and I wished that didn't fill me with such warmth.

Kian had decided we should go the Marquee, probably to impress Tanya with his unexpected coolness. Maybe because I was already in a pissy mood, a wave of resentment swamped me. He'd only gone to this place because of me, and now he wanted to show it off to someone else, the girl he'd secretly liked for years. *Whoa, rein it in. You can't be like this.*

Taking a few steadying breaths, I stepped into the lobby bar, where Kian was already waiting, despite the fact that I was ten minutes early. He beamed at me, so sweet and excited that it hurt me to look at him. On him, happiness held an unexpected sheen, lending him this puckish, irresistible charm. Yes, he was still too young, gangly and awkward, but this was how he should've been all along, before his life got twisted up by supernatural gamesmanship.

"You're here." He took a few steps with bright smile in his eyes; then his gaze diverted to the door, where Tanya stood in a white jacket, a white knit cap on her tawny hair like a princess in a fairy tale. I almost expected to see a diadem of snowflakes when she pulled her hat off, officially proclaiming her the snow queen.

Then she bounced on her toes, turning into a normal teenage girl. "This place is so awesome. Are you sure we can swing this?"

As she said this, a staffer came over. "IDs, please."

Tanya froze. I whipped mine out, as did Kian. We got a cursory check; then the guy looked at Tanya pointedly. She seemed like she might panic, and Kian stepped in. "She forgot hers. But come on, do I look like a cradle robber? We just want to watch the movie anyway."

As the dude hesitated, someone dropped a drink tray, and a whole lot of cursing commenced on the other side of the room. A big guy was shaking spilled liquor off his combat boots, looking like he might put the clumsy waiter through a wall. This server dashed off, presumably to mitigate the damage. Tanya exhaled slowly.

"Sorry, I was too nervous, I guess. I almost screwed things up." She smiled at Kian like he was some kind of super hero.

Wow, this sucks more than expected.

"Will Colin be here soon?" Kian asked, checking his watch.

Before I could answer, a pair of arms slipped around me from behind. "Present. Shall we get a table?"

I shook him off, but that didn't stop him from settling a hand in the small of my back in a distinctly proprietary fashion. Kian didn't even seem to notice, as he was one hundred and ten percent Tanya-focused. He shepherded her through the dark room to the same booth we sat at the last time we came, but he slid in after her, probably hoping for some incidental contact.

Thankfully, the preview reel started, sparing me the need to make small talk. When the Harbinger put an arm around me, I elbowed him. Undeterred, he whispered, "You're not playing your role with much conviction tonight. Why are you so angry?"

The truth spurted out of me like lotion from an over-squeezed tube. "Because you're keeping someone as a pet, and I was enough of an asshole to forget."

In the faint, shifting light, something like surprise . . . and relief flickered over his too-handsome features. "Is that all? When I decided to share your story, I set him free."

"What?" I stared, unable to credit what I was hearing.

"I tweaked his memories and gave him into human hands. It would've been cruel to leave him alone so much while I focus on you, no?"

In my book, keeping someone as a pet at all qualified as cruel, but I couldn't deny the relief flooding me. "Whatever."

He kissed my temple, more Colin pretense, right? "This pleases me, dearling. I thought . . . well, that it must hurt you to see this."

Across the table Kian was whispering to Tanya, taking advantage of the setting. She didn't seem opposed to his closeness, either. While she might not be ready to date just yet, I had the feeling that in time, this could turn into something. I waited for the pain, but it was muted, a low thrum of inevitable acceptance edged in longing for what I'd lost. *He is not mine*, I thought, and this time, it carried the unmistakable knell of truth.

When the Harbinger reached for me a second time, I let him pull me in. Settling against him felt disturbingly like coming home.

THE POLARITY PRINCIPLE

Tuesday after school, new minions awaited me. A pair of men in sunglasses and black suits stood with arms folded, just beyond school property. The taller one opened the back door to a silver town car and gestured for me to get in. It wouldn't be Wedderburn, so I climbed in and found the interior balmy like a sun-drenched beach. I recognized the god at once, but panic careened along my nerve endings because I had a sword made from Dwyer's heart wrapped around my wrist. Aegis tingled as if in awareness of the paradox.

The car pulled away from the curb, and through the tinted window, I glimpsed Kian, staring after me from the school parking lot. *He'll have questions for sure.* Putting that aside for the moment, I shifted to face Dwyer. His aura stung my eyes, so tears drizzled down my cheeks. Tawny gold like a surfer, he looked a little out of place in a suit. I could easily picture him sprawled in board shorts on a lounge chair.

"You're not what I expected," he said in greeting.

There was no point in deploying the confused-schoolgirl impression; he clearly knew I was more than I seemed. "Oh?"

"Someone capable of getting the better of Buzzkill, thwarting the winter king, and enchanting the Harbinger."

"You don't think I did all those things?" I'd probably choose a word other than *enchant*, but otherwise, fair enough.

"No, I have evidence to the contrary, but I'm baffled as to how."

"Is that important?"

He wore a musing look as he shook his head. "Perhaps not. Would you explain to me how a human girl came to possess a legendary blade forged by Govannon?"

"I'd rather not." Dwyer reached for my bracelet, like he recognized the base material on some level, and I snatched my hand away. "Bad idea."

"You pose quite an intriguing riddle, girl. But that's not why I've asked for a moment of your time. Do you know who I am?"

"Wedderburn's opponent, the sun god." It would do no good to feign ignorance anymore, and it might only serve to piss him off.

Since I was barely surviving as it was, I couldn't deal with two powerful immortals gunning for me. He smiled, and I strangled the urge to throw myself on the floor of the vehicle in helpless obeisance. It actually hurt to keep myself upright, beside him on the seat, as if we were equals. *No wonder people thought these creatures were gods, back in the day.* His smile tightened a little when he realized I had resisted.

So that was an intentional power play.

"How fascinating," he said.

"Would it be impolite to ask why you wanted to meet? There's someone waiting for me."

"Yes, I can feel his birds circling. But they can't report back on what happens in the car, for it is *my* domain." That statement felt like both a promise of privacy and a subtle threat.

Since I was making an excuse, surprised flared like a match in complete darkness. Sometimes I forgot how seriously the Harbinger took his promise to protect me, though I wondered if that encompassed all of his interest. He seemed far too vigilant for someone merely honoring a deal.

"That's good, I guess." If he asked, I'd tell him what happened later.

"Since you've taken it upon yourself to impede my enemy's progress, I propose an alliance of sorts. I can extend my protection and make Wedderburn think you're one of *my* agents. That should grant you the opportunity to do some damage. In fact, it wouldn't surprise me if you managed to complete your offensive against him."

"What makes you think I have an endgame?"

"Intuition," he said, smiling.

The car slid smoothly across a bridge, taking us away from downtown. The streets widened, and the houses got a little bigger. If we continued north, they would expand into subdivisions instead of neighborhoods, and beyond that lay a smattering of McMansions, like the one the Jake Overman lived in. Cross Point wasn't a huge city, but it had all the problems and perks of a larger one like Pittsburgh, only in miniature.

"Well, it's true I'm trying to accomplish something, but to be honest, foiling Wedderburn's plans is incidental. If that's fine with you, I could agree to an alliance." More protection sounded good, as long as it didn't come with restrictions.

"He is not the forgiving sort. Once you cross him, the encounter can end only in one of two ways."

"You think he'll wipe me out," I guessed. "But you're hoping I'll do some more damage before he gets me."

Dwyer shrugged. "Does that seem heartless? But my offer will buy you time, something you mortals always find to be in short supply. Your intervention has ruined multiple plans for Wedderburn, and I would like him to judge me more formidable and unpredictable than he previously estimated."

"You want me in your deck as the wild card."

"That is an excellent summation."

"What are you offering exactly?"

"Primarily, a bodyguard. But I'll also let it be known that you're doing my work. That will drive Wedderburn mad."

"I don't want someone obtrusively following me around," I objected.

"Selena knows her business. You won't even know she's around unless you're about to be jumped by the winter king's lackeys."

Pondering, I tried to see any potential drawbacks, but off the top of my head, I found none. But just to be sure . . . "What are my obligations in this arrangement?"

"Just keep harrying Wedderburn. Keep him frustrated."

"Because while he's focused on me, you can make moves that he won't notice, or come up with methods to counter."

Dwyer smiled. "Now I see it."

"What?"

"The reason for the Harbinger's interest. You're a clever creature, aren't you?"

It didn't seem right to agree, so I took that as a rhetorical question. "My mission is to save someone he's determined to acquire as an asset."

"Yes, I've noticed. Since I intended to deploy agents to ensure that asset's destruction, it was a most entertaining development. Your advent had the same effect as my original plan, only you caused Wedderburn considerably more chagrin."

"Because he didn't know who I was working for or why I appeared?"

"Precisely."

"If I only need to keep doing what I'm doing and act like it's on your orders, that seems like a fair deal," I said.

"So we have an agreement?"

"Absolutely."

His answering smile nearly blinded me. "Excellent. I'll let Selena know at once. She'll find this most promising."

"Excuse me?"

"She's been waiting for an excuse to tangle with the hag in Wedderburn's employ. With Buzzkill out of commission, he'll send her after you at some point."

I remembered the nightmare creatures with the metal claws and shivered. "She has a strange idea of fun."

"So I've said more than once." Dwyer seemed pleased to have his opinions validated even by someone like me. "Would you like to meet her? If only to avoid misunderstandings."

"I have time."

He rapped on the partition between the seats and leaned forward to give instructions to the driver. The car changed course and delivered us to an upscale coffeehouse in the suburbs. With a big, mostly empty parking lot, it was an odd place for a supernatural meeting. We went inside, and Minion A got us both cappuccinos without asking what we wanted. Dwyer chose a seat by the window in a cluster of overstuffed armchairs, and I noticed how everyone in the café perked up, like flowers facing the sun. Since he had his aura dialed down to a minimum, I could only imagine how people would react if he came at full charge. The two guards sat down at a neighboring table. Eventually the patrons went back to their phones, laptops, and quiet conversations, leaving me in awkward silence with Dwyer.

Twenty minutes after we arrived, a young woman dressed all in black stormed into the place. She rocked a unique look at the intersection of Goth and punk, lots of metal studs, a few spikes for good measure. Her lips were red as blood, and she had on an amount of eyeliner usually preferred by tween girls. Her hair stood in green-streaked peaks, an impressive amount of hair product there. Marching over, she hauled a straight-back chair toward us, spun it around backward and straddled it, aiming an angry look at both Dwyer and me.

Right, she looks completely enamored with the idea of guarding me.

"What's so important that I had to drop everything and heel like a dog?" she demanded.

"I told you about her already," he said. "I thought you'd want to meet the thorn in Wedderburn's side."

"This human offed Buzzkill?" Her tone said *bullshit*.

"I had help." There was no way I'd admit that the Harbinger had taken control of my body and used my epic sword.

Though to be fair, I ended him on my own in the other timeline.

Her entire demeanor changed, becoming avid. She folded her hands on top of the chair and leaned forward. "What happened?"

"When he died, you mean?" This was decidedly a weird avenue of inquiry, unless she was testing me. If so . . . "He faded into dark smoke. In my experience, the immortal's nature determines the light show. If they're mostly good, then it's golden sparks. Evil? Black smoky swirls, all the way."

Two pairs of shocked eyes locked on me. Selena spoke for both of them. "You've killed immortals other than Buzzkill?"

Damn. Maybe I said too much.

"I don't remember asking you this many questions," I said. "The nature of a wild card is that you don't understand it fully."

Please let that be enough. I can't piss Dwyer off too.

To my relief, the sun god laughed. "Well said. I'll take your knowledge as a reminder to be wary."

"Good plan," Selena muttered, seeming unconvinced. But she set aside whatever misgivings she had to get down to business. "I'm not sure if you recognize me. Probably not, I suspect. Mighty huntress, goddess of the moon? Contrary to popular opinion, I'm not much for mysteries, and I'm definitely not into virgins. People seem to think this idiot is my brother. Sometimes I agree. Let's see . . . what else . . ."

Bemused, I listened to her rattle off a list of true and false. Finally, she concluded with, "But the huntress thing is spot on. I miss the Colosseum."

"You can see why I put her in charge of your protection," Dwyer put in.

"The picture is forming."

"I'll have your back when shit gets real." Selena seemed eager for that to happen. "When Wedderburn finds out you ended his favorite clown, his head will explode."

"That would solve a lot of problems for me," I mumbled.

She grinned. "Figuratively. I thought you'd understand."

"I'm glad to see the two of you getting along. You'll need that goodwill until things are resolved, one way or another."

I half thought Dwyer would bail right then, but to my surprise, he tipped his head at one of the guards, who got Selena mineral water and, inexplicably, a cup of olives. Neither of them seemed in any hurry to leave, and I sipped my cappuccino, waiting for the other shoe to drop. I noticed the guards were attentive, watching the door with a focus I found faintly unnerving.

"Are we expecting trouble?" I asked, low.

"Hoping is a better word," Selena answered.

Half an hour later, the door blew open on a wintry breeze, and an elderly woman stepped in. Something about her seemed off, though I couldn't put my finger on it. When she bared yellow teeth in our direction, I realized this must be the human camouflage for Wedderburn's hag. Dwyer raised his nearly empty cup with a smirk of knowing amusement, while Selena just stared, likely cataloging the creature's strengths and weaknesses.

Clad in a yellow hat and muffler, the hag stepped closer. She smelled of copper and seaweed, a combination that caused a stir in the other customers. "This is an interesting coffee klatch. I'll have an update for the cold one after all."

"Make sure you mention how I'm going to tear your throat out with my bare hands," Selena said softly.

"Enemies better than you have tried," the hag snarled back.

"Let's keep it civilized," Dwyer said. "We have an audience after all. Feel free to run along back to your master. You've learned what you came to uncover."

"Not quite. I have a question for you first."

"Go ahead," the sun king allowed.

"How did you entice the clown away? What prize did you offer?"

Choking on a laugh, I covered by taking a sip of my drink. The other two had better poker faces, so other than a fresh glint of humor, Dwyer gave no sign of how wrong this guess was. Selena rolled her eyes and tipped her head at her "brother." He responded with a lazy twirl of one hand.

"Why should I enlighten your master? It will do him good to wonder when that loyalty began to erode, how many small betrayals led up to this final one."

"So you admit that Buzzkill has come to you?"

Selena cut in, "If you want to dance, let's do it. Otherwise, get the hell out of here."

The immortals exchanged a long glance, and then the hag inclined her head. "I'll see you soon. Next time there will be no parlay."

"Enjoy your promotion," Selena shot back. "Too bad Buzzkill had to defect for you to get some recognition. That must sap the joy right out of it."

I actually saw the hag's jaw clench. To me, it was amazing that none of the people peering at their laptops noticed anything weird about our group, as it seemed so obvious. But nobody glanced up when the old woman left without ordering. At that, Dwyer stretched lazily, like a cat that really enjoyed his nap in the sun.

"Well, that's an unexpected bonus," he murmured. "That misunderstanding will greatly aid our plan to keep the winter king distracted."

Selena snickered. "He'll be searching everywhere for Buzzkill, trying to find out what you have him doing."

"And to punish him for the treachery," I added.

Dwyer nodded, then turned to me. "Truly a superb red herring. Stay alive, won't you? I have irons in the fire depending on you as a successful diversion."

Before I could reply, the doors blew open, glass banging on glass. Some customers started, and a few others lingered because the Harbinger in his Colin guise qualified as pure eye candy. Truthfully I wasn't surprised to see him, only that it had taken this long. He strode toward us, violin case in hand.

"You must already know that I don't like others trifling with my things," he said, perching on the arm of my chair.

"Easy. It was only a conversation." Selena studied us, as if she couldn't figure out why the Harbinger took such an interest in me.

"Did you sign anything?" he asked, ignoring her.

The sun god faked a yawn. "No need for that. A verbal agreement is more than enough. I have no further business with our girl, so I'll leave her in your capable hands."

Dwyer signaled to his entourage, and the guards followed him out. Selena lingered only long enough to remind me, "I'll keep an eye out for trouble."

As if I could forget.

"A verbal agreement?" The Harbinger's tone was dangerously quiet as he watched the others file out. "*Our* girl? I am . . . quite provoked."

"It's not like that," I said, though I didn't really know what "like that" would entail.

Quickly, I explained what went down before he could blow a fuse. Oddly, he didn't move from the arm of my chair the whole time I talked, and I fielded more than one envious glance. It must have been an unconscious gesture, but he stroked my hair like I was his pet in truth. Once, I tried to scoot away, and he made a sound that sent shivers through me.

Yeah, he's pissed.

"I'm doing my best to control myself, but I am not pleased," he said eventually. "Dwyer will use you like chewing gum and spit you out when the flavor is gone."

Mustering my courage, I touched him on the arm. "I know. But he can help me buy the time I need. It's not that long by immortal standards; I just need Wedderburn trying to solve the wrong problems for a bit longer."

"It's your life." The Harbinger sounded tremendously unhappy about that fact. "But don't trust him, or the moon-mad Selena for that matter."

"I don't trust anyone. Except you, maybe a little."

He gentled, his hand slowing on my hair. "You shouldn't. Not me. Not even a little. But I'm happy you said so."

"It's the truth." *Ill-advised as it might be.*

The Harbinger relaxed further, as if I'd said the magic words somehow. "If you have time next Friday, I'm calling your debt due."

Worry warred with curiosity, underscored with amazement that he cared about my schedule. *Since when . . . ?* Since I'd promised, of course I said, "I'll be there."

SONGS OF LOVE
AND DEATH

When I agreed to the Harbinger's request, I didn't realize, but the Friday he'd chosen was Valentine's Day. All day at school, student council representatives ferried roses around; you could buy one for a couple of bucks and have it sent with a handmade card to someone you liked. It was a little cheesy, but the cool thing was, they had different colors: red for romance, pink for showing interest, and yellow for friendship. Those might not be the agreed-upon definitions with the floral society, but as a school code, I admired the simplicity.

I got a couple yellow ones, one from Kian, one from Carmen, and three pinks. Judging by the way Wade Tennant made eye contact and waggled his brows as I went by, he must've sent one. Reading the card confirmed my hunch. *We should get to know each other better, new girl.* The other "interest" roses didn't have cards attached, so it looked like I had secret admirers. I dropped that in the bin but kept the flowers. Together, the five blooms made a pretty bouquet.

Tanya had over a dozen, clutched in her arms like she'd just won a pageant, and they were predominantly red and pink with one sole yellow, probably from her best friend, whoever that was. I hadn't paid that much attention to her social circle, though she didn't limit herself to people at the popular table. From what I'd observed, she was fairly nice to everyone.

I sent yellows back to Kian and Carmen at the last-minute sales table, mostly because I hadn't known "friend" roses were a thing on V-Day. At lunch, everyone seemed pleased with their haul, as nobody in Devon's group came up empty-handed. Devon had a single red rose, but he didn't divulge who it was from, despite good-natured teasing from everyone else. To my surprise, Kian had a pink one, and he was practically vibrating.

"I need to talk to you," he whispered.

"Let's go get chocolate milk."

Walking to the cafeteria line offered some privacy, but he still checked over his shoulder. "Vonna sent me a pink rose."

"You have a lot in common. Thoughts?" Personally, I suspected his feelings for Tanya were basically a crush, but I couldn't just say "get over her already."

"I want to get to know her better," he admitted. "I've been tutoring Tanya in science and the more time I spend with her . . ."

"Yeah?"

"I don't know, it's not like I expected. I never thought I'd say this, but . . . there's no spark. I mean, she's nice and everything, but we don't have a lot to talk about."

It was kind of amazing that he realized that. "So maybe tell Vonna you'd like to hang out and see where it goes? You don't have to promise to be her boyfriend until you figure out if there's chemistry."

"She's cute," he said. "And I love her sense of humor. Plus, the fact that she can talk about classic movies is a huge draw."

"Sounds like you're sort of into her already." Saying that gave me a twinge.

My fingers ached. *Okay, that's a strange reaction.* But no other description fit, as invisible needles pricked away beneath my nails. I checked but didn't see anything that should be making me feel that, though I did glimpse that golden ghost light from before.

"Maybe I am. I guess I just didn't want to admit I devoted so much time and mental energy to a girl I basically invented."

"Cool. Now you can try living in the real world."

My turn in line came, and I bought chocolate milk to lend credence to our absence. "You want that?" he asked.

"Not really," I said.

For some reason, I hadn't been hungry lately. Food didn't taste the same, sort of bland, and the textures seemed wrong too. Kian plucked the carton from my fingers and headed back to the table with a spring in his step. He squeezed in beside Vonna, forcing Nathan to give way. The boy I'd met six short weeks ago wouldn't have had the courage to do that. Melancholy, I chose a seat across and a few chairs down. Vonna laughed at something Kian said, her dark eyes sparkling. Today, she had on jeans, a red open-weave sweater over the top of a sparkly tank top.

"You're watching him like you just found out he's got a terminal disease," Devon said.

"I don't mean to." I pinched some bread from my PB&J and formed a tiny ball of dough.

"If you like him, tell him."

"He's just a friend," I muttered.

"If you say so." Devon didn't sound convinced. "You have a boyfriend anyway, or at least that's what I've heard."

"I'm seeing him later." That was meant to distract him since he saw *way* too much.

"That's sweet. I'm boycotting commercial romance day."

"Someone will be disappointed." I eyed the red rose beside him.

He sighed. "It's from my ex. I've told him it's over repeatedly, but I guess it's just not sinking in."

"Breaking up sucks," I said, determinedly *not* watching Kian.

The rest of the day went at a crawl. Everywhere I looked, there were happy couples, starting something or celebrating the continuation of it. After school, Vonna and Kian left the building hand in hand. I ambled out five minutes later to find the Harbinger waiting for me. *Right, I promised him today. Wonder what's happening.*

He seized my hand like it was his and led me away from half a dozen milling students. Instead of whooshing through space, however, he took me to the bus stop. I raised a brow. He carried his violin case, and something about his expression troubled me.

"You okay?" I asked.

"Not really."

"Did something happen?"

"It's more what *will* happen," he said softly. "But I'm determined not to think about that. Today is ours, you promised."

"So I did." I stared at our joined hands.

He tugged me onto the next bus. I didn't recognize the route number, and it delivered us to the main terminal, where we got on another. Good and lost, I sat next to the Harbinger watching Cross

Point stream past. Ten stops later, we hopped off across the street from an upscale shopping plaza. The streets were busier here, and people hurried into the mall to get out of the unseasonable cold. By now, the snow on the ground should be a slushy mess, paving the way for spring, but Wedderburn had a choke hold on this city, so it still looked like a greeting card that could be called Winter Wonderland.

"Why are we here?" I asked.

He ignored the question, setting up near an outdoor heater operated by a restaurant with a terrace for smokers. Behind him, a fountain hissed and shimmered, jetting icy water into the air. It was kind of miraculous that it didn't freeze. When he brought out his violin, I heard a woman say, "Oh my God, he's back."

Attracting an audience should've been impossible in this weather, but as soon as the Harbinger started to play, people flocked to him like moths to a flame. I had to admit, his sound was exquisite, a sort of aural ravishment. His arm moved with the purest passion I'd seen in him, drawing an ardent wail from his violin. I didn't recognize the song, but it didn't matter. Money dropped into his case, not just coins, but wads of bills. Five songs later, I was nearly frozen, but I didn't even care. If I died while listening to him, it would be worth it.

The Harbinger finally spoke, drawing an audible sigh from his enthralled audience. "I have a special treat for you this evening."

"What is it?" someone asked.

"I brought my lady to sing."

Excuse me? My eyes widened as I jolted from the near trance his music had put me in. Shaking my head frantically, I resisted as he

217

pulled me to the center of the crowd. The Harbinger leaned his head against mine and whispered, "You promised."

True. I did.

Even if I had no talent, I should comply with this odd request and count myself lucky he wasn't asking anything worse. *What's a little public humiliation between friends?* The Harbinger cupped my face in his hands and stared into my eyes so long that I suspected he was trying to hypnotize me. Apparently the audience agreed, because a guy shouted, "Kiss her already."

My breath hitched. "I'll sing. Let's do this."

He played the opening bars of "Danny Boy," and while I'd heard the song, primarily in old movies, I didn't know the words by heart. Except . . . I did. And the voice that came out of my mouth didn't sound like me: husky, beautifully on pitch, and rich with emotion. The crowd quieted as if the punishment for interruption was death. Though the Harbinger hadn't gone over the program with me, I knew every song he played. The strangeness of it made me shiver, but I sang on, like that cursed girl who couldn't take her dancing shoes off.

An hour or so later, he played the final bars, and we received thunderous applause from the crowd that was closer to a mob. As shivers took me, I noticed that mall security guards had come out, but nobody had attempted to disturb us. He packed up while I trembled, and the audience parted like the Red Sea to let us pass. They didn't disperse until the Harbinger went into the restaurant nearby. Inside, it was blissfully warm. The hostess didn't ask if we had a reservation despite the people waiting. She just led him to a table for two near the back. Valentine's Day decorations gave the place a cheerful, romantic air, aided by the warm lighting.

"I don't understand what just happened," I said.

But as the Harbinger shrugged out of his jacket, I could tell that he looked better. There was color in his cheeks for once, and he looked as close to human as I'd ever seen. Even in his Colin guise, there was a certain warmth he couldn't muster. *Does that mean . . . ?*

"That's how I've been feeding," he said softly. "Taking only the admiration that's freely given, nothing they wouldn't offer any talented musician. I haven't played in a hundred years, but for you, I broke an old promise."

"Excuse me?"

"When Saiorse died, I swore I wouldn't make music without her. I wanted you to know how important you've become to me."

"Is this a . . . declaration?" I couldn't decide how to feel or react.

The waitress came over then, interrupting the moment. "Can I get you started with something to drink?"

"Hot chocolate for me," I said, though I was cold, not thirsty.

"Black tea." When the Harbinger smiled, I feared the girl might pass out.

Somehow she rallied. "Coming right up."

He went on as if we hadn't been interrupted. "Not in the usual sense. I thought it might reassure you to know I've turned over a new leaf. Well . . . as much as I can. I've had periods of peaceful benevolence before."

But then your nature overwhelms your good intentions. I understood that he didn't want to cause pain; rather, it was a compulsion, a sickness, even. Tenderness welled up in me as I gazed at him through a flicker of candlelight. How could a creature so old be interested in me? On any level. The mystery didn't clarify, no matter how I considered it.

"What are we doing tonight?" I asked.

"This is your gift to me . . . no questions. I've asked for tonight, I will explain nothing. Can you offer this much, dearling?"

"Of course."

We ate dinner together like any normal couple. I hadn't even known the Harbinger could eat. I didn't taste much, but the warmth slowly seeped into my frozen bones. He fed me bites of chocolate cake with an inexplicable sorrow building in his eyes. Curiosity tried to chew its way out of my sternum, but I'd promised to let him be, just for tonight. Maybe this was a sort of macabre anniversary, and he didn't want to be alone. Though I knew Saiorse had died of natural causes, I had no idea what day. If she'd passed on February 14, it seemed beyond cruel.

I mean, losing someone you love on Valentine's? Too far, universe. Too far.

Maybe busking was what he used to do with her, and he just needed me to be her stand-in. That possibility didn't thrill me. Yet I contained all the questions, finishing the meal with a hot cup of tea. The Harbinger paid for our meals with some of the bills we'd collected singing outside. A bit later, we emerged to the strobing lights of the fountain, bathing everything red, then blue and green. The shifting colors lent his countenance a melancholy elegance.

"Will you stay the night?" he asked.

I nodded. It seemed highly improbable that he was asking for sex. While immortals definitely had libidos, dependent on their stories, he didn't need me for that. This seemed like a deeper question, and even if I hadn't promised him my time and understanding, I couldn't leave him alone. *Fragile* was an odd word, but it fit him tonight.

He took me to a small studio apartment, much nicer than my room at the Baltimore. The place was clean and modern, a renovated unit in a historical building. The walls were painted a sunny shade of cream, warming the space even without the brick statement wall. From the dark leather furniture to the Murphy bed, everything had its place. This area could be called gentrified, lots of restoration in progress. There was an organic market up the street, such a contrast from the bodega, but I preferred José and Luisa's store. Since I'd imagined he popped in and out from his moldering mansion on the New England coast, this was quite a revelation.

"Do you like it?"

"Definitely. The breakfast bar is nice." There was no need for a table, as the counter space could double as an eating area.

Not that he needs to worry about that.

"It's yours," he said simply, proffering a key. "That is, if you decide to stay."

I stared at the ridged brass implement. "With you?"

With a sad half smile, he shook his head. "I won't ask that. Soon, we will have an important conversation. I suspect I already know your answer."

"What—" I cut myself off before I could frame the inquiry.

You promised, no questions.

"You have more self-control than most, but you're ridiculously easy to read. No, I didn't devise this to torment you. I just ask that you contain that curiosity for tonight."

"I can do that. But . . . you make it sound like you're leaving."

"That's a question in the form of a statement." He opened his violin case and counted the cash remaining, a couple hundred dollars. "I want you to have this. Since you were with me when I earned it, you can't doubt where it came from."

Why burbled on the tip of my tongue as I accepted the money, tucking it into my backpack. If he truly meant for me to live here, things would be a lot easier. The building was secure, no creepy clerk watching my every move, no threat of home invasion from the rusty fire escape. Before, I might not have believed he'd offer such generosity without strings. Now I trusted him, and the more he warned me not to, the more my faith stretched.

"Thanks. But . . . this feels more and more like loose ends wrapping up."

"You're too clever for your own good." Which was not exactly a convincing denial.

I ached with unspoken curiosity laced with concern. He had refused to leave more than once. *So what happened? What's changed? Or maybe—*

The Harbinger traced cool fingers down my cheek, as if he could memorize me. "Don't. Let's pretend there is no tomorrow. You promised me tonight, and I'll hoard every last second."

"Okay," I said.

Anyone else might have kissed me then, but he was closed and odd, none of his usual excess. I sat beside him on the sofa and didn't wait for him to pull me close. The way I nestled made his eyes widen, but he put his arm around my shoulders. His embrace held a familiar weight now, and I sighed as I tipped my head against his shoulder.

"You loved her." Not a deal breaker, not a question—I knew.

He didn't ask who I meant. That would be disingenuous. "The heart is a house with many chambers. She was one of many."

Phantom pain flared again, hot spots all over my body, and as if he felt it, he held me closer; I closed my eyes against the inexorable pull of morning.

NORMAL IS A TOURIST TOWN

A week after the weirdest Valentine's Day ever, Devon used a carrot stick like a laser pointer, aiming it around the table for emphasis. "We should try another meet-up, this time without the hallucinogenic roofies."

Carmen nodded. "Sounds fun."

"Everyone free tonight?" Vonna asked.

The best part of hanging around with freshmen and sophomores? Few of them had part-time jobs. In another year that would change, cutting into the time the group had for another. By graduation, they'd probably be ships passing in the night, and once everyone split for college—I checked the depressing thought. It wasn't like these were my friends; this was Kian's life, and I was only auditing for a while.

"I can't," Amanda said.

"Hot date?" Nathan poked her.

I kind of suspected he had a crush, based on how he treated her.

Ignoring that, she shook her head. "Grandma's birthday party. Have fun for me too."

Everyone else could show up, though, and we agreed to hang out at Carmen's, whose place had a big basement with a TV in it. The address she texted wasn't that far from my new apartment. I'd moved into the studio two days before, not like that was a huge endeavor, as everything I owned fit easily in the used backpack I'd picked up at the House of Style. There was no question that the cash the Harbinger had donated would make my remaining time here easier.

"Be there around seven," Carmen added. "My mom works the night shift as a nurse, so she'll be up by then. She leaves the house at like ten."

"Wow, that's rough," Devon said.

Carmen made a face. "Sort of. It means I'm in charge of the house while she's out, so my brothers and sisters might pester us, if they're not asleep."

Kian smiled. "We'll survive."

"I can't wait. I'll bring some awesome DVDs." Nathan seemed eager to handle that, but I wondered if his choices would entertain everyone else.

Still, when was the last time I'd enjoyed a simple movie night with friends? Honestly I couldn't remember, unless you counted the nights at Kian's place, but even then, it wasn't a big group. With Selena looking out for me from the shadows, it should be safe for me to go.

"You look excited," Devon said.

"Maybe."

"Trust me, Carmen's family room isn't that thrilling."

"I heard that." She frowned at him from a few seats down the table.

Smiling, I let the conversation flow over me. The rest of the school day doddered by like an elderly couple. Despite less than stellar attendance and little effort, I had a B average in all my classes, nothing to alarm the teachers. After the day ended, I headed out to my stop. I still wasn't used to boarding the new bus, and I'd gotten a surprise when I realized Kian lived farther along the new route. He climbed on after me and slid into a window seat. I plopped down beside him, rationalizing, *Better me than a stranger.*

"When are you inviting me over to see your new place?" he asked.

"I'm not sure." For some reason, reluctance percolated through me, maybe because the flat was a gift from the Harbinger. To bring Kian in seemed disrespectful or something.

"Is there some reason I can't come?" He really was too perceptive.

I shrugged. "It's just . . . I share the place with my boyfriend. So I should check with him before inviting anyone." That was more or less true, though I hadn't seen him since he dropped me off at the Baltimore on Saturday morning.

"Wow. But . . . is that a good idea? From your descriptions, I wouldn't exactly call Colin reliable. I mean, I haven't seen him around all week."

For some reason, this pissed me off, and I found myself defending him. "He travels for work. You know he's a musician, right?"

Kian shook his head. "Sorry, I forgot. You don't talk about him much. But it makes sense that he has an irregular schedule if he's

226

traveling for gigs." He seemed self-conscious about the last word, as if he wasn't sure he'd used it correctly.

"He's not a saint," I said. "But he's been there for me during some pretty rough times. I can't forget that."

"Makes sense." He gave the impression he was placating me, but I let it go.

"How are things with Vonna?" It wasn't a great conversation shift, but honest curiosity made me ask.

"Good so far. But it's only been like a week and we haven't done anything but hang out at school so far."

"Maybe you can spend some time together tonight."

He flashed a bright smile. "I hope so."

My stop came up shortly, so I waved and got off the bus. It was incredible to key in a code so I could enter the foyer. The attendant waved at me as I went to the elevator and took it to my sparkling-clean fourth-floor unit. My brass key opened the apartment door, as it had for the last week, and I shook off the fear that it would suddenly morph into a live worm, and that I'd find I had been squatting in a cardboard box for the last two days.

There was no sign the Harbinger had been here in my absence. Fighting disappointment, I fixed a snack, as he'd left me a fully stocked fridge. If I was careful, I wouldn't need to buy food for another two weeks, and that didn't account for any of the canned goods in the cupboard. In my quiet, clean, and safe apartment, loneliness knocked at the door, but I didn't let it in.

Instead, I took a shower and then did all my homework. *You can take the geek out of her timeline, etc.* That killed a few hours, and then it was time to walk to Carmen's. She was eight blocks farther out, not worth getting on the bus. The weather had gotten warmer. Either nature was asserting itself over Wedderburn's fit of pique or Dwyer was showing his strength to make a point. Regardless, my hoodie and jean jacket was enough even at night.

Carmen lived in a ramshackle blue Victorian-style house that was tall and narrow with a sagging porch. As I came up the steps, I could hear a couple of kids yelling inside. When I rang the bell, the doom theme from *Star Wars* played. She opened the door a minute later, looking slightly harried.

"Sorry, the little monsters are being stubborn about dinner."

"I want pizza," a boy about seven yelled.

"How does your mom sleep through this?" I wondered aloud.

"Necessity and practice. Come on in." She turned to address her pint-size critic. "If you eat the soup, I'll let you have Popsicles."

The boy exchanged a look with a girl a year or two older. "Deal. But we get as many crackers as we want."

"I don't care, just get in the kitchen and eat. The baby's already down for the night," she added to me. "No thanks to these two."

"Is this why you invited us over?" I asked.

"Because I couldn't go out otherwise? Basically, yes. That Saturday we went to the party was a rare exception and my mom had the night off."

Obviously, I wondered about Mr. Maldonado but if she didn't mention him, I figured she must have a good reason. I followed her into the kitchen to supervise her siblings. This time, they ate the chicken soup without complaint, but I noticed an impressive number of oyster crackers went down their gullets as well. Two orange Popsicles later, she banished them to play in their rooms as the bell rang again.

She sighed. "My older brother's idea of a joke. So far we can't figure out how to change or disconnect it."

Kian and Vonna stood on the porch, as if they'd come together, and they were holding hands. I ignored the sinking sensation in my stomach and summoned a bright smile. "Hey, guys. I hope you're ready for some cinema magic."

Vonna stepped in first, and he helped her out of her jacket. "With Nathan in charge? I bet we'll get a Scream fest."

"Could be worse," Kian said.

"Yeah, he could dig up all the I Know What You Did movies." Carmen beckoned to us and led the way down the basement stairs.

Like most old houses, the steps were scary, skeletal wood, but downstairs, the cement room had been painted a cheerful yellow and filled with comfortable furniture that looked like it had been lifted from various grandmothers. On one side, there was a red floral overstuffed sofa that somehow didn't look hideous with the green plaid love seat or the orange armchair. There were also giant pillow seats and like five beanbags. This was clearly a room where people could crowd in and still feel cozy. Our apartment wouldn't have allowed me to invite this many friends over, and a small pang went through me. A spark of light shot from my fingertips, and I hid them behind my back, heart thumping like mad.

Did anyone see that?

"It's a mess, I know," Carmen mumbled.

Based on the minivan, it was cleaner than I expected. All the toys were piled in the box, and the super fluffy gray rug looked as if it had been vacuumed recently. Cushions in all hues lay scattered on the floor, tempting you to curl up like a puppy. As for the TV, it was a big box unit, but when she flicked it on, the picture was good. She left us watching music videos when the bell rang again, and I busied myself inspecting the family photos that lined the wall near the stairs. While Kian and Vonna quietly tried to decide where to sit, I was third-wheeling up a storm. I'd almost decided to go back upstairs when Carmen returned with everyone else.

"So this is the family room," she said, juggling DVDs presumably from Nathan.

"Nice," Elton said.

I wandered around inspecting everything while Elton promptly claimed the orange chair. Once I picked the love seat, Devon sat next to me. That left the couch for Kian and Vonna. Nathan yielded the last spot to Carmen and flopped in one of the beanbags. She dimmed the lights and started the first movie. Everyone had guessed wrong, as it was a terrifying Japanese import. I jumped more than once and covered my eyes for about half of it. At least pure terror kept me from staring at Kian, who had taken the opportunity to wrap an arm around Vonna. Even I had to admit they made a cute couple.

"You're the only one who will be unhappy if you keep quiet," Devon whispered.

I jumped at his proximity, not realizing he was paying attention. Dismissing the idea of a flippant *whatever*, because anyone this astute deserved better, I leaned over to make sure nobody could hear. "Timing is everything, you know? And sometimes we just can't have what we want. It would be selfish of me to say anything when I can't stick around. It's better for him to be happy. Just look at how she makes him smile."

Vonna must have cracked a joke because Kian's shoulders shook with silent laughter. Devon watched them for a few seconds before nodding. "I get you. And I can respect that."

"Don't say anything, okay? It would only make things awkward, and I honestly want things to go well for them."

"I'm definitely not the meddling kind. Plus, I've known Vonna since first grade. She deserves somebody who will treat her right."

"She'll never meet anyone sweeter or more devoted." Tears stung my eyes, and I blinked them away. *Who knew it would feel so awful to give the blessing for your first love to be happy with someone else?*

I focused on the movie again, though the terror had lost some of its grip on me. Carmen brought drinks and chips down during intermission. Her younger siblings put in an appearance, and she had to go read them a story. That left Elton flipping channels while Devon called suggestions.

"We're not watching Lifetime," Nathan snapped.

"Women's tennis." Vonna seemed comfortable tucked against Kian's side, not self-conscious now that the lights had come up.

The guys didn't seem disposed to tease her, either. I'd noticed they were protective, courtesy of a shared past I knew little about. *I wish I had friends I'd known since grade school.* But when my parents transferred me to Blackbriar, I lost touch with my classmates, and in all honesty, I hadn't been close with anyone before the move. Regular students saw me as a kiss-up while the smart ones considered me a rival for the position of teacher's pet. Doubtless poor social skills contributed to my friendless state, but if I could rewrite history, I wouldn't go to a fancy private academy. My parents could save their money, and I'd enroll in a science-focused magnet school.

But that was pointless speculation. In my timeline, I'd graduate from Blackbriar on independent study and go to college with only my father to celebrate my achievements.

Presuming I survive this and can return.

Contemplating the future that awaited, a wave of pain wracked me so hard I doubled over. I hadn't let myself picture returning before. Maybe part of me hoped that this future would replace my old one, but the Harbinger made it clear time travel didn't work that way. There was no way to wipe the slate clean. Creating a new world wasn't a minor feat, though. I should be proud, right?

Devon touched my shoulder. "Are you sick?"

Managing to smile, I shook my head. "Sorry. Ate too much salsa, I guess."

"Carmen's pico de gallo is no joke if you're not used to it." He rubbed my back until I felt a little better, not from the fictional stomachache, but due to simple human contact.

"Thanks. I'm okay now."

My smile faded when I realized Kian was watching Devon and me with an odd expression. I didn't know what to make of it, but I hadn't done anything wrong. Carmen hurried down the stairs, out of breath from coming down two flights in a rush. She leaned against the wall to rest, breaking the spell. I glanced away to find that Elton had turned on a Cinemax soft-core. The resultant panting and moaning made everyone supremely uncomfortable.

"Enough of that." Carmen snatched the remote and switched it back to the DVD player. "Sorry, guys. We should be good for another movie. They'll pass out soon."

"It's cool," Devon said. "I'm an only, so I like seeing how the other half lives."

"You want to swap?" Carmen offered.

He shook his head quickly as she started the next flick. Nathan's second pick was an action comedy, two cops played by Martin Lawrence and Will Smith. Humor matched the explosions, and I enjoyed it a lot. More important, I wasn't completely freaked out when it came time to walk home.

"This was awesome," I said, standing. "Thanks for having us over."

"It's not even midnight." Nathan seemed affronted. "We have two more movies to watch."

"Some of us have curfews," Vonna said.

Kian added, "I need to catch the last bus."

Despite Nathan's objections, the party broke up at twenty minutes to twelve. I waved as I headed out. The others went toward the bus stop, leaving me to walk home alone. It hadn't seemed spooky earlier, but despite the streetlights, I couldn't shake the sensation that someone—or something—was watching me. Touching Aegis for reassurance, I quickened my pace, practically sprinting between pools of the light. The shadows seemed deeper where the brightness didn't touch, like it was filled with sentience. My skin prickled. There was no safety. If something was chasing me, getting back to the apartment wouldn't help.

My mom died at home.

Footsteps rang out behind me. *Okay, so it's not my imagination.* That helped. I forced myself to calm down. By reacting like prey, I'd make whatever this was even more anxious for the kill. *I'm not a victim anymore.* While my skills might be a little rusty, Aegis would take up the slack. The sword vibrated on my wrist, its thirst drying my mouth. For a moment, my vision went white with the need to fight.

Sensing my pursuer behind me, I whirled and swung. Selena barely sidestepped my strike. A lock of her hair dropped to the pavement, and she stared at me hard. "Killing the messenger isn't cool."

"You scared the shit out of me. What're you *doing?*"

"I'm keeping you safe, moron. I'm not the only one tailing you tonight. Weird old git, smells like death and camphor, big burlap sack, two creepy kids. Ring any bells?"

"Crap."

He works for Wedderburn. He killed my mother.

"I thought I'd only have to deal with the hag, but the winter whatsit has a serious hate on for you."

"That's not news," I admitted.

"Just . . . be careful. Big Bro gets pissy when he loses, not that you'll be around to suffer those consequences." Her gaze locked onto my sword, and I hastily deactivated Aegis, but from her speculative expression, it was probably too late.

"Noted. Thanks for the warning."

I wondered what she'd tell Dwyer when she got back. *Guess what? The girl you have me guarding has a sword made out of . . . well, you.* Somehow I suspected our alliance might break down if he discovered that truth. But no point in fretting about it now. Folding my arms, I waited for her reaction.

Selena tapped the side of her nose, and her smile gained layers, like an exquisite stained glass panel. "Something tells me this job will be *way* more interesting than I thought."

A BURST OF
BITTERSWEET

Over the next two weeks, I played hide-and-seek with the bag man, but Selena kept him at bay. I didn't imagine the monster would be content to stalk forever, so once a day, I shifted all the furniture to the wall and practiced the katas Raoul had taught me. I also applied myself to fitness with renewed dedication. Weirdly, my body didn't respond as well as it once did.

It was early March before I saw the Harbinger again. I'd gotten used to leaving school alone, so it was actually a surprise when I came out and found him waiting like he used to. Without meaning to, I hurried toward him, like I'd forgotten that he wasn't my boyfriend, a musician who went on a low-rent tour. But my eagerness colored his reaction, so when I cleared the parking lot and reached the streetlight where he waited, he caught me around the waist and whirled me, before catching me close. He smelled of lightning and cordite, as if he had been firing automatic weapons in a killer storm.

"What a lovely greeting. I take it you missed me?" His eyes held an amusement that managed to impart a sense of melancholy.

"Maybe," I mumbled, feeling like an idiot.

"Do you have time for me tonight?"

"Yeah." My plans were the same as they had been for the past two weeks—hang tight, work out, and hone my sword skills, just in case shit went horribly wrong. Maybe I was paranoid, but I couldn't shake the feeling that this was the calm before the storm.

"Are you staying at the flat?"

I nodded. "Moved in a week ago."

"I'm glad you didn't tarry in that hovel out of misplaced pride. It could give you dysentery." He seemed quite pleased.

But the feeling lingered that everything wasn't as it should be. A shadow or something settled over him, muting his aura. It wasn't like the time he'd spent most of his power liberating me from the Black Watch, so I couldn't decide what to call this intuition.

"It wasn't that bad," I protested. "But the new place is definitely a lot better. Thanks."

"Your appreciation is a panacea, dearling."

The Harbinger scanned the street, and in reflex, I did the same. A couple of people loitering across the way dinged my warning bell, but I couldn't be sure if either one might be the bag man. But the thing would have to be insane to start something at 3:15 in the afternoon with teenagers everywhere and another immortal holding me like I was precious. Shyness wreathed me, and I shoved until he let me go.

"Such modesty," he mocked.

"Let's go before you start a hormonal riot."

Without answering, he took my hand. I expected him to whoosh us at the first opportunity, but he strolled to the bus stop and boarded when the big blue vehicle juddered to a stop. This was like Valentine's Day, only more ominous. The driver smiled when we passed, as I had been riding at this time regularly for a while now. Once we settled into an open seat, I surveyed the Harbinger from beneath my lashes. He was preoccupied enough that he didn't seem to notice my scrutiny.

Or so I thought, until he said, "Something on your mind?"

"It's weird you're on the bus again," I admitted. "I didn't take you for a fan of public transit."

"My way of prolonging the inevitable."

"Excuse me?"

He sighed a little and turned my hand over to inspect my palm. Since I didn't believe in that, I pulled free. "Stop it. You're freaking me out."

"Do you remember when I said we would have a serious conversation?"

"Obviously. It wasn't that long ago."

"Are you certain? Seems an eternity to me." With that weirdness, he fell silent and wouldn't say another word.

When he reached for my hand again, I laced our fingers together. A little shiver went through him, impossible to imagine it was because of me. There had to be a thousand other explanations, only I couldn't think of them with him looking so somber and sad. We didn't speak until we got to the apartment, and instead of bridging the serious subject, he checked out the minute changes I had made.

"Do you like it here?" he asked.

"You mean this place or this time?"

"Clever. Both, I suppose."

"Yes and no."

"The place but not the time? It's like extracting bone marrow to get you to confide anything." For the first time, he sounded truly human, his words limned in frustration and some hidden darkness.

"Sorry. It's just . . . I'm used to hidings things because, with everyone else here, I'm keeping so many secrets."

"But I'm not everyone else," he said, as if that should be obvious.

"Right. Well, the studio is fine. And I'm happy to be forging a new future for Kian, but I can't say I *like* it here. This isn't my time, so I feel weird. Itchy."

"Have you considered coming home? Set your watch. We can go back to right after you left. Your father won't have missed you yet."

"Thanks to the simulacrum you left." I considered that, but the scientist in me needed more information. "What happens if I do?"

He shrugged. "This world exists. Events will unfold with or without you."

"Does that mean Kian could still die on his birthday?"

"You've altered that course, but that doesn't mean some other crisis couldn't arise later. Life doesn't come with certainties or guarantees. But I think you've done enough. So take my hand and let's go back."

It was tempting. But if I went now, I'd never know for sure how things played out. "Not yet. Sometimes being here kind of hurts, actually. But . . . this is worth doing."

"It hurts." The Harbinger actually paled, and he closed his eyes for a few seconds, talking more to himself than me. "So it's begun already. Damn." The mild curse contained anger sufficient to fuel a much stronger word.

"Can we have that vital convo already? All this mystery is getting on my nerves." More to the point, anything that could affect him like this nearly froze me in place.

"Yes, it's time."

I collapsed on the couch more than sat down, angling my body to face him. "Whatever it is, I can handle it."

"At this point, dearling, in the simplest terms, the universe has taken note of you, and nature abhors a paradox. Remember what happened with my pet?"

Space-time parasite, check. Despite my intention to be brave, I shuddered. "Yeah."

"You don't belong in this timeline, and if you linger, you will be erased. The pain you mentioned is the start of that unbinding."

"Like, I'm coming unglued at a molecular level?"

Wow, that's so much worse than I guessed.

He nodded, unable to hold my gaze. "You will simply . . . disperse, if you remain here long enough. And that's presuming one of the immortals gunning for you doesn't get you, or you don't have a terrible accident first."

"You're saying the world itself will eventually start trying to kill me, not just Wedderburn and his ilk."

"I've never known anyone to linger in the wrong time stream for so long, so I can't be sure. But all the data I've uncovered points to yes," he said softly.

"That's where you've been. Researching this for me?"

"For all the good it does."

"No, I'd always rather have all the facts."

"That's why I'm asking you to stop now. You've done enough for atonement, given your beloved boy a second chance. It's time to go home."

Anguish sank its teeth into me and wouldn't let go. "There's still three months left. Wedderburn could still hurt Kian, and who the hell knows what Dwyer will do if I renege on our deal? He might take it out on Kian."

The Harbinger balled up a fist. "Will you erase yourself for him? That's what it will amount to in the end. There's only one way you can stay here safely."

"How?" I demanded.

"Go to Boston. Find your younger self." His smile became malevolent. "And then kill her. Two copies of the same person cannot exist in one world. If you eliminate her, then you can take her future for your own."

My breath went in a pained rush. "*No.* Obviously I'm not doing that."

"Then you will cease to be. Do you understand, Edith Kramer?"

"You just said you don't know how long the breakdown takes. It's possible that I can hold it together long enough and still go home."

"Use your allegedly excellent brain," he bit out. "It's been two months, and the pain is already starting. Based on that ratio and other factors, do you think you'll be fine in June?"

Empirical evidence suggested otherwise. "Probably not."

"Why are you so reluctant to go home?"

I closed my eyes against fresh grief; I had been blocking it by focusing on Kian's situation. "What's waiting for me there? Kian's dead because of me. My mom's grave? Oh wait, maybe it's all the ghosts of the Blackbriar students who died because I made a stupid wish."

"There, that's the truth. You don't want to go back to your old life."

"Not really," I muttered.

"You hoped traveling back could make everything untrue—that you could still be with Kian and see your mother again."

"So what if I did?"

"Face reality. You must leave the boy to handle whatever fate has in store. There's no question that it will be different than what happened in your world, but perhaps he is simply marked for extremis."

"I don't accept that."

"And you're willing to sacrifice everything for him?" The Harbinger's disapproval could not be clearer if he red stamped my forehead. "Your father will grow old and die alone, wondering what happened to you."

"The simulacrum . . ." I realized I didn't know much about the illusion I'd asked him to send to keep my dad company.

"Is fading even now. The energy will last until you go to college, then it simply disappears. So you never reach university, and he won't understand why you vanished. Between that and your mother's murder, your father's future looks bleak indeed."

"You're just saying that to get me to stop," I accused.

He rubbed a hand over his chest. "Didn't you once say I'm cruelest with the truth?"

Direct hit. The devil's choice I feared before wasn't between Kian and the Harbinger but Kian's future and my own. Staying here might condemn my father to God knew what in my own timeline, but then I'd never have any peace, because it wasn't like I could look up what happened to this Kian on the Internet. Tears spilled over as I buried my face in my hands.

The Harbinger pulled me against him, and for long moments, I cried against his chest. He stroked my hair with a tenderness I wouldn't have believed possible. There was no heartbeat to comfort me, but somehow his proximity took the edge off. Eventually I shuddered into quiet, unable to decide what I should do. Abandoning my mission felt like quitting, but I didn't really want to dissolve, either.

I should go home and take care of my dad. My world sucks, but it's because of my failures. So maybe I should give up and live there.

But some small part of me wondered if my father would be happier without me. Time was supposed to heal all wounds, so maybe he'd fall into his work and eventually meet some scientist who would enjoy eating his healthy, bland food. Without me around to remind him of Mom, maybe he'd remarry and move on, even start another family. *Maybe I'd be the albatross around his neck, if I came back.* Before I jumped, he certainly acted like I was more of a bother than a bright spot.

"I can hear you thinking," the Harbinger said. "It's so loud."

"Since when?"

"When we killed the clown as one."

"You didn't see fit to mention this to me before?"

"It would only have agitated you."

"To say the least," I mumbled.

He let me shift, but he didn't relax his hold on me. His aura washed over me in a muted tingle, soothing the phantom pain I'd gotten used to in the past weeks. I didn't even realize how uncomfortable I was until it stopped. My head rested on his shoulder, as exhaustion swamped me. If he wanted to treat me like an actual pet, I'd let him.

"This is the part of the talk I wanted to avoid," he said.

"Why?"

"You see, dearling, I got impatient, so I skipped to the end. And I'm afraid I can't stay."

"Huh?" I mustered the energy to sit away from him. Of all possibilities, I hadn't envisioned this one. The Harbinger had been my one constant, my protector and friend.

"Unless you surprise me. Unless you come home with me. The world you left has little to recommend it, but without you, it will be less." He extended his hand in a symbolic gesture, but if I took it, we'd be gone before I could whisper *good-bye*.

I pushed away from him and stood up. "I'm sorry. I can't. You might not understand, but I have to finish what I started. If I'm still in one piece in June, I'll go then."

"If," he repeated. "And so you choose his future over yours. This is precisely what I saw coming, but I hoped I could change your mind."

"Because it ends badly?"

He showed me his teeth in an expression that couldn't rightly be dubbed a smile. "It always does, dearling. But even I must draw the line somewhere. I've watched so many people die. You can't ask me to witness your passing too."

"I'm not," I whispered.

"Your eyes are. But I'm not listening anymore. It's rarely been so disheartening to be right. You *did* break my heart." There was no levity in his tone as he stared at me.

I retreated a few steps from the hand that wanted to save me. Now I fought the urge to take it. It was hard as hell to accept that this path might mean the end of me and that I must walk it alone. But he had done enough; I should let him go freely and without tears.

Yet they rose to my eyes anyway. Stubbornly, I blinked them away. "Thanks for everything. Maybe . . . think about making some friends instead of keeping people as pets. There's no reason you should be so alone."

"When people are my pets, they need me, not the other way around," he said in a broken voice. "And when they leave, it doesn't make me wish I could die of it."

"But you're going, not me."

"Only because I can't stay for the last act, dearling. I couldn't survive it." Normally, I'd accuse him of hyperbole, but the stark pain in his expression stopped me.

"I'll miss you."

It was the sole truth I had to offer. While my feelings for the Harbinger were twisted as two trees grown into one shadow, I knew that beyond any doubt. Knowing he'd no longer sweep in unexpectedly, never wait for me, and that I'd never hear his music, an invisible fist squeezed ferociously at my heart.

"Must you be gracious? It wouldn't hurt if you asked me to stay. I won't, of course. But somehow I want to hear it."

"I can't," I said, low. "I'm trying not to be a selfish asshole."

His lips twitched in a rueful half smile. "Of course not. You've got altruism to spare. Perhaps that's why I couldn't resist you from the start. The devil always loves what he lacks."

Loves. My insides quivered over that word, but I ignored it. Some questions were better left unspoken.

"I'll ask for a parting gift, however."

That surprised him. "Greedy thing. The flat wasn't enough?"

"Will you play me a song? One last time."

"You appreciate my music that much?"

"It reveals a really lovely soul." I couldn't meet his gaze, so he closed the distance between us and tipped my chin up.

"Shall we call this your requiem?"

Oh, that was unkind. But I didn't have time to fret over the injury. His violin appeared in his hands, and he sailed into a song so gorgeous that it stole my breath. The music poured over me like liquid fire, cleansing and healing. Yet beneath the passion, a purple thread of loss laced through, breaking my heart a thousand times before he finished. I didn't even realize I was crying until he dusted my tears away with gentle fingers.

"You honor me so. If I might, I'll claim a gift in parting too."

"I don't have anything." I sniffled and swiped my hand across my cheeks.

"Untrue. I'd count a kiss from you as a treasure to cherish."

If he wasn't leaving for good, there was no way I'd agree. But since he'd granted my final request, it seemed stingy to deny his. So I lifted my face and closed my eyes. I expected a chaste peck, but instead, long fingers cupped the back of my head and his mouth took mine, cool and firm, intimate as if he knew exactly what I wanted. I moaned a little, and he deepened the kiss, savoring me until my knees nearly buckled. Then I wasn't just receiving a kiss; I gave it back with everything I had. I wrapped my arms around his neck and fell into him like a river.

"You don't taste of innocence," he murmured against my lips. "How delicious."

I had no idea how to respond, so I hid my face in his shoulder. *I can't believe I kissed the Harbinger. I can't believe he's* leaving *me.* Right then I almost begged him not to go. Almost. But I held the words in my mouth like medicine it would kill me to swallow.

Touching his cheek, I said, "Good-bye," instead.

And then he was gone, my arms empty.

I fell apart.

NATURE ABHORS A VACUUM

I t was dark by the time I recovered.

Turning on the lights, I noticed something new on the break-fast bar. The Harbinger had left me a gift he hadn't mentioned, a laptop. I traced the rectangular edge, wishing I could tell him how much this meant; it was invaluable to the next stage of my plan. But then, since he'd been part of me, he probably already knew.

Trembling, both from emotional overload and low blood sugar, I fixed some food and ate it without relish. There was no joy in understanding the reason why the flavor had leached from my favorite dishes. Based on what he'd said, it wouldn't be coming back, either. A pain quake shivered through me, a warning of how bad it would get. I switched the laptop on and found it was already set up with the Internet connection ready to go. In a real sense, before he left, the Harbinger gave me the world.

That knowledge settled me enough to carry the computer to the sofa. I brought up an anime forum I'd belonged to back in the day and searched, then sure enough, I found my username, NamiNerd.

At this point, I only had forty posts or so, most of them about One Piece, as I was completely into pirates at twelve, and it didn't hurt that Luffy was adorable in a goofy way, exactly what junior high girls enjoyed. Skimming the messages gave me a weird feeling as I remembered my old life. Back then, school was tolerable; it didn't get horrible until high school, but I didn't have any friends, so most of my human contact came from the Internet. As long as people left me alone, it was all right.

It would be awesome if I could issue direct, specific instructions, but if I approached my younger self in a weird way, she'd cut me off. So I had to build a rapport, somehow. The Harbinger had been wrong about one thing; I wasn't *only* staying for Kian. Now that I had him on a better path, I had the chance to teach prior me a few things. Maybe I could steer my own life in a happier direction. While I couldn't erase the badness, I could try to ensure it didn't happen in this world too.

Wedderburn will hate this.

Maybe his entire game plan didn't hinge on Kian and me, but he'd already demonstrated that he was a poor loser. With a wry smile, I registered on the site and created a profile for TimeWitch. *People are always strange on the net,* I figured. *Might as well put it in the username.* I chose NamiNerd's most recent post, just a few days back, and responded to her comments with excited agreement. Then in the General Chat subsection, where people could talk about anything they wanted, I found a post I had forgotten I'd written. *I don't like my new school. People are snotty. I wish I had magic powers to make me stand out.* Traffic was less outside the anime sections, and so it sat with a goose egg for replies.

Time to change that.

Maybe you should ask your parents to switch schools. They won't know you don't like it unless you tell them.

Resisting the urge to haunt the forums, I closed the browser tab. If I replied to too many of her messages, she'd wonder, *Who's this weirdo and why is (s)he suddenly so obsessed with me?* The need for patience sucked when I had no idea how long I had. At base, the Harbinger had just informed me I had two months or so to live. I stumbled to my feet, but fear crimped my chest, making it hard to breathe, and that incited another wave of phantom pain. The intensity left me curled on the floor with tears streaming down my cheeks.

I crawled back to the couch and, with shaking fingers, searched for *chronic pain management*. A few sites offered suggestions of meditation, deep breathing, and exercise. These tips were intended for people with fibromyalgia and the like, not those falling apart at an atomic level, but maybe it would help me cope. Unwilling to sit and feel sorry for myself, I changed into sweats and put on my sneakers.

This building had a small fitness center, and fortunately, one of two treadmills was free, so I set it and climbed on. Running for an hour and not going anywhere seemed like a metaphor for my current existence. In the end, I came off the machine sweaty, and the aches retreated some. A middle-aged man lifted his chin at me as I scrubbed a hand towel over my face.

"That was intense," he said. "You looked like something was chasing you."

"Could be."

He reacted like he wasn't sure if I was funny or crazy, so he cracked a halfhearted laugh, playing along with the joke he didn't entirely get. I was in no mood to make small talk, so I headed to my apartment. It had only been a few hours, but I kept wanting to check the window. Any minute, the birds would land all along the ledge, right? Then the Harbinger would sweep back in and say he couldn't leave. But . . . he'd also been the first to tell me not to trust him.

God, what's wrong with me? Before, I couldn't wait to get rid of him.

My phone pinged with a text from Kian, distracting me. *Just watched Fantasia for 10th time. Lil cousins love it. Wassup?*

Time to pretend everything's okay.

But I hesitated, unable to thumb-click the lie on the phone the Harbinger had given me. Shit, I'd have nothing here without him, and he'd taken care of me so slowly and subtly that I didn't balk at accepting his gifts. Shit, when he called in his "debt," I only spent the night with him in the platonic sense. Suddenly, I wanted to cry again.

Existential crisis, I finally texted back.

What's wrong? came the immediate reply.

I didn't mean to tell even a version of the truth, but my fingers had a mind of their own. *Broke up with Colin.* Kian's answer took almost ten minutes this time. *Be right over. Address?*

He must've been explaining to his aunt or uncle. Since it was after eight on a school night, he probably had to do some fast talking to get permission. Things being better at home meant more supervision apparently. Staring at the screen, I hesitated. While it would be nice to let him comfort me, I probably shouldn't. In Vonna's shoes, I'd be pissed if my boyfriend zoomed over to some girl's house the minute she had an emotional problem.

So I replied, *It's fine. I'll talk to you tomorrow,* and turned off my phone. Still, Kian's concern made me feel better, enough to shower and pull down the Murphy bed. I read on the laptop until I fell asleep. In the morning, I ate out of habit more than from hunger. Probably a bad sign, but I ignored that as I packed a basic lunch.

For some reason, it was unseasonably bright and warm. I liked to think Dwyer was behind it, invoking weather *fu* as a sort of immortal *in your face* to Wedderburn. The walk to my stop went down warm and sweet, like good chai tea. The people already waiting had dragged out their pastels in hopes of enticing the sun to stick around. With the winter king in ascendance, Cross Point had seen some record lows and terrifying blizzards this year. When the bus whined to a stop, I waited for everyone else to board.

The driver had a smile for me as I swiped my card. "Early spring, looks like."

"Hope so."

Mornings were always crowded, so I didn't take a seat, though I could've wedged in. At the next stop, a little old lady claimed the spot I hadn't, and that small moment, along with the sunshine, cheered me enough that I was smiling when I got off at school. Kian was already waiting for me, and he seemed pissed. *Oh, right. I shut my cell off.*

"You know how worried I was about you?" he demanded.

"Sorry, I wasn't in the mood to chat."

"It's really hard being your friend. You're so flipping secretive."

The Harbinger had said something similar, just before he took off. *What are the odds?* But I pretended that didn't cut too close to the bone. "You can't make people feel like socializing, dude. Commercials imply girls always want to be with their BFF and eat a pint of

251

ice cream while weeping copiously, but some of us are more like wild animals."

"You'd rather lick your wounds alone and then emerge strong enough to attack again?"

I grinned. Kian always did get me, better than I knew myself sometimes. "Basically."

"Okay. But . . . when you went radio silent, I thought you might disappear again. This time for good." His soft tone didn't disguise that real fear.

The part of me that would always love him melted. "Ah. I'll make you a promise. When I'm ready to move on, I'll say good-bye in person. I won't just vanish. Deal?"

Unless my molecules just go whoosh. In macabre bemusement, I wondered, *Will I go in gold sparks or black smoke?* Or maybe that was reserved for dying immortals, and I'd just wink out of existence like a snuffed candle. Hoping my expression didn't show these thoughts, I managed a smile as Kian studied me.

Then he seemed to relax. "Deal. That makes me feel better. But sometimes the way you talk, it's like I'll never hear from you again. You're going to Miami, right, not Mordor?"

"One does not simply walk into Mordor," I said, deadpan.

He grinned. "You're not walking to Miami, either."

"True."

We headed into school together, as we crossed the parking lot, dodging skateboards, girls showing off chunky heels and short skirts in honor of Dwyer, he said, "Want to talk about it?"

"Not really." There was no question he was asking about my broken relationship.

"Well, what happened?"

252

"Basically, he got tired of my nonsense," I said. "My shitshow of a life and my poor choices. He said he couldn't stick around to watch it end badly."

Kian stopped, eyes wide. "What an asshole."

My defense came out on its own. "Nah, just honest. And . . . he's not wrong. It was always his choice to stay, and now he's chosen to go. I respect his decision, and I don't fault him for it."

"You must love him a lot," he said softly.

"Maybe. It's—"

"Complicated."

A quiet laugh escaped me. "Exactly. Now you're up to speed."

"I'm here if you need to talk about anything or hang out. Oh, there's Vonna." With a parting wave, he hurried to meet her.

She stood in front of the school with a bright smile, looking cute as hell in red walking shorts. When they joined hands and went in together, my heart only hurt a little. Every time I saw them together, he felt more hers and less mine. *Glad I made the right call last night.*

Finally, however, I knew what I could do mitigate the damage I'd unwittingly inflicted on Jake Overman. Today, he looked better, less furious and bitter, and he didn't seem to care that people were ignoring him. But I understood how much pain an apparently imperturbable façade could hide, so after I stopped at my locker, I headed for his.

"Want to have lunch with me? I have a proposition for you."

"Sounds interesting. I'm game."

"Okay, see you then."

On the way to class, I noticed Tanya holding hands with an upperclassman, one of Wade Tennant's cronies. She'd moved on with a quickness, so my plan wouldn't trouble her. But this wasn't all for Jake's benefit; with the best intentions, Kian would probably tell Vonna my depressing news and maybe ask her to cheer me up girl-style. She wouldn't think it was some big secret, so the rest of Devon's group would know soon enough. Based on gossip patterns at Blackbriar, I predicted anyone who cared would know I was single by the end of the day. And Wade seemed like the kind of guy who would pester me, unable to process the fact that I was indifferent to his charms. I mean, shit, the guy sent me a rose back when I had a boyfriend. Ergo, the problem the Harbinger had solved initially still existed.

When lunch rolled around, I went to find Jake, who was standing like a pillar outside the cafeteria. I raised my brown bag. "Got mine here. What about you?"

"Yeah. I've been in the library lately. We're not supposed to eat there, but if you hide behind a book, leaving no mess, they usually don't crack down."

"We can't talk in there."

"Roof?" he suggested.

"Are we allowed?"

"Not really. But nowhere else will be as private."

"Then let's go. I'm not afraid of breaking a few rules." That came out sounding cockier than I intended, and Jake shot me a look.

"Come on. The back stairs are usually unlocked."

This time proved no exception, and we slipped upstairs with no challenges. A few cigarette butts hinted that people liked to smoke here, probably teachers and students alike. Jake led the way around the corner, past a knot of pipes. Here, there were actually ratty cushions that didn't smell very good, but I plopped down anyway. For ambiance this was -10, but as he'd mentioned, the privacy couldn't be better.

"So here's the thing," I started.

"I'm not loaning you money."

I raised a brow. "Excuse me?"

"Just wanted to get that out of the way first. Sometimes people who have seen my house go there, even if it makes no sense."

"That's not what this is about."

"Then go ahead."

"As I see it, we have similar problems with a symbiotic solution."

His forehead crinkled. "You lost me. Nobody thinks you roofied an entire party."

"Let me explain . . ." I outlined my plan.

Jake listened with a growing expression of incredulity. "You want to be my fake girlfriend for a month? You're such a weird girl. If you're into me, just ask me out. We can hang out, see where it goes. If it doesn't work, no harm, no foul." Sometimes it was really obvious he played basketball.

"Not a chance." Sighing, I tried again. "It's obvious to *me* you're still in love with Tanya, and I just broke up with someone. We don't need a relationship; we need a rebound. More to the point, you need other people to see that I believe in your innocence."

"Huh?"

"If I thought you were guilty, we wouldn't go out, right?" This felt like pulling teeth. Who knew it would be so complicated to make him see the benefits? When I thought this scheme up, it seemed straightforward.

"But you're *not* dating me," Jake protested.

Oh God.

"Don't be so literal. I'm offering to do you a favor. Yeah, we'll hang out, but as friends. But everyone else will think—"

"That we're together. Okay, I kinda see the advantage for me, but what about you?"

"You act as a buffer basically. I don't want to be bothered. Wade was hitting on me when I first got here, and he only stopped when he found out about Colin."

"Yeesh. Yeah, he's kind of a stat counter."

"What?"

"You know. Wade likes being the first to tap a new girl if she's hot. He comes on strong until she puts out, and then he never calls again."

"Charming," I mumbled.

"Most girls go for him eventually, though, unless somebody gives them a heads-up in the first week."

"Well, that's gross, and I don't need the complication."

"If I agree to this stupid idea, which seems like it comes straight out of a manga, by the way, you can't fall in love with me." Jake smirked, like this was a real danger.

"Not a problem. You shouldn't get attached, either."

"So one month, fake dating status. Should we write a contract?"

I shook my head, grinning. "That's where they go wrong. Someone always finds it; then there's blackmail drama, and I'm trying to simplify both our lives."

"Then let's work out terms, verbal agreement only."

"Physical contact as necessary to sell the story. We tell no one about our deal." I thought for a moment. "We should probably hang out at least once a week. Anything you want to add?"

"Can we have an option to re-up the contract?"

"I can't promise," I said. "But sure."

"Our breakup has to be mutual. Dating you won't help my reputation if you make up some crazy story about how I like to have sex in front of my grandma's portrait."

When the snicker escaped me, a wash of red colored his cheeks. "That's oddly specific. But definitely, one amicable split, coming up."

"With or without hot fudge?"

"I'll get back to you."

"What are we doing about lunch?" he asked, opening his.

"Where to sit?" At his nod, I considered. "I'm pretty sure we can wedge a chair in Devon's table. People would think it was weird if I suddenly spent all my breaks hiding on the roof with you."

I halfway expected him to object since he'd once sat at the popular table, but Jake seemed relieved. "That's better than the library. Thanks."

"No problem."

"Not just for the lunch-seat offer, for all of this. I still think I'm getting more out of this deal, so I'll be a good boyfriend, I promise."

MY BODYGUARD

The next day when I showed up at the lunch table with Jake in tow, I got more than a few odd looks. But nobody protested when I squished a chair in for him. That left us thigh to thigh, but since we were supposed to be together, I couldn't elbow him away. Plus, I didn't mind because he wasn't taking advantage of the chance for under-the-table action like another guy would've, Wade Tennant for instance.

"So when did this happen?" Devon wasted no time in asking for the scoop.

I exchanged a look with Jake, and at his slight nod, I answered, "Yesterday at lunch. We're just seeing where things go for now."

"Unexpected," Carmen murmured.

Elton stared at me down the table. "You're one of those code-pendent girls, huh? Can't go one day without a boyfriend."

I laughed. "Clearly."

Jake seemed nervous, something that reminded me of Kian's first day at this table. *Man, I'm building networks all over the place.* I remem-

bered the silent woman at the Baltimore and how the Harbinger—
of all people—reminded me that we needed connections to survive.
The friendships I nurtured today likely would outlive me. That stunning, melancholy thought arrested me mid-bite, and it took some
effort to choke down half my sandwich.

At the next conversational lull, Jake said, "I want you guys to
know that I didn't do . . . whatever went down at my party."

"It was probably somebody who wanted you out of the way,"
Nathan said.

"What?" Jake stared at him.

"Oh God help us, he encouraged Nathan." Amanda put her head
down on the table in a parody of despair.

The reason behind her reaction clarified when Nathan expounded
for ten minutes on how the junior now dating Tanya probably
bribed someone to make Jake look bad. By the time he finished the
conspiracy theory, Carmen was pelting him with pickles and
Vonna couldn't stop laughing. Even Kian cracked a smile, though
he hadn't been in their group any longer than me. Still, there was
something hilarious about Nathan's outrage.

"What? You know I'm right. It totally makes sense. I mean, Jake's
sitting with us now, and his girl's off with someone else. It—*ow*.
Why'd you hit me?" He glared at Amanda.

She scowled right back. "You act like our table has leprosy. Plus,
Jake's already with someone else."

"It's not the dumbest idea I ever heard," Jake said, narrowing his
eyes.

Devon shook his head. "Don't go down that road."

"That's probably wise. Whatever." Jake shrugged and inspected
how much was left of my lunch. "You're not hungry?"

"I'm not a big eater." *Anymore*, I added silently.

"Then can I have it?" At my nod, he pulled my leftovers toward him with a ravenous joy that made me laugh.

"So when you get popular again, are you planning to drop us like hot potatoes?" Elton wondered aloud.

Between his lack of tact and putting on porn on movie night, I suspected Elton might be the socially awkward one in the group. Someone kicked him under the table, but Elton must have been used to this because he dodged. While everyone glared, Jake fielded the question.

"You probably won't believe me, but I'm done with them. I'm looking for low-key, no drama and minimal backstabbing."

"That's us." Carmen lifted her soda can for a mock toast.

Initial hurdle passed, the rest of lunch went quickly, as did afternoon classes. Jake came to my locker in his practice clothes, likely to lend credence to our hookup. We attracted some looks from people leaving school, but when I made eye contact, they hurried by. He shook his head with a faint sigh.

"Lemmings, am I right?"

He nodded. "So lunch was fun. Maybe we can do something this weekend. Can I come over to your place?"

"Why not?"

Suddenly, he shifted from casual to intense and his voice got louder. "Anyway, I have training camp after school all this week. We didn't make state finals, which is where we should be this weekend. So Coach scheduled extra sessions to help us." He used air quotes around the word *help*. "Feels like punishment."

And you're telling me this why?

"Uh-huh . . ."

My tone must've said, *I fail to see how this pertains to me*, because he went on, a little louder. "Normally, I'd take you out, so I thought you should know it's not that I don't want to." Jake shifted his eyes slightly to the right.

When I glanced over, I spied Tanya doing a crappy job of eavesdropping. So I fell into my role with enthusiasm. Going up on tiptoe, I put my hand on his shoulder. Obligingly, he leaned down so I could whisper in his ear, "You're seriously trying to make her jealous?"

His grin made his eyes sparkle. "Maybe. Is that wrong?"

"Hey, you're broken up. She can't mind what you do."

"Exactly." He straightened and tapped his finger twice on his cheek. "One for luck?"

Why not? It wasn't like my lips were gold-plated, and people in all over the world greeted complete strangers with kisses. But when I went in, he whipped his face toward mine so my mouth landed on his. And we both froze, me from plain shock, him probably that such an old trick worked.

Then he cupped my face in his hands and took it to the next level. *Wow.* Jake was a really good kisser, and I didn't have to be crazy in love to enjoy making out. We both got a little more into it than we expected. I forgot Tanya was watching, and I suspected he did too because he looked kind of flummoxed when I pulled back.

"That should tide you over," I mumbled.

"Maybe. Let's make sure." He leaned down for seconds, and I shoved at his chest.

"Go run sprints and do crunchies and herkies or whatever you athletes are into."

He laughed so loud he almost snorted. "Sprints, yes, and I think you mean crunches. Herkies sound like an STD, but those are cheerleader jumps."

"Bet you can't do one."

"You would be right." Jake tousled my hair as he went by, a gesture that should pass for real affection.

Three, two, one . . .

Tanya didn't disappoint me in the speed with which she rounded the corner, but she didn't stop to chat. Instead, I got a nod. Her expression didn't tell me much, but at least she wasn't the type to act like a fool over a guy she left. Turning, I found Kian ten feet away. Guilt surged through me until I remembered he wasn't my boyfriend . . . and he shouldn't be looking at me with that odd mixture of hurt and confusion.

"What's wrong?" I asked.

"That was some PDA. Are you sure you're not rushing this?"

I shrugged. "That's the least of my worries. Jake knows I'm not looking for some big serious thing and that I'm on my way out." Well, that last part, not exactly, but he understood our deal was temporary.

"I'm more concerned about him," he muttered.

"Huh?"

"You have this alluring, unattainable quality." He struggled for words, like he couldn't figure out how to articulate it without pissing me off. Finally, he settled on, "Even when you say, *I'm leaving soon,* you make people want to be the one who can make you stay."

People? You mean you? I fought the urge to ask. There was zero chance of a happy ending between Kian and me, so I had to keep him at arm's length.

"You can't *make* someone stay," I said softly. "They have to want that."

He let out a slow breath, clearly conflicted. "And maybe I shouldn't admit this, but it bothers me that you invited him over so easy after you told me no. Twice, actually. We're supposed to be best friends, but—"

"Whoa, hold up. My circumstances have changed. Colin doesn't live there anymore." Not that he ever did—with *me* anyway.

"Oh, you kept the apartment? I'm glad. Your room was so shitty."

I ignored his commentary about the Baltimore. "So if you want to come over, it's fine. The main reason I hesitated the other night is because I didn't want to give Vonna any reason to distrust you when you're just starting out."

"Oh, shit." It seemed like Kian hadn't even thought of that. "I'm pretty new to this stuff. Maybe I should talk to her before we make plans?"

"If it was me, even if there was nothing to worry about, I'd still want to be kept in the loop. It's respectful. Not like you're asking permission, more that you care about her feelings."

Kian smiled, the shadows fading from his gaze. "I feel like you're tutoring me in how to be a decent boyfriend."

"Vonna will handle the advanced classes."

After that, I went home to find two messages on the anime board—from myself. That was pretty trippy, but I still read them eagerly. I continued the conversation about One Piece and then skimmed what she'd said about the school issue.

God, it's odd referring to myself in the third person.

Per the timestamp, she'd written this one first, so it had a more formal tone than our mutual squeeing in the anime thread. *Hi Time-Witch. (Cool handle btw. Which show is that from? I'll check it out.) Basically there's no point in telling my parents anything. They never listen to a word I say. They nod along and then tell some story from childhood that has nothing to do with anything. It's hopeless. Maybe college will be better.*

I could tell that young me was purposely trying to sound older. Smiling, I typed, *Then make them take you seriously. If they respond to facts, compile some. Also, parents love deals. Tell them you'll do one year at your current school to make them happy, but if you're still miserable at the end, then they make you happy by sending you somewhere else. P.S. Have viable alternatives lined up, as it's always easier to sell a concrete plan. Good luck!*

That was more than enough. If she couldn't get out of Blackbriar with the suggestions I'd provided, then I'd be disappointed in myself. To keep from looking like a potential stalker, I posted in a few other random threads, ones that hadn't been started by Nami-Nerd. Afterward, I clicked over to a few sites that Ryu and Vi had mentioned frequenting in their misspent youths, but I didn't know their usernames. Probably just as well, I shouldn't muck around in their timelines. They might both be better off not meeting me.

Around nine, my intercom went off. Since nobody but the Harbinger knew where I lived, my heart quivered to life. *He wouldn't come back this way. Not his style. He loves big entrances and pageantry.* There was no way he'd just come home and ring the bell.

Heh. Home.

Yet I still rushed to the panel and pressed the talk button. "Yeah?"

"It's me. Can I come up?"

Oh.

Selena's voice shouldn't disappoint me this much. I buzzed to open the front door. "You know what floor I'm on?"

"Of course."

I opened the door when I heard her footsteps in the hall. "Welcome, I guess."

As usual, she was Goth-punk fabulous. She surveyed the room before taking a seat on the sofa. "I want to talk logistics."

"About?"

"Our hunt. The way you reacted to me shadowing you says you're not a victim, plus that glowing sword of yours? I'm *dying* to see it in action. You can't be willing to let the bag man set the rules of engagement." She sounded more like a teen girl talking about the newest cell phone than an ancient, immortal being.

I considered. "Makes sense. And no, I don't really want to fight on his turf and terms."

"You've got good instincts. Back in the day, you could've been one of my acolytes."

"Pass," I said.

Seeming offended, Selena got up and went to rummage in my fridge, returning with a bottle of mineral water. "That wasn't on offer."

Something about her manner seemed familiar. "Wait, do you know Allison?"

"Who?" A blank look met mine as she cracked open her drink.

"Lilith. I bet you'd know her as Lilith."

"Shit, yes. We're hunting buddies. Or . . . we used to be anyway."

"Huh. Small world," I muttered. "Did you fight or something?"

"She took to prowling for easy meat in schools, and that's so not my scene. It's hardly sporting to take down prey that's constantly in a hormonal state of flux that equates to a lapse in faculties. Like fish in a barrel, you know."

"You think teenagers are mentally impaired?" Since I didn't want Selena hunting with Allison, I decided to leave it that. *Better not to argue sometimes.*

"Aren't they? Anyway, back to the bag man. I propose using you as bait. You wander around, somewhere that we've scouted. I'll hold far enough away that he doesn't sense me. Then when he thinks you're helpless, we spring our trap and glorious combat ensues."

"I like the idea of turning the tables, but won't he wonder why you're suddenly not guarding me anymore?"

Selena tapped a long black nail against her white teeth. "Good point. Maybe Big Bro could let slip about my 'new top secret orders' to interested parties?"

"Are we seriously using gossip against immortal entities?"

She grinned. "We come from humans after all. So . . . duh."

"This is a separate issue, but . . ." I hesitated, wondering how far I could trust her. Buzzkill helped me, until Wedderburn ordered him not to. Selena was probably loyal to Dwyer, who might or might not be her brother. "What do you plan to tell him about my sword?"

"The feeling I get from it, I'd sound crazy if I tried to explain it to him. So I intend to take credit for any of our victories. Got a problem with that?" She chugged the rest of her fizzy water and let out a burp that could've leveled a small town, then giggled. "Damn, that's fun. Only reason I ever drink anything."

Whoa.

With some effort, I directed the conversation away from her gaseous hobby. "I don't, actually. For me, that's a best case scenario. Don't worry, I won't be around long enough to cause trouble for you."

"Trouble? I thrive on it, so that's the last thing you should worry

266

about. But I'm suddenly fascinated by where you might go that one of us couldn't find you."

"No comment," I said.

"As long as you make it possible for Big Bro to win this round, it's fine by me. He's betting heavily on you, by the way. It's been like a hundred years or something since he beat the winter whatsit."

"A round is a hundred years?" I asked, astonished.

"No, dummy. But he's lost the last ten. Forfeited somewhere in there because of a big fire, no, that was more than ten rounds ago . . . maybe it was an earthquake? Regardless, he's so thrilled that you have his opponent this agitated."

"It's a gift."

But her careless words put into perspective what I was up against, the scale of what these creatures had seen and the span of time they planned over. To Wedderburn, I must feel like a bug on his windshield that just wouldn't die. It was . . . staggering. Selena talked a little more in a disjointed fashion, and then she sprawled on my couch.

"Um. I'm going to bed soon."

"Go ahead. I think I'll stay here for a while. Safer for you, cozy for me." The concept of privacy or personal space seemed alien to these creatures, and I couldn't piss her off when she was keeping a dangerous secret for me.

Great, looks like I have a roomie. Kian would be hurt if I told him not to come over again, so maybe I could get her to leave temporarily or explain her as my cousin. *Whatever.* I showered, put on sweats in the bathroom, and pulled down my bed to the soothing sounds of a chain saw on the TV. Selena seemed to thrive on the screaming and the blood spatter, which explained why she'd been good hunting buddies with Allison. It would have been normal for me to struggle to fall asleep, but in a weird way, her presence was comforting.

For the first time in a while, I slept like a rock. When I woke up, she was curled up like a cat on my sofa, TV off. I skipped breakfast and quietly slipped out for school. I found Jake Overman waiting for me in a chauffeured car. *What the hell?*

"What're you doing?"

More important, how did you find me?

He gazed up at the building with a curious expression. "I'm not actually here to see you."

Ducking his head with a faint sigh, he explained. "I *own* this property. My dad makes me check in with the building manager every so often, and I don't have time after school, so—"

"That leaves early mornings. Got it. Also, holy shit, you own a building."

"It's to build my portfolio and gain real experience handling assets," he mumbled.

I gave him the best mock sympathy money couldn't buy. "Rich-people problems. It's so sad when all you want to do is kiss girls and play basketball, probably not in that order."

"You're the only one who understands me."

"It's not hard. Your subtext is written in crayon on big line paper."

"Harsh. Listen, if you want to wait in the car for ten minutes, I'll take you to school with me after I talk to the manager."

Pretending to shrug, I acted like it was no big deal to ride in a Rolls or whatever the hell this was. "Sure, if you want."

Just then, Selena came running out with no shoes, her eyeliner smeared wildly. "How can you just leave without saying anything?"

She checked when she saw Jake, but his brows were already trying to climb his forehead to reach Mount Top of Head. *Awesome. My fake boyfriend thinks I have a real girlfriend.* And I was trying to simplify, not add drama. The silence was excruciating.

"I'll . . . let you guys talk," he said finally.

ALL THE WRONG
REASONS

As soon as Jake disappeared inside, I couldn't contain my laughter. "His expression was priceless. What did you want to talk about?"

"We didn't decide when we're scouting or the day of the hunt." From her annoyed moue, I should've known that.

In my admittedly limited experience, Selena did have something of a one-track mind, so I wasn't surprised she thought this was urgent business. "Whenever. Just keep me posted."

"Excellent. This hunt is in the bag." She seemed really pleased with that pun.

So I chuckled, and she brightened up as she headed for the building. Jake came out a few minutes later, seeming relieved that the encounter wouldn't be repeated. He opened the back door for me, and we both slid in. Though this wasn't a stretch limo, there was a partition in back.

He lowered it partway to say, "School, please."

"Right away, sir."

No joke, it was all kinds of weird to hear a fortysomething guy address Jake like that. When the frosted Plexiglas went back up, I said, "So you're basically Lex Luthor, huh?"

"Why do I have to be a supervillain? Besides, I'd much rather talk about the girl whose heart you broke last night."

"Pics, or it didn't happen." I invoked the twenty-fourth rule of the Internet.

"I can't believe you're already cheating on me." Jake let out a mournful sigh. "But you're wrong in your assessment of my subtext."

"I am?"

"I'd rather be playing basketball and kissing people, not just girls."

That surprised me, mostly that he was telling me out of the blue. In my experience, people needed to know you longer before opening up, but hell, we already shared a secret. So maybe this was a demonstration of trust?

He went on. "So you don't have to lie to me. That girl's clearly not your cousin. It's cool, I get where you're coming from. Plus, I'm aware that there are no family units in my building. Those are all studios, so you must be living with her, not your parents. Did they kick you out?"

Wow, he was ready to dive into my business. Sadly, it wasn't an outlandish assumption; too many parents reacted that way to learning their kid wasn't purely straight. I could probably use this to my advantage somehow, but since he was being so open on his end, I couldn't do it. Instead, I gave an honest response.

"I haven't seen my folks in a while," I admitted. "But actually I'm the one renting the studio and she's staying with me, but not because we're together."

"Sorry, I thought you were bi." The unspoken *like me* hung between us, and his expression slid toward awkward chagrin. Jake seemed to realize he'd misunderstood and that there was no reason for him to have confessed out of solidarity.

I found myself saying, "To be honest, it hasn't been that long since I've been remotely datable for reasons I won't go into. Back in the day, my self-esteem was so low that I think I would've gone out with anyone who asked. I was basically that lonely."

His eyes swept me from top to bottom, obviously wondering why I'd thought so little of myself. "I'm glad you're not in that place anymore."

Nodding, I added, "That said, there have been a few times when I've thought certain girls are really pretty and even wondered—"

"So . . . you *are* bi?"

I shook my head. "I think . . . I could probably be attracted to anyone, under the right circumstances and if our personalities are a good fit."

The Harbinger came to mind. He usually presented as male, but he'd indicated that he could be female during one conversation. Since he didn't have mortal limits, he could be whatever he wanted or something entirely new. Yet my feelings wouldn't change, no matter what he looked like. It was the crazy, chaotic, yet tender heart that moved me.

My feelings . . . what are *they?* I shied away from examining them, as it didn't matter. He'd gone, leaving me to face what lay ahead alone.

"Ah, that's pan. It's cool you realized it. But you're not the person I thought you were."

It's mutual. This was *not* the conversation I expected from Jake,

272

who was deeper than I'd realized. When I first met him, I saw only a jock, but he definitely had layers.

"You too," I said. "How come you're not at some pricey prep school?"

"My father thinks they're a waste of money. He's self-made, and he got where he is without paying for a fancy education. He says it's up to me to capitalize on opportunities and to learn what I need to master life on my own, if necessary."

"Wow. He sounds hard-core."

Jake sighed as we turned down the street the school was on. "Exhausting, more like. He's always traveling for work, and I get e-mail bulletins with sudden work assignments at the weirdest times. Like, he'll be in Dubai and decide I have to check on our properties in Phoenix, and never mind the time difference or the fact that I have school."

"That sounds awful."

"Most people only see the house and the car. Don't get me wrong, it's better to have money than not, but my life's definitely not my own."

"What about your mom?" Honestly, I expected to hear that he was on stepmother number four, and she was only five years older than him.

"She travels with my dad, mostly. I had nannies when I was younger, but last year I convinced them I didn't need constant supervision."

"Huh. Well, I bet a lot of people at school would like to swap lives so they can try your problems for a while."

He smiled at that. "Sometimes I'd take that deal."

The driver pulled up the semicircle in front of the school office, and Jake got out without waiting for the door to be opened. I didn't expect so many students to be out front, but since it was a bright morning, another happy smile from Dwyer, everyone was sprawled on the cement, faces turned to the sky like blossoming sunflowers. It also meant tons of witnesses to report on the fact that I'd arrived with Jake. The whispering started straightaway.

"Looks like your plan is working." He plucked my grubby back-pack from my shoulder and carried it inside along with his.

Hurrying after him, I tried to repo my stuff, but he didn't stop until he reached my locker. "I don't need a porter."

"It's just one of the many services I provide."

"Great line." When I turned, Wade Tennant stood nearby. "I have a bone to pick with you, dude. I saw her first. I even sent her a damn rose on Valentine's. So I should've been first on deck. So why are *you* with her?"

"Because I have free will and get to choose?"

But Wade ignored me. I might be a butterfly on a pin for all the notice he took. Instead, he glared at Jake, like any of this made sense. God, would it kill him *not* to add my notch to his bedpost? If we were last people on earth, I'd choose a boulder instead of him as my life partner because at least it would be a good listener. But this bullshit was exactly what I wanted to avoid and part of why I'd offered to help Jake. Wade had a real entitlement problem, as I shouldn't need a guy's stamp on me to be left alone. My own *hell no* should be sufficient, and it pissed me off that it wasn't. Since Wade was a senior, he seemed to think Jake should just give way.

Like I'm not even a person.

"I'm not a moon rock," I said loudly. "It doesn't matter who saw me first. There can be no dibsing on me, you get that? Now piss off."

My voice attracted the attention of the passing counselor, whose eyes narrowed when he realized it was the grieving student. "Is everything all right, Chelsea?"

That name gave me a jolt since I'd gotten used to Nine. "Fine. Jake was about to walk me to class."

Now I sound like Tanya.

But Jake took the cue I lobbed and escorted me without complaint. "That was . . . weird. I've only known Wade a few months, but I've never seen him so single-minded. Usually he's fairly laid-back, part of his charm."

Wedderburn. A little shimmer of horror went through me. He'd driven Tanya to be uncharacteristically cruel and then to kill herself, so maybe he was twisting Wade's normal conquering instincts into something more sinister. Maybe I was overreacting, but it was hard not to hear the winter king whisper, *I'll have you raped and killed.*

Concerned, Jake touched my shoulder. "Don't let him get to you."

Easier said than done, maybe. But I'd be vigilant.

So I spent the day dodging Wade and stuck with the crowd as we left school in the afternoon. In his basketball clothes, Jake walked me out, ever the attentive fake boyfriend. He paused on the front steps, smiling down at me.

"This is as far as I can take you."

"Look out!" someone yelled from the parking lot.

Jake reacted with an athlete's reflexes and yanked me away, back toward the building, and where we had been standing, two huge cement blocks smashed to the ground. My breath wheezed in my lungs, starting another wave of phantom pain. He didn't let go of me, probably because I shook so hard, gritting my teeth against the anguish, that I would've fallen down. Fortunately, he took the episode for sheer terror, so he rubbed my back and told me I was okay.

"What the hell are they doing on the roof?" A teacher whose name I didn't know sent someone to check it out.

Kian arrived a few seconds later, his face pale. "Are you all right? What happened?"

Jake filled him in while I tried not to bite my tongue. My fingers glowed gold again, so I hid them in Jake's practice shirt, tangling in the fabric like I couldn't get close enough to him. He was big and protective for sure, and I wished I could thank him for taking the focus off my near incapacitation. From what I gathered, strong emotions made things worse. So fear, anger, passion—all of that needed to stop. I'd last longer if I remained calm.

The principal came out a few minutes later. By then I'd settled enough to give my version of events. He listened with a worried frown. *Probably afraid I'll sue.*

"I'm truly sorry, Miss Brooks. I'll personally oversee the investigation and ferret out the responsible culprits. If this was meant as a prank, it is spectacularly unfunny."

"It's okay. Jake has fast hands."

"That's what she said," a guy called from behind us.

The principal fixed a stern look on him and then turned back to me. "I'll be happy to chat with your parents and give them my personal assurance regarding your safety."

Oh, shit.

"They're pretty busy," I mumbled.

"I'm sure they'll make time when they learn how serious this could've been."

Time for some scare tactics. I lowered my voice. "Actually I wasn't planning on telling them. Having two attorneys in the family sucks sometimes. They tend to be . . . litigious."

The wheels started turning in the principal's head, and I could see him mentally listing potential lawsuits. "Well, if you think that's best. But my office door remains open anytime."

Jake waited until the crowd dispersed somewhat before calling me on my bullshit. "I thought you'd hadn't seen them in a while."

To borrow a word from Selena . . . "Duh. Don't you need to get to practice?"

"I'll be late. Coach will make me run twenty laps. Big deal."

"Are you sure?" If my muscles didn't feel like cooked spaghetti, I probably would dismiss him. This was getting a little too close to a real relationship.

"Definitely. People would think I was an asshole if I abandoned you that fast."

Right. And we're trying to fix his reputation.

Just beyond, the janitor piled broken cement fragments into a rusty wheelbarrow. From his expression, he'd like to go upside the head of whoever created the mess. Since there was no blood, people lost interest and went about their business. Jake wrapped an arm around my shoulders and led me to a bench just inside the front doors.

"Thanks," I said.

"No problem. Let me get you a coffee from the vending machine. How do you take it?'

"I didn't know we had one." I'd seen the soda ones, of course.

"It's in the teacher's lounge, but there won't be anyone in there right now. Teachers are either bugging out for the day or in the clubs they sponsor."

"Then light and sweet please." The sugar might help, even if I didn't taste it.

"Be right back."

True to his word, he appeared with a small cup of hot liquid that might well be horrible. I drank it all while he sat beside me. I got up and threw it away, enjoying the energy rush. "Seriously, I'm fine now. Go be an athletic star."

"Okay." He dropped a casual kiss on my forehead, and while I wasn't in love with him, it was easy to pretend he actually cared— that this wasn't part of the show.

"That was crazy," Kian said.

For maybe the first time ever, I hadn't noticed him hovering nearby. *Does that mean I'm getting over him?* Now he stepped away from the wall and came toward me, radiating muted concern. I nodded as we headed to the bus stop together. *The universe is officially trying to kill me.* Did that mean it wasn't safe for me to ride public transportation? But that accident would've only injured me, so I guessed I didn't have to worry about massive disasters. That would be like nuking a roach from space.

As we reached the stop, he said, "Word is, there was no construction going on today, so it must've been students."

"How do you know?"

"While you were making Jeffers stand down, I asked around. Did you piss someone off?"

Wryly, I shrugged. "Hard to say, but all signs point to yes."

"This isn't funny, Nine. If you know who it is, speak up. You nearly died today." He scowled until the bus came, refusing to talk to me.

I followed him on board and sat next to him, despite the backpack he put in my way. "Don't be mad. I really don't know. Maybe it was people who think dropping rocks off overpasses is fun."

"Idiots," he muttered.

There was no way I could tell the truth. *Nobody did it. The world is trying to murder me.* Just picturing how that conversation would go made me shake my head. Kian caught the movement in his peripheral vision, and he touched my arm, his demeanor softening.

"Sorry. I'm not upset with you. Honestly, I'm pissed that someone tried to hurt you and I can't do anything about it."

I leaned my head against his shoulder, friend-style. "It's enough that you want to."

"Sure, and Jake gets to be your hero."

On some level, it seemed like Jake and me bothered him more than Colin had. *I wonder why.* So I asked.

Kian sighed. "I wish I knew."

"You don't like Jake?" That probably wasn't the reason, but I chose not to encourage any sparks of latent attraction. Obviously, we were good together, but not in this world.

It can't happen, I told him silently. *Sorry.* But part of me exulted over the fact that on some level, he sensed that maybe we *should* be together. That had to be hellaciously confusing.

"It's not that. Never mind. I'm probably just being sensitive."

That's part of what of what I loved about you. Time to change the subject.

"I didn't see Vonna today. Is she okay?"

"Sore throat. She messaged me this morning. Would it be weird to show up with lozenges and soothing tea?"

Somehow I'd become his relationship coach. *I can live with that.* Considering, I shook my head. "But text first. I know you want to surprise her, but she might prefer not to see you if she's feeling puny. People are cranky when they're sick, so your good intentions might get lost."

"Good idea," he said, already typing on his phone. He let me read over his shoulder as the chat happened, and it was incredibly cute.

Kian: *Missed U today. Feeling any better?*

Vonna: *A little. Miss U 2. Will try to make it tmrw.*

Kian: *Want a care package later?*

Vonna: *Ur sweet. Y, if U want.*

At that point, I stopped reading. Apparently, she was okay seeing him now. Maybe it wasn't a big deal to her, but it seemed like one to me. This was such a contrast to the time we rode the bus together and listened to his music, sharing his earbuds. Once he finished, he showed me a picture he'd taken of Vonna when she wasn't looking. The camera on his phone was shitty compared the ones I'd left behind, and selfies weren't a thing yet.

"Isn't she pretty?"

"Definitely," I said.

My stop came along as he got another text, so with a feeling of bittersweet inevitability, I left Kian in Vonna's capable hands.

GOOD WITCH HUNTING

Morning meditation seemed like a stupid idea at first but it settled me, so I started the day on an even keel. I wrapped up and climbed to my feet to find Selena watching me while she rummaged in my cupboards. She had been here for over a week and showed no sign of vacating anytime soon.

"You don't have any olives," she told me.

"I hate them. So no, I don't."

"I could eat them by the jar, especially the ones that are a little fishy." Her disappointment carried a tangible weight.

"I'll pick some up on the way home."

"Don't forget that we're hunting tonight."

"I got it." We had scouted a locale about a mile from here, the biggest park in Cross Point, and after dark, it was ideal for our purposes.

Snagging my lunch, I waved as I went out. Jake and his driver were parked at the curb, one of the perks of our fake relationship. He didn't take me home in the afternoons since he had a later pickup, but cutting my daily bus time down by half rocked. The ride was quiet as Jake thumbed through a textbook.

"Test?" I asked when he glanced up.

"Did you forget?" He held the book up, and I recognized it from the class we had together.

"Kind of. But I'll be fine."

"I'm torn between admiring your confidence and hoping you fail."

"That's not on the list of acceptable boyfriend behavior."

He smirked and ruffled my hair. Once the driver dropped us off, we made our usual entrance together and then went our separate ways. It was normal that he'd stop walking me to every single class as time went on. Too much hovering sent the message that things were shaky or that somebody was feeling needy.

God, I'm tired of high school.

The two and half months I had left seemed interminable. My life didn't improve when the counselor flagged me down the period before lunch. I was walking with Devon, and he cocked his head, silently asking what was up. I shrugged slightly and followed Dr. Miller into his office. According to the certificate on his wall, he had a PhD in school psychology from the University of Houston. He indicated the seat on the other side of his desk.

"I just wanted to touch base. It's been a while since our last chat. How are you doing?"

"Better," I said, because that was he wanted to hear.

Actually, Doc, I'm falling apart. Literally. I might go poof in your office if I let myself feel sad. Or happy. Or angry. Or . . . anything at all.

Constantly seeking inner peace might sound like a good thing, but after all, it seemed a lot like going emotionally numb. He wrote something down, and I noticed he had my file open on his desk. *Doesn't he have other students to worry about?* I clenched my teeth and tried not get pissed off. If I had an attack in here, God only knew what would happen.

"Are you working on the journal like I asked you to?"

"Yeah. It's a real relief."

"Obviously, this is your choice, but I'd be happy to—"

"No, thanks. I mean, the only way I can write what I feel is knowing nobody else will ever read it. It's so liberating." I headed that offer off at the pass.

The flattery seemed to ease his disappointment at not getting a peek at my inner workings. "That's all I wanted. I'm glad you're making progress. Your teachers say that your work is solid."

"That's good to know." This would probably thrill him. "I was thinking . . . when I'm done writing, I might collect some things that remind me of my mom and bury them along with my journal, kind of a like a time capsule. Is that dumb?"

He perked up, steepling his hands. "Definitely not. That's a great step, Chelsea. When you feel stronger, you can examine these emotional artifacts."

"Yeah, maybe in five years or something." *Time I don't have.*

Minus the journal, I wished I could do this. But I'd have to go to Boston and rob my old house, and that would likely create all kinds of weird ripples. Hell, who knew what the universe would do if I got too close to my double? The Harbinger had said I could steal her future by killing her, but the world might swat me a like a bug first.

"I feel like you're in a much better place. Let me write you a pass, okay?"

"Thanks."

The halls were deserted when I stepped out of the guidance office. I hurried toward my next class, already in session, when Wade Tennant sauntered out of the bathroom. He cut a look at the door I'd just come out of and then smirked, folding his arms across a broad chest. Aegis prickled on my arm, an early warning of how bad this could get.

"So a girl really does need to be crazy to turn me down," he said, evidently thinking that was clever. "Why else would you be with Overman?"

"Leave me alone." I tried to go around him, but he grabbed my arm, and Aegis sent a shiver-shock from fingertips to elbow.

Let's kill him, the sword whispered.

Well, that's new. Was it possible that part of Dwyer's personality survived the forging and I had what amounted to a sentient weapon? *Disturbing.* I used a move I'd learned from Raoul, grabbing his hand and twisting Wade's arm so it could pop out of socket if he resisted. The pain startled him, so he swung at me.

No, you did not. I'm so tired of putting up with shit like this.

Pouncing, I kicked his legs out from under him and activated Aegis with a whisper and a touch. Gold sparks enveloped me as the pain started. *Right, anger bad, sword pretty.* With a twist of my lips, I touched the tip to his throat. "This is as clear as I can make it, asshole. Don't mess with me again."

I didn't count on him nearly pissing his pants and screaming his head off. Doors banged open as I hid my weapon. The big idiot scrambled away from me, huddling against the wall, and when a teacher popped his head out to see what was up, Wade went off on

284

an incoherent rant. The way he spoke reminded me of Nicole the day she snapped.

Something's definitely messing with him.

"Nine beat me up," he babbled. "Then she threatened to kill me and she was glowing all over, and she's got a sword."

Dr. Miller came out in time to hear that, and he signaled to the teacher in some professional code that he'd take charge of the situation. "Calm down, Mr. Tennant. I just had a conference with Miss Brooks, and I can assure you she's unarmed."

"Damn, he's seriously tripping," someone said, peeking through where a teacher had left the door slightly ajar.

"Take your seats," the counselor ordered.

A series of clicks followed, until it was just the three of us. Miller tried to calm Wade, but he only repeated his outlandish claims. Jaw set, Miller turned to me for a sensible version of the story. Possibly wrong, but I'd enjoy this. I hadn't entirely lost my taste for revenge.

My gaze dropped to the floor. "He's been bothering me, off and on, since I started here. Today he was waiting for me to pass by and said some mean stuff about my boyfriend, Jake. When I tried to leave, he grabbed me. I was about to yell for help when he suddenly fell over and started acting weird."

"That is . . . bizarre," Miller said.

"Tell me about it." With a hesitant smile, I tugged at my hoodie. "I can take this off if you want to check me for a blade."

As expected, he laughed. "You obviously don't have a broadsword in your back pocket. Go on to class. I'll take it from here."

"Okay. I hope he feels better."

"That's generous, if what you said about his prior behavior is true."

"Don't take my word for it, ask around." With that, I headed to class, which should've been the end of it, but everyone was riled up, whispering questions as I tried to slip in quietly.

"Did Wade Tennant really freak out?"

"Was it drugs?"

"Is he being suspended?"

"They should send him to rehab."

The teacher slammed her book on the desk to settle the students. "Enough. Chelsea, please give a quick summary so we can move on."

I repeated a version of what I'd told Dr. Miller, best to stick with the same story. The whispering finally died down when the period was nearly over. We didn't cover as much material as planned, and people were still gossiping when the bell rang. During lunch, I hid in the library, partly because I was done talking about Wade, plus I had no desire to pick at my food and pretend to find it delicious. Nobody found me, either, which was the best part of the day.

After school, I avoided both Kian and Jake, who were canvassing the school. After turning off my phone, I went out a side door and sprinted for the bus stop before they realized I'd already gone. My luck held; the bus was starting to pull away, but I bounded up and slapped the glass; the driver stopped and let me on. Wheezing, I fell into a seat and got off six stops up, then transferred, heading downtown. I still shopped at the bodega because I preferred it to the upscale organic market. Plus José and Luisa had been so good to me, they should get my money now that I had some.

This bus reeked of curdled milk, and the driver was surly. I found a seat near the back, and a homeless guy plopped down in front of me. But when he shifted, I recognized his profile. *Raoul? Is this the Black Watch starting some new shit with me?* The Harbinger and I had pretty much ransacked one of their outposts, and I hadn't spotted Raoul watching me, but maybe he'd gotten better at surveillance. *Where the hell is Selena?* Possibly Raoul didn't trip her alarm since she was watching for supernatural stalkers, like the bag man.

"Don't speak, just listen for a moment first."

I sat quiet, doing as he suggested.

"There's been a change in leadership. After some heated debate, I have new orders. They've decided that the cost of further engagement is too high."

"What about Kian?" There was no point in feigning ignorance.

"Not my problem anymore. I've been assigned elsewhere, so I'm leaving Cross Point tonight. I've also been asked to convey our formal apologies and hopes there will be no escalation on your part."

Is he kidding with this? But maybe they thought I had the guns to go to war, if they still believed the Harbinger had my back. Not to mention, I'd been running with Selena lately too, which meant ties to Dwyer and, by association, Fell. As far as the Black Watch knew, for unfathomable reasons, I could have an immortal death squad at my command.

Pun intended.

Obviously, I quoted Jensen from *The Losers*. "'As the ancient Tibetan philosophy states, "Don't start none, won't be none!"'"

"That's not Tibetan philosophy," Raoul said.

"Never mind. My point is, I have other things to worry about. I accept the truce."

"I'll let them know." At the next stop, he got off the bus.

287

As the vehicle trundled on, lightness suffused me. I hadn't realized how many things were weighing on me until one of them disappeared. Now I only had a handful of immortals trying to end me—oh, and the world. *Can't forget that.* The Harbinger perched at the edge of my mind, whistling a somber tune. *What did you see? What was bad enough to make you leave?*

Dark thoughts held me hostage until I reached my old neighborhood. The sunshine cheered up the streets that had seemed so desolate during the winter god's reign. Under Dwyer's management, the trees had budded early, and shop owners were scrubbing down their windows until they shone. First I popped into the store to do some work for José; then we chatted a little.

"How's life uptown?" he wanted to know.

"Good. But I miss people around here. I might be moving south in a few months, but I'll stop by before I go."

"Whereabouts?"

"Miami," I said, paying homage to Kian's assumptions.

"I got family there. Nice place, too humid for my tastes, though."

"We'll see."

Before I left, I bought Selena's olives and turned down the food José offered. When I first got here, the smell of Luisa's tamales made my mouth water. Now the scent might be dirty shoes or stamp glue for all the interest it aroused. I was getting by on protein bars and vitamins, but I was starting to look hollow-eyed, as if the world was devouring me from within.

Last stop, I went to House of Style to pick up some gloves. People would think I'd developed a weird affectation, but it seemed best to cover the glimpses of gold as best I could. There was no solution for my face, but hopefully any witnesses would think they'd imagined it. Devon's mom made cheerful conversation as I shopped.

"It's been a while. How have you been?"

"Good. And you?"

She gestured at the store, which she seemed to be trying to organize. "Oh, you know. Devon talks about you sometimes. Says you're funny."

"I think he's cool too."

Once I had a pair that would work, I paid and put them on. With a wave for Mrs. Quick, I headed home. Two bus rides later, it was dark by the time I got to the apartment. Selena waited upstairs, watching a dance competition program. When she saw I had olives, she beamed.

"Thanks! You're not so bad for a clay pot." That was probably meant as a compliment. Without hesitation, she cracked the jar open and dug in with her fingers.

"What time do you want to head out?"

"Around half past eleven? That'll put us in the park at the witching hour."

"That's midnight? I thought it was three a.m."

"It's whatever time the witch says," she snapped around a mouth full of olives.

"And that's you, I take it."

"You dance naked under the moon? Didn't think so."

"I'll put it on my bucket list," I mumbled.

"Point in fact, devil's hour is three a.m. But that's not important now. Are you ready to be a damsel in distress?"

"Yep. It's better than being a damsel in a dress cuz I don't own one."

Unlike Raoul, Selena appreciated my humor, cackling as she

dumped the rest of the olives in her mouth. "Let's watch three epi-
sodes of *SYTYCD*, then go kick some ass."

Shrugging, I settled in next to her. "Hit it."

At half past, she switched off the TV. "Okay, it's time. Do you
need to limber up or something? Your bodies are so weird."

"Probably not a bad idea." I ran some katas and calmed myself
until the phantom pain eased. These days I had discomfort pretty
much all the time, like a low-grade headache all over my body that
no medicine could touch.

"Set?"

I nodded.

"Then I'll give you a five-minute head start. Do it just like we
discussed, and try not to die before I get to you. That would piss
Big Bro off, and then he sulks."

"Yeah, because that's my primary concern," I muttered, dodging a shoe.

Outside, the weather was calm and clear, plenty of moonlight.
Since it was warm, it wasn't weird that I'd be out. As I walked, I pretended to be nervous like a normal girl would be a night. I looked
at my phone a lot and glanced around—up, down, across the street,
behind me—until my neck felt like it might snap. A chill down my
spine halfway to the park suggested I'd caught an immortal tail.

A bench mostly hidden by the trees offered the perfect for an
ambush. And the bag man must be thinking it was his lucky night
as I paced and stared at my text messages, doing my best impersonation of someone being stood up. The scrape of boots on pavement sounded nearby, but I didn't see anything. Aegis tingled on my
wrist, but if I drew it before the trap snapped shut, our targets might
get away.

I whirled in a slow circle. "Jake? This isn't funny."

Seems right to talk to my fake boyfriend while feigning terror.

The bag man materialized behind me, and honest to God, he *did* scare the shit out of me. My heart skipped, until I realize his aura must be swamping me. It had been a while since I fought him, and the wrong timeline had weakened me. Diving, I rolled away from his claws, only to find the two creepy children on my legs. Their tiny teeth sank into my flesh, and I screamed. *Holy shit, that stings.* Unlike an attack animals, they didn't just lock on; instead, they *chewed,* as if they'd eat me alive. The boy-thing spat out a mouthful of me, his mouth stained red. Then he went back for more.

Come on, Selena. Where are you?

His face a horrible rictus of anticipation, the bag man stalked closer. *This creature pulled off my mother's head.* Killing it twice wouldn't be enough. On the verge of activating Aegis in a panic, I held off somehow, even as the girl-thing ground her teeth. Another step, and the old one would have me.

Then Selena dove from above. *How the hell's she in the trees?* No time for wondering—I called Aegis and executed both the children before they could blink away; they vanished in a swirl of black smoke as she spiked a knife into the ancient monster's chest. Her weapon paralyzed but didn't kill. She seemed to realize the children were *gone* then.

Yeah, it's permanent. Not sure what you were expecting.

Limping, trembling, I copied the bag man's awful prowl and beheaded the thing in a clean sweep. One more puff of dark smoke, and Selena narrowed her eyes.

"You have to tell me about that sword now," she said.

AN ECHO OF
LONGING

The silence stretched taut between us on the way back to the apartment. But we'd agreed that it would be unwise to have a conversation in the park past midnight. On her end, I suspected it was more the inconvenience of being questioned by human authorities than actual fear. As we walked, I frantically tried to decide what to tell her. Selena's jaw was set, her expression grim. Unsurprisingly she made me get into the lift first.

When the studio door shut behind us, she said, "Talk."

There's no chance she'll believe this.

I couldn't come up with a more plausible story on the fly, though, so I just recounted everything that had happened since Kian first found me on the bridge, including my fight with her big bro in the other timeline and ending with my time jump. Her eyes widened as she listened, and when I finally stopped talking, it was past one in the morning. Selena sat quiet for a whole minute, obviously analyzing my story.

"You're serious with this? Govannon forged that sword and it's actually . . ." She trailed off with a faint shiver. "Looks like we underestimated you."

I stressed, "I never met you in the other timeline. And we're not enemies in this one. Your brother has nothing to fear from me."

"Because you already yanked out his heart," she muttered.

"That was when I had a truce with Wedderburn. Here, he wants me dead, remember? That's why your side approached me."

"True," she said, thoughtful.

"What are you going to do?" It was impossible not to sound anxious.

If she revealed all of this to Dwyer, my life would get even more complicated, and I didn't have the time or energy to deal with another enemy when the world itself was trying to kill me. *Maybe I should tell her that too.*

"I don't know yet."

Acting on instinct, I added what the Harbinger had told me and how two cement blocks nearly crushed my skull not long ago. Shitty for me, but that information seemed to reassure Selena. Relaxing visibly, she went to the fridge to get mineral water. From what I'd seen, she only consumed fizzy drinks and olives.

"So . . . you'll be gone soon, either way," she said.

"The goal is a bit over two months away. I'm trying to last that long."

"That's like . . . a nap. I won't say anything, but I'm making you swear a blood oath that you won't try to harm me or mine." She eyed my bracelet as if she'd like to cut off my arm and take it by force.

"What does that entail exactly?"

"You offer blood in my name and make the promise. Believe me, I have sufficient power to make it binding."

"But . . . you could double-cross me. Then I wouldn't be able to defend myself without invoking the curse or whatever."

Selena shrugged. "You'll have to trust me. I mean, you're asking *me* to believe you won't take your immortal-killing sword and annihilate me on a whim. If you don't accept this offer, I'm heading straight to Big Bro to let him decide how to proceed."

"We both know he'll try to kill me on principle."

"He's pretty hotheaded," she agreed. "The downside of being a sun god."

"If I agree to your deal . . . ?"

"You get that sliver-of-grace time you asked for, and I keep your secret while watching over you, both for your protection and to make sure you're not planning anything dire."

This was probably as good as it got. I'd already sacrificed so much; it would be absurd to balk now. *Whatever it takes.* "Okay, let's do it."

Selena snapped her fingers and a battered silver chalice appeared in her hands. "Come with me."

Surprised, I followed her to the building's roof. Since it was a clear night, the moon shone bright, three-quarters full, overhead. Clouds offered a wispy fringe flickering about the lunar face, and she tipped her face back in visible pleasure. Odd, but I'd never seen an immortal react so strongly to a component from an origin story.

"What should I do?"

"Slice your palm with this." She proffered a curved knife, and I complied.

My blood trickled into the cup; then Selena followed suit. Her hand yielded light instead of bodily fluid, yet instead of dissipating, it mingled with the red of mine, until it looked strangely phosphorescent, glowing like I had some radioactive ailment. She swirled light and blood together, and then she cupped my hand around the chalice, covering it with her own.

"I pledge to protect you and keep your secret," she intoned.

"I promise not to harm you or yours." That sounded overly simple, but once I finished speaking, a shudder rocked the roof and a tone rang out, almost too low for me to catch.

"Good, our vows are locked in."

"Wait, so you're accountable too? You didn't tell me that."

"Duh. I was testing you. But yeah, it's reciprocal. Basically, according to the old ways, I just accepted you as my priestess. Try not to let it go to your head." She stretched, popping her neck. "Damn, it's been a while since I did that."

"Really?"

"Like a thousand years or something. But I feel better about keeping my mouth shut. This way, you can't decide go for a dual wield or something."

"Thanks, Selena."

"Let's go back. You need to clean those bites before they turn putrid."

Shuddering, I followed her advice and patched up as best I could. By then it was close to three, and I didn't much feel like going to school in four hours or so. So I finally turned on my phone to find over forty texts and almost that many missed phone calls. Most were from Jake and Kian, though I had some from Devon, Carmen, and Vonna too. It surprised me how persistent Jake was in trying to get in touch, not like our audience could appreciate how devoted and loyal he was via cell service. I skimmed, opting to ignore voice mail. The gist was that they were all deeply concerned about my tendency to vanish.

Dark amusement flowered. *You think that's impressive? Just wait for the grand finale.*

But . . . if I don't answer, it will just get worse. So I texted them the same basic message: *I'm OK, don't worry. But not feeling school tomorrow. See you the day after.*

With Jake, I added, *No need to pick me up.*

Devon was either an insomniac, a night owl, or both, because he responded. *Damn, girl. U had everyone so worked up.*

Sorry, I was dealing with some personal stuff. Unrelated to school drama.

As I crawled under the covers, my phone buzzed again. *That shit was crazy. Word is, Wade had a breakdown. His parents took him to county for mental help.*

Whoa. Tell everyone U talked 2 me, OK? Switching phone off so I can crash.

Will do, Devon sent back.

Then I plugged it in and powered down and passed out for ten hours. The apartment was empty when I woke, past one in the afternoon. Probably I should feel bad about Wade's breakdown since Wedderburn was just using him as a pawn, but hopefully removing the school's star athlete from my orbit would let him recover. Grudgingly I ate a protein bar, showered, and then checked messages. I answered the urgent ones and then vegetated in front of the TV until the bell rang.

Selena must've forgotten the code again. For an immortal, she could be surprisingly absentminded. I buzzed her up and schlepped back to

the sofa. A few minutes later, my bell rang. Weird, she usually fina-
gled the doorknob, though modern digital security was beyond her.
Sighing, I got up to let her in and found Jake standing there with a
paper sack.

Shit. His gaze skimmed down my legs where the bandages were
clearly visible in the lounge shorts I had on, and then he took in
the gauze wrapped around my palm. "Aren't you going to invite
me in?"

"I wasn't planning on it."

"That's just rude when I skipped out on practice to cheer
you up."

"Nobody asked you to do that. You understand that we're not
really together, right?" I started to shut the door.

"Please," he said. "You said yourself, I'm still pining for someone.
But it's clear that you're going through some shit and could use a
friend."

"Maybe. Fine, you can watch TV with me, but forget about
cooking. I already ate."

"This isn't food," Jake said.

"Oh?" He had my attention.

"Magazines, mostly, a few DVDs. There are also some tissues
and cold medicine." He shrugged, seeming self-conscious. "I thought
you were sick."

"Just of school."

He stepped into the apartment, taking it in with a curious air.
"Okay, I suspected before, but you obviously don't live with your
parents."

I sighed. "What about it?"

"You're a seriously mysterious girl. Do you plan to say anything about all those injuries?" Jake took a seat, looking ready to hang out for a while.

"Nope. If you hadn't showed up uninvited, I wouldn't have to. So let's skip ahead and pretend I made a plausible excuse and you accepted it."

"Fine."

That acceptance set the mood between us. My emotional spine softened, so we just watched TV in silence. When he left, I wasn't even mad that he'd stopped by anymore. Selena came home late, but she didn't mention where she'd been and I didn't ask. Since it was made of moonlight, our truce might not sustain heavy scrutiny.

The next day was a mess at school, as expected, but it blew over within a week. People gradually stopped talking about Wade's meltdown and forgot my role in it. Anonymity suited me just fine, and with my chief agitator gone, the time trickled away with a sweetness that made me ache, even as I savored it. All this average joy, everyone else took for granted. Sometimes I glanced around the lunch table and wished this was my real life.

But I'm living on borrowed time. Literally.

Before I knew it, April Fools' arrived with pranks and cries of, "Oh my God, you asshole, I thought you were serious." March had come in like a lamb, and the days warmed further, more like a purring cat than tentative spring. Wedderburn must be reeling from Buzzkill's supposed defection and the disappearance of his next-favorite murderous minion.

A week later, Jake pulled me aside at lunch to whisper, "You know what day it is, right?"

"Yeah, are we breaking up now?"

He shook his head. "Tanya's still dating that asshole. But lately she's been watching us more. I think she's almost ready to crack."

"You're diabolical. So I take it you want an extension?"

"Unless you have other plans," he said.

"No, it's fine. It's not like we don't get along well enough."

He grinned and brushed a strand of hair away from my face, dropping his voice so I had to come closer to hear. "I've had shorter relationships."

I caught the unspoken *real* in between *shorter* and *relationships*. Smiling, I took his hand and led him back to the table. Sure enough, Tanya was watching from the popular table, but she didn't look angry, just . . . sad and sort of heartbroken, like she'd gobbled down a huge plate of regret for breakfast. We joined the others in the middle of a debate about what classic movie was the most underrated. Jake didn't have much to contribute, and I caught him stealing looks at Tanya when she glanced away.

"You two are adorable," I whispered.

"A normal girl would at least pretend to be jealous," he shot back.

"Normal is for suckers."

Devon aimed his fork at us. "I don't care if you're the happiest couple, secrets are rude."

"Actually we were talking about asking Vonna and Kian if they want to double." The idea came to me in a brilliant flash.

For the last two weeks, Kian had been hinting, unsubtly, that he wanted to see my new place, but I didn't want to invite him over alone. Anything that might make Vonna feel uncomfortable was off-limits, and I had been careful to keep him at friend distance for a while now. But this way, I could make him happy without coming off sketchy to his girlfriend.

"Sounds fun," she said. "When?"

"How about this weekend?" Jake was apparently down with this plan.

Kian eyed him. "No offense, but I'm not going to your place again."

"None taken. Why don't we hang out at Nine's apartment?"

Fortunately, nobody else realized he meant *my* place, not the family home, and I kicked him in the ankle. "Stop being a butt."

"They'll find out soon enough," he muttered.

Hardly. I can make excuses not to invite everyone else over for a little longer.

• • •

Two days later, I had take-out tamales and other snacks from the bodega on the counter. I'd asked Selena to vanish for the night, as I had no idea how to explain her, and Jake had already rejected the cousin story. Kian and Vonna showed up first, so I welcomed them with a nervous smile.

"Welcome to Casa Nine. I'd give you a tour, but there's not much to see. Bathroom's over there, though."

"Whoa, how many people live here?" Vonna asked.

I understood her surprise. "Two. This is temporary housing, and my dad works a lot." That was true before I left anyway. Some days, I hardly saw him. Pain twisted me into knots, and my nerve endings ignited. Turning a gasp into a cough, I added, "Help yourself to the food. Those tamales are the best thing ever."

Jake rubbed my back. "You okay?"

I nodded.

The others fixed plates, so I did too. My tamale tasted like heart-break, but I chewed and swallowed until it was gone. In my gut, the food felt like it might expand until my body couldn't contain it. *Hope I don't explode into light confetti tonight.* Flexing my fingers, I reassured myself that the gloves would hide any telltale signs.

"I noticed you wear those all the time lately," Kian said.

"Poor circulation. I'm always cold."

That seemed to be enough, and I turned on an old movie after that, the one we'd decided was the most underrated. The film riveted Vonna and Kian, who snuggled up on the couch. I chose a seat on the floor and leaned against Jake's legs, avoiding greater intimacy. Every now and then, he stroked my hair, but it seemed like the absent attention you'd offer a dog.

Yeah, he's definitely not falling for me.

Once the movie finished, we deconstructed it over a tin of Danish sugar cookies. These still tasted sweet, so I ate a bunch, greedily savoring the last hurrah of my dissolving taste buds. Jake contributed more than I expected, analyzing the themes with a deftness that proved again he was far more than a handsome athlete. No joke, by the time he finished dissecting the sacrificial motif from all angles, he seemed a hundred times hotter.

"I never thought of that," Kian said, "but maybe you're right."

Vonna was nodding. "It's so common for women to die tragically in old movies."

"Usually to save someone else," I muttered.

And here I'm doing the same thing. But to be fair, he died for me first.

"I just realized I don't know much about you." Vonna smiled at me. "I've heard some from Kian, but you're pretty reticent."

Her sincerity made me feel shitty, so I couldn't quote the fake

301

bio I'd worked up. She deserved something real. "Okay, let me dig deep for something nobody else knows."

She rubbed her hands together. "This should be good."

"I'm secretly a huge nerd. You can't understand how much I love anime. When I was twelve, all I did was post on anime forums, watch anime, read manga, and so on. Oh, and I semimarried my rock tumbler that year too."

"Oh, man," Jake said with a muted groan. "Why does this information make you cuter?"

"Did you have a geode collection?" Kian wanted to know.

"Obviously."

His gaze met mine, and a small jolt went through me, an echo of longing. "Me too."

"Too funny," Vonna said. "What forums did you hang out on? And what's your favorite anime? I don't even know what I should ask first."

My cheeks heated, and it was weirdly like standing naked when I showed them the forum where NamiNerd was currently chatting with me about One Piece. They crowded around to read, and Jake nudged me.

"You're TimeWitch, right? So your anime love didn't die off." He wrapped his arms around me from behind, and I didn't resist, until he dug his fingers in to test if I was ticklish.

Squirming away, I mumbled, "Shut up."

"Would I like One Piece?" Kian asked, once we closed my laptop.

"Probably. It's a fun series. Also, it has pirates." Thus encouraged, I talked about the story and characters for a good five minutes.

Funny, it had been forever since I'd been honest with anyone about the real me.

"Want to check it out with me?" Vonna leaned her head against Kian's shoulder.

Nodding, Kian smiled at her, not me, and that was exactly as it should be. *So why does it hurt so much?*

KILLING TIME

Near the end of April, Jake's driver dropped me off in front of the school and then circled to the gym entrance, while Jake waved through the back window. *Now that's service.* Tons of people milled around outside, radiating an air of excitement. In the mob, I recognized Devon.

Tapping him on the shoulder, I asked, "What's up?"

"Word is, Wade's coming back today."

"Is he doing any better?" I had mixed feelings, considering how peaceful life had been since he went to county. Still, it wasn't his fault that Wedderburn twisted him, amping up his worst traits.

"No idea. But his fangirls are out in force."

True, now that he'd pointed it out, I noticed that by percentage, girls dominated the crowd hanging around out front, probably freshmen and sophomores. They bounced on the balls of their feet and monitored the parking lot like a boy band was about to roll up any minute. Shaking my head, I squeezed through and went inside. Devon came after me a few minutes later.

He found me rummaging my locker. "Lose something?"

"Only my mind."

"Funny."

"I can't find my English essay. To be honest, I can't even remember if I wrote it." That had been happening more often lately, and I wondered if my mental acuity might be breaking down too.

"That's not a good sign at your age. You have twenty minutes to scribble something, though. Better than a zero."

Nodding, I went into the classroom early and got going. It wasn't hard to dash off a couple of pages, though this was by far the messiest and least complete assignment I'd ever turned in. When the time came to pass our papers forward, I hid behind the guy in front of me and silently cringed when my work ended up on top of our row's pile. Fortunately, the teacher collected those from the door and went toward the window, so mine got buried in the middle of the stack.

I didn't see Wade or hear anything about him until someone stopped me in the hall, one of his friends, based on the guy's size and letter jacket. "Wade would like to speak to you." His tone was odd and formal.

"Okay," I said. "Where is he?"

"I'll go with you." Jake came up behind me, and he didn't put an arm around my shoulders, but he made it pretty clear that refusing him wasn't an option.

"No problem." The guy led us out front.

Wade stood in a circle of girls, fielding their questions with a brittle smile. Despite his size, he carried a fragile edge, as if some of his bravado had shorn away under the scalpel of self-reflection. He flinched a little when he saw me, but I didn't react. Jake threaded our fingers together in a comforting show of solidarity.

"I'm fine," Wade was saying as we approached. "And I need to talk privately for a minute, so why don't you get some lunch?" He spoke kinder to his fans than I'd expected.

A gaggle of girls shot me dirty looks as they darted past. I stopped five feet away and waited to learn what this was about. Wade's crony took off, leaving Jake and me alone with him. I expected an angry outburst, but instead, Wade lowered his eyes.

"I'm supposed to apologize," he mumbled.

"What?"

"It's called making amends. My therapist says that once I clear my conscience, I'll feel better. I know I was acting weird, but to be honest, *I'm* not even sure why I was so obsessed with you. Anyway, I'm sorry. I won't do it again, and I'll stay away from you from now on."

Not if Wedderburn has any say in it.

Now I did feel bad. Wade might be a player, but he didn't seem like a villain. "Accepted. I'll stay out of your way as much as I can. I'm not looking for trouble."

"And, Jake, I'm sorry to you too, bud. What I did was disrespectful. I've never gone after somebody else's girlfriend before."

"Everybody screws up," Jake said. "The important thing is, you're willing to learn from it and you want to do better."

When I turned, ready to end the conversation, I spotted like twenty people in the foyer, likely trying to eavesdrop. Sighing, I elbowed Jake. "I'm headed to the roof. I can't deal with people today."

"It'll blow over when they realize nothing's up."

Still, guilt had me in a choke hold. Maybe Wade would come out of this a better person, more respectful of women, but I feared

306

my intervention might have derailed his future somehow. If Wade ended up totally screwed four years from now, did that make me any better than the immortals? They wouldn't balk at sacrificing one human to get what they wanted. Inner turmoil cracked the nerve quakes to life, and I nearly fell down.

Pale and sweaty, I hugged the wall until I got to the bathroom. For the rest of lunch, I sat on a toilet and cried, not even entirely sure why I hurt so much. And it wasn't just the physical stuff; my soul twisted inside me until it might snap. *This is what the Harbinger couldn't watch. I miss him. I hate that I miss him.* Instead of buckling down, I crept out of school and ditched afternoon classes.

I wanted to talk to Selena, but she wasn't home. My gloved hands shook as I powered the laptop on. *Guess I've come full circle, dying of lonely, and looking for company on the Internet.* I checked the anime forum next. NamiNerd was chatting with more people in multiple threads, conversations I never had, and someone named GreenKnight had chimed in on her school post, adding to my advice. She'd responded, *Okay, you guys convinced me. I'll definitely talk to my parents. Will keep you posted.*

Reading that offered some comfort, but it didn't make the pain go away. I remembered how I thought hard at the Harbinger and he came to shut me up. Curling up in the fetal position on the couch, I focused, trying to turn longing into a tractor beam. A scrabble at the window pane made me jump up, but when I got there and raised the sash, there was only a single raven flying away. A black feather wafted in and landed on the floor. I picked it up and twirled it in my fingers, feeling less alone.

"Are you hot?" Selena asked, shutting the door behind her.

"Not really." I closed the window. "Can I ask you a favor?"

"Sure, but don't think being my priestess earns you automatic perks. I'm not wasting my energy for nothing."

"There's a guy at school . . . Wedderburn had something riding him, and it kind of drove him over the edge."

"Extreme behavior?" she guessed.

"How did you know?"

"It's probably Bess."

"You know who does this kind of thing?" That alone could be invaluable.

"Sexual obsession is a specific skill set, and Bess has been known to do contract work for the winter whatsit from time to time."

"Well, can you do anything? Maybe give me a charm or something that will help him resist that pull? It doesn't have to be long-lasting, just over a month will do. Once I'm gone, Wedderburn will probably turn his attention elsewhere."

"That's easy enough," she said. "But I need a bucket of grave-yard dirt, some dust from a church, two bird bones, and a lock of virgin hair."

My mouth fell open. "Really?"

"Idiot. No, not really. Unless you're in the mood for a weird scavenger hunt." She smirked at how gullible I was.

Reluctantly, I smiled back. "Pass."

"I'll just infuse this with some of my energy. It might make him a little more aggressive, but he won't go off half cocked like before." She closed her eyes and a glow suffused her palms. When it died away, she handed me the pen.

"Thanks. I'll slip it into his backpack tomorrow."

"No problem. As favors go, this one was simple, and anything that thwarts Subzero counts as a win for Team Sun and Moon."

Selena opened a jar of olives as she settled in front of the TV. "I'm kind of getting used to you. Pity you'll be gone in like a day."

"Four weeks, three days," I mumbled.

"Close enough. Want to watch more *SYTYCD*? This show is magical."

"Why not?" I ignored my buzzing phone, and this time, it stopped much sooner. *This is for the best,* I thought. *They'll miss me less when they accept that I'm flaky and disappearing is what I do.*

Hours later, when I finally went to bed, I realized I was still clutching that stupid feather. I almost threw it away, but instead, I tucked it between the pages of one of the magazines Jake had brought when he thought I was sick. Like an idiot, I fell asleep thinking of the Harbinger.

Suddenly, I found myself in an open field, but it was no place I had ever been. The soil smelled of sulfur, and the trees were all dead and twisted. Ten ravens circled overhead, keeping formation. I didn't see him anywhere, but I sensed him. The low-grade ache eased. *I know you're there,* I said. Or rather, tried to say. No words came out because I had no mouth. My eyes went next, so the world went dark. Wind on my face, smelling of soot and decay, but I couldn't call out or find my way back again.

Why are you here, dearling? The deadlands are not for you. His mind touched mine, filling me with familiar warmth, and my visceral terror receded.

A hard pinch jolted me awake. The clock on the microwave read 3:00 a.m., and Selena stood over me, cranky-faced. "You were squealing in your sleep like a baby pig. Stop."

"Sorry."

She returned to the couch, but I couldn't relax. *That was just a dream?* Until dawn, I watched the window, hoping for a bad omen bird that never came. A hot shower burned away some of my yearning, and I scoured the rest away with a coarse sponge. To Selena, a month might be a day, but for me, it was starting to seem interminable. My head rattled with ball bearings yet I felt light as air too, as if my bones had gone hollow. Without my goal to tether me, I might just dissolve now.

Maybe I've done enough.

As I thought that, a shiver of gold sparked from my skin and it went translucent, just for a second, and I choked out a shuddering breath. *No. I'm not ready yet. I'm not done.* For a shivering, anguished minute, my face flickered in the mirror. Wet hair, big eyes, gaunt frame, and nothing stared back at me. Like a vampire, I had no reflection. Touching the door to prove I existed, I dug my thumbnail in my palm. The pain caused a shiver in the mirror, and then something else was looking at me. But she pointedly turned and walked away.

"Heh. Even the monster in the mirror doesn't want my life."

A few seconds later, my image came back, but it was weird and distorted, light streaks raying throughout my body, a bad psychedelic trip. Breathing hard, I shook the whole time I put on my clothes. One good thing about Selena, she didn't care how long I took in the bathroom. Any other roommate would be pounding on the door by now.

I stumbled out and paged through a magazine, pretending I wasn't a hot, microwaved mess. By seven thirty when Jake arrived to pick me up, I'd pasted myself together with grit and determination. How long that would hold, I had no idea. He helped me into the car and didn't say much on the way to school.

Today, the driver dropped us both at the front. "No morning practice?"

"No. Coach is taking it easy on us for the rest of the year. Listen, can we talk?" His somber tone gave me the first clue.

Oh, wow. It's time, huh?

"Sure. What's up?" Since I'd never actually played a breakup scene, I had no idea how to react. Crying would probably be over the top, no longer than we were together.

"I've had fun hanging out with you, but . . . I don't think it's going to work."

"Yeah. I didn't know how to tell you, but I'm moving at the end of the year. So I'm glad you said it first." A smile felt wrong, so I made eye contact, surprised to find that he actually seemed a little sad to hear it.

"No shit? I'll miss you, but . . . I'm not over Tanya."

She walked up just in time to hear that and just . . . stopped, her eyes wide. From Jake's satisfaction, he'd seen her coming. *Well played, sir.* But I didn't want it to seem like he was breaking my heart.

So I said, "To be honest, I dreamed about my ex last night."

"Jake . . . ," Tanya said in a small voice.

That was my cue; I hurried inside the school so they could make up. *Damage control unlocked.* After I slipped this pen-charm into Wade's backpack, I'd call it good regarding the problems I created by enrolling at this school. If I'd learned anything at Blackbriar, it was that shit could spiral out of control *so* fast.

Jake came to my locker after lunch, probably for the last time. "Thanks again."

"You guys are back together?"

"Yep. She broke up with the a-hole a week ago."

"Aren't you mad she believed that bullshit gossip and dumped you over it?" Technically, none of my business, but since I'd played a role in their reunion, I indulged my curiosity.

"At first. But the more I thought about it, it was actually a relief. When people know my background, sometimes it's hard to be sure . . ." He trailed off, shrugging.

"Because when she thought you were a scumbag, she left. Money didn't make her stay."

"More or less. We can build mutual trust, but if she'd stuck around, even when she didn't believe in me, *I* would've had to go. If that makes sense."

"Completely."

"And that would've really sucked because I do love her." His gaze locked on Tanya coming down the hall, and I swore he glowed.

Happy endings are awesome.

"You probably shouldn't spend too much time with your ex," I said then.

"That's actually why I'm here. Tanya said our table looked really fun from across the room. So she was wondering—"

"Wow, really? Instead of taking you away, she wants to join?"

"Is that okay? I meant it when I said I'm done with that crowd." Clearly, Jake put some stock in the rumor that someone had sabotaged his party to steal Tanya.

"Fine by me. It may be crowded until I leave. There will be more space next year."

He ruffled my hair. "Don't say that. You'll make me emotional."

"What will?" Tanya gave me a tentative smile, as if she wasn't sure where we were on the social spectrum.

"We were just talking about my imminent relocation. My dad's been transferred." That was a good lie, right?

Just then, Kian and Vonna came down the hall, and if I had to third-wheel with a happy couple, they were a much better choice. Vonna glanced over shoulder as we walked away. "That looked pretty civilized. You okay?"

"Yeah. We were basically just killing time." I swallowed a laugh at the accidental pun.

"You still miss the other guy?" she asked.

Hating myself a little, I nodded. When she hugged me, I leaned in, and it was good, though I feared dissolving in her arms like a wicked woman in a bible story, nothing left but sparks and salt. *Maybe not even salt.*

"Thanks. But I'll be all right. I'm really used to good-byes."

"You shouldn't be," Kian said.

There was nothing I could say to make him understand, so I just listened to the pep talk about how modern life made it easy to keep in touch until the bell rang. *Not long now.*

• • •

Two days later, I had failed in every conceivable way to get this damn pen into Wade's backpack. It was becoming a maddening, impossible quest. The thing was always in his locker; he rarely carried it to class. *So how the hell . . .*

Oh, shit. My mind is going. I can't believe I didn't think of this.

Embarrassment practically immolated me. Putting that aside, I strode toward him, pen in hand. "Hey, Wade."

He drew back on instinct. "Hey."

"I just wanted to give you something."

"What is it?"

I handed him the pen. "Just a symbol that we're cool."

In his huge hands, the thin blue cylinder looked even smaller, which made his reticence pretty funny. "This is exploding ink, right?"

"Nope. It's just a decent pen. See?" I got out a notebook and wrote *Chelsea Brooks has no grudge against Wade Tennant.*

"Oh, it's gel," he said.

"They write really smooth. Just be careful, they can smear if you touch the ink too soon."

Wade clearly didn't know what to make of this slightly odd "gift," but he seemed to conclude it was a harmless gesture. "Okay, cool."

Lowering my voice, I added, "I'm proving to everyone else that we're fine too. See how they're watching us?"

"Right. Morons." He'd had enough attention lately, it seemed.

As I walked off, I mentally high-fived myself. *All the pieces are falling into place.* But I shouldn't have celebrated so early. That was the fastest way for things to go horribly wrong.

And they did.

RUNNING RAGGED

May came in like a day at the beach, plenty of sunshine, but there were also sand mites and uncontrollable itching. These days even my skin hurt, and I often had to drag myself out of bed. I bought a bunch of makeup to camouflage how shitty I looked, and Selena taught me to apply it with a heavy hand. I went for video vixen style, and my friends were too busy criticizing my new look to wonder why I'd suddenly switched it up.

I can't have them asking if I'm sick. Just need to hold together a little longer.

But the truth was, I couldn't stand looking at myself in the mirror. Beneath the foundation, my skin seemed papery and odd, showing gold sparks, and I'd gotten so thin that I could hardly wear the clothes I'd bought when I first arrived. Selena brought home a belt, and I made the pants work and covered with hoodies that were more oversize than ever.

She scrutinized me. "Are you going to make it?"

"I don't know." My whole being was locked on the goal, but sheer will could only take you so far in overcoming physics.

"I could give you a focus, like I did for your school friend."

"Would that help?"

"Not sure. To be honest, I've never run into a time traveler before. At any rate, it can't make things worse, right?"

I accepted her offer, and when I took the paper clip, some of the pain did recede, like it had when the Harbinger was nearby. Back then, I'd imagined it must have to do with our connection, but apparently immortal energy had the power to buffer the effects of cellular decay. *Glad Selena likes me.* Apart from Rochelle, she was the nicest supernatural I'd met.

"I might live," I said.

"Good to hear. The end of the round is coming up, so stay sharp. Coldsnap will absolutely make a move before then."

"I'm loving your nicknames for him."

"It's best not to drop names unless you want attention," she told me.

"Huh. So J.K. Rowling had that part right?" I remembered Kian also cautioning me against calling things that might refuse to leave.

"Who?" Selena asked.

"You're not a big reader, I take it."

"Kidding. Harry Potter, the boy who lived. I've seen all the movies like three times."

And I'm the girl who won't.

Despite my dark mood, I laughed. "Okay, I'm off."

The bus ride wasn't bad, but I missed arriving in Jake's town car. Now that he was back with Tanya, I doubted she'd appreciate it if I kept mooching rides. Today, summer was holding an early launch party in the parking lot. The skateboarders were going nuts, and someone was blasting music from his car, plenty of thumping bass.

Hot as it already was, I should have been sweltering in my sweat-shirt and gloves, but I couldn't get warm.

Only three more weeks.

As I crossed, avoiding knots of students, a skateboarder careened off course right into the path of a car pulling into the lot. The driver panicked and jerked the wheel, so instead of hitting a person, he slammed into the light pole. It toppled toward me and I dove out of its path, but I couldn't predict the trajectory of the broken, snap-ping electrical wires. The pole hit hard only a few feet from me, whereas the wires jerked, inching ever closer. I scrambled away from the current, gloves scraping over the pavement. To me, it looked like the cable had a mind of its own, determined to fry me with thousands of volts. I stared at the twitching wire, crackling power as it thrashed closer to my legs. I scrambled backward. All around me, people screamed, and someone was asking driver and skate-boarder if they were okay.

If I move too much, somebody else might get hurt.

At my movement, the wire reacted like a live snake, curling back to strike. *Yeah, this is definitely not normal.* Kian grabbed me from behind and hauled me away from the tangle of copper and fire. Something popped, the power box maybe, and smoke poured from the downed pole. *Probably the world, then, not Wedderburn, if it backed off hurting any-one but me.*

"Are you all right?" he asked.

"More or less." But I was shaky as shit.

I'd come so close to being flash-fried that I appreciated the new bruises and the bloody scrape on my knee. Kian supported me all the way to the front of the school, where the nurse took charge of me. As we went inside, sirens wailed in the distance.

She checked me over, then said, "You were lucky. It could've been a lot worse. Do you want to call home?"

Shit, not this again.

But this "accident" had been so much more serious than the one with the cement blocks and other people could've been hurt. It would be abnormal if I didn't want go home, hug my parents, and cry. So I input a fake number and waited while pretending to listen to it ring.

"He's not answering," I finally said.

"Is there anyone else you can call? I can't send you home without a parent coming to pick you up." Her sad eyes said she felt sorry for me, but that she wasn't surprised to find a kid who couldn't get ahold of anyone who cared in a crisis.

I shook my head without meeting her gaze. "It's just my dad and me. He works a lot."

"Let me take care of your knee," she said gently. "You can rest on the cot for a while if you like and try again later."

"Okay."

An hour passed, and I went to sleep to avoid dealing with my messy reality. An announcement that the situation had been handled came on the PA; then the principal added, "There will be no loitering permitted in the parking lot, before or after school. This is not a skate park, and the rules will be strictly enforced going forward."

Groans came from neighboring classrooms. I pretended to be asleep when the nurse checked on me. A few minutes later, the principal came to the mini-clinic to ask about me. But he wasn't interested in my welfare as much as concerned about a lawsuit.

"I need to speak with Miss Brooks."

"The poor kid's been through enough." The nurse sounded irritated.

"Since the personnel reduction, we've been lax about monitoring the side lot. Her parents are lawyers, Clara. This could get ugly."

"Really? Just now, she said it was only her dad at home."

Shit. There goes the first thread unraveling.

Incredibly stiff and sore, I rolled off the cot and went to wrangle damage control. "My parents are divorced. They're both attorneys, but I don't live with my mom."

Sorry, Mom and Dad. I know you were happy together.

"See?" the principal said meaningfully.

The nurse sighed. "Fine. You can talk to her since she's awake."

"Would you please come to my office, Miss Brooks?"

"No problem." But it was likely to be a huge, insurmountable one.

He started the conversation with an apology and an explanation about budget cuts. They'd laid off two security guards who normally prevented nonsense like what happened this morning. In conclusion, he felt sure I could agree it was all an unfortunate accident and would I mind explaining this to my parents?

"Not at all. I'll talk to my dad tonight," I said.

"Excellent. When can he come in to discuss the incident and to sign some simple documentation for the school?"

You want a promise not to sue, huh?

But my heart sank. I'd painted myself into a corner by saying I lived with my father because I didn't know anyone who could fill in. If the Harbinger hadn't gone, he could've slipped into the Mr. Brooks persona with no problem, but José was the only older guy I knew, and he'd think I was out of my mind if I showed up with such a sudden, random request. Possibly Selena could shift her appearance like the Harbinger, but I'd already gotten two favors from her.

Plus, it was hard to pretend things were normal at school day after day. So I made an irrevocable choice. "Actually, we're moving. My dad's already in Miami. I stayed to wrap up the school year and pack up our apartment, but considering what happened today, I think he'd want me to come now. I'll talk to him about it when I call tonight."

"You're leaving?" He sounded as if he couldn't decide if this was a good thing.

"Yeah, I don't feel safe here. If my dad flies back, it won't be to sign stuff." *Shots fired.*

In five seconds, my meaning registered with him. "Do whatever you think best for your family, Miss Brooks."

"The nurse said I can't leave unless he picks me up. So what am I supposed to do? He's in court right now."

"We don't want to make your father get on a plane over a skinned knee." The principal was probably imagining how pissed my fictional self-absorbed, high-powered attorney papa would be under those circumstances. "I'll make an exception and sign off for you."

"Thanks. I need to get home and start packing."

"I'm sorry this happened, but I'm relieved you're not seriously hurt. We'll expedite transcripts and transfer papers when the request comes in," he added eagerly.

You'll be waiting a long time.

Five more minutes of apologies, and I had a pass permitting me to take off. *Wow, this is the last time I'll be here.* Unlike the other times

320

when I just vanished and turned off my phone, I texted everyone I thought might care. *I'm done at this school. You know how to find me.* By the time I got home, my friends were having lunch, and they flooded my phone with questions.

Devon: *Did U get suspended? That's BS. How's that your fault?*

Kian: *What's wrong? What happened?*

Carmen: *U okay? Want to come over?*

With most of them, I just kept it vague, but I wrote a longer message to Kian since he knew more about me. *They wanted to talk to my parents. I had to bail.*

Ah. So RU going to Miami early?

Nah. Studio's paid until June. Not smart to waste money.

He sent back, *Cool. So you'll be here for my b-day?*

Of course, I thought. *That's what I'm waiting for.*

But I couldn't tell him that. *Depends. When is it?*

June 3.

Oh definitely. Will probably take off right after, though.

I'll miss U, he texted.

Ditto.

For a while, I thought that was the end of the convo, but eventually he sent, *It's gonna be weird without U at school.*

U can always come over as long as Vonna's cool with it.

I'll talk to her.

• • •

For the first week after I left school, I just vegged in the apartment, but then it hit me. *Anything could happen to Kian. And Selena even warned me to be vigilant.* With me out of the picture, Wedderburn could do whatever the hell he wanted. That fear took hold and wouldn't let go, like a dog with a locked jaw. I considered checking in via text, but I wouldn't feel secure until I saw him in person.

The second week in May, I stalked him, harder than it sounded. Unlike Boston, where he followed me around, the crowds weren't as dense in Cross Point and I constantly had to dodge aside and hide around corners. Kian definitely had the sense something was up because his attention sharpened, as if he sensed I was watching. But then, I didn't have any cool tech to help me with the mission.

School was another problem, however. Against my better judgment, I sent a request to Devon. *Do me a favor?*

Depends. What?

Watch out for Kian. And ping me if you see any weird, shady types hanging around.

A long silence followed. Finally, I got, *U, not the cops. RU in trouble?*

I debated a long time before answering, *Unsure. Just want to be sure U guys R OK. Help me out? Pls.*

U got it.

That message relieved my mind. If anything went down at school, I could tag Selena and we'd ride to the rescue. Instead of going to class, I studied at the University of Kian. In the morning, I watched him from the shadows across the street. He smiled a lot more these days, usually while checking his phone. *Must be messages from Vonna.* Once he left his house, I ran to the stop before his and got on just before. Since he tended to sit near the front, he never saw me hunkered down in the back. The aching emptiness of just observing, nothing more, hurt more than usual, and even meditation couldn't make it go away.

Is this how he felt, watching me?

I'd done a good job of smothering it, but I did still love him, for all the good it did. *At least he's still alive in this world.*

As he got off at school, I twitched into a full-on seizure, and maybe because I looked weird, nobody tried to help me. When I came out of it, my head lolled against the window and blood trickled from my lips. I got off at the next stop, disgusted with humanity. *Really? They'd just let me die of whatever was wrong rather than get involved.*

My mouth tasted of copper, but it was actually a pleasant change from nothing. As usual, I killed time at a nearby park and slept in the sun, waiting for school to end. I woke to a text from Devon. *Might B nothing, but . . . past 2 days, a weirdo seems 2B stalking UR boy.* My nerves crackled to high alert. Aegis quivered on my wrist.

Description? I sent.

Old woman. Scary, not sure why.

With that news, I ratcheted to high alert. *Has to be the hag. No time to find Selena, I have to handle this.* I remembered our fight in Wedderburn's compound . . . and back then, I'd had Allison's help. Weak as I was now, it couldn't be a straight up battle. I had to catch the monster unaware, or I'd lose.

If I lose, Kian dies. This has all been for nothing.

Terror and urgency created an adrenaline cocktail, and I raced faster than I ever had. I spotted Kian leaving school alone, headed for the bus stop a few blocks down. There were a couple of decent ambush points—I'd scouted them a week ago while on silent watch—and if I was the hag, I'd be lurking in one of them. Gathering my full strength, I pushed to a sprint, feet slamming against the sidewalk. I dodged people like I'd just stolen someone's purse and vaulted over a bench, determined to get ahead of him. Wheezing, I reached the first danger point and found it empty.

Only one other spot she could be.

I changed directions, circling to enter the alley from the next street. *Can't stop.* My chest burned; full body pain threatened to cripple me. Somehow I pushed on, despite feeling like I could shake apart at any moment. A woman yelled at me for nearly bumping into her, but I couldn't stop. Seconds might separate the distance between victory and defeat. My knee still hadn't healed properly, and running broke open the scab, so blood trickled down my shin.

Here, she has to be here.

I charged in from the back of the alley, startling the creature lying in wait. She lashed out, but I already had Aegis drawn. Dizzy as hell, I whirled in and delivered a wound to her gut. She hunched over, raking my back with her iron claws as murky fumes boiled out of her belly. I ate that pain too and spat it back at her, slashing in a vicious swing that would determine who lived.

In a golden shimmer, Aegis arced like a throat-seeking missile as it sliced through her neck. She dissolved in a swirl of dark smoke.

I collapsed.

For a few seconds, I just curled up on my side and waited for the pain to implode me. But it receded, leaving me more or less in one piece, though I shed gold sparks like a lizard molting from its old skin. After a while, I staggered upright to find a small boy staring at me wide-eyed. There was no way to gauge what he'd seen, but adults never believed little kids anyway. So I put my finger slowly to my lips, and he ran off in the opposite direction.

So . . . I killed Buzzkill twice. The hag too. Screw you, Wedderburn. I beat you. Again. He'd be so pissed when he found out. But I couldn't savor the triumph. My brain felt like liquid oxygen sloshing around in my skull as I stepped out of the alley.

Recognizing me, Kian stared, taking in my sweaty dishevelment. "You look like shit."

Which was concrete proof that he wasn't in love with me. *You're welcome*, I thought. But it was also gratifying that he had the confidence to say something like that. Before, he was so skittish and timid that it hurt my heart.

"Rough run. I haven't worked out in a while."

He appraised my jeans and sweatshirt with a dubious eye. "Maybe put on exercise clothes first next time?"

"That's just a gimmick to get your money. Did cavemen wear track pants when they ran after saber-toothed tigers? No, they did not."

"God, are you doing that Paleo thing? My aunt won't shut up about it and now there's no bread in the house. No wonder you're acting weird. Want to get something to eat?"

How am I supposed to act after killing the thing that meant to murder you?

Mentally, I shrugged. "Okay. Let's have coffee."

THE DEATH
OF WINTER

"You smell like violence," Selena said when I got home a few
hours later.

Exhaustion overwhelmed me, and my legs went watery. It had
been pure hell to hang out with Kian with the claw marks burning
on my back. I'd been careful to keep him in front of me to avoid
awkward questions, but the pain made it difficult to focus. A text
from his uncle finally prompted him to head home, so I wearily did
the same.

Now I have to break the bad news to Selena.

"I had to fight the hag."

"Without me? That's *so* mean. You know I wanted a go at her."
She radiated pure petulance, like I'd set out to rob her of a battle.

"There was no time to find you and still save Kian. It's not like
you have a phone."

She sighed. "True. Maybe I should get one. Are you hurt?"

"Yeah. If you're feeling sympathetic, you could patch up my

back." The gouges still hadn't clotted fully, and my T-shirt beneath the hoodie was sticky-crunchy with blood.

"You know I'm not a healer, right?"

"I meant the regular way—iodine, bandages, or whatever's in the first-aid kit."

"Oh, sure, that I can do." She got up and went over to the cupboard that held the supplies. "I can't wait to tell Big Bro that we took out another of the big chill's minions."

"You're taking credit for this too?"

"Of course. Immortals are starting to avoid me. The rest bring offerings." She pointed at a pile she'd dumped by the door: statues, ornate and gilded treasure boxes, plus a case of olives and high-quality mineral water. *Whoever sent those knows her best.* "Nobody's sure how I'm suddenly so lethal, and it is *awesome.*"

A half smile was the best I could do. "Glad you're having fun."

That makes one of us.

We headed to the bathroom and I stripped out of my layers to reveal my bare back. Gritting my teeth, I managed not to whimper as she dumped something sting-y and astringent on my wounds. Selena sucked in a breath as she leaned closer. I craned my neck and failed to see what had alarmed her. The motion made my wounds feel even worse.

"I don't want to alarm you . . ."

"But?" Her bedside manner sucked, and despite her intentions, I was already freaking out a little. What could bother a moon goddess who lived to hunt and kill things?

"You're not just losing blood," she said.

"Huh?"

"You're losing . . . mass too. Part of your back's missing. It's like . . . I don't know what it's like. A bandage will *not* fix this."

I angled my body to try to glimpse the problem in the mirror, and there were just slashes of darkness, not injuries as much as tiny dimension rifts. "Do the best you can. I'll cover the rest with my shirt."

While she wrapped up, I tried not to worry about how long I had. Patients with a terminal illness never knew, either. The doctors might predict three months, and people hung on much longer than anticipated. Eventually I washed up, careful with the gauze, and crashed for the rest of the day. In the morning, mild astonishment filtered in with the dawn sunlight, surprise that I was still around.

Selena wasn't, however. I'd gotten used to her disappearances, so I just went about my usual routine of avoiding my own reflection while I got ready to guard-stalk Kian. This time, I stopped cold, shocked by my own face. Pallid skin, deep bruises beneath my eyes, and the expanse of my forehead showed flecks of golden light. I had the look of someone struggling with a fatal illness or maybe radiation poisoning. *Right, almost forgot the makeup.*

Late now, I rushed out to make my morning rounds. But before I made it ten steps toward the bus stop, I passed through . . . something. A sliver of ice pierced me, and I fell forever, until I landed hard in a snowdrift. My hands already hurt, and my heartbeat slowed in the extreme chill. The blood in my veins turned sluggish as my eyeballs froze in their sockets. There was nothing I could fight, just the slow death of winter, and only an endless desolation of snow, as far as my locked gaze could see.

Wedderburn's voice rumbled from all around me. "You are pathetic, less than nothing. *How* have you blocked my will, vermin?"

Frozen like a statue, I couldn't reply or even glare. Aegis thrummed on my wrist, but in the heart of this pocket plane, likely similar to the one where Dwyer had brought me when we fought in the other timeline, my sword lacked the strength to free me. *So close, I was so close.* The winter king prowled into my field of vision, every bit as terrifying as I'd once thought him. He was all insectoid ice, dead eyes, and long, spidery fingers that dragged down my frigid cheek like he'd peel my skin as one would a grape.

"I shall savor this. While your pain cannot possibly offer sufficient recompense . . ." He circled me with a playful menace, examining me from all angles. "I can break you into pieces first, perhaps carve your face into a new shape."

Aegis, I thought.

A hot spot formed on my wrist, burning my flesh, and it glowed gold beneath the blue-white ice, but I could only wriggle my wrist, no way to activate it fully. *Not enough, not nearly enough.* Wedderburn traced the slope of my shoulder, the curve of my hip, and I couldn't shudder, could only taste the bile in my throat, and then it froze too.

"Losing a nose to frostbite is exquisite agony," he said.

Stop toying with me.

Now that he had me helpless, the monster meant to torture me. His curved claws drifted closer to my face, flicking back and forth between my staring eyes. "Perhaps I'll pluck these out, one at a time, or I could have your teeth first. They'd make a lovely necklace."

Then he gestured, and my mouth thawed. "I'm weary of such a one-sided conversation. If you answer to my satisfaction, I might finish quickly."

"Screw you," I said.

Possibly not the wisest decision I ever made.

But before he could retaliate, a brilliant flash of light blinded me. Wedderburn swore in a language so alien it hurt my ears. The pain faded, not a good sign, and sleepiness set in. I recognized this feeling from when I escaped from the Black Watch compound with the Harbinger, only this wasn't mild hypothermia.

I won't last long.

"Couldn't have said it better myself," Selena called, swinging a leather bag over her head like a bola.

The sack opened, and five searing coals flew out, bright enough to burn like miniature suns. Three of them hit me, and the other two nailed Wedderburn. Between that heat and Aegis, I broke free and dove away—or tried, rather. Numb and clumsy, I flopped in the snow instead. Wedderburn let out a scream of sheer rage. In this eerie landscape, icicles speared the snow in the distance, and an avalanche began, millions of tons of snow hurtling toward us.

Holy shit.

"Move fast," Selena snapped.

In response, I stumbled to my feet and activated Aegis. It was impossible for me to approximate a battle-ready stance; all my strength went into positioning the blade before me. *Human determination can only go so far.* Yet she nodded approval and raced across the snow like a lightning strike, slashing and weaving at the winter whatsit until it was all he could do to block her, likely knowing her blade had the power to paralyze.

And that's all I need.

"How?" he roared at her. "*How* are you here? This is my domain!"

"I can always aid one of my oath-bound acolytes." Selena laughed and dodged an ice lance hurled at her head.

Their clash sped past in bursts I could hardly track. Mostly, they showed as blurs and bursts of light, interspersed with Selena's laughter and Wedderburn's snarls. Inching closer, I waited for my opening. My feet felt like they were encased in ice. While this might be fun for Selena, I just wanted to survive. The need to hold on until Kian's birthday defined me now. Icy knives rained down from above, and I slashed at them with Aegis, clumsily, missing most. The move almost put me on the ground, so tempting to just let it happen. The cold would take me—

No.

Disjointed scraps of a Dylan Thomas poem surfaced, lending me strength. *Do not go gentle into that good night. Good men, the last wave by, crying how bright . . .*

I whispered, "I will not go gentle."

"Now!" Selena shouted.

Her dagger lodged in his chest, and he stood frozen, just as he'd done to me. I didn't trifle with him; I rushed in a graceless stumble and rammed Aegis through his chest. The winter king didn't die easy. He exploded in a shard of ice and snow, whirling into a blizzard all around us. Snow got in my nose and mouth, stinging, blinding.

Somewhere nearby, Selena shouted in triumph, "Winter is *not* coming, bitch!"

Footfalls crackled toward me. I cleared my ice-frosted lashes in time to see the pocket world imploding. She latched on to my wrist; her steely grip hurt, and then we flashed out in a beam of light so bright it burned my eyes. The sensation of free fall hurtled my stomach into my throat, and then we hit the ground hard in an alley near the studio.

I shook uncontrollably for a full five minutes while Selena communicated with someone using runes or stones or who the hell knew what. No way could I process all of this; it was still early morning, and the sun shone like a lemon drop overhead. Even the sky seemed surreal somehow, the blue of an Impressionist painting. When I stared at the passersby, I feared their faces might be melting off. The sad part, nobody spared us a glance. I'd gotten it right when I thought before that homeless people were invisible.

When my tongue thawed sufficiently and she finished clacking her stones, I mumbled, "Did you use me as bait again?"

"Not on purpose. I came as fast as I could. But holy shit, who could've known he'd set a snare and handle you in person? He hasn't left his fortress in centuries."

"What *was* that, exactly?" I hauled to my feet, aware that the pavement had chunks of dried vomit nearby.

"A trapdoor, kind of, attuned to you. A thousand other people could've walked over that patch of ground and nothing would've happened."

"If he could do that, why did he waste so much time sending goons after me?"

"At first, I'm sure he didn't view you as a real threat. Look at yourself."

"I'm really not. I'm more of a finishing move." Which made me a valuable ally, but I didn't have the strength or stamina to go toe-to-toe like she did.

Selena shot me a dirty look. "Don't interrupt. As I was saying, that construct requires a *serious* outlay of power . . . So does the pocket dimension. That would be like you building a mousetrap out of a nuke. Would that be *your* first solution to a rodent problem?"

The analogy made me grumpy, but I got her point. "No. Did we actually—"

"Yep," she said with relish.

Two timelines, one without Winter and the other sans Summer. The balance seemed right, though what I knew of such things could fill a thimble. I was too young and ignorant to have this much power. Rochelle's words about my sword echoed in my head, and it appeared she was probably right. *This is a curse . . . I was just too thick to realize.*

"If you're up to it, Big Bro would like to see you." She steadied me as it looked like I might pitch forward.

"I suppose it wouldn't do to piss him off."

Selena shook her head. "He's euphoric at the moment, so this is the right time to pay your respects. Once he levels out, he'll have questions. Luckily for you, he'll celebrate for longer than you'll be around."

That should've cheered me up.

It didn't.

Dwyer gave us the royal treatment, fetching us in his personal silver town car. We got so many weird looks when we ambled out of the alley looking like twice-baked shit and got into this luxurious beast. I tilted my head back against the buttery leather upholstery and wished I had an appetite because I'd try all the gourmet snacks. It seemed pointless now since it would all taste the same.

"Your bro promised I'd never know you were around, by the way. I feel like we have different definitions of obtrusive."

"Please," she said, smirking. "You'd be lost without me."

Probably. Even carrying her token, I was already silently trickling into oblivion. Closing my eyes, I dozed the rest of the way. When I perked up, I saw that the driver had brought us to the same coffeehouse where we'd met before. The writers and housewives stared longingly at Dwyer, who was all gilded elegance in a dark suit and sunglasses. He rose when we headed toward his seat by the window.

"Welcome," he said warmly. He greeted Selena by kissing both her cheeks, and then to my astonished discomfort, he did the same to me. His aura washed over me like a hot bath, instantly soothing my chapped skin and mild frostbite.

"Thanks."

Selena chose a chair, and I fell into the one next to her. Since I just wanted to get this over with and maybe sleep for a week, I let them do the talking. She ordered his henchmen to get her some fizzy water through a series of hand gestures. They paused to ask if I wanted anything, but I shook my head.

"Today, you two are my favorite beings in all creation," Dwyer said eventually. "Ask for anything, and if it's in my power, it will be yours."

"Gimme your—"

"No," he said.

Selena sulked. "Winter is dead. And you *said* anything."

"I'm being magnanimous and benevolent. Stop making me look bad."

"You're doing that on your own."

Okay, maybe they are siblings.

Quietly, I cleared my throat. The bickering stopped.

"My apologies, little one."

It was amazing that he could still patronize me when I'd delivered the killing blow to his archrival, but whatever. I should scram before I lost my patience with his self-aggrandizement and solar-size ego. Gritting my teeth, I smiled and nodded, pretending this wasn't a colossal waste of time and my back didn't feel weird.

There's a hole in it.

Selena poked me. "Go ahead, don't be shy. What do you want?"

Maybe . . .

"I promised someone I'd stick around until June third, but that may prove problematic."

She did me the favor of explaining how I came from an alternate timeline while conveniently leaving out all the details that would make him want to turn me into bacon. He listened with growing fascination and incredulity until she finished. Dwyer quieted, the wheels clearly turning in his head.

"The weapon . . . ," he began.

"It goes with her." Selena half got out of her chair, seeming ready to fight.

The immortal-killing sword won't be a factor for much longer, so none of your rivals can use me against you.

"So then . . . what's your request?" the sun god asked at last.

"Can you fix her?" Selena cut in.

Her dark eyes said she cared—that she wanted me to be okay. I smiled, wishing I could express her how much she'd come to mean to me in such a short time. Without her, I might have died of loneliness, not disintegration.

Dwyer sighed. "I did say anything in my power. Sadly, that's far beyond my abilities. Wouldn't you prefer me to thaw a glacier instead?"

"That would flood the world," Selena snapped.

Oh, man. I hope she keeps him out of trouble after I'm gone.

Since I didn't expect he could heal me, I suffered no disappointment. So I considered and then made what I hoped was a reasonable request. "Maybe . . . a token, like the one Selena gave me?" Maybe their combined energies could bind me long enough to keep my promise.

The coward in me fought the urge to set the watch and bolt. I couldn't—for two reasons. First, I had no idea if going back would heal the damage I'd already suffered, so I might just continue dissolving once I got there. If that was the case, it would be a fitting punishment. Plus, my scientific side wondered if I was too far along in this chemical process for reversal to be possible. Second, that pledge was all that kept me going through some truly desolate moments. I'd be damned if I abandoned it now.

No, I'll stay. I'll finish what I started.

The sun god nodded, seeming pensive. "That's easily done. But it's such a trivial matter, it hardly seems enough in payment."

"It is to me," I said gravely.

In response, he pulled a battered coin from his pocket and offered it to me. "I have carried this for two thousand years. It . . . means a great deal to me, so I hope you'll care for it."

"As long as I can."

When my fingers closed around it, a shiver ran through me. Instantly, strength suffused me, and while this was the equivalent of shooting up, it took the edge off my constant pain.

I shot Dwyer a blissed-out smile. "Thanks."

"No, thank *you*. We won't meet again, I think. Live well, little one." That might've been sarcasm since I had less than three weeks, but maybe the sun god meant it.

"Let's get you home," Selena said, standing. "I'm taking your car."

"Is that your boon?"

"Don't even try." She escorted me out, and the driver took us straight back to the studio.

We didn't make conversation, mostly because I had no idea what to say. Circumstances forced us together, but now I wasn't ready for her to go. *Not ready for another good-bye.* Sometimes it felt as if the atoms that built my world had the word *farewell* etched in fragments, until a pattern of loss emerged. The other Selena—the one in my time—was she angry and alone? I got the feeling she had a yin-yang relationship with Dwyer. I'd never ever considered that I might've left someone grieving for eternity when I took the sun god's heart. This Selena might not hold it against me since it didn't happen here, but in my actual life, this goddess would never protect or befriend me.

Some of the glow wore off.

We got out of the car in front of our building.

"I hate this," she muttered.

"What?"

"Beginnings are fun. Middles are sometimes slow, but the finish is always a pain in the ass. What am I supposed to say?"

"The truth."

"Then . . . you were the best priestess I've had in five hundred years." She hugged me so hard, my ribs might give way.

"But all we did is watch *SYTYCD* and kill things."

337

"Exactly," she said. "Plus, you're also the only priestess I've had in twice that long."

Fighting tears, I choked out a laugh. "And you're the only moon for me."

We held on for a few seconds more, and then she streaked into the sky, leaving me as a meteor breaking apart on the ground.

MINE AND MINE
ALONE

When I pulled myself together enough, I stumbled upstairs. How could such a small studio seem so empty without her? I collected all the fizzy water bottles and olive jars to stare at them. *This is pointless.* It took all my strength to haul down the Murphy bed. Now that I lived alone, maybe I wouldn't bother putting it away anymore. Crawling into it, I rolled into the covers like a cocoon. *Possibly I'll emerge as a butterfly.*

Sleep took me.

A familiar voice whispered near my ear, "You smell of the sun and moon, dearling. But you're mine and mine alone, are you not?"

Disoriented, I jolted awake, my mouth dry as old bones. Though I searched the apartment thoroughly, I found no sign of the Harbinger, inside or beyond the window. Like a junkie, I checked the magazine and found the black feather, a pitiable excuse for evidence that he hadn't abandoned me. *It could've come from a random bird, genius.* Still, I put it back carefully.

After that, I lost five days in a near comatose haze. My injuries couldn't heal properly, but it didn't matter anymore. I wandered the studio intermittently, ate and drank enough to stay alive, and slept more than ever before. Every now and then, I answered texts so my friends didn't panic. Fortunately, they were busy with finals and didn't focus too much on me.

Devon proved the exception, but he just wanted to know about the tip. *Did U take care of business? What happened w/ the old lady?*

Yeah, I sent back. *All good now. Won't blow back on any of U. Thx.*

He seemed satisfied without further details, so I left it there and dozed more. When I finally came out of the soporific state, my body felt stronger than it had in months, and my mind had a sharpness and clarity that had been lacking for a while. Many terminal patients experienced a surge of revitalization known as "the last hurrah" right before the end.

That's where I am.

Tucking the two tokens in my pocket bolstered me further. On a whim, I got on the anime forum, probably for the last time, and found GreenKnight still chatting with NamiNerd, who had exciting news. *I did it, you guys. It took nonstop persuasive persistence, but my parents agreed to the deal. I only have one more year, and then I can change schools. They promised.*

I smiled and touched the screen. *Way to go, young me.*

Then I typed a response: *That's fantastic. Congratulations!*

GreenKnight had beaten me to it, though. *What'd I tell you? Before, I thought it was futile too. But if you don't even try, you can't complain if your life doesn't change.*

The thread continued for a while with NamiNerd extolling the virtues of the science program at the magnet school she'd selected. I noticed she was careful not to let it slip that she was still in junior high. With a surge of nostalgia, I responded to a few more threads, and then I shut down the laptop. I slipped it into my backpack and headed out. The bus driver seemed pleased to see me, at least.

"It's been a while," she said.

I smiled as I went by and took the seat I'd occupied with Kian while we shared headphones. Touching the empty space beside me, I let the tears fall. With nobody who knew me nearby, I had no reason to pretend. Impulse impelled me to return to my old neighborhood, where they were decorating for some kind of street festival. Luisa must've taken a rare day off work because she was setting up a booth outside the bodega.

"Nine," she called, genuinely pleased to see me.

Her face lit up in a smile, and she hurried toward me to give me a powerful hug. *So different from my mom.* I could count on both hands the number of times she'd held me like this. But I missed her. When she died, we were just starting over, tentatively building a different relationship. I wished I had the time to go to Boston to see her face, but it probably wouldn't be smart to get that close to young Edie, even if I did.

"You've been busy with school?" Luisa guessed.

"It's done now. Can I help you?"

"If you don't mind. José is minding the store, and I have a stack of things just inside the door that I need brought out."

"I'm on it."

The bell tinkled when I stepped in, and José waved from behind the counter. If he noticed how wan I looked, he was polite enough not to comment. "You can't stay away, huh? How are things uptown?" That was his favorite question, as if the city might change wildly between my visits.

But I knew what he was really asking and fought the urge to answer, *Terrible. I'm there all alone and I'm dying.*

"Okay. I brought you a present."

When I fished out the laptop, his eyes widened. "Are you kidding? This is probably worth five hundred bucks. It looks new."

I won't need it where I'm going. In truth, terror dogs nipped constantly at my heels. I had no idea if there was an afterlife waiting for me. *What happens to people who perish of time sickness?* With some effort, I regulated my breathing and didn't panic.

"My dad bought me a better one," I said. "Things have turned around for us. That's part of why I'm here . . . to let you know we're moving. I promised to stop by, before."

"When?" José asked.

"Next week."

He still hadn't accepted the laptop. If he didn't, it would trouble me . . . because I literally had nothing else to offer. Kindness like his should be rewarded somehow, and my resources were limited. But his eyes admired it.

Finally, he said, "Are you sure? Your old man's okay with this?"

"Definitely. He ate the food you sent too. Before he got this new job, things were pretty tough. Without you guys . . ."

His cheeks colored. "We all just do what we can."

"You and Luisa, more than most. Speaking of which, she's waiting for this stuff." I angled my head at the pile of boxes by the door.

"Better get moving before she comes looking for you," he teased.

I left the laptop on the counter and went to work. Three trips later, I'd delivered all the supplies so Luisa could continue prepping the booth. She included me so gradually that I hardly noticed I'd been deputized as her assistant. Some of the stalls were just folding tables with slow cookers sitting on them, but the street smelled amazing with foods from twenty different countries. Since everything tasted the same to me, I contented myself with deep breathing.

"What's this all about?" I asked Luisa.

"It's a tradition. Since we're so multicultural up in here, it started as a pride fair, kind of, but we're starting to get some recognition. They did an article in the paper last year, and I hear some food bloggers are coming incognito this time." She peered up and down the street as if she could figure out who it might be.

Under other circumstances, this would be amazing. *Hell is a food fair when you can't appreciate the culinary wonders.* As the day wore on, Luisa got busier, so I helped her by plating up the tamales. She had ten plastic bins full of them in various flavors: chicken in green sauce, pork in red sauce, mushroom, cheese and peppers, bean and cheese, and the list went on, types I'd never heard of or tried. We also had beans and rice; I sold them by the scoop. Down the street, there were gyros, kebabs, falafel, pizza, puff pastries full of meat and potatoes, yogurt drinks, and cups of mixed rice. A woman with a wok above a grill was selling street noodles, while her husband made fish cakes on a stick.

"Whew," she said, downing some water and swiping her forehead. "This is a lot busier than last year. We've actually got some out-of-towners."

Scanning the street, I estimated there were a couple hundred people roaming around, and the police were having a field day with the lack of parking. "I'd call this a resounding success."

Another wave of people came, so I got back to work. Mindless, repetitive, so I was startled when a familiar voice said, "I didn't know you work here."

Glancing up, I recognized Jake. Tanya wasn't around, though. Instead, he was hanging out with Devon, who waved. "Me either."

"Introduce your friends." Luisa nudged me.

Relief shaded her smile, probably because this was the first remotely normal behavior she'd observed. As a social worker, she must've wondered if I was a runaway. I silently thanked her for not digging too much into my fustercluck of a life. Smiling, I did as she requested.

"This is Jake and Devon."

"Pleased to meet you." But when they tried to pay, she waved off the bills.

Devon laughed. "If you knew how loaded this guy is, you'd double your prices."

Luisa smiled, but she didn't relent. "It's fine. I can afford to feed Nine's friends. If you want to take a break, you can eat with them."

Before I could demur, she fixed a plate for me too. After some searching, we found a spot to eat on the steps of a nearby apartment building. With three of us, it was a bit of a squeeze. *Good thing Devon and me are small.* The guys practically inhaled theirs, while I struggled to finish one. They both eyed my remaining food with hungry eyes, so I split it between them.

"This is heaven." Devon gazed worshipfully at his plate.

Jake licked his fingers. "Thanks for bringing me. It's my first time here."

"Mine too," I admitted.

And the last.

"So how long have you worked for José and Luisa?" Devon asked.

"I'm just helping out today. How did your exams go?" *Time to change the subject.*

Jake shrugged. "Not bad. My father doesn't care about grades anyway. 'Money is where it's at, son. You can buy better marks if you're rich enough.'"

"He sounds like a fun guy." Devon shook his head and carried his plate over to the trash can on the corner.

I followed suit. "Luisa is probably swamped again. I should get back."

Jake stopped me with a hand on my arm. "Hold up. You're coming to Kian's surprise party, right?"

"Nobody invited me." I twinged hard over that. Funny how fast you got deleted from plans when you weren't part of the daily social circle anymore.

"Relax. I would've," Devon said, nudging Jake. "We're still figuring out the logistics. *He* wants to host, but everyone's nervous for obvious reasons."

"Come on, dude. How can I prove myself if people won't cut me some slack? I'm not inviting any of the assholes who were there before, I promise. It'll just be our core group."

"Welcome to my world," Devon muttered, turning to me. "What do you think?"

Pretending to study Jake, I kept quiet until he squirmed. "Come on, Nine."

"It'll be fine," I predicted.

Since Wedderburn ruined his last party, this should be awesome. Plus, since he had the biggest house, it made sense to let him host, if he wanted to. When I first arrived, I never could've predicted that things would work out like this. Some of the weight anchoring me trickled away. Soon I'd just float into the stratosphere, all ties untethered.

"Then maybe we'll give him a shot. I'll text you," Devon promised.

With a wave, I headed back to Luisa's booth. Sure enough, she had a line again, and I hurried to help her catch up. I spent the rest of the day assisting, so it was close to ten by the time we finished cleaning. Her cash box bulged with bills, and she was glowing when José came out to check on us.

She beamed at him too. "Fantastic, right? We can probably take that vacation we were talking about."

He smiled at me. "She should open her own restaurant, tell her."

"Please." She acted like this was an old argument. "My government job is steady, and we don't have to worry about start-up failures or health care."

When they turned to me, I struggled to find words other than good-bye. "Thanks for everything. I won't be around after this, so take care, okay?"

They exchanged a look and I could see José promising to explain after I left. That silent communication reminded me of my parents. Aching, I rubbed my chest.

"You too," Luisa said.

They enfolded me in a two-sided hug, and for a long moment, I leaned, soaking it in. I noticed they didn't offer to pay me this time, and it leavened my heart. *Maybe they think of me as family.* I waved and headed out. On the bus ride home, I stared at my flickering face reflected in the window. It came and went according to the shift of internal and external light, but it felt like a sinister, predictive version of a child's game with flower petals.

Now you're here. Now you're not.

That last week, I used my library card hard. Not only did I read the two novels I'd checked out before, but I paid the late fine and took out more. I worked on the list of *100 Books You Must Read Before You Die*, mostly because I wouldn't have a chance later. In the middle of number twenty-eight, I got a text from Devon.

Friday night, Jake's place. If U need a ride, meet at usual place, 7pm for Carmen car pool.

I sent back, *See U then.*

Three days before my personal D-day, Selena's token dissolved in my hands. I guessed I'd drained it and let the silver dust trickle through my fingers into the trash. So far, Dwyer's coin was holding out, but it didn't warm my palm as much as it used to. That meant the return of my old friend pain. Surprise surges doubled me over at random moments, cramping my hands into claws, and my skin was simply . . . gone, in more than one spot, not showing muscle or meat beneath but a freaky *nothing* inside.

I don't have long.

Once again, fiction saved me, or I might've cried myself to death.

• • •

The day of Kian's surprise party, I cleaned the studio and washed my clothes. I folded them neatly and stowed them in a small trash bag. *Wow, I really don't have much.* With a tremulous sigh, I checked the move-out list to make sure I hadn't missed anything. Then I realized the absurdity of it. Jake's building manager would have a hard time finding me or the Harbinger to charge us extra. Still, I pulled all linens and bedcovers and set them on the washer, as requested. Then, for the last time, I did my makeup so I didn't alarm my friends and dropped the cosmetics into the bin afterward.

"I can't believe *this* is how my story ends," I whispered.

Yet, while fear gnawed at me like hungry rats, on some level, I was also ready for it to be over. Exhaustion hung over me like a cloudy day that never ended in rain. It felt symbolic as I walked the six blocks to the Goodwill donation box. Without hesitation, I pushed everything I owned into the chute. *Now I have only what I'm standing in, just like when I arrived.* That felt right. In my pocket, I had two fake IDs, a cell phone, and the remainder of the cash the Harbinger had left.

With two hours to kill, I walked aimlessly. Somehow I ended up on the bus, riding to the mall where the Harbinger and I had busked before the fountain. The plaza looked much different during the day, especially beneath the dazzling sunshine. Another musician had taken the Harbinger's spot, but he hadn't attracted much attention. He was young, probably my age or younger, and scruffy as hell. The song he strummed on his battered acoustic guitar seemed to be original, or at least, I hadn't heard it before. I listened until the end and then dropped five bucks in the case.

"Thanks," he said.

I repeated José's words then. "We just do what we can."

And sometimes that had to be enough. *That's why the Harbinger left.* Something like peace flowed through me, blocking the intermittent pain. In that moment, I stopped waiting for him to return. My heart ached, a welcome change from physical pain. Everything hurt except the creepy rents in my flesh. At the convenience store across the way, I bought a sandwich and offered half to the musician. Since he'd watched me take it out of the package, he took it and gobbled it down. I chucked the filling of mine and went to a nearby bench to crumble up the bread for the birds.

Soon I had a small avian army at my feet: fat-breasted gray pigeons with glimmers of blue and green, tiny brown wrens, one white dove, and a huge crow with greedy, beady eyes. I focused on him for obvious reasons, pretending he represented someone else. Pinching a huge crumb to lure him closer, I tossed it, and he strutted to claim it with pure bird swag.

"You can hear me, right? This always was your favorite way to spy on me."

"Mom, is that lady talking to the birds?" a little kid asked.

The mom shushed him. "Don't point; it's rude."

They hurried past as I laughed quietly. From across the way, the guitarist called, "Don't feel bad. I talk to animals too."

"You're Dolittle, right?"

He laughed and continued playing.

As for me, I was way beyond caring what random strangers thought, so I continued my conversation with the crow. "I want you to know, I'm okay. Everything's all right now, and I'm in a good place. You made the best choice you could, and I don't blame you." I hesitated, but since I was talking to myself, I added quietly, "You were my hero, by the way."

I waited for the tears, but they didn't come. A smile formed instead. The black bird sidled up to me and snapped the remaining bread from my fingers, and then it flapped away to stare balefully from a nearby wire. *It's not him. He doesn't know.* But now that I'd dumped my emotional purse, just like I'd given away all my belongings, I could brace for the hardest good-bye of all. Just then, my phone alarm went off, reminding me to meet Carmen and company for Kian's surprise birthday bash.

Okay. Time to party like it's the last night of my life.

THE LAST NIGHT
OF MY LIFE

Today I arrived last and took some scolding from everyone else. Kian was missing, though. "Where's the guest of honor?" I asked.

"Jake's picking him up," Devon explained. "He said he needed some tutoring."

I crawled all the way to the back, next to Elton. He didn't glance up from the PSP in his hand. Nosy, I leaned over to check out the racing game he was playing. He elbowed me without looking up. Carmen checked to make sure everyone was settled and then took off. She must be used to driving with distractions if she ran errands with her brothers and sisters in the car.

"Also, we're being sneaky." Vonna turned to face me, arm on the back of the seat.

"How so?"

She grinned. "Technically today's not his birthday."

"Really?" I'd completely lost track of the date, so I'd take her word for it.

"So we pretend nothing's up until midnight?"

"It's genius," Amanda said.

"You're welcome." Devon had shotgun, but his voice carried.

Amanda and Nathan were snuggled up together in the seat ahead of me, so I suspected they'd finally moved beyond the picking-on-each-other stage of the relationship. No need to ask since that would highlight the fact that I'd been out of the loop for a while. It hadn't been all bad that I left school early, as it gave Kian plenty of practice dealing with people on his own.

Seems like he's doing great.

They talked around me, discussing end-of-year stuff with context I didn't share. Nobody noticed that I didn't talk much, pumped up with the prospect of surprising Kian. *Five months ago, you thought he was beyond weird. Now you're giving him the best present since his dad died.* As we pulled into Jake's impressive drive, I remembered the last time we were here.

It'll be fine. Winter is gone, and for now, Summer loves me.

Dwyer's coin also seemed to keep the murderous universe at bay, so hopefully, I could hang out with my friends one last time without anything exploding or catching fire. The gate buzzed and swung open. True to his promise at the food festival, no other cars lined the drive. Carmen parked right by the door, and we rang the bell. Jake answered with a harried expression.

"Help me, guys. Tanya got here early, so Kian's already suspicious."

"Trust her to screw this up," Devon muttered.

Amanda smacked him. "Don't be like that. You know how hard she's trying to make you like her."

He shook his head. "Girl just can't accept that she's not the princess anymore."

"Guys," Jake prompted.

I thought fast. "Right. Tell him you tricked everyone into coming over because you want to clear your name." Since that was the truth, it made for a good cover.

Jake brightened and hurried inside. Keeping up with his long strides wasn't easy, so it took the rest of us another minute. Kian and Tanya sat at the long dining table with the chandelier on dim. This house impressed me all over again, though it still struck me as somewhat soulless. *This is what money without heart buys. I hope Jake has a happier life than this.* He was at least as well off as the elite at Blackbriar yet considerably kinder than most.

"You're all here?" A smile started on Kian's face, as he was too smart not to know when something was up.

It had been a while since I'd seen him, long enough for me to catalog the differences. He'd filled out a shade, and his skin had cleared up some. I could well imagine how he'd look at twenty, not supernaturally beautiful, but smart, attractive, and comfortable with himself. I must've stared too long because he locked onto me and we exchanged a long look. I had no idea what he was trying to tell me, but I smiled.

"Actually," Jake said then. "I have a confession to make." He proceeded with my suggested explanation.

Kian's shoulders slumped slightly. *He's going to be so shocked later.*

Either not noticing or pretending not to, Jake went on. "Don't worry, it's a low-key hangout tonight. My mom's in the other part of the house, but she won't bother us."

"Doesn't she usually travel with your dad?" Nathan asked.

"They're fighting right now. He recommended she get some cosmetic surgery; she accused him of secretly wanting to trade her for a younger model." He seemed remarkably unconcerned, but I had the impression he didn't spend that much time with them anyway.

"So you don't actually need tutoring," Kian said, sounding annoyed.

But I knew what was bothering him. The others probably did too, but we couldn't let on until midnight. Jake showed us to the home theater, a room that was a small VIP cinema, complete with recliners and a huge screen. I pictured Jake in here watching movies alone, and it was sad somehow, worse than curling up under the covers with a laptop and Netflix.

"What movies do you have?" Nathan asked.

Much discussion ensued, and eventually, since he'd done such a good job entertaining us at Carmen's place, we agreed to let him pick a movie this time too. At some point, Vonna and Kian disappeared. I had no intention of playing creeper, but my body still processed liquids fine and I needed to pee, so I headed out to find the guest bathroom. Instead, I stumbled on what sounded like a private conversation. The minute I realized that, I should've backed out of the hall, but I was nosy enough to linger.

"So . . . you want to break up?" Kian whispered.

Holy shit, that's taking the bit too far.

"More of a hiatus. I'm going to Long Beach to stay with my cousin for the summer, and it's better if we're both free to have fun. When I get back, we'll see. I mean, I like you, but we're not married, you know?"

354

"That makes sense. We're pretty young to be all serious anyway."

"You're not mad?" She sounded anxious, so maybe this wasn't a joke.

"I'll miss you, but how can I be mad about you getting an awesome vacation?"

"See, this is why I'm into you. Well, that and your poetry."

For a few seconds, my heart froze in my chest as I imagined him reading to her from his private book, the one only I'd been privy to before. But those memories belonged to Vonna now. I wondered if she liked the firebird poem, if it spoke to her. The last line came to me in fading echo of a past I had to let go:

It must fly or die.

"I thought girls only liked bad boys," he murmured.

"Only the dumb ones."

The sounds of kissing followed, and I slipped out of earshot to complete my bathroom quest. When I got back, the movie had started. Vonna and Kian were curled together in the back, so he must be okay with the summer break request. *Hell, maybe, he'll date other people too.* When he started college, he'd likely be a lot different than the person I loved.

Better. Stronger. Happier.

After the comedy Nathan chose, we pigged out on snacks Jake's housekeeper had prepared. Rather, they did. I watched with hungry eyes—not the food—but the interaction. Such a wealth of warmth and friendship filled me up, so I couldn't eat a bite. Devon came up beside me, his hip bumping mine.

"You okay?"

"Sure."

"I hear you're leaving soon."

"Jake told you?" Other than him, I didn't think I'd mentioned it to anyone else.

Well, Kian, of course. But even he didn't know that this was my last night. I planned to put Dwyer's coin in a safe place and just . . . let go when morning came. *I'm so tired. Tired of fighting. Tired of begging and bargaining for just a little longer.*

"Yeah. We hang out quite a bit these days. He's not nearly as much of a douche as I initially thought. I see why you dated him."

I stifled a laugh. "Maybe *you* should give him a shot."

Devon slid me a sideways look. "I don't think he's into my type."

"Actually he might surprise you," I said absently. I realized my mistake too late and bit my lip.

He gave the basketball star a long look. "Oh, really? Well, he's pretty into Tanya at the moment, but I'll keep an eye on the situation. You're not messing with me, right?"

"Definitely not, though I shouldn't have told you. It's not common knowledge."

"Yeah, it's not okay to out someone. You're lucky I'm a pro at keeping secrets."

When Devon smiled ruefully, I recalled how worried he'd been that people would find out his mom owned Madame Q's House of Style. These days he seemed cool with it, a sign of greater maturity. After all, most teenagers went through a period of being embarrassed by their parents for one reason or another.

By this point, Kian had relaxed, and he truly seemed to have no clue we knew his birthday arrived in less than two minutes. Precisely at 12:01 a.m., Jake carried a cake in with fifteen candles glowing on it. The perfectly frosted layers reflected the unmistakable touch of an experienced baker, likely the housekeeper. Kian stared, speechless, as presents appeared out of purses and backpacks. I had only cash and my fake ID, so I gave him twenty bucks wrapped around the card.

When he cocked his head at me, curious, I said, "Something to remember me by. And you can buy another rare album at Psychedelic with that. I wouldn't have known what to get."

"Thanks." He leapt up and hugged me.

But he didn't linger. In his eyes, I was just another friend, while Vonna was the girl he'd miss most. And I didn't even mind; that meant I'd done my job. He hugged everyone, even Elton, who put up a halfhearted struggle and mumbled, "Get off me, man."

"Admit it," Devon said around a mouthful of cake. "We got you."

Kian grinned so wide it seemed like his face might crack open and shower us in rainbows. "You played me perfectly."

Jake refilled everyone's glasses with some kind of punch that held just a hint of a kick. "And I proved that my parties don't all end in disaster."

"Two thumbs up." Carmen matched words to gesture.

A little later, Jake turned on some music, and we were all loose enough to dance. I had an awesome time just being silly and free, trying not to think about what came next. The liquor helped with that, making it easier to watch as the songs slowed, and the group coupled up: Vonna and Kian, Nathan and Amanda, Tanya and Jake. So I drank more with Dev and Elton, until the world was pleasantly fuzzy, and I couldn't hold my head up anymore.

When I woke, it was late morning, and everyone was sprawled on the floor in various awkward poses. Elton and Nathan ended up spooning somehow; I must've missed that. Stepping over them, I fixed my face as much as possible, but with part of my makeup smudged off, I didn't look quite right, already fading. I met Jake in the kitchen, staring vacantly into the fridge.

"It won't take you to Narnia no matter how long you wait," I told him.

He startled, shutting the door on reflex. "Man, what a night."

"It was fun. You threw a great party. Kian really appreciated it." I paused, wondering if I should ask. *Yeah, he's the best choice.* "Would you do me a favor?"

"Sure. I owe you. Your stupid manga plan paid off big-time." Finally, he got a bottle of water and chugged half as if he'd remembered why he opened the fridge in the first place.

"Wrap this up so you can't tell what it is. Then drop it off for Dwyer at this coffee shop." I wrote down the address, along with some basic directions, though Jake's driver would take him and he probably knew Cross Point like the back of his hand.

"That's it?" He took the coin, turning it in his fingers. "This looks ancient."

"Don't ask, okay?"

Jake sighed, shaking his head. "That's like your motto or something. And there's your good-bye face again."

"It's time," I said.

But I didn't realize I had an audience. Somehow I didn't picture a bunch of tearful farewells, but that was how it went down. I got all the hugs and promises to keep in touch from hungover people. By the time we all piled into Carmen's minivan, I felt scraped raw by their feelings, hard enough to handle my own. But they rebounded, recapping the night's high points so we didn't have to focus on the fact that this was it.

At the drop-off point, we hugged one more time. It was tough for everyone to get to me in the vehicle so they all hopped out. Carmen grabbed me first. "Promise you'll text."

Amanda squeezed me next. "When can I come visit?"

The guys elbowed in, and then, finally, Vonna gave me a long, hard hug. "Won't be the same without you around here, girl."

It took the last of my restraint not to break down. *Oh God, they'll honestly miss me. They care that I'll be gone.* Now, poised at the edge of extinction, I'd come full circle from that dark night on a bridge, feeling sure nobody would. Ironically, now that I wanted so much to survive, that path no longer existed for me.

But I made my choice. It's time.

Dazed, I headed for my bus stop out of habit. To my surprise, Kian went with me. I arched my brow.

"I'm seeing you to the station. But . . . don't you need to swing by and get your stuff?"

"It's in a locker," I lied.

He kicked a rock so hard that it ricocheted off a nearby building. "Right. How long does it take to get from Miami from here?"

I shrugged. It wasn't like I was actually going. "Are you okay?"

"With you leaving? Not really. But it's not like you hid the fact that you'd be moving on. I've been braced for it from the start."

Which is probably why he protected his heart. Clever Kian. Thank you for not letting me hurt you. Again. It's the last thing I could stand.

"I actually meant about you and Vonna."

He stumbled a little over an uneven spot in the sidewalk. "Oh, you heard? I asked if it was part of the joke, but . . . apparently not. It's a surprise for sure, but I'm glad she went this route instead of cheating on me."

"You could have a summer fling too."

Kian laughed. "Please. I barely know how to handle one girl."

"Practice makes perfect," I teased.

For the last time, we rode the bus together, and he offered his earbuds, as he had before. The music was different this time, an interesting mix of old hits, classic jazz, and modern R & B. Already Vonna's influence was shaping him. Through my lashes, I watched him.

You're going to have an amazing life. Promise me.

All too soon we reached the station terminus, and the long-distance bus depot was three blocks down. Kian walked me all the way there. Without Dwyer's coin, pain came at me in waves like enemy soldiers. I wouldn't be able to control this much longer.

This has to end. Oh God, it has to.

Gritting my teeth, I covered the distance while Kian talked about summer plans with his uncle, mostly house renovation stuff. He pretended to flex. "Maybe I'll come back so buff in the fall, nobody will be able to resist me."

I couldn't stop staring at his smile. *Happy birthday, baby. In my world, you tried to die today.*

"You're already potent enough."

Thinking that was a joke, he laughed. "Whatever. Oh. Here we are." From his tone, he'd been putting on a front too, refusing to acknowledge the inevitable.

"Thanks for keeping me company."

"It's me who should be thanking you. I mean, damn. Basically, you changed my life."

That was the mission. But I only gave you a nudge. You did the rest.

This moment shone brighter than all the diamonds I'd never wear, tasted sweeter than all the meals I wouldn't eat. Kian reached for me then and pulled me close with a desperation he'd clearly been concealing. I wrapped my arms around him as tight, burying my face in his chest. It was a small miracle that I could. Somewhere down the line, *someone* would have a beautiful life because this boy survived.

"I can't believe the only picture I have of you is that stupid fake ID," he whispered into my hair. His hand tangled in the short strands like he couldn't help it, and it hurt a little.

Parts of me, the missing bits hidden beneath my clothes, couldn't feel him at all, and that terrified me. I held on harder.

"Sorry. But it's something, right?"

"Sometimes when I look at you, I get this feeling . . ." He sighed, and it tickled the side of my face.

No, I don't want him thinking that.

"By the way, if I go quiet, please understand it's not that I wanted to. But—"

"Your life is complicated," he finished.

I should be relieved that he accepted the excuse so easily. After all, I'd be conditioning him for months to let me go. But it hurt like tearing open a wound when I finally pushed back and stepped out of those comforting arms. *He's not mine. This isn't my time.*

"Give the man a prize."

"If you insist." He swooped down and kissed me, not the deep kisses of the past but an almost-more tease of a kiss.

Shivering, I pretended he wasn't better at that than when we dated. *He's already learned a lot.* "Not sure your girlfriend would approve," I mumbled.

"We're on a break, remember? It was her idea."

A deep breath allowed me to say impossible, unthinkable words. "Okay. I have to go."

WHERE THE
END BEGINS

"I refuse to say bye. So message me when you get there." With another kiss, this one on the cheek, Kian walked away.

I watched until he rounded the corner, disappearing from sight.

You thought nobody could ever love you, but I did. I loved you as you were in our world, perfect and tormented at twenty, and I loved you as you are at fifteen, awkward and unsure.

Good-bye, my beloved boy.

He thought I had a bus to catch, but rather, I'd run out of time. My heart hurt, but it was the good, clean ache of a job well done. *I did it. I chose the Potter's Future and made it true.* I'd fixed everything here that I possibly could.

Waiting five minutes convinced me he wouldn't double back out of misguided chivalry, so I left the depot then. My steps were aimless, Aegis heavy on my wrist. Since there was no reason to hide anymore, I peeled off my glove and studied my hand. Gold glimmered from my skin, light showing through the thin spots where I'd begun to fade. Soon my particles would abandon all cohesive bonds, returning me to subatomic dust. Echoes didn't leave a body behind. They just . . . stopped. This was the universe balancing the scales.

And I was done resisting.

Glad Kian won't see this. The most critical bit was that the future stretched wide open, free from immortal interference. Though the monsters played on, even the immortal game had a few immutable rules. And while I couldn't say I won exactly, I didn't lose, either. In this timeline—or alternate universe, whichever—Edie Kramer still had her mom and dad, plus I'd given her enough guidance online that she shouldn't make the same mistakes as me. She was learning how to make friends, which was more than I knew at her age, and she communicated more effectively with her parents. A small pang went through me. That could've been *my* future, under different circumstances. But he *died* for me in the other world. So my life in exchange here in the summer timeline was a fair price.

Dissipating into sparks of light, however, wasn't something I should do on a public street. I chose a random office building and headed through the lobby. Nobody questioned me. They seldom did if you looked like you knew where you were going. My hand trembled, a thing of light and shadow more than form; I barely had the physical substance left to open the door to the stairwell. It wouldn't be long. Running, I dashed up all the flights and burst out onto the roof. It seemed more fitting for this to happen up here, closer to the sky.

I wonder if Dwyer will get his coin back. Wonder if Selena will miss me.

The door slammed shut behind me, and I moved toward the protective wall built to keep people from falling. I noticed the first black bird then, eerily similar to the one I'd spoken to in the plaza.

Soon the ledge was covered with them, at least a hundred, and despite fearing what lay in store, I smiled. They regarded me with bright, unblinking eyes. None of them shifted or preened; they all just watched me.

"You can come out," I said.

After everything we'd been through, the Harbinger's arrival only invoked joy and relief. Astonishing, actually, how much I'd *missed* him. He appeared in a shimmer of gray smoke, striding toward me like an incarnation of war. His black cloak fluttered behind him, and I recalled when the sight of him summoned visceral dread, preventing me from noticing the details. I took in the red satin waistcoat and the silver chain usually tethered to some improbable artifact. These days, his familiarity qualified as comforting.

I won't die alone. He's come to bear witness.

"You're not angry," he said.

I shrugged, unable to manage a smile. "Thank you for seeing me off."

"You think that's why I'm here? Silly girl. Well, you'll understand soon enough."

"Are you here to . . . absorb me?" He fed on me in the other world, both to replenish his energy and keep part of me with him. We'd gotten even closer in this timeline, nearly one person in some ways. At this point, it didn't seem entirely awful that what was left of my natural life should go to the Harbinger. He'd saved me so often that it felt right, like repaying a debt.

"Is that what you think?" His lightning-in-the-dark eyes locked on me, not human enough to show certain emotion but I sensed . . . disappointment laced with hurt.

I started to speak, but it was too late. My mouth filled with light, and my eyes popped in molten sparks. In that moment, I dissolved and there was terminus, endless nothing—a moment where all music ceased. It was a silence that could swallow the universe, but something followed the nothing, and for a few reeling moments, I couldn't parse the change.

How am I still here?

"I don't understand."

Flexing my fingers, I stared at my hand. It looked the same, but slowly I noticed the difference. Slowly, I set my fingertips against my wrist. *No pulse. I'm not human anymore.* Trembling, I raised my eyes to the Harbinger, whose expression was delicately amused.

"Welcome to the choir angelic," he said.

"How?"

"There are stories about you already, dearling. I only helped them along, sharing with those most likely to believe."

"That's where you've been," I realized aloud.

Awe surged in a giant wave. When we said farewell before, I thought it was the last time and he'd forsaken me as a lost cause, along with all other amusements that lost their shine. Instead, for me, he played Martha Jones's role, spreading my story far and wide, until it reached the tipping point, until the legend was enough to deliver me. This was what Martha did with her unrequited love for the Doctor; she roved the earth endlessly, carrying his message. I suspected it was easier for the Harbinger, but the sweetness at its heart felt the same.

"Indeed. The nine-fingered Fury with her golden Aegis? Or do you prefer the warrior-queen who killed the sun? The tale practically writes itself. When you add the story of the girl who loved a boy who died for her, so she made up her mind to shift time itself and die for *him* . . . well, the audience was beyond captivated."

"You gamed the system," I whispered, numb with astonishment.

All this time, I was bracing for my own end, but I *never* prepared for this.

Careless, he lifted a shoulder in a graceful half shrug. "Hardly. This is an age desperate for heroes, but they've forgotten how to create them."

I imagined him repeating the stories at various firesides over and over, a stranger come to entertain for an evening. But there must've been enough who believed him, or I wouldn't still be here. Well, an incarnation of me anyway.

I'm here. I'm still here.

"What does that make you?" Such kindness lurked beneath all that desperate, hungry cruelty. When he begged me to kill him and I couldn't, it forged a bond between us, one it appeared couldn't be broken.

"A clever devil."

"I guess I can't argue that." Softly, I added, "You saved me. Again."

"It's become a habit. Or should I say that I'm still bound contractually . . . ? No, I doubt you'd believe that. My best lies are generally wasted on you." The Harbinger's light tone yielded to a silky somberness. "Someone like you should exist . . . to keep something like me in check."

"You're not a monster." No creature that cared so much about my survival, one who did the impossible in my name, could be completely evil.

Pure whimsy laced the way he vaulted up onto the ledge, scattering his birds in a flutter of black feathers, and he spread his arms, as if he would tumble backward. The illusion of shadowy wings wreathed him. "Rather, a dark angel instead?"

"I'm sure you already know, the birds tell you everything, but—"

"Yes, I heard your little speech. You made it damned difficult to do my job. Do you know how many times I wanted to rush back? And in the worst moments, I questioned if I could do this, if I could save you."

"Is that why you didn't tell me?"

He paced the wall in measured steps, avoiding my gaze. "Why I left? Yes. It seemed better to let you think ill of me rather than offering what might prove to be false hope."

Suddenly shy, I couldn't look directly at him, either. "I dreamed about you a lot."

"How fascinating. I'll expect a detailed account." He paused, leaping lightly to the rooftop. "But . . . you don't hate me for making you as I am? For you, that could've been the end. Now I've pushed the infinite upon you."

I smiled. "Remember, I'm quite young. I wasn't ready for the ride to stop."

"I'm so glad." There could be no feigning such relief.

Stretching, I luxuriated in a pain-free body. "My work's not done, now that you've returned. Your story still needs some revision. There must be others who would write about the Harbinger, granting you a brighter nature."

He strode toward me, not stopping until his face was close enough that I could see how weary he was. "Is that your new mission?"

"What?" I didn't back off.

"Saving me." His tone revealed nothing of how he felt, if that were the case. Often there was no way to tell with him what he truly wanted. The Harbinger *was* the master of misdirection.

"Well, it feels like I owe you."

He almost smiled, a faint twitch of his mouth. "Eternity is a long time. We'll work it out."

"You say that like I'm staying with you."

No doubt the Harbinger was lonely, not that anyone cared to interrupt his self-imposed solitude. Even immortals remained wary of his capricious nature, and he broke most humans like a child too rough with his toys. I had read enough of his stories to understand his rage and grief. Humanity burdened him with too much tragedy and then abandoned him amid the wreckage.

"Will you?" he asked.

"That depends. Does a cage factor into this offer?"

He shook his head. "Our circumstances have changed. You're no longer qualified to be my pet." In a musing tone, he added, "Perhaps you never were. So if you stay, it will be because that's the path you chose freely."

"That's basically what I was fighting for all along," I said softly, "But I'll admit, this wasn't the ending I expected."

"Disappointed?" He thought the answer was yes, I could tell, that my surprising survival was a consolation prize.

"Not even a little. But let's talk terms. If I'm not your pet, what am I?"

"You truly enjoy these negotiations." But the joy I'd felt at seeing him on the rooftop echoed in his voice too. "Must we define it?"

"Call me curious."

"Then let's say . . . companion."

I grinned at that. "How very Doctor-ish of you."

"Doctor who?" His eyes twinkled, nothing but delight.

A happy Harbinger—I never thought I'd see the day. "I can't believe I gave you that opening. Anyway, I think you should be *my* companion."

"I'm willing to be flexible on the terms. But it's time to leave this world. The one you came from still needs you."

I nodded and set the timer on my watch. "Did you peek ahead again?"

"I'm not telling."

Touching his arm, I begged, "Come on, give me a hint."

His smile lit me up like a neon sign. "If you show your face often enough for your father to move past his guilt, he does eventually remarry, but there are no more children. In time he comes up with the theory behind the chronometer you're wearing, but it will be generations before the tech is perfected and viable."

"What a relief. I can play human often enough to ease his mind, right?"

"It's never been a problem for me." His tone carried a faint edge.

"You don't have to pretend with me," I said softly.

But . . . once I leapt, I would never be able to speak to my friends again. I must've shown some reluctance because the Harbinger sighed. "You're thinking like a human. Time doesn't have the same hold on you anymore, so if you want to visit, you can."

"And the world won't try to erase me?"

"Of course not. You're a legend now, not a person." His expression darkened. "Like me, you're at the whim of your creators."

"We'll cope," I said softly.

If I could keep in touch with the friends I'd made, it would be amazing. I'd probably have to play the flaky, mysterious loner who popped in and out, but it was more than I had *ever* expected when I made the jump. Happy as I was, however, I wouldn't head to the Harbinger's depressing pile of rocks on the New England coast and molder.

"But . . . I won't simply vegetate. I want to *do* things."

While a human life was impossible, it didn't render my existence devoid of meaning. Rochelle dedicated her immortality to healing the sick. Her power might be insufficient to cure the whole world of its ills, but that didn't detract from her purpose. Maybe the Harbinger's unhappiness came from feeling as if the world had passed him by. If necessary, I'd drag him by force into the modern world and show him how to connect, how to care again. After all, he was the one that taught me how much that mattered, back in the dingy room at the Baltimore.

"Such as?" A globe appeared in his hands, and he spun it. "There's a rather interesting war building here. Or we could destabilize the economy in this region. The people are starving here because the soil's tainted. And—"

"Why don't we *help*? You said you're tired of wearing the black hat. Show me where it's worst, where they could use heroes the most."

Bemused, he stared at me. "It has been written that I will *destroy* this world. One day, the seas will rise; mountains will crumble. Why would I ever work to aid the humans who hated me so? It has been my greatest pleasure to torment them, oh, these thousand years."

"Did it make you happy?"

"No." It was a clipped and brooding concession, reluctantly given.

Gently, I set a hand on his arm. "I *know* that's not what you want, and there are no stories about us yet. The Nine-Fingered Fury and the Harbinger? Our tale is yet to be written. And we can ensure our actions drive the narrative, not other people's ideas."

His eyes widened, locked on mine. For a long moment, he stared at where I was touching him. Freely. "I think you truly believe that."

Sliding my fingers down his forearm, I laced our hands together. "The only way to find out is to try. Like Lewis Carroll said, believe in six impossible things before breakfast. I mean, holy shit, I was once fragile human flotsam and now I'm a nameless immortal."

The Harbinger gave a wry smile, shaded with regret. "My apologies. Naming is clearly not my forte, else I should certainly have gained more than a title at some point in the last aeon."

I smiled up at him. "It's enough that you gathered followers for my legend. What's in a name anyway? If I call you Harbinger, and you call me Nine, isn't it enough? That's the whole point anyway, that we make our own meaning."

Suddenly, I was in his arms, enveloped by his darkness, but I could still feel the burning heat at the heart of him. It was a hungry embrace from a being so long alone that I smelled the centuries in which he'd gone untouched. Time pressed on him like an unrelenting hand, a sort of pain that left me mute in response. I breathed him in—essential wildness that was like igneous rock charred by lightning.

"You have such a ferocious spirit," he said then.

"I didn't always. It grew in me, a little at a time. Some traits can be cultivated."

"Do you think so?" he asked.

And I understood all the layers of that question. *Can I become more? Can I write my own story?* I nodded. That was the key to winning the immortal game—first one must choose not to play. And in that way, together, we stepped off the game board for good.

He lowered his head, but I went up to meet him. This kiss tasted of promises; it was the warmth of the hearth at home combined with longing that lit me up like kindling. My toes curled. When he pulled back, he pressed his lips to the curve of my neck. I shivered.

"Will that newfound strength let you remain with me, unbroken?" In the question lay a thousand years of anguish, a trail of bones from those he'd loved and lost.

Does he love me? His devotion would be beautiful and terrible, like a storm over the open sea. I had feelings for him, powerful ones, and I'd missed him so much it hurt, but right now, I was brand-new, and we had time to burn.

So I only answered the question he asked, not the ones swirling between us unspoken. "Most definitely. The better question might be, will you go adventuring with me?"

In a flicker, he had us up on the ledge, one arm still around me. The sky opened before us, deep as a bruise. I knew no fear because falling couldn't kill me, bizarre to think that the only thing that *could*, I currently wore as a fashion accessory. And there might come a time when I'd be ready to fall on my sword to end the ennui. I couldn't imagine it, however. No matter what, giving up was no longer a choice I could make. As the Harbinger noted, like a flower in the cracks of the sidewalk, I had grown a ferocious, unstoppable spirit.

"Start your watch now," he said.

I did. And together, we leapt. The wind rushed up to meet us, and I swallowed a scream as the sensation of free fall caught me. *This is how I leave my old life forever.* Before hitting bottom, though, we flickered, and when we reappeared, it was in a village in a country

I had seen only in pictures. There were no power lines, no cell towers, either. The people were thin and sad, terrified because they lived on ground that more powerful groups coveted and clashed over. Bullet holes riddled the buildings and divots in the earth showed where shells had exploded.

This is my world. Welcome back.

"Here," he said, "is where they need us most. I had nothing to do with the poverty and chaos, by the way. Humans have done all the work for me."

Only when one story ends can the next arise.

A rumble sounded in the distance, clarifying into engine noise. Someone fired an automatic weapon in the air, warning shots or a promise of violence. The townspeople scattered. As an army truck full of troops approached the village, I called for Aegis, and a flock of angry ravens appeared from nowhere. They circled the vehicle as storm clouds formed overhead, shrouding the whole area in darkness.

The soldiers cried out, already alarmed, and the fighting hadn't even started. Good thing there were no rules preventing immortals from killing humans as they pleased. Some people needed it, and Govannon had given me the power to play executioner. He'd meant for me to wield Aegis against the immortals, but in a place like this, I'd raise my blade in defense of the innocent as well. For now, we would shield this village, and from this, our legend would grow. Not the old myths, new ones born of kindness and hope.

Our choices drive the narrative.

I smiled at my Harbinger and said, "This is where we begin."

POSTSCRIPT

Edie Kramer checks her reflection in a small compact. Her new purple glasses are cute, and she's never worn this plaid cardigan before. Combining science-themed T-shirts with a layering sweater qualifies as geek chic, she decides. She isn't wearing makeup, but she has good skin, nice eyes, and she's heard more than once that she has a pretty smile.

There's no reason to be nervous as she's been talking to Kian online for four years. He's GreenKnight; she's NamiNerd. They met in an anime forum—he was branching out from old movies—so she schooled him on what to watch, and he gave her good life advice. They went from board posts to direct messages to messenger chat to texting. Since he starts at Tufts in a few days, today she's meeting him in person for the first time.

He's sent pictures, of course. She made a collage of them in graphic art, but this isn't a big deal because she did the same with photos from other online friends. TimeWitch in particular travels to the most fascinating places, and occasionally, she sends visual evidence of her adventures. Edie likes the one of TW in a long-haired man's arms, perched atop an elephant. Her favorite photo of Kian is just a close-up of his smiling face. Sometimes she thinks of him as her online boyfriend, though that's not official. She's well aware that he's older and he usually has a girlfriend. *He probably sees me as a little sister.* Since she's a junior and he's starting college, Edie is prepared for this to go nowhere, though friends say he must like her, as her phone is constantly buzzing with messages. Right then it does too.

Turn around, the text reads. Nervous, she spins, spotting him across Copley Square.

Their eyes meet, and the future unfurls.